MAGNET OF DESIRE

When Alisa Amsell fell under the spell of Riordan Daniels' animal magnetism, she could measure his danger by the fierceness of her own naked desire. And as his passionate lips burned hungrily over her soft, pliant body, she found herself in an erotic web of love from which there seemed no escape . . .

FIRESTORM OF LOVE

Never before had Alisa known such rapture, as Riordan's kisses burned up and down her body . . . as his hands kneaded her willing flesh, caressing her, tantalizing her, until he could finally claim the very core of her. And as they were swept up in this frantic hunger for each other, Alisa knew she was bonded to this lusty scoundrel for eternity. . . .

SATIN EMBRACES

Passionate Historical Romances from SIGNET

SATIN
EMBRACES

by Julia Grice

A SIGNET BOOK

NEW AMERICAN LIBRARY

PUBLISHER'S NOTE

This novel is a work of fiction. Names, characters, places, and incidents either are the product of the author's imagination or, if real, used fictitiously.

SIGNET TRADEMARK REG. U.S. PAT. OFF. AND FOREIGN COUNTRIES
REGISTERED TRADEMARK—MARCA REGISTRADA
HECHO EN CHICAGO, U.S.A.

SIGNET, SIGNET CLASSIC, MENTOR, PLUME, MERIDIAN AND NAL BOOKS are published by New American Library, 1633 Broadway, New York, New York 10019

First Printing, November, 1984

1 2 3 4 5 6 7 8 9

PRINTED IN THE UNITED STATES OF AMERICA

For readers interested in Chicago, I would like to recommend two fascinating picture books: *The Great Fire: Chicago, 1871*, by Herman Kogan and Robert Cromie; and *Chicago, A Pictorial History*, by Herman Kogan and Lloyd Wendt.

Special thanks go to Al Zuckerman, my hardworking agent, and Hilary Ross, my very gifted editor. Also to Bambe Levine, Margaret Duda, Joyce Campbell, and Teane Ames. To my parents, Jean and Will Haughey, and last of all, to my sons, Michael and Andy Grice.

1

Alisa Amsell slapped the buggy reins, urging the chestnut mare to a brisk canter. It was a glorious May morning, the sky deep sapphire, the Illinois sunlight brilliant, full of the glare and promise of spring.

She would *not* worry, she told herself. Not yet, not until she actually faced her father and found out the worst.

She veered the buggy toward the corner of State and Monroe streets, where Chicago's solid-gray Palmer House Hotel dominated the street like a frowning uncle. A liveried doorman helped an elaborately dressed lady to alight from a carriage. Circling the woman's wide skirt, an apple peddler eyed Alisa boldly, lifting up a bright red apple to wave it at her.

Alisa drove on, drawing a deep breath. The air was full of rich city scents. That apple, the last of winter's storage. The French perfume the woman had worn. Horses. Mud. Sawdust, the stockyards, smoke, and the hint of a river stench that on hot days would become formidable.

This was her city, Chicago, where she had been
born, and to which her father's steel mill contrib-
uted some of the full-bodied flavor to the air.
Papa. . . . Again the worry nudged at her, but she
pushed it away, for she didn't believe in fretting.

She was a tall young woman with upswept honey-
gold hair tucked under a pretty straw bonnet, and
the erect posture of a princess as she drove in lone
command of her buggy. Traffic was heavy. Skillfully she aimed the jaunty vehicle through a narrow space that opened between a horse-drawn
wagon groaning with lumber, and a draper's van.

The van driver cursed at her as she made it
around him. Women who drove! Alisa grinned
and kept going. Two years ago, her father had
bought her the buggy for her seventeenth birthday.
Dutifully, Eben Amsell had cautioned her about
the dangers of a runaway horse, and the possibility that, on a rainy day, the mare might skid on
the slick wooden blocks with which the streets of
the city were paved.

Then he'd taught her all the driving skills he
knew, until she could handle a buggy as deftly as
any coachman or cabdriver—and better than most.
It was vast amusement to Eben, who laughed and
said that Alisa's driving put all the dull, timid
society ladies to shame, not to mention a great
number of men. Too bad she hadn't been born a
boy. She would surely have shown Chicago a thing
or two.

But even though she wasn't a boy, Alisa loved
driving her own buggy. She had the freedom to
go where she pleased, to explore the fascination
of the city, with its dozen wooden bridges that

spanned the river, its grain elevators, stockyards, the McCormick Reaper Works, and the ramshackle hovels of Conley's Patch and Kilgubbin that contrasted with hotels of marbled elegance.

It was a freedom that, in 1870, few upper-class girls possessed.

"Racing about like a hellion, like some wild boy, putting her pretty nose into manufactories and lumberyards and heaven knows where else!" Cousin Malva Eames, who had tried to oversee Alisa's upbringing since the death of her mother, would sigh gustily. "Thank heaven she has intelligence and some sense. Otherwise I'm sure I don't know what would become of her."

That remark had been made only yesterday at a tea given by Malva, a leading Chicago hostess. It held some truth. What *was* to become of her? Alisa was nineteen now. Her education at Mrs. Soames's School for Young Ladies had included a smattering of French, history, needlework, piano, singing, economics, and literature, all subjects considered essential for the well-brought-up girl who intended to enter society.

Unfortunately, Alisa hated the piano. She couldn't sing, and only tolerated needlework. But her French was superb, and she had excelled at history and mathematics.

"If you were a boy . . ." The headmistress had sighed, unconsciously echoing Alisa's father. She had looked at her charge with mingled regret and speculation. "But you aren't, are you? No . . . Still, you do have certain qualities. Energy. A wild spirit that may serve you well."

"Yes, Mrs. Soames," Alisa had murmured, pleased

at the compliment, which the teacher, frowning, immediately took away.

"Of course, you are much too prideful. Pride is not always a virtue, Miss Amsell. Sometimes it can be a grievous fault."

After graduating first in her class of twelve, Alisa had then been "finished" with a trip to Europe, a gift from Malva, and had returned, under her older cousin's sponsorship, to plunge into the whirl of debutante balls and parties, intended to introduce her to society and to possible suitors.

And suitors there were. Perhaps even an indecent number of them, for Alisa was considered one of the season's beauties. She was tall, her hair rich honey, her skin the color of peaches and milk, its fine-pored delicacy the envy of Malva, who said in exasperation that the sight of Alisa's skin was enough to make a woman of forty-eight throw away her creams and lotions in despair.

Alisa's eyes were an intense shade of cobalt blue that could sparkle with interest or flash with anger, and occasionally intimidate a less-than-forceful suitor.

A few said she was too tall, of course. Some claimed that she was too outspoken, and some middle-aged Chicago matrons whispered over tea that Alisa's father let her go entirely too wild, that a husband would have to work hard to force Alisa Amsell back into line again.

Still, Alisa thought now, as buggy wheels clattered over paving blocks, these flaws did not seem to deter the men who sought her out. Men who paid calls and compliments, who took her driving and to the opera, ice skating, or on jaunts to stagecoach inns outside Chicago, where a supper of wild game could be had after a bracing ride.

Yes, Alisa had her beauty to draw them, and her blue-blooded lineage, for Eben Amsell could trace his ancestry back to the *Mayflower* and beyond, his family intermarried with Jeffersons and Adamses. Alisa's mother, Tessa Biddle, had been a beauty in her own time, related to the Biddles of Philadelphia, another venerable name.

But on the debit side, Eben Amsell's fortune was not very large. True, he owned the Amsell Steel Mill and a few other holdings, and the Amsells lived in a new corner house on Michigan Avenue. Alisa drove a smart little runabout, and her father a larger equipage pulled by a pair of matched grays. Still, for reasons Alisa could not fathom, money always seemed to be a problem.

"I don't suppose you could marry for money, could you, chicken?" Eben had jested once, ruffling up his daughter's hair. Then he had laughed at himself. "Don't listen to me, sweetheart, not a word. Marry for love, for passion. Never think about crass money . . . it'll only put frown lines in your pretty forehead, eh?"

Still, it had been an effort to swing Alisa's debut, to furnish her with the large wardrobe that was required, and if Malva had not paid for the trip to Europe, they could not have afforded it.

"We're poor but blue-blooded," Eben said. "That means we survive on our wits, using what faint glamour our name still possesses. And our looks," he added ruefully, for at forty-three Eben was still handsome, and with one of his slow smiles could turn female heads in any drawing room.

But Alisa didn't want to survive on her looks—or use her name either. She wanted to do things for herself, to ... But impatiently she slapped the reins, shutting off the thought. The truth was, she didn't really know what she wanted. What was there, in Chicago in 1870, for a pretty girl to do, if she didn't wish to marry?

Alisa dropped the thought as another buggy rounded the corner. Its driver swayed in the seat, urging his horse, a large gray, to a strong trot. The second buggy rumbled up beside her own, then veered past her so closely that Alisa could smell the leather of its fine-tooled seat and quarter-top, and hear the jingle of silver ornaments. A set of initials was elaborately scrolled in silver on the gleaming black body.

But she did not get a chance to decipher the initials or to get more than a glimpse of the buggy's driver, a craggy-looking man in black whose top hat marked him as belonging to the ranks of the rich. Wheels rattled, and then she was looking at the back of the carriage, which had passed her as easily as a greyhound lopes past a mongrel.

Alisa felt the color flood to her cheeks. She hated being passed. She hated being bested, and she adored a challenge.

"Ah, come on, Dancy," she shouted in a clear voice to her mare. She used a small buggy whip to lightly flick the horse's flank. The mare, bred of racing stock, instantly increased her speed.

"Go, Dancy! Go on, girl, show him!" Alisa shouted. She cracked the whip in the air, and leaned forward, the wind blowing her hat askew.

The mare seemed to catch Alisa's excitement, and forged ahead faster. In a moment they pulled beside the other buggy. Its driver flashed her a look from dark, smoky eyes. Alisa saw a shock of curly black hair and a flashing white grin.

"Two dollars says I can beat you to Lake Street!" she cried.

Black eyebrows raised. "Ten says you can't."

Ten? It was a huge increase, the difference enough to buy the smart little dress Alisa wore, her hat, and new garnet earrings besides.

"You're on!" Recklessly Alisa cracked the whip again and swung her buggy around a large muddy depression in the road, positioning her vehicle so that her opponent would be forced to hit the bump head-on.

He did, spraying water. His grin vanished, to be replaced by a scowl.

She laughed aloud as she gained a few feet on him. Gleefully she swerved to avoid collision with a phaeton filled with young ladies on a shopping expedition. The girls shrieked and Alisa shouted to her mare, totally swept up in the excitement of the race. She loved it! She could hardly wait to see his crestfallen expression when she beat him.

The buggies slammed down the crowded street, battling for position. This was the commercial district, and the sidewalks were thronged with women shoppers, businessmen, stevedores, fish sellers, newsboys, beggars, many spilling out into the street to cross at random.

Alisa had to circle two men lugging a wooden crate, losing a few feet. She cried out with annoyance—*he* drove with the arrogant skill of a stagecoach driver.

Another block put them neck-and-neck. Then, inexorably, he pulled ahead. She saw his wide grin, and he had the effrontery to tip his hat to her, the gesture one of assured victory.

Alisa screamed at her mare. She half-stood in her seat, slapping the reins, wild with frustration. Faster . . . was this all the faster that Dancy could go?

They hurtled toward Lake Street, possessing the entire road by sheer virtue of their speed, pedestrians jumping back to allow them to pass. Suddenly Alisa saw a blur from the corner of her eye. It was a newsboy, making his erratic way down the walk, hawking copies of the Chicago *Tribune*.

No, she moaned to herself. *No, don't, not now!*

But the boy, intent on a customer, was repositioning his bag of papers and didn't see them. Alisa shouted out a warning and heard her opponent's angry cry as he was forced to swerve to avoid hitting the boy.

She pulled ahead, winning by default.

Alisa drove to the tall wooden lamppost and telegraph pole that marked the corner of State and Lake. In a few seconds the other driver pulled up beside her. She noted, to her hot satisfaction, that the shiny black paint of his buggy was mud-spattered, the silver initials soiled. He looked annoyed.

"Do you always drive like a fire wagon on the way to a blaze?"

"Whenever I can," she responded pertly, enjoying herself.

She eyed him from under her lashes. He was a tall man in his mid-thirties, with eyes so black and bold that they seemed to glisten like dark jewels. He had high-carved cheekbones, a jutting nose, and a firm, willful mouth. He hated losing, she saw. It made her feel glad.

"Too bad you had to avoid that boy," she called. "But I'm the winner! By a length at least."

He scowled. "Indeed you are. I suppose you want payment?" He fished in a pocket and pulled out one of the huge paper bills of the period, handing it to her. As their hands touched, she felt the sudden electrical contact of his skin, and involuntarily jerked away.

He grinned slowly. "I won't bite you, you know."

"Of course not. Don't be silly!" But she was uncomfortably aware of the interest in those jet-black eyes.

"I'll challenge you again sometime," he promised. "But next time there'll be no newsboys to interfere. And I'll win."

He'd said it so confidently, as if, of course, there could be no other outcome, that Alisa lost her temper. "Not without a battle—a damn good one!"

" 'Damn'?" he mocked. "Ah, such language, my dear. You must learn to win with more grace. However were you brought up? By ruffians?"

"By . . ." Alisa felt herself turn six shades of furious pink. "I was reared by my father, who is a *gentleman*. You are the one who is rude! And I'd say that you're probably a ruffian, too!"

As he reddened, she straightened her spine and slapped the reins firmly, signaling the mare to go. After all, she was a lady, although she certainly hadn't proved it today. Marshaling what dignity she could, she drove away.

She didn't look back, although she imagined she felt the heat of his angry glance centered in the middle of her back.

As Alisa drove home, she tried to settle her jangled nerves. Why had she acted like such a fool? First she'd raced the man like a daredevil stableboy. Then she'd jumped away from his touch as if it had been fire. Finally she'd promised him a good battle and sworn like a . . . a livery-stable thug.

Hot color flooded her, racing up and down her veins.

And who was he, anyway? His dress and attitude plainly marked him as wealthy, yet she'd never seen him in any of the drawing rooms she knew. He must be from out of town, she decided. Or a confidence man or impostor who was not accepted into society.

She tried to calm herself, trotting the mare at a brisk pace. Anyway, what did it matter who such a rude man was? She had to hurry, or she'd be late for luncheon with her father. And she mustn't arrive tardy and disheveled, for she had to talk to Papa, had to persuade him to tell her what was wrong.

She left the business area and drove into the residential streets, where tender green leaves arched overhead in the season's first pale green. Pink-white fluffs of cherry blossoms spilled perfume, and flowering crab apples were an explosion of pink.

Alisa neared her home, slowing the mare. Big square mansions lined the street. These homes—

all new—boasted wood trim and mansard roofs, but despite their size, were crammed so close together that the residents lived practically wall-to-wall.

But it was all considered stylish, and the biggest homes had ornate cupolas jutting up from their flat roofs, crowning the dwellings like odd brick hats. The Amsell home also possessed such a decoration. Now Alisa glanced up at it, thinking of Papa's amusement the day when, at eight years old, she had told him they lived in a house with a hat.

"A *hat,* my precious? Is it a bowler or a top hat or maybe even a fez or a stovepipe? You must make up your mind, eh?"

Alisa had decided that the cupola was a top hat, tall and elegant.

She pulled her buggy around the corner to the back alley, where a row of carriage houses served the dwellings. What was wrong with Papa? For something certainly was. For weeks he'd been too busy even to eat meals with her. She'd actually had to send him a note in order to get him to take luncheon with her today. And that wasn't like him.

She drove into the carriage house, which was shadowy dark and smelled wonderfully of straw, leather, and horses. A collection of buggy whips, prizes won by both Papa and herself in buggy and cutter races, hung on one wall.

"A good ride, Miss Amsell?" The stableboy was waiting to unhitch.

Alisa suppressed a stab of chagrin at the thought of the man with the bold black eyes. "Oh, yes, Billy, a fine ride."

She didn't wait for Billy to help her down, but swung out of the buggy herself, landing lightly on the wooden floor. She started toward the house, brushing at the street dust on her skirt. Somehow, that mud puddle must have splashed her, too.

"Ah, miss, your dress is filthy! And your hair! *Vraiment*, it is a disgrace!" Alisa's French maid, Fifine, pulled out the pins from Alisa's honey-blond mass of hair and began to brush its tangles vigorously.

"Ouch!" Alisa grabbed the brush and began to do it herself. "Honestly, Fifine, must you yank and tear at my hair as if you wished to pull out every lock by the roots?"

"I am only brushing. *Alors*! Such a hoyden!" Fifine had been with the household since Alisa was a child, and believed this gave her the right to scold. She went to the closet and began laying out dresses.

Alisa sighed and tugged at the brush, impatient with her thick mass of hair that required constant discipline. Why couldn't she have easy, biddable hair, instead of this mane of streaked gold and saffron and tawny that always tumbled out of hats and fell out of pins by its sheer weight?

"What dress shall I wear?" she called to Fifine.

Fifine, who had worked at a *couturier* house in Paris as a girl, grimaced. At thirty-five, she still had sharp good looks that were set off by the black taffeta uniform she wore, a white lace apron pinned to the front. "Do you wish to be elegant?"

"I don't know. I suppose so." Alisa put the brush down. "By the way, what sort of mood is he in today?"

The woman shrugged eloquently. "He is ... autocratic. A tyrant. What else? He is as always."

Frowning, Alisa walked to her bed, where four dresses awaited her selection. A dark green, a blue silk, and two others. Papa, she thought. No one else understood him as she did, his pride, his volatile temperament, his deep love for her. He was a wonderful father. She adored him and always would.

She pointed to one of the dresses, a white piqué trimmed with a cloud of ruffles and lace. "That one," she said.

"Very well."

Fifine helped Alisa out of her riding dress, a chore that required the unfastening of dozens of tiny jet buttons and the release of several hidden ribbons and ties. Then she busied herself with the piqué, taking out the fine tissue paper with which it had been padded to guard against wrinkles, and undoing its long rows of pearl buttons. Alisa stood in her corset cover and petticoats and worried about her father.

"How is he autocratic?" she asked. "In what way?"

"He shouted at Mary, that silly little downstairs girl, and he threatened to fire the gardener. Ah, he was in a mood."

Alisa frowned. Papa usually ignored the servants, expecting them to act as well-oiled machines, serving the household. "What else?"

"He was sick this morning, too."

"Sick?"

"*Oui.*" The woman pantomimed nausea.

More worried than ever, Alisa stood with the

dress loosely pulled around her, staring at her maid. Perhaps it was only servants' gossip, to be discounted. To the best of Alisa's knowledge, Eben Amsell, tall, blue-eyed, and handsome, had never succumbed to illness. He refused even to admit it existed.

"Hurry!" Alisa struggled into the yards of cloth and turned her back so Fifine could reach the buttons. "Oh, do hurry with this, Fifine. And think up something for my hair. I *have* to talk to Papa!"

Ten minutes later, Alisa descended the stairs in a silken rustle of petticoats, her shoulders proudly held back, as Mrs. Soames had taught all her girls. The headmistress had despaired of Alisa's long stride, unfashionable for a woman, but Papa had assured her it was all right. Alisa, he said, walked with the sinuous lope of a young tigress. What real man, he wanted to know, could complain of that?

She reached the bottom of the stairs and turned right toward the library. This was where she knew she would find her father, bent over papers and ledgers that he had brought home from the Amsell Steel Mill.

"Papa?" She rapped at the door.

But there was no response, so, knowing she was expected, she pulled open the door and entered the library. It was a large sunny room that faced south, its walls lined with books.

"Papa, I raced my buggy today, and I won."

She stopped. Eben Amsell sat at the desk with his back to her, his luxuriant blond hair mixed with gray, his neck stalwart and handsome. He did not seem to have the slightest idea she had entered the room.

"Papa! I'm here . . ." She darted forward to slide her arms around her father's neck, nuzzling kisses into the starched back of his collar. But instead of returning her kiss, her father started violently. His muscles flexed with such force that his hand crumpled the papers he held.

He had never reacted like this to her before. Alisa's blood went cold. "Papa, whatever is wrong? I . . . I did knock. I didn't mean to startle you."

Slowly Eben Amsell turned. His face, which had been drained gray, gradually regained its color and became handsome and familiar again, the father she adored.

"Do you always walk up behind men, scaring them half into the next world?" he teased. But Alisa thought she still saw a white edge to his lips.

"Papa . . ."

"Nonsense, my girl, enough of this fussing. Didn't we have an agreement to have lunch? Or was that note you sent me merely a lark and a lie? Whitefish," Eben Amsell went on in his deep voice. "I ordered whitefish. Poached. Does that sound agreeable to you, my sweetheart?"

"It sounds . . . very good," she managed to say. She waited while her father rose from his desk and put the stack of papers away, pretending she didn't notice that the top ones were creased from the violent pressure of his hands.

Something *was* wrong, she thought as she followed him out of the library. Something dark and bad, she could tell by the shiver that prickled the nerve ends of her skin, and that would not stop, even when Papa smiled at her.

2

They lunched in the conservatory, an octagonal-shaped room paved with pink Italian marble and containing high floor-to-ceiling windows that were hung with dozens of plants, their fronds falling down in a wild profusion of greenery. Among the green stood a Greek statue of a small laughing boy. As a child, Alisa had been fascinated by him. She'd imagined him as a real boy, caught and turned to stone by some witch.

Now she sat poking at her whitefish, pushing it around and around her plate with her fork. Mary, the Irish maid, served them, scurrying back and forth with trays, her face wearing the cowed look of one who expects to be shouted at again. Alisa felt sorry for her.

"Mary seems distracted today," she ventured to say at last, after she had exhausted all the luncheon topics she could think of—today's race, a recent fire, a velocipede that she had seen in a shop window at Adams and State streets.

"Distracted? The girl is empty-headed! She can't even comprehend the simplest of orders. But what can anyone expect? She probably spent her life living in a sod hut with the pigs and the cows."

Eben Amsell's prejudice was typical of Chicagoans toward immigrants, who had flooded the city for years, forming a large, poor segment of its population. But they would work long hours for low pay, and Germans, Swedes, Irish, and Italians now populated all the servants' quarters along Michigan Avenue and Terrace Row, and were employed in the city's stockyards, reaper works, tanneries, distilleries, and flour mills.

"I'm sure she's doing the best she can to learn our ways," Alisa said diplomatically. She pushed back her plate. "Papa . . . this isn't like you, none of it is. Shouting at a poor Irish girl. Threatening to fire a gardener—our only gardener, by the way; who will do the grass and flowers if he goes? And do you realize that I had to send you a *note* in order to have lunch with you? You've hardly been home at all in three weeks."

"Ah. My Alisa, my beautiful treasure." He pushed aside his own untouched plate to gaze at her with sad eyes. "What have I done to you?"

Something about his expression made her uneasy. "Oh, Papa. You've had things on your mind, I suppose."

Sad eyes! Eben Amsell had never looked sad in his life, not even at her mother's funeral. He had raged then, ranting at the huge injustice of fate that could take a woman away in childbirth along with her infant.

She reached across the table and took her father's hand. She didn't want him to be sad. She wanted the old Eben back, the one who'd taught her to drive like a hoyden and gloated over her victories. Who had taken her to the mill with him and treated her like a boy. She searched for the proper words. "Do you wish to talk about it?"

Mary returned to clear their plates, taking them away on a big wooden tray to the kitchen again. Eben looked at her, and suddenly the sad expression in his eyes turned to anger, and the handsome mouth twisted. "What is there to talk about? What's done is done. There are predators in this world, you know. Sharks. Human ones, that prey on those who . . . buck the tiger."

Alisa's father often used expressions like that. "Papa, what are you talking about?"

"We are prey, Alisa. Food for them, for the ones who stalk the jungle of the business world."

This talk frightened her. "Papa!"

Then, as if sensing her distress, Eben Amscll sighed, giving a small, tight laugh that Alisa didn't even recognize. "God, honey. Oh, God. Don't pay any attention to me, I think I've been burning the midnight candles for too long and too hard. Don't mind my little jokes. Or the fact that I indulged in a tiny jot of brandy before you came to the library to fetch me."

"I see." Alisa looked over to where the marble boy laughed in perpetual happiness. So Papa had been drinking. Of course. That was why he talked and acted so strangely.

She relaxed in her chair and listened while Eben began a long, involved story about something that had happened yesterday at his club. Apparently a mule had been dressed in top hat and cravat, led in through a back door, and given a place in the dining room, as a prank. Two members, both regulars at one of Chicago's gambling clubs, had had a wager.

Eben finished the story and laughed heartily, leaning back while Mary brought their dessert, a sour-cream-and-raisin pie. "So you won another a race today, darling?"

"Yes, I did."

He made her repeat all the details, and questioned her on who her opponent had been.

"I don't know, Papa, I didn't recognize him."

"Oh, well, many new people arrive in this city every day. The industries draw 'em. Upstarts . . ." For an instant Eben looked distant again. But he shook the sad look away. "And you won by a length?"

"Yes . . . but, Papa, it was because of a newsboy who got in the way—he had to swerve to avoid hitting him. So I suppose that I really—"

"Never mind about that. It was his bad luck, not yours. I want you always to win, Alisa. Make them sit up and take notice—you can do it, aren't you Eben Amsell's offshoot? You *did* win. And just for that," he added expansively, "I think I'll give you a little victory reward. How would you like a brand-new runabout? Handmade, the best, with a good hardwood frame."

Alisa hesitated, her unease somehow still not laid to rest. "But I already have a fine buggy."

"Then you shall have another one, my darling. And I'll buy you a beautiful Arabian horse with the clean, fine lines of a champion—because *you* are a champion, Alisa, you are clean and fine, too, the very best."

Alisa turned her attention to the pie, eating quickly. She was almost relieved when Mary bustled in again with a letter, which she handed to Eben Amsell.

"Man came deliverin' this, sir. Said you were to have it straightaway."

"What is it?" Eben looked at the letter but did not take it.

"Why, 'tis a letter, sir."

After the maid left, Alisa watched while, with slow, deliberate movements, Eben Amsell slit open the wax-sealed envelope. As he read the letter, his face drained of color, and by the time he had finished, his skin was pale and sallow, dotted with perspiration.

"Papa?"

But it was as if Eben did not even hear his daughter's cry of alarm. Crumpling the letter and jamming it into his pocket, he pushed back from the table.

That night Alisa couldn't sleep. She tossed and turned restlessly, listening to the creak of boards as they settled and adjusted in the night, a mouse scurrying somewhere in the rafters, the distant clip-clopping of a horse, sounds so familiar that she usually never even heard them. Tonight the moonlight streamed into her window like a curtain of silver gauze, an empress's veil.

She flopped over on her stomach and tried to sort out the strange and confusing day. The hot joy of winning the race. The way that strange black-eyed man had challenged her. And then the bewildering lunch with her father, that had ended with him stalking out of the conservatory.

She'd even run after him, calling his name. But he had gone into the library again and closed the door firmly behind him, and this time she didn't dare pursue him.

Rebuffed, she'd finally plunged from the house and gone walking down Michigan Avenue—striding block after block, past the mansions into the area to the west, where small frame workers' houses teetered in the mud, alive with swarms of children, dogs, and chickens. Tired-looking women stared at her from doorways, envying her dress, her beauty, her freedom.

What, oh, *what* was wrong with Papa, turning him into a sad-eyed, frightened stranger?

Finally she'd turned back, and she'd dined alone in her room. Then, in the fragrant spring dusk, she'd gone riding with Matt Eberley, the most persistent of her suitors. Matt was Eben's attorney, a well-to-do widower of thirty-four who was much in demand by hostesses for his sandy-haired good looks, his well-bred manners, and his willingness to serve as "extra man" at dinner parties. She and Matt had talked, as usual, about books, gossip, and some of Matt's legal cases, which he enjoyed discussing in tiresome detail.

Now she was glad to be home again. She lay in bed, consumed with a terrible feeling of foreboding that only seemed to grow heavier and more oppressive as the night hours passed.

She turned on her side. She bunched up her pillow and buried her face in it, and then she tossed the pillow aside and lay on her stomach again, staring at dust motes that floated in the beam of moonlight.

Suddenly an explosion shattered the air, so loud, so ear-splitting that it sounded as if a cannon had been fired off in her ear, splintering her thoughts, rending apart her very brain.

What was it? Almost before the sound had stopped, Alisa had jumped out of bed. She raced for the door, running as fast as she could, yet she felt as if she struggled through molasses.

Everything seemed to happen in slow time. Wearing a nightgown, her maid, Fifine, was somehow in front of Alisa, blocking her way into her father's bedroom. Alisa surprised herself with her strength as she threw the woman aside and yanked open the door.

"Papa . . . no . . . no . . ." She didn't even hear her sobs as she rushed inside. Behind her, Fifine was crying in French.

Eben's room was semidark, the air tainted with a strange, powdery, metallic stench. Alisa gasped in realization. She knew that smell! *Gunpowder.* She had smelled it often, on the Fourth of July, a rowdy holiday when men and boys sometimes shot off guns in the streets, and prudent people stayed indoors.

Wildly she looked around. *No,* she thought. Her father's bed was empty. A chair by the window stood empty, too, outlined in calm, silver light.

But there was . . .

Oh, there was . . . On the floor near the chair . . .

Papa's body, clad in a dressing gown, was sprawled loose-limbed on the floor, like a pile of abandoned clothes.

His hand still clutched a pistol and there was blood on his head, and blood on the floor, shiny with moonlight.

Alisa screamed. She screamed and screamed. She rushed toward her father and threw herself on top of him, refusing to leave him until Fifine and Mary and two other terrified servants finally came and pulled her away.

He had killed himself. With a pistol that Alisa hadn't even known he possessed, he had gone away and left her, he had deserted her, *he had killed himself*. Alisa fought her grief and rage and shock all night and all the next day, refusing to let anyone into her room.

She heard servants' knocks and calls, and once Malva's voice, but she had slammed the bolt shut. She huddled on her bed in a fetal ball, weeping until her eyes burned, then lying still in a stupor of suffering. Her father . . . her father . . . *Papa!*

She couldn't understand it. Why had he done it? Why? Had he possessed worries that dark, that serious? Why hadn't he told her? Was it her fault for not trying to talk to him more? Perhaps she should have followed him into the library. Hugged him, kissed him, reassured him of her love.

She rubbed her temples. She had cried so much that her eyelids hurt and her head throbbed painfully. Still in her terrible shock, she replayed it again, those endless minutes. Herself in bed. The explosion of the pistol shot. Herself racing down the corridor. Fifine . . .

Fifine had been in the hall too, wearing only a nightgown. But the servants' quarters were on the third floor, and so how could Fifine have gotten down a whole flight of stairs so quickly, when Alisa herself had just managed to race out of her nearby bedroom?

Then, numbly, Alisa retreated into her dumb, animal pain. What difference did such a small detail make when Papa was gone forever?

By noon of the second day, Alisa's young, healthy body rebelled against grief. She had cried her eyes dry, and her stomach was beginning to rumble with the normal hunger of an active young woman.

Slowly she rose from the bed and pulled off the nightgown in which she had lain for the past thirty-six hours. Moving like an automaton, she found a corset and laced herself into it, putting on a camisole, petticoats, the armor of undergarments worn by all women from childhood on. Blindly she went to her closet and took out the first dress her hands touched—a plain blue serge school dress that she had worn at Mrs. Soames's school.

Her fingers managed the buttons automatically. Then she ran the brush through her full, thick curls that did not seem to know there had been a death, but bounced up eagerly to her touch. She found a hairnet and stuffed her hair into it, extinguishing the honey-colored light.

She went downstairs, averting her eyes from the door of the conservatory, ajar on a view of greenery and the mindlessly laughing marble boy. She could smell ham frying, and the scent of yeasty bread.

"Alisa. Oh, my sweet girl." Malva was waiting in the mahogany-paneled dining room, clad, as always, entirely in black, a magnificent full-busted dowager who wore that dark hue like a royal mantle. Her cousin enveloped her in a hug that smelled of heliotrope perfume. "Poor, poor baby."

"Malva," Alisa whispered, choking.

"There, there. It's all right. I've been here since last night. You poor little girl, shame on you for locking yourself away."

Malva held her and petted her, as a mother might have done, and for an instant Alisa gave herself up to this comfort, biting her lips against fresh sobs. Finally she became aware of a second, male voice.

"You have my sympathies, Alisa. It is a terrible blow," Matt Eberley said. Alisa pulled away from her cousin's embrace. Had Matt been here all along? She hadn't even seen him. Her mind felt thick, damaged by grief.

Matt hugged her too. They converged around her, saying the empty, sympathetic things that people always say. Finally Alisa sat down at the table and let Mary bring her a hot platter piled with fried ham, eggs, biscuits, sausage, and toast with strawberry preserves. There was a pot of coffee, and plenty of thick top cream. Automatically Alisa began to eat, surprised at how good the food tasted. Salty ham. Sweet preserves with seedy little bits that crunched slightly between her teeth. She ate greedily, and felt guilty for doing so, and could not stop eating.

Finally Alisa was sated, and she pushed her plate away with revulsion.

"Well, at least you're eating again," Malva said briskly, going on to tell Alisa of the arrangements that had been made pending her approval. She

finished, "Alisa . . . there is something that Matt
Eberley has come here to say. I know it comes at a
terrible time, but it is necessary for you to listen."

Alisa froze, her throat suddenly closing up. Matt
was Papa's attorney; she'd forgotten that. And
now she saw that he'd brought a briefcase with
him.

"I could come back later," Matt offered. He was
tall and thin and sandy-haired, with a face that
tended to freckle, and skin that reddened with
exposure to the sun.

"No, please talk to me now," Alisa begged.

"Very well. Under the circumstances . . . That is,
you know how legalities are . . . That is to say . . ."

Alisa held on to the edge of the dining table,
feeling the hard mahogany hurt her fingers. She
looked at Malva and saw pity in the older woman's
eyes. "Don't *dawdle*, Matt! Just go ahead and tell
me!"

At her fierce cobalt-blue glare, the attorney
cleared his throat, taking some papers out of the
case and shuffling them. But at last Matt said,
"You're penniless, Alisa."

"What!"

"I'm sorry to have to say it so bluntly, but it's
true. Your father made some . . . ah, business
errors. Big ones. He has lost everything, including
this house. You'll have a few weeks to pack and
get out, of course. I'm sure the new owner will be
kind, he is not a monster after all. But all the safes
must be opened, and your father's other holdings
put on the block as well. And the mill," Matt went
on inexorably. "The Amsell mill. That too is gone,
of course."

"Not the mill," she whispered. The Amsell mill. With its huge puffing smokestacks and eerie, glowing red light from the blast furnaces, it had been part of Alisa's life from the time she was a baby. How many times had Papa brought her there to visit? A hundred times? A thousand? They all knew her name, they'd remembered her birthday.

"I'm very sorry," Matt was saying.

He had said so much, so fast, that she could only make sense out of about half of it. Errors? What errors? The house gone? *Penniless?* Oh, surely this was all a prank, like the mule at her father's club.

Alisa shook her head, her mind resisting. She looked imploringly at her cousin, who was biting on her lower lip. Matt, too, looked distressed, his blue eyes anxious.

With a sinking squeeze of her heart, Alisa realized that he had not been lying to her—it was all true. And then her mind made a further, instinctive leap. *This* was the terrible thing that had worried Papa for weeks. This was what he had spoken about when he had referred to human sharks and predators.

"You'll never be in want, Alisa," Malva promised, her voice seeming to come from a long distance away. "You'll come to live with me, of course. I'd be delighted to have you, you can help me plan the summer season. And I always need help with my orphan girls." Like many society women, Malva had her pet charity, a small orphanage for homeless girls.

Alisa nodded, wondering when she'd start to

feel the pain of all this fully. Right now she felt
numbed, unable to absorb it. Her beloved father
was dead, and she was to be left with nothing, not
even a house to live in. And it was someone's
fault, it had to be. Why couldn't she shriek, cry,
rage with anger?

Matt began to talk knowledgeably about speculation, credit, and bank notes, but Alisa burst
through his explanations. "Who?" she demanded.
"Who did this to my father?"

Matt and Malva glanced at each other. "Why,
no one, Alisa. It was his own doing. He—"

"Stop protecting me! Stop looking at each other!
Tell me the truth!"

"I have, Alisa."

She was suddenly feeling again; anger, white-
hot and frantic. "No, you haven't. He talked about
predators, men preying on other men in business.
I have to know! Who is the one who treated Papa
like this, who made him want to kill himself? This
wasn't just a matter of my father making a business mistake or two, was it? I can tell by your face,
Matt Eberley."

Matt moistened his lips, but it was Malva who
spoke up. "Now, Alisa, darling, you're terribly
overwrought. This has been a dreadful ordeal.
Come upstairs with me, and we'll hunt through
your closet for some mourning clothes suitable for
the funeral. And you'll need more things, too,
some good black serge and French bunting. I have
a wonderful little dressmaker who—"

"No!" Anger went flowing through Alisa like a
spring freshet. "No, I won't be fobbed off like a
child. I want to know who did it." She glared at

Matt, deliberately using the strength in her deep blue eyes. "Matt! If you don't tell me, I'll find out for myself. I swear it!"

Matt sighed. "Oh, very well, Alisa. You *are* strong-willed, aren't you? Still, there is nothing you can do about it now. Your father did try, but he was unable to prevail."

"Prevail against whom?"

"Why, against Riordan Daniels. It was he who pressed the matter."

Riordan Daniels. The name whirled in Alisa's head like a tornado, forcing her to sink into a chair, her fingers gripping its arms. She spoke through stiff lips. "Who is this man?"

"He is new to the city, coming from New York, where he still maintains interests. He bought the Eglinton mansion, I believe. Alisa, do you really think this is a matter for you to concern yourself with? You should take Malva's advice, and—"

"Tell me about him, Matt."

"Well, he is rich, very rich, one of the wealthiest men in the country, they say, with holdings in construction, railroads, lumber, steel. Now," Matt added as Alisa started to burst out, "I don't want you to be upset, because there is nothing you can do. Do you hear me? Over a period of more than a year, your father speculated wildly. Finally his debts were astronomical. He gambled he could repay them and lost. The man to whom he owed insisted on collecting, as was his legal right."

She shoved back her chair and jumped up. "No! My father never gambled! It's a lie, Matt, a . . . a misunderstanding! Papa would never have risked everything so foolishly."

"Well, he did." Matt turned to Alisa's cousin. "Are there smelling salts, or perhaps some laudanum? She must be calmed, and I really think—"

"I don't want smelling salts!" Alisa shouted. "I don't want laudanum!"

"Well, you need them." Matt reached into his briefcase again. "I didn't want to give this to you now, but I suppose I have no choice. Your father left you a note. One of the servant girls found it this morning and handed it to me as I came in, since you were locked in your room."

"A . . . a note?"

Alisa stared at the letter, and finally took it. Matt and her cousin both began to talk at the same time.

"Dear, take the sedative—" Malva began.

"If you'll come to my office in a few days—" Matt said.

"No!" Alisa whirled away, clutching the letter from her father to her chest like a talisman. "I . . . I won't do anything, I . . . I won't take laudanum, I . . . Oh . . ."

Her control, like fragile eggshell, had suddenly cracked. She turned and blindly fled to her room.

Upstairs, she sank down on a window seat that overlooked the street and stared out at the pink flag of a flowering crab apple, gorgeous with heavy blossoms.

Riordan Daniels. Her lips formed the name of her father's betrayer. She didn't pay much attention to gossip, but hadn't she heard of him? Yes. There had been talk about some newcomer from New York, indecently rich, with a background tainted by scandal. It was said he'd even fought a duel, in an era when gentlemen of quality seldom indulged in such braggadocio.

The pink of the blossoms seemed too deep, too beautiful. Alisa looked down at the letter she held, and finally she slit it open, her father's angular script jumping out at her, bringing him back as nothing else could have.

She scanned words and phrases: ... *my darling girl, daughter of my heart ... There is so much I wanted for you ...*

Her eyes stung with tears as she clutched the paper, forcing herself to read on. *And now my mill, the house, everything are going to be unfairly taken away. It all rightfully belongs to you, and I cannot bear to see my darling stripped of everything.*

Get it back, if you can, Eben wrote, his handwriting becoming more angular, more agitated, as if the gunshot was now only minutes, seconds away. *Get the Amsell mill back, Alisa. And remember that I love you dearly and always will. Forgive me for any wrongs I might have done. I was thinking only of you.*

And then the postscript, tensely scrawled, urgent: *Get it back.*

Alisa stared down at the pages she held in her hands. It was a letter, she thought, written nearly from the grave, its impact as binding as a deathbed wish. *Papa, yes,* she answered him in her head. *Oh, yes, I will.*

She reread the letter again, then a third time, committing it to memory. Finally she folded it and tucked it inside a drawer, knowing she would take it out again, dozens of times, would treasure it until it fell apart, until its words were engraved on her very soul.

Get the Amsell mill back. Papa had begged her, literally from the brink of death. And she intended to do as he wished.

3

An hour later, Alisa stood defiantly in front of her mirror, clad in daffodil-yellow shot silk. The changeable fabric, lush as spring, caught the light as she smoothed the flowing sleeves with their triple tiers of cream lace.

She refused to wear black. No, she simply would not. Papa had hated her in that shade, insisting it sapped the color from a woman's complexion, making her look sallow and uninteresting. Once he had jokingly told her that if she ever had to mourn for him, he expected her to wear black only for the funeral. After that she was to remember him with flower colors, the colors of joy.

Again her eyes flooded with tears, but quickly she dashed them away.

She leaned toward the mirror, afraid that her eyes might be puffy from crying. But, thank God, they weren't. If anything, she decided, they looked larger, more luminous, their deep blue color striking against the pallor of her face. Good, she thought grimly. She needed to look her best.

Drawing confidence from what she saw, she

moved around the room, collecting a pair of kid gloves, a parasol that matched the wonderful yellow of the gown. She pulled over her high-piled curls a bonnet of pale green velvet and surah ribbon.

She finally left the room and hurried downstairs. From a closet she took a cashmere fitted jacket. Matt and Cousin Malva had left, so Alisa was able to depart by the back entrance for the carriage house without anyone to stop her.

She paced about while Billy hitched up the buggy. Outside, it was beginning to rain, a fine, light spray of droplets. This, she knew, combined with the usual slick of horse droppings and axle grease on wood paving blocks, would make the streets slippery and hazardous.

When Billy wanted to put the rubber storm shield over the buggy seat, Alisa refused. "It isn't raining, it's only misty. I just want to *go*, Billy! Please, will you hurry?"

Impatience seized her, but at last she was in the buggy, her hands slapping the reins, glad for the road conditions that would force her to concentrate. Twenty minutes later she stopped in front of the large, showy Eglinton mansion located in the North Division.

She pulled up the mare to stare at the home of the man who had destroyed her father.

The three-story marble structure, the only one on the block, dominated the street. Arched colonnades lined a massive porch that stretched for the full front of the building, reached by an impressive double flight of steps. There were outsize arches, balconies, decorative fretwork, all of it crowned by an enormous cupola set with windows.

Just seeing the house made Alisa's heart pound hard with indignation. While dressing, she'd forced herself to comb her memory for all the gossip she'd ever heard about Riordan Daniels. There was the duel, of course, in which an opponent had nearly died. There were whispers of actresses and shopgirls, ownership of a gambling establishment, bribes paid. Riordan Daniels was reputed to have nearly stolen the wife of a prominent railroad magnate. When confronted by the furious husband, he had laughed and told the man that his wife was a shrew, and not worth the fight.

All these incidents and more had set the blood of Chicago society aboil.

And then there was the house. Daniels had purchased it from a reclusive widow. Within a month, he had spent more than five hundred thousand dollars on furnishings—a sum staggering in its enormity in 1870. The home, gossips whispered, possessed not one, but *two* ballrooms. Daniels had installed a billiards room and a bowling alley. In the gleaming kitchen there was reputed to be a trio of faucets, one equipped with hot water, one with cold, and the third with iced champagne.

Riordan Daniels, Alisa told herself indignantly, could drink champagne at the twist of a wrist, while her father killed himself in grief and despair.

By the time she hitched Dancy to a post, Alisa had worked herself into a fury. She descended from the buggy in a swirl of skirts and marched to the front door. There were teardrop windowpanes set in a semicircle above the door. The knocker was of rich polished silver in the shape of a lion rampant. That figured; a predator, Alisa thought, lifting it to knock with unnecessary violence.

"Yes, miss?" A uniformed butler stared down at her. He was middle-aged and beefy, his shoulders straining at the seams of his black livery, which was trimmed with silver buttons.

"I am Alisa Amsell," she explained, "and I would like to see Mr. Daniels at once."

"Are you expected?" The man's expression was forbidding, and Alisa knew that if her clothing had been less obviously expensive he would have told her curtly to go around to the servants' entrance. In 1870, women did not pay calls upon strange men unannounced—not if they were ladies.

But she was her father's daughter, and she had no intention of being intimidated by a butler.

"Yes, I'm expected," she told the servant firmly.

The butler nodded, ushering her into an entrance hall of rococo splendor. Alisa forgot everything to stare around in amazement. There were decorative pillars, deeply scrolled and embellished with gilt. A plaster ceiling was molded into deep octagonal figures. A wide, imposing staircase led upward, its balusters heavy with gold-leaf plaster flowers and fruit.

Ornate dark furniture was everywhere. There were rich red-hued Persian rugs, one of them depicting mythological beasts. More rooms of equal opulence could be seen opening off the main hall.

Why would any man living alone need so much? The very sight of the house made Alisa more and more angry, although she knew full well that her own father would have possessed such surround-

ings if he could. It was an era for show, for flaunting wealth. But already she hated Riordan Daniels
for doing so. It was like gloating over her father,
she thought.

"Come this way, miss, you can wait in the library."

"Very well." She kept her voice cool, tried not to
be impressed by the thickness of the rugs, the
high ceilings, the *riches*. The library was more of
the same. An improbable canopied couch was cushioned in lush red velvet, its intricately carved woodwork made of black walnut.

The butler left her and she began to pace the
room, soaking in the arrogance of it, the sheer
magnitude of the money it represented. The walls
were covered in wine-red morocco, and there were
more rugs—Turkish, Persian, Chinese—each one
a jewellike work of art that drew the eye irresistibly.

And books, Alisa saw, her anger growing. Tall
glass-fronted shelves were crammed with leather
volumes. There was even a book lying on a table,
a place marked with a leather marker. She peered
at the title. *Civilization*, by Ralph Waldo Emerson.

Furiously she moved away. A robber . . . a predator . . . a shark . . . who *read*! She couldn't believe
it. She didn't want to believe it.

The minutes ticked by as Riordan Daniels kept
her waiting.

"Well?" a voice said behind her, its timbre low
and rich. "To what do I owe this unexpected
pleasure? I don't believe we have been introduced."

He had entered the library without her noticing,
his footsteps muffled in the thick rugs. Alisa turned
as if drawn by an invisible cord. That voice—she'd
heard it before.

"*You!*"

"Ah! And you." As shock pummeled her like fists, he gave her a wry mock bow. His black eyes gleamed at her. "My avid little racer. Might I ask how you managed to find me? Don't tell me that you are here to offer me another challenge? If so, I assure you you have committed a folly. For I certainly intend to win."

She stared at the man against whom she had raced her buggy only two days ago, the man whose touch against her skin had been so violently electric. "Do you really think that I came here because I want to race you?" she demanded in the coldest tones that she could muster.

"Well, didn't you?" He was plainly amused and intrigued by her presence.

"Perhaps you didn't catch the name that your butler gave to you. My name is Alisa Amsell. *Amsell.*"

"Yes, of course." Smiling, he moved toward her with a lazy, lynxlike stride. He was far taller than she had thought, dwarfing even Alisa with his six-foot-three height, like some Saxon king. The bones of his face jutted ruggedly, his high-bridged nose looked as if it might once have been broken, and his eyes were very black. But his smile was unexpectedly sweet, a phenomenon that shook her composure.

"What do you mean, 'yes, of course,'" she mocked. "Do you mean that you *did* expect me? Is that why you kept me cooling my heels for more than a half-hour, like a servant for hire?"

His voice was still amused. "I was with one of my accountants. Please, calm down."

"No, I won't, I won't calm myself. I'm Alisa

Amsell, *I'm Eben Amsell's daughter*. And I've come here to tell you that I'm going to get it back—*all* of it. And I'll make you pay for the crime you've committed—if it's the last thing I ever do."

"What crime?" Black eyes inspected her, the smile in them fading. "That's a serious accusation, Miss Amsell. I had business dealings with your father, true, but there was no crime involved. It was simply a turn of the cards. In this case, luck was on my side."

"Luck! A turn of the cards!"

"You, of course, are a sheltered girl of good family, and probably understand little of business, or of men either. But I assure you, Miss Amsell, what transpired between your father and myself was perfectly legitimate. He made a wild gamble ... and he lost." Riordan Daniels shrugged. "It happens a hundred times a day, it's nothing unusual. It's part of the money game. But he'll eventually recoup his losses, you may be sure of that."

Alisa stood rigidly, staring at him, her pounding heart crowding up into her throat. "Do you mean ... that you don't know?"

"Don't know what?"

"Why, my father's dead."

"What!"

"He killed himself two days ago with a pistol shot to the head."

Riordan Daniels' face paled and he took an involuntary step backward, letting out an exclamation. "I'm sorry, Miss Amsell," he said, regaining control of himself. "I've been holed up in my office working eighteen hours a day. I didn't know, truly I didn't."

But Alisa, worn out from the strain and grief of the last days, had held herself back long enough. Her voice was ragged with tears as she cried, "How ... how could you not have heard? I'm sure it was in all of the papers. I won't accuse you of gloating over Papa's death—surely even you wouldn't stoop that low. Still, I don't think you really care, do you? To you he was just another victim."

"A victim! Come, Miss Amsell, you're being outrageous and insulting. That's hardly fair." Riordan Daniels caught Alisa's arm in his own strong hand. She could feel the warmth and strength of the man, the hearty vitality. "I'm terribly sorry this happened. He didn't seem the type. He was a man's man, or so I thought—"

"You never thought at all!" She shook herself away from him as if he were a pickpocket or a thug. "And my father was certainly not a ... a common gambler, not as you imply! Please don't give me your sympathy or your excuses. I don't want them. I'm going to get the Amsell mill back from you. It was my inheritance, he meant for me to have it!"

She could talk no more; her voice was breaking. In a moment she would humiliate herself by sobbing on the shoulder of her father's enemy. She pulled away, gathering up her skirts, and ran out of the ornate library.

For Alisa, the day of her father's funeral passed in a mercifully blurred state of numbness. Malva made all of the arrangements. Somehow Alisa found herself wearing a black crepe dress and heavy black lace veil, nodding to the hundreds of people who offered sympathy. She could tell they felt sorry for her, that word of what happened had spread throughout Chicago. And she was glad, glad that Riordan Daniels' deed would be known to the world.

She overheard two distant Amsell cousins whispering to each other.

"What's going to happen to Alisa now?" one wanted to know.

"But of course she'll go to Malva," the other said. "Until she marries, at least. And thank God there will be no trouble with that. She is pretty, indecently so, if you ask me. And she's going to need her looks, now that she has no fortune. Of course, there is the Amsell name and that's worth something. And her mother was a Biddle."

Prominent Chicagoans were present: Marshall Field, Potter Palmer, Philip Armour, Cyrus McCormick. Girls with whom Alisa had made her debut gave her swift, embarrassed hugs. Men with whom she had danced at balls and cotillions murmured condolences. Felix Morgan, the manager of the Amsell mill, was openly weeping. The household servants sat at the back of the church, Fifine among them, her eyes also reddened with tears.

Yesterday's mist had turned to a steady, penetrating drizzle as Alisa huddled under Matt's umbrella at the gravesite, listening to the dull, plopping sounds of raindrops on silk. Papa, she remembered, had loved to watch a storm coming in over Lake Michigan, the sky bunched in low, mean, dark clouds that finally burst forth in washes of water.

He'd have loved to have a glorious storm sweep down upon his own funeral cortege, sending him away with a flourish. But not this drizzle, she thought. This was just damp and miserable, and she noticed that the mourners were shifting their feet uneasily, anxious to get back to dry parlors in which an unseasonable May fire would probably be lit.

The minister intoned the stark final words of the burial service and finally it was over. Efficiently Matt held the umbrella over them both and guided her around puddles of rainwater back to the carriage. She could tell by the pressure of his arm that he hoped she would lean on him, overcome with grief.

Proudly Alisa took her arm away from his and walked by herself.

As they reached Matt's carriage she saw Riordan Daniels, standing alone under an umbrella, by his elegant black runabout. Alisa stopped in her tracks. He had not been in the church, and she had not seen him at the grave, either. Had he just arrived? And how dare he attend at all?

"Alisa? What's wrong?" Matt had not seen this unwanted mourner yet.

"He . . . *he* came!"

"He?"

But Riordan was already approaching them, his stride large, loping, and aggressive, his black eyes fixed on her, as if daring her to snub him. Alisa caught her breath, feeling a wave of sickness. This was the man whose *luck*, whose *turn of the cards* had killed her father—indirectly, at least. He,

Riordan Daniels, was the cause of this whole funeral, the reason they all were here.

"Miss Amsell," Riordan Daniels began. "If you need any help, anything at all, I am prepared to give it. Your house, for example. I've had my attorney draw up a life lease for you—"

"No!" Ice froze in her veins, shards of dangerous crystal. "I won't take your charity, or anyone's. All I want is what's mine by right."

Instantly his face hardened. "You already have what is yours 'by right,' Miss Amsell—nothing."

They glared at each other, challenge leaping between them like hard electricity, just as it had on the day they had raced their buggies. In that instant Alisa read him utterly. He was a predator who gloried in the battle, the *game*, as he called it, who asked for no quarter and gave none.

No doubt he fought his battles with men, she thought furiously, and not women. But there was going to be a change in that!

"I want what you took," she told him evenly, giving him an angry smile. "I intend to get it, too."

As his lips twisted, she took Matt's arm and almost dragged him toward their waiting carriage. Her head held proudly, she allowed Matt to help her inside. They drove away, Alisa burningly aware of the tall dark man who stood in the rain scowling after them.

On the following day, Alisa rose early and drove to Matt Eberley's office, which was located on Lake Street over the quarters of a prosperous bank. True to what she considered her father's wishes, she had dispensed with mourning costume, and today wore a dress of cream and hyacinth, a matching bonnet giving a defiant gaiety to her appearance.

Matt looked startled when he saw her. "Alisa! You're not wearing black."

"And I don't intend to. Papa hated black, and so do I. I'm mourning—in my heart, where it counts. But I didn't come here to talk about that," she went on. "I came to find out what I can do to get my father's mill back."

Matt showed her into his inner office, a rather untidy room crowded with legal volumes, containing long tables stacked high with case folders and wooden file boxes. A photograph on the wall depicted Stephen Douglas, who had run against Abraham Lincoln and had spoken, in 1858, at the Tremont House.

Alisa sat on a horsehair sofa, and Matt slumped into a leather chair. He looked at her, a freckle-faced man with a reputation for caution and reasonableness whose law practice was just beginning to thrive.

"I've already told you, Alisa, there's nothing that you can do."

"I refuse to accept that."

"Well, it's true." Matt rose from his chair and went to the tall windows, where he stared down at the jostling traffic of Lake Street. "If it was just money . . . Alisa, you're only a girl, you don't understand. It's a tough, competitive world out there, and men like Riordan Daniels aren't in it for the money. No, to them it's a game, a huge, all-encompassing, exciting game, and to acquire a lot of money is only a symbol that they've won in the competition."

"It wasn't a game to my father." Alisa set her mouth stubbornly.

"It was. He played, too, on a smaller scale. Alisa, don't you see? Your mill isn't even important to Riordan Daniels, except as a symbol of his power."

As Alisa said nothing, Matt Eberley went on. "Reality is reality. The Amsell mill isn't yours anymore. Riordan Daniels took it in payment on your father's debt to him. And I hope you realize that Daniels is still writing off thousands of dollars as a loss."

"What? Then . . . then I'm taking charity from Riordan Daniels?" she demanded incredulously.

"In a way. There simply isn't any more property left to pay off the debt."

Alisa reddened, blood filling her cheeks painfully. She finally jumped up and strode to the window too. Down on the street two delivery men were arguing about something, their fists waving pugnaciously in the air. She wondered if they were going to come to blows. Men always battled, she thought dully. Two women would have settled their differences peaceably.

But *she* had to fight a man.

"I'm going to do something," Alisa said at last, surprised at her own tenacity.

"What can you do? Haven't I just explained it? You don't know anything about business, not even the simplest things. And you're a lovely girl, why should you have to?"

"Stop it! Stop patronizing me!"

"Well, it looks as if I'm going to have to. Alisa, Riordan Daniels is a powerful man, and you're a helpless young woman without money, without any resources to fight him. And even if you did have funds, you couldn't possibly have enough. The man is one of the richest in the country! He could buy and sell any of the men who were at your father's funeral. *Any* of them, Alisa, and that includes me!"

Matt's voice gentled, and he took both of Alisa's hands in his. "No, you'd better forget the whole thing, darling. You're helpless. You have no money, your house will be sold soon, you need somewhere to go, a place to live. Your best solution is simply to get married and let a man who loves you take care of you."

By the way Matt gripped her hand, by the way his eyes sought hers, Alisa knew that he meant himself. "Matt, oh, Matt. You know I can't."

"Marry me, Alisa," he urged. "Let's do it soon, within a few weeks. I'll take care of you. My mother has been caring for the children for me, but she has been wanting to go to live with her sister, and you would make a wonderful mother for Henry and Julia."

Even though Matt's children, Julia and Henry, eight-year-old twins, were adorable, Alisa swallowed hard at the thought of acquiring a ready-made family when she had barely grown up herself. She pictured embracing Matt, sleeping in bed with him, giving her body to him, giving him more children. . . .

Gently she pulled away from him.

"I can't get married yet—I just can't, not to anyone. I know I'm in a helpless position right now, but I don't want to take Malva's charity, nor do I want to depend on you. I've already thought about this, and I've decided what to do."

Matt smiled, although she could tell he was hurt. "Alisa, you're so determined, it's admirable. I've never seen a girl like you. But in this case—"

"There are some jewels of my mother's—we kept them in a secret box in the library paneling. They are mine, not Papa's, to do with as I wish. I'll sell them today. I'm going to open a small business of my own. And somehow I'll make enough money to buy back my father's mill, and pay back his debt, too." And beat Riordan Daniels at his own game, she added mentally.

"It's a ridiculous idea, Alisa!" Matt exploded. "What kind of business could you run?"

"I don't know yet."

"Girls of good family simply *don't* run businesses of any kind. Whether you know it or not, you've been pampered all of your life. You were your father's one child, he doted on you, solved every problem for you. Besides"—Matt took another tack—"I'm sure your Mrs. Soames never taught you bookkeeping or accounts, did she?"

"No, of course not."

"Then . . . you see? Do you know about supply and demand? Bills of credit, stock losses, pilferage, leases and contracts?"

"No, I don't, not yet."

"Do you have the stamina to put in a twelve-hour workday, to set a good example for clerks and employees, to arbitrate their disputes, to hire and fire when necessary without flinching?"

"Yes, I think I do." With dignity Alisa stood to her full five-feet-eight, so that her eyes were almost level with Matt's. She remembered the flaunting, challenging look that Riordan Daniels had given her, and felt an odd surge of energy. It flowed in her veins, bubbling like the finest French champagne. It was a wonderful feeling.

"I think I have a lot of good business qualities in me, and I intend to find out what they are. You're right, I *have* been pampered, I *am* young, I have been blind to the real world. But I'm not anymore. I don't care how big Riordan Daniels is, how rich, or how powerful. I intend to challenge him somehow. I'm going to play his game, too."

4

"What? You want lessons in accounting and book-keeping—from me?" Matt Eberley was both flattered and annoyed when Alisa showed up in his office two days later, wearing a simple dove-gray foulard dress that she considered suitable for business.

"And why not you? Plainly you know those things, or you wouldn't have scoffed at me for *not* knowing them," she retorted. "I'm not asking it as a favor, however." She reached in her purse and pulled out some bills, putting them on the desk. "I'll pay, Matt."

To his credit, Matt Eberley flushed scarlet. "Why, I couldn't charge you, Alisa. It's just that—"

"I want to learn. I'll read anything you tell me, do anything you tell me, I'll work fifteen hours a day if necessary."

"But, Alisa, you're not . . . you've never . . ."

"Are you afraid I'm not strong enough to work fifteen hours a day, Matt?" She gave a rueful laugh. "Look at me. I'm taller than some men, and I'm as healthy as a horse. Have you ever seen me give way to fainting spells or have the vapors?"

"No."

With a flourish Alisa removed her velvet-trimmed hat. "Well, then! When shall we start?"

So, protesting, Matt gave in, and to his astonishment and her own satisfaction, Alisa absorbed everything quickly, taking voluminous notes and asking many questions.

Grimly she put to the back of her mind all thoughts of Riordan Daniels. In one thing, at least, Matt had been right: she wasn't equipped to face him yet. She needed time, knowledge, strength.

Two weeks later, she bought her shop. Although Matt insisted she should lease, Alisa craved the feeling of ownership, of permanency. She fell in love with the little ground-floor store, with its charming shingles and large plate-glass display windows. Merchants were just beginning to move to State Street, and she was able to buy the building cheaply.

She painted the exterior federal blue and installed blue-striped canvas awnings. Over the entrance she hung a carved golden eagle with outspread wings that seemed almost to flap with arrogant pride.

Inside were the workroom, a small office, and a luxurious showroom area where customers could preen themselves in ornate gilt-encrusted mirrors or relax in Chippendale chairs arranged on a Brussels carpet of soft blue tones that would not take away from the glory of the bonnets sold.

Yes, the hats! Knowing that Fifine had worked as a girl for a Parisian couturier and milliner,

Alisa had decided to make millinery her trade. Carefully she had stocked up on Tuscan straw, ostrich feathers, lace, satin ribbons, and all the other paraphernalia of trimming women's hats.

However, the stuffed birds and real spread birds' wings that were so popular on ladies' bonnets, peeking out from among the piled-high decorations, filled Alisa with revulsion. She herself had always refused to wear a hat for which a bird had had to die. She decided not to sell bonnets of which stuffed birds were a part.

"You're a fool, then," Fifine sniffed. "It's all the rage, you know, all the finest ladies are wearing them."

"Perhaps they are," Alisa said firmly. "But if our customers want birds, we'll give them *papier-mâché*."

Already Alisa's former maid often tried her patience. Sometimes Alisa wondered if Fifine had been her father's mistress. Why, otherwise, would the Frenchwoman have been so close to Papa's room on the night he killed himself? But always she pushed such uneasy conjecture out of her mind. Fifine was undeniably attractive, in a dark, sallow way, but her father would never have glanced at a servant in his own house.

Further, in her tart, almost resentful way, Fifine had begged to be kept on, promising to sew, cook, do anything. And Alisa realized she did need the skills the woman possessed.

Fifine was a natural hat-trimmer. She had a love of the lush and ornate, skill with the needle, and a zeal that could produce dozens of bonnets, ball and evening hats, airy little breakfast caps, knitted fanchons, and even a selection of velvet and satin bows for the hair.

A glass-enclosed brass display case could be moved each day to the sidewalk in front of the shop, and here Alisa arranged Fifine's most elaborate creations, their cost more than a hackman or clerk could earn in months of labor.

But on opening day, to Alisa's stunned disappointment, they had only two customers, neither of whom made a purchase. In the next eight days, only a few more women ventured through the door, causing the little musical bell to ring. Two of these were "soiled doves," prostitutes from the Tenderloin in search of gaudy apparel in which to ply their trade. Fifine gloated at selling them several hats, but Alisa's heart sank. Were these to be her only customers?

The shop floundered along for another month, on the verge of failure.

"It's public opinion," Matt Eberley told her, frowning. "Alisa, your real potential customers— the rich women, the women who move in society— just don't approve of you. They aren't going to patronize you."

"They will, Matt, give them time."

"Time? You should hear my mother talk, Alisa. She is indignant because you are 'in trade,' as she calls it. She says no young woman of good station would lower herself to handle money. Darling, when will you realize that this is all a costly, foolish mistake?"

"It's too soon to tell yet," Alisa insisted stubbornly.

Still, she feared he was right. After her father's death, society had at first felt sorry for Alisa, pitying her for losing her house to that upstart Riordan Daniels. They had expected her to move in with Malva and to marry within a few months—after all, wasn't that what any of *their* daughters would do?

But Alisa had not done the expected. She had rented a small house near the courthouse and moved into it, with Fifine as her chaperon.

And when it was learned that Alisa had actually bought a millinery shop and intended to run it herself, many were scandalized. As Ida Eberley believed, work was for poor girls of the lower classes, for impoverished widows, not for beautiful young women with relatives to go to and men who wished to marry them.

Suddenly Alisa found herself ignored at small teas, receiving fewer and fewer invitations.

"Alisa! It isn't that we're *snubbing* you," Cordelia Landsdowne explained. Alisa and Cordelia had made their debuts together, both of them considered beauties of the season, Cordelia a fluffy blond, Alisa tall and honey-haired. "It's just that . . . well, there's hardly *time* anymore, is there? You're working all the time, just like a man. You hardly belong to our life anymore."

Alisa stared at her friend. "Then what life do I belong to?"

Cordelia shrugged prettily. "Who knows? I'd say you're outside the pale. You're not really anything now, are you? Except a milliner, of course."

Furiously Alisa drove home from the tea where she had encountered Cordelia. She was as close to despair as she had felt since Papa died. She missed Papa with a deep, aching pain, rereading his last letter almost daily, imprinting its message indelibly on her memory.

What if her shop did put her "beyond the pale," as Cordelia put it? She was trying to avenge his death the only way she knew how—by work. She didn't want to be a burden on anyone, and was trying to support herself honorably.

Why did society look on this as a crime?

"Darling Alisa, they don't think of it as a 'crime,'" Malva explained patiently after Alisa drove to her cousin's house to explode with frustration. "They are merely shocked, that's all, by your daring. You have to understand, dear, that those women are not like you. They are not strong. They have always depended on men to take care of them, they know nothing else. Gossip, public opinion, and social pressures rule them utterly. It's almost a game they play, with rules that aren't written down, but which everyone follows precisely. And those who flout the rules somehow threaten *them* and everything they stand for."

Alisa started, remembering what Matt had told her about business being a game to Riordan Daniels.

"But I'm *not* threatening them!"

"You certainly aren't, and I intend to see to it that this snubbing business stops at once. I'm giving a party, Alisa—a big one—and it's going to be at your shop. I'm a pretty powerful player in this society game, and you, too, possess power of your own, if you would only see it. Your mother was a Biddle, and your father an Amsell. You have lineage, Alisa. The best. Remember that."

So Malva gave the party, and throngs of women attended, and somehow "Alisa's" was properly launched, and Alisa had her friends back again. Even Cordelia now came weekly to the shop, and brought a group of girls who considered Alisa to be "daring" and "brave."

Within a month, the shop had more society business than it could handle, plus a clientele of actresses, whose profession required them to buy all their own costumes and street dress. Alisa was forced to hire six more trimmers, immigrant women who chattered happily as they worked in a mixture of German, French, Yiddish, and Polish.

Alisa owed her cousin a tremendous debt, and decided to repay it in hats. Once a month she packed into a hatbox the most stunningly elaborate bonnet that Fifine could devise, and sent Billy, her delivery boy, off with it to Malva's.

"Alisa, my dear, the last thing I need is another hat, wonderful as they all are," Malva protested after the March delivery, a bisque-colored straw covered with a profusion of pink rosebuds. "My closet is stuffed full of them. Why don't you desist?"

"But, Malva, you've done so much for me—"

"Pooh. What have I done? I gave a party, got you a few society customers, talked your shop around—that isn't much. If you want to give away bonnets, why don't you make them for orphaned girls? I happen to know of a few who could use something pretty, and I'll take all you're willing to give."

Now it was April again, 1871, a month when women were ordering hats for promenading, for summer resort wear, and the seaside. The air was soft with the odors of thawing earth and melting snow, and Alisa had planted masses of hyacinths in pots to decorate her shop. These had sprouted glorious purple blossoms.

"If only we could put *you* on a hat," Alisa murmured to the hyacinths one dreamy afternoon, feeling giddy somehow with the moist promise of spring. "But you'd wilt, wouldn't you? And then how furious our customers would be!"

Smiling to herself, she put aside her books and walked through to the cluttered shop workroom. As usual, the room was a bustle of activity. All surfaces were littered with scissors, scraps of lace, and bits of silk. Fifine was bent over a flower-maker's catalog, frowning at the prices, while the six trimmers sat at their long table, each with a half-finished bonnet on a stand before her.

Billy, formerly Papa's stableboy, was busy packing fifteen children's hats into boxes for delivery to Malva's girls.

"After you finish those, Billy, I have ten other deliveries for you," Alisa said briskly. "Here are the slips, and be sure that you're prompt. These are important customers."

"Yes, miss."

"Then, when you come back, the display cases need polishing and there are more boxes to be unpacked and sorted."

"Yes, miss." Billy touched his cap with more respect than he'd shown her as a stableboy. Alisa worked all her employees hard, but she herself put in as long hours as they did, and she paid decent wages.

Alisa looked up as the silvery bell jingled, indicating a customer. She smoothed her powder-blue work dress, trimmed with a discreet lace collar, and hurried into the showroom.

The customer was a petite, sulky-looking brunette. Fashionably dressed in forest-green silk, a flowing cape about her shoulders, she was already taking one of the bonnets off its display hook and settling it on her own head.

"Good morning, miss," Alisa said. "May I help you?"

The brunette gave a little half-smile, barely acknowledging Alisa. She turned in front of the mirror, eyeing herself with narcissistic fascination. The hat she had selected was pale green, with white, fluffy ostrich tips, swirls of satin ribbon, and a lace mantilla draped around the bonnet itself, to fall casually onto the shoulders. It was one of the shop's most elaborate.

"The shade is most becoming to your brunette coloring," Alisa began automatically. "And the style—"

"Oh, I don't know. Maybe I should have something more rich-looking."

Richer-looking than that hat? Alisa smiled to herself wryly. But it did not do to offend a potential customer. "Then perhaps something in this silk surah?"

She began taking down other models, and it was as she was turning, a bonnet in each hand, that she heard the silvery tones of the shop bell again.

She looked up to see Riordan Daniels stride into the shop.

Alisa stood frozen, clutching at the hats as if they were glued to her fingers. She'd forgotten how handsome he was, a tall dark man whose well-tailored suit coat hinted at lynxlike muscles beneath. A rough energy seemed to emanate from him, almost to crackle around him as he filled the showroom with his maleness.

Even the brunette customer seemed to sense it, for she pinkened, preening herself in the plate-glass mirror like a vain little peacock.

"May . . . may I help you?" Alisa approached him, angry at herself for the way her voice cracked over the words. She had not seen Riordan Daniels in nearly a year. As far as she knew, he had returned to New York shortly after her father's death, with only brief visits back to Chicago for business purposes. And she'd been glad. She wasn't ready to take him on yet—she'd had plenty of daydreams and fantasies, but had no notion of how to put these into reality.

Riordan's grin was slow and easy, his teeth flashing white. "So this is what happened to you. I wondered."

"I opened this shop, if that's what you mean," Alisa snapped. "Do you want to buy a hat? Is that why you're here?" She could feel herself trembling all over; if she'd had fur, it would have been crackling.

But before he could respond, the customer in green turned lazily. "Oh, miss, he's with me. What do you think of this one?" she asked Riordan as an astonished Alisa tried to recover her composure. "I don't know about the color. Garnet. So drab, don't you think? Not very gay at all."

"I don't know about hats, Linette," Riordan said, still smiling at Alisa.

The girl sighed with displeasure and plopped the garnet-colored bonnet down on the display case. A cloud of musky perfume drifted around her every movement. "Really, miss, this one isn't right. Don't you have something with a little more flash? Maybe some of those changeable birds I've seen, with the spread wings? They are awfully smart."

"We don't sell stuffed birds," Alisa told her. "Ours are *papier-mâché* and quite lovely."

"Oh, well, your *own*," Linette said disparagingly. "Come now, show me some more hats, will you? I haven't much time, have I, Riordan? I have a matinee to give today."

So this Linette was an actress, Alisa thought. No wonder she had wanted a more showy hat; actresses usually craved attention.

As the girl tried on hats, a succession of satin and lace that never seemed to end, she kept demanding opinions from Riordan. Was this one too dull? That one unflattering? Riordan discussed the merits of each bonnet, his tone light, as if this entire situation amused him very much.

Alisa didn't find it humorous. The more hats Linette tried on, the haughtier Alisa became, waiting on her customer with chilly courtesy. But inside, she fumed. She was being treated like a servant by this vain, silly creature. Worse, it was all happening in front of Riordan Daniels.

How dare he bring this actress into her shop? And to have the temerity actually to *enjoy* it, leaning over Linette to help her fasten a frilly ribbon, then looking up to meet Alisa's eyes?

Finally six hats were lined up on the counter.

"Oh, dear," Linette sighed, apparently surfeited with the pleasures of choosing and discarding. "It looks as if I am going to have to take all of these—is that all right with you, darling?"

Darling. The word grated on Alisa like fingers clawing along slate. She stood at attention, waiting for the decision.

"Six bonnets?" Riordan drawled. "Whatever will you do with so many?"

"Why, wear them! I *know* you can afford them," Linette added archly. "You could buy me this whole shop if you wanted to, Riordan, and probably the entire street."

"But why would you want an entire street?"

"Oh, honey-poo," the actress cooed, realizing she'd aroused his displeasure, "I was only teasing. But I would like all of these." She pointed to the array on the counter, indicating they should be boxed. "Deliver them to my dressing room at the Chicago Theater. I'm only in town for two weeks, so don't dally. Send him the bill."

"Very well," Alisa managed to say evenly.

"We don't have to wait, do we, honey?" Linette hung on Riordan Daniels, pulling possessively at his arm. "Come on, let's go back to the theater. I want to sit down and relax before I have to go on. And maybe have a little drink."

They were gone in a flurry of tinkling shop bell and Linette's giggle, of perfume and the rustle of green silk skirts. Alisa smacked the first bonnet into a box. She stuffed tissue paper around the elaborate creation and shoved the lid on the box.

Then, her temper still not released, she strode

to the door of the shop and slammed it shut as hard as she could.

The act gave her little satisfaction.

That very day, Alisa began to gather information on Riordan Daniels. Arriving home to her small house, still seething from the encounter with him and his actress, she began culling through a stack of newspapers that she had been too busy to read.

Almost at once—four times in one issue of the *Tribune*—she found his name. "DANIELS ACQUIRES NEW BANK INTERESTS," one headline read. Dutifully Alisa clipped it out, and finding a large envelope, began her collection.

In the days to come, she found that her position as proprietor of a fashionable shop gave her an ideal position from which to hear the city's gossip. Alisa wrote down everything she heard about Riordan Daniels, whether large or trivial, and added it to her envelope.

Within weeks she had formed a picture of a hard-driving man who traveled frequently between Chicago and New York. He worked twelve, fifteen, even eighteen hours a day in his office at State and Randolph, although he could well afford to do nothing at all except go to the gambling houses and horse races, activities he also enjoyed sparingly.

Riordan Daniels had apparently made his first money in the West, in silver mining. There were stories of rivalries, even a few fistfights. Later he had returned to New York, dealing astutely on the stock market and acquiring several ironworks. He enlarged these, making a fortune providing artillery for the Union Army. Now he was owner of horse-car lines, railroads, banks, lumber mills—to Alisa the list seemed endless. And, of course, to the spoils was added her own father's mill.

"Is he really as powerful as they say he is?" Alisa dared to ask Matt on one of what had become their regular carriage rides on her Sundays off.

"Who?"

"Why, Riordan Daniels, of course! Whom did you think I meant?"

"I thought you'd forgotten about him months ago, Alisa."

She stared at Matt, whose sandy hair, beneath his top hat, was neatly combed and pomaded. Dressed in well-tailored afternoon garb, Matt Eberley looked exactly what he was, an ambitious young attorney with hopes of further riches.

"Of course I haven't forgotten him. I ... I think about him every day. About how to vindicate my father, of course, I meant," she added awkwardly.

Matt frowned in annoyance. "I told you before, Riordan Daniels is no one to fool with. Get it through your head, Alisa. He's *rich*. Rich in a way you've never known, never imagined. He pays no taxes, owes nothing to anyone, and all of his money earns other money. And *that* money makes more money. Even if he worked fifteen hours a day, he couldn't spend everything he possesses, because his money grows *faster than he can spend it.*"

Alisa could hardly imagine such a thing, but it sounded vastly exciting to her, like a cup that never emptied. She looked up at the vehemence of Matt's expression. "That's really incredible, Matt."

"It is. Men like Riordan Daniels go through life scot-free. They buy politicians, they buy favors, they buy women, horses, steel mills, whatever they want. If they want to get rid of someone, they can do it. They can—"

"Stop!" She was shivering. "You make him sound terrible."

"Just forget about him, Alisa. Hope that he doesn't cross your path again. That would be the best thing."

Fifine went to the theater with a group of her cronies, one of whom was a wardrobe mistress, and returned with juicier tidbits. "*La!* He is quite a womanizer, they say. He likes actresses especially. He sends them notes and pretty gifts and sometimes they come to his house."

"Oh?"

Fifine went on, gesturing as she talked. "I also heard he was once in a duel over a lady's honor."

"I heard that too," Alisa encouraged cautiously.

"Ah, *oui.* That was in New Orleans, where such things still happen. It is said that he shot the other man in the thigh. He was lucky to survive it. If that man had died, Riordan Daniels would today be a murderer."

Alisa swallowed. "Go on, Fifine," she pressed. "What else did you hear about him?"

"He was jilted once."

"What!"

"But that happened years ago, when he was poor. The girl belonged to one of the rich New York families and she thought he wasn't good enough for her. *Oui,* I wager she would change her tune now," Fifine added.

Alisa nodded. She couldn't picture any woman turning Riordan Daniels down—except for herself, of course.

"And what about these actresses?" she probed. "Isn't there one named . . . yes, Linette?"

On the occasion several weeks ago, Fifine had been in the back room and had not seen Riordan bring in the brunette actress. "Linette Marquis? *Oui.* She is back in New York now, with a part in some new musical. They say she is a minx, that she toys with him like a cat with her prey."

"Indeed." Alisa, who had been brushing her thick hair, flung down the brush and stared straight ahead, into blank air.

"I thought you wished me to tell you everything." Fifine smirked. "Don't you want to hear how pretty she is? They say she is *très belle.*"

"I . . . I think I will get ready for bed now," Alisa said faintly.

"Ah! Are you jealous, *petite*? Why else would you be asking me all these questions? You, too, are smitten by him."

"No . . . no, I'm not!"

"If you are, you're a fool," Fifine pronounced. "Anyway, collecting snippets of gossip will do you no good at all. He is a man. He'll do as he pleases, eh? That is the way of all of them. *We* have no control over that."

5

Alisa stood in the doorway of her shop, shading her eyes to gaze onto State Street, where late-afternoon sunlight glared off awnings and plate-glass windows, making the eyes ache from brightness. Even the muffin boy who usually hawked his wares from this corner had gone indoors, and only a few shoppers walked the wooden sidewalks, their stride listless.

It had been a blazing hot summer and a dry, hot October, a month plagued by small fires that had ignited all over the city, many of them in barns that were tinder-dry. In fact, only an hour ago Alisa had heard a newsboy crying out the news of a fire in a lumber-planing mill on the West Side.

She rubbed her eyes and went back inside the shop. It was Saturday. Even if they had no customers, there were always the accounts, and a large shipment of artificial flowers had arrived and must be unpacked and sorted. Only two more hours, she thought, and she'd close the shop. They could all go home to enjoy the remainder of the day, and Sunday.

One of the immigrant girls, Helga, was courting, and would probably see her suitor. Nella, a widow with two boys, would spend all her free time cooking and cleaning. Fifine gathered with her cronies for long sessions of gossip and squabbling.

As for herself, there was Matt Eberley, who usually took her for a drive in his carriage. Often they ended with dinner at the Tremont or one of the city's other large hotels.

She sighed, thinking of Matt. Lately Matt had been insistent that his two children, Henry and Julia, be included on some of their outings. He wanted her to "get to know them better," as he put it. Matt had come to regard her millinery shop as a temporary thing, a project she would drop as soon as she was ready for marriage—to him, naturally.

In the workroom Fifine was scolding one of the girls, her voice strident. The day had been hot, Alisa realized. The entire summer had tested tempers, and for three weeks there'd been no rain to cool the city down. She walked to the door of the workroom.

"Do you think *you* are a real hat trimmer?" Fifine was demanding of Nella. The plump German widow looked stricken. "Pah! *Ça ne vaut rien!* You know nothing about hats!" Pettishly Fifine swiped the woman's half-finished evening hat off the worktable onto the floor.

"But . . . it was only a slight smudge—"

"It is enough! Do it again. *Stupide!*"

As the trimmer burst into tears, Alisa walked briskly into the room. "We haven't a customer in the shop—not one." She pretended she didn't see

Nella sniffling into her hands or Fifine angrily sorting ostrich tips into storage bins. "It's Saturday, and I think we should close the shop two hours early. And we'll come in on Monday morning two hours late—how would that suit everyone?"

Nella looked up, brightening, and several of the women cheered. Fifine, her back to Alisa, said nothing.

"Well, that's settled then," Alisa said, smiling. "Straighten up your tables, everyone, and I'll see you on Monday. Get going, now, before I change my mind!"

Nella's teary face burst into a wide grin, and all of the immigrant women whooped and applauded. Within seconds, scraps of lace and silk had disappeared from the tabletops and scissors were neatly placed in storage boxes. Half-done hats were shielded with muslin to protect them from dust.

As the women hurried out of the shop, the bells ringing gaily, Fifine walked over to Alisa, who was locking up. "If *I* owned this shop, I would not allow short working days," she announced.

Alisa looked at her. "I see nothing wrong with it."

"When they are out courting their *beaux*, nothing gets done here. Their minds go . . ." Fifine struggled for the word. "Flibberty."

At the awkward word, Alisa stifled a smile. "The women are human beings, not machines who can work endlessly. They suffered through the hot summer days with few complaints. Now I have given them four hours' extra holiday. That really isn't very much."

Alisa put the day's money in the safe beside the

small packet that contained the remaining pieces of her mother's jewelry and closed and locked it. As they left, she also locked the front door behind them. They started off, picking their way on wooden plank sidewalks that were still coated with a layer of dry summer dust.

"You are too lenient with those girls," Fifine began as they turned the corner. "When I was in Paris—"

"But you are not in Paris now. You are here in Chicago."

Fifine said nothing for a moment, and finally sighed. "It has been too hot."

Alisa knew this was an apology and decided to accept it as such. She, too, had been sharp-tempered, she supposed. "Well, at least it's October, and any day now we should get rain. That will cool things off and make everyone happier."

They smiled at each other, the tension between them gone.

That night Fifine went out with her friends, and Alisa sat with a novel, cutting pages as she read in absorbed concentration. The following day, Sunday, dawned hot and dry again, the streets seeming almost to shimmer with sunlight. Dead leaves blew in the streets, their color drab brown, as if the unseasonable weather had dried all the sap and life from them.

"What's wrong with you?" Matt demanded when he came to pick Alisa up. He helped her into his surrey, settling her on the seat, then swinging up on his own side.

"What do you mean, what's wrong with me?"

"You seem ... distant somehow. Distracted, Alisa."

"Perhaps I am," she sighed as he turned the surrey toward the Chicago River, lined with lumber schooners, their masts tangled against the sky. A middle-pivot wooden drawbridge would take them to the West Division.

They crossed the river, weaving through a tangle of wagons, delivery vans, stevedores with hand trucks, and pushing, gesticulating men. The big Sturgis and Buckingham Grain Elevator towered over everything. As always, at the sight Alisa caught her breath, feeling a surge of excitement. She loved the river. This was Riordan Daniels' world, she thought. A world created by money and trade, at which she herself stood only at the far fringe.

"Oh, Matt," she burst out. "I'm not sure that running a millinery shop is what I really want to do."

He stared at her incredulously, nearly dropping the bridle in his astonishment. "I thought ... The way you've pushed and pushed it, forcing me to teach you bookkeeping ... and you don't like it? Alisa! *I* never thought you fitted in the millinery business. I never wanted you to work at all. Marry me. Oh, darling, marry me."

This was not his first proposal to her.

"Matt," Alisa began. She had to raise her voice to be heard over the din of a lumber wagon that churned past them. "You're a wonderful man, of course, and it isn't that I'm not fond of you ..."

He sighed. "I know, I know. You're just not ready yet. Well, I can wait until you are. Meanwhile, we might as well enjoy our drive. We'll go to Lincoln Park, all right? The pond there is pretty."

"Very well," Alisa agreed, relieved to have the issue of marriage safely shelved. Matt was dull, safe, predictable, and he didn't know her at all. He certainly didn't know that she thought the sight of the crowded, busy, smelly Chicago River far more interesting than Lincoln Park with its lagoon where tame swans paddled.

She had been dreaming of a tall dark-haired man clad in black, who drove a carriage at breakneck speed, hurtling over ruts and raising a huge cloud of dust. The dust was stifling, choking her.

Alisa stirred, half-awaking to struggle up in bed. With an odd feeling of something being wrong, she turned on the gaslight to see what time it was.

One o'clock. Strange; something must have awakened her. Slowly she realized that the courthouse bell, only two blocks away, was ringing stridently. *Clang. Clang.*

She rubbed her eyes, which seemed to sting oddly, as if irritated from the dust in her dream.

The insistent, clanging peal did not stop, but if anything grew more urgent. Alisa's heart gave a little squeeze. The courthouse, only a block away, was a sprawling, ungainly structure with a wooden central portion and two wings made of limestone. It was topped by a tower that held a five-and-a-half-ton bell, and an outside walk for a watchman whose duty it was to scan the city's skies nightly for signs of fire. There had been plenty of those during the summer, and even during the rainless past three weeks.

Like a knell of disaster, the bell continued to ring.

Realizing it was smoke she smelled, Alisa crawled out of bed and stumbled to the window. She threw aside the damask curtains. For an instant she stared, at first not comprehending. The sight that met her eyes was incredible, like a fever-dream come to life.

The sky to the south glowed red. Huge clouds of smoke billowed along the street, carrying red sparks. Even as Alisa gasped, one of the sparks sailed like a firefly, veering toward her own window. It touched the glass, flaming like a tiny furnace.

Dark shapes were moving in the street and Alisa's eyes widened as she realized that the shapes were people. Dozens, hundreds of them, *running*.

She breathed in a shallow gasp of fright. It had to be a big fire, she thought feverishly, to drive out so many people. How long had the bell been ringing?

Most of Chicago was built of wood, Alisa knew. The houses, the public buildings, the drawbridges, rickety wood sidewalks, even the streets, with their miles of wooden paving blocks. Thousands of tons of dry lumber were stacked along the riverbanks. In addition, there were coal heaps everywhere, and thousands of barns and stables, each filled with tinderbox straw, which needed only an overturned lantern to ignite them.

"Fifine!" Alisa screamed, suddenly coming to her senses. She backed away from the window, letting the drapes fall shut again. *"Fifine, there's a fire!"*

* * *

Fifine was a stubbornly deep sleeper, and burrowed angrily away from Alisa's tugging hands. Alisa beat her fists on the woman's shoulder, and finally the Frenchwoman sat up, her brown hair straggling onto her shoulders. Quickly Alisa blurted out what was happening.

"F-fire?" The woman seemed not to grasp it.

Her first hysteria gone, Alisa felt eerily calm. "Yes, a big one. We have to leave right now. Sparks are carrying the blaze this way."

Leaving Fifine to struggle out of bed on her own, Alisa half-ran to her own room. She pulled on the blue work dress she had worn that day, skipping stockings and petticoats to yank on only the essentials. She fumbled for her shoes, her mind working quickly. Perhaps she was worrying unduly—after all, the city did possess fire equipment such as the "Long John," a horse-driven steam fire engine named for a former mayor. In fact, its newest steam engine, the "Williams," could throw seven hundred gallons of water a minute, and the *Tribune* called it the most modern fire fighting equipment in the world.

Still, was it her imagination, or had the smell of smoke grown even stronger? Alisa coughed as she quickly fastened her shoes. She grabbed several handkerchiefs from a drawer—they could be held over her mouth to guard against smoke.

Three minutes later, she had a terrified Fifine in tow, pulling her out of the house and onto its tiny front porch. Fifine looked up at the sky and screamed. Alisa, too, felt her throat close in fear.

* * *

Red. The sky was a lurid, billowing red, the color of flames, of furnaces, of a gigantic pyre, lit by tongues of leaping light. A hose cart careened by, pulled by one frantic horse. Two sweaty firemen clung behind. A riderless horse galloped past, its heaving sides lathered with white. Then came a fleeing family, the mother cradling an infant, the father dragging two wild-eyed toddlers. A fiery spark settled in the hair of one of the babies, and the mother batted it away, shrieking.

Everyone was screaming, Alisa realized. It was one A.M., and she could see as clearly as if it were daylight. And a heavy wind whipped erratically between the buildings, driving sparks before it.

She shook away Fifine's hysterical grip and tried to think rationally. The fire was coming from the south. That meant they'd have to flee in the opposite direction. But had the flames fanned out wider? How many streets or blocks did it cover? Had it leapt any of the bridges yet? She felt icy with fear. That hose cart had seemed awfully tiny in contrast to the huge malevolent sky that burned before them.

What if the fire couldn't be stopped? What if it reached State Street, where her shop was? Her mind clicking with strangely lucid calculation, Alisa remembered the small safe she kept in the millinery shop. Not only did it contain the week's income, but it also held the few remaining pieces of her mother's jewelry. These were the only assets, aside from her store, that Alisa still possessed.

She eyed the glowing sky again, vivid sparks whipped by an increasingly high wind. State Street was east. Maybe the fire hadn't penetrated there yet. Maybe there was a chance she could water down the roof of her shop, guarding it from sparks. Anyway, she had to try. If only Fifine had kept her wits about her, instead of dissolving into fright. Alisa could scarcely believe this sobbing woman was the same person who had lorded it over the immigrant trimmers.

She coughed, gagging on the bitter smoke, and pulled Fifine into the street.

They joined the throngs of terrified citizens who were running from the blaze. People fled on foot, on horseback, or in frantic overloaded carriages. They carried babies, strongboxes, puppies. One weeping old woman even clutched a basket of newly washed laundry. Screaming hotel guests dropped luggage from balconies, trunks and suitcases smashing to the sidewalk. One woman dropped a valise, then threw herself after it, hurtling downward in a flutter of white nightgown and bared legs.

Nightmare, Alisa thought. She was in a numbed state far beyond terror. The wind whipped at their clothes, a vicious devil that gusted savagely from a dozen directions, hosing sparks in blazing showers along the pavement. Alisa gripped Fifine's arm, forcing her out of the path of yet another runaway livery horse. Apparently the city's horses had simply been turned loose to escape from the blaze as best they could.

They struggled on, veering around a group of drunken men who were raiding a saloon. A bearded old man danced a tipsy dance, cradling an armful of bottles. Liquid from a spilled whiskey barrel flowed into the street. As Alisa and Fifine hurried by, a spark ignited the whiskey, creating a ribbon of blue flame.

"Oh!" Fifine gibbered. *"Oh . . . mon Dieu . . . we'll die . . ."*

As they cut across the courthouse square, they saw that the prisoners were being released. An anxious-faced little man, apparently a jeweler crazed by the disaster, was handing out rings, watches, and bracelets to the freed convicts as they poured across Randolph Street.

Fifine stopped her screaming and actually started in his direction, as if to get some of the free jewelry for herself.

"No, you don't! Come *on!*" Alisa yanked at her former maid's arm.

State Street was pandemonium. The wind had heightened, and the great red maw of the fire seemed to breathe at them from only blocks away. The raw stench of smoke was overpowering, and both Alisa and Fifine were choking and gagging into their handkerchiefs.

A woman and a teenage boy staggered past, bent under the burden of a dozen bolts of damask and silk cloth. Looters, Alisa thought, feeling chilled.

At last they reached the millinery shop. Eerily, it looked just as it always had before, an elegant little store with neat striped awnings, lit now by lurid red.

"Look . . . look . . ." Fifine clutched Alisa as a huge scrap of burning cloth sailed over their heads, almost hooking on the wings of the gilded eagle. The fireball skimmed over an awning, emitting trails of lesser sparks, and then was gone, sucked away by the wind. But soon, Alisa knew, feeling sick, there'd be another one.

She fumbled for her key and, shaking, inserted it in the lock she'd turned only hours ago. She pushed open the door and both women hurried inside.

Immediately Fifine let out a keening moan. Alisa, too, suppressed a scream. The interior of the shop glowed orange, lit by the fire outside. Ghostly red hats hung on hooks and were arranged in the showcase, light flickering off lace and satin. For the first time, Alisa admitted to herself that she was going to lose her shop. Secondary fires, fed by the wind and sparks, had already spread to State Street. The whole street would go. *Was going now.*

An icy calm filled Alisa as she ignored Fifine's sobs and hurried through the showroom to her little office. She knelt down by the steel safe, engraved with a scroll-like design. In a moment the door swung open, revealing a cigar box half-full of money, and the jewelry packet.

Alisa stuffed the bills into her dress. But as she pulled out the oilcloth packet, it spilled open its contents, a shimmering double rope of pearls, a bracelet of diamonds set *en pavé*, an emerald ring, some smaller items. Even the green gem seemed changed by the fire to an evil red.

"*Mon Dieu!*" Fifine suddenly screamed behind her in warning.

Alisa turned. Approaching through the shop, dressed in a torn black broadcloth suit, was a looter.

*   *   *

The man was about twenty-five, mousy-looking, with protruding ears and gingery hair. He looked as if he had spent his entire life perched on a stool in some dim insurance office, writing in ledgers.

But the fire had released impulses in him, Alisa saw, for his eyes glittered wetly, and he was mouth-breathing with excitement. A tangle of gold watch chains hung from his pocket, indicating that this was not the first store he had visited.

"I thought you only had hats. Rich hats." The looter grinned, his eyes fixing on the rope of pearls, which seemed transformed by the eerie firelight to pink.

"Get out of my shop," Alisa snapped. She rose to her feet, nudging her hip against the safe door so that it swung shut. Thrusting the pearls into her bodice, she edged into the narrow workroom with its long tables. "Get out of here, *right now.*"

But he did not move. "Everything here is gonna burn. Yes, even you, you could burn up too. So why not give that stuff to me? Save you the trouble of carryin' it, eh? Give it to old Charlie. He needs it more than you do."

The looter advanced on her, his hand extending. Plainly he expected her to be afraid and to hand the pearls over.

Something snapped inside Alisa. It had been a long year, a hard one, and now her shop was going to burn. She was trembling violently. "No! I won't!"

"Oh, yes, you will, honey."

Alisa knew her shop, every corner of it, intimately. She backed up against the table, the space where Nella usually worked. Like the other girls, Nella kept her supplies in a wooden sewing box. Alisa's frantic hands found the box lid, fumbling inside.

The looter apparently was enjoying the spectacle of Alisa's fear. "Do I make you mad, pretty milliner? Eh, you're pretty when you're mad. Give me those pearls, honey."

As he advanced on her, Alisa's hand snaked forward, aiming a pair of scissors like a knife. She jabbed them forward, into the soft, fleshy part of the clerk's arm.

"*Ahhhh!*" He let out a yelp of outrage. Choking back her terror, Alisa withdrew the scissors and brandished them, indicating her willingness to strike again.

An ugly moment hung between them, and Alisa feared the man would lunge at her.

"*Bitch!*" the looter muttered, the bravado leaving his face. Abruptly he bolted, one of the stolen watches falling out of his pocket as he slammed the shop door behind him.

"He was . . . He wanted . . ." Fifine stood shivering like a child in the doorway. She had picked up one of the bonnets, Alisa saw, a creation of leaf-green velvet and loops of Chantilly lace, and stood clutching it to her chest.

"He was a damned looter," Alisa snapped. "And he might not be the last, either. There isn't any law anymore. Come on, Fifine, we've got to arm ourselves."

She rummaged in Nella's box until she had found two long hat pins and another pair of scissors. But Fifine refused to take either, clinging persistently to the green bonnet.

"Fifine . . ." Then Alisa gave up. The looter had

been right, the fire was near, there was no possibility that the shop could be saved. They were going to have to flee for their own lives.

"My hats, my hats!" The Frenchwoman was wild-eyed as Alisa dragged her out of the shop, her babble disjointed. "I worked for them . . . I earned them . . . *my hats!*"

⚜ 6 ⚜

The two women clung together in the doorway of the shop, clutching each other in fear. Even in the short time they had been in the shop, the fire had surged further out of control. More stores on State Street were now on fire. And the main fire itself had blazed closer. Huge, billowing red, wind-whipped, and devouring, it was now beyond human intervention.

No fire engine in the world—not the Long John, not the Williams—could fight such a conflagration. Where were they to go? How could they get away from it? With horror Alisa realized that the crowds in the street also seemed confused. Like a disturbed nest of ants, people were beginning to run in several directions, as if uncertain where to go. In which direction had the eating red flames not yet spread?

"We'll die, we'll die!" Fifine sobbed. She had not let go of the velvet hat.

"No, we won't."

But how was she to save them? Alisa wondered, mentally going over the map of the city in her mind. The south and north branches of the Chicago River divided the city into thirds, and to the east lay Lake Michigan. To the north was Lincoln Park, with its lagoon and blue vistas of water. Had the fire gone that far, would it? Could flames leap onto the city's wooden drawbridges and cross to the far side?

But there wasn't time for more thought—they had to run somewhere, had to do something. Alisa decided to run north. She took Fifine's hand and tugged at her, guiding the other woman onto the wooden sidewalk.

Suddenly a group of youths in workclothes staggered past them, two of them lugging a keg of beer, the others cradling whiskey bottles. Plainly their last stop had been a saloon. More looters, Alisa thought; and these were drunk, by the sound of them. Rough curses and snatches of song rippled from them, incongruous among the cries of the fleeing crowd.

Alisa took Fifine's hand to pull her back into the shop, but she was too late, for they had been noticed.

"Eh, girlie? What you got there, eh, what's that sticking out of your neckline?"

Alisa looked downward in horror to see that her mother's pearl necklace had somehow come loose, revealing itself at the neck of her bodice. She darted a hand up to cover it, but the young toughs had already surrounded them, shouting raucously.

"Pearls, pearls!" they shouted. "Hey, give us what you've got!" One of them grabbed Alisa, wrenching her toward him.

He was wiry and thin, sporting the first stringy

mustache of young manhood, the sour stench of whiskey and vomit thick on his breath. Alisa gagged, crying out as she struggled to push herself clear of him. But he was far stronger than she. He yanked her close to him, planting a wet kiss on her mouth and at the same time roughly thrusting his hand down her bodice.

Alisa felt his fingers dig at the tender flesh of her left breast. She screamed out for Fifine, her voice shrill with anger and fear.

It all happened quickly. From the fleeing crowd appeared a man shouldering a large strongbox. He lunged toward them, dropping the box as he came.

A long hard arm shot out to grip the drunken youth. He shook him as if he had been a terrier, and finally flung him from Alisa, bowling him into the center of the group of looters with such violence that two others fell down under the impact of the youth's flying body.

"Get out!" her rescuer shouted. "Get away from these women or you'll live to regret it!"

One of the shaken youths stumbled, groaning, to his feet. The one who had manhandled Alisa was bleeding at the nose.

"Go!" Alisa's rescuer roared. All Alisa could see of him was his aggressive stance, the massive width of his shoulders, and an untidy shock of black hair. "Now—at once—or I'll take all of you on, and don't think I can't!" Bunched massive fists swung at the air menacingly.

As the youths fled, a shaken Alisa turned to thank the man who had saved her. The words froze on her lips. "It's . . . *you!*"

"It does seem to be, doesn't it?"

"But . . . it can't be. It just can't be." Her eyes focused on a sooty, torn white shirt, open at the throat to reveal a tangle of dark curly hair. Riordan Daniels' face was smudged with ashes, and there was a jagged cut along one cheekbone, still oozing a few drops of blood.

"Are you all right?" he demanded.

The fire, the night, and the looters had created a maelstrom of reckless emotions in Alisa. "No!" she shouted. "No, I'm not all right. My shop is going to burn down and I've just been attacked by . . ." Her eyes suddenly found the strongbox where it lay on the ground. "Are *you* another looter?"

"Do I look like one?"

"Maybe you do."

They glared at each other, something, some unknown force, leaping between them. Then Riordan grabbed her arm, yanking her onto the walk. An anxious Fifine trotted behind. "Don't be a little idiot. I'm no looter, girl; I have better things to do than rob a milliner. Come on."

"What! With *you*, the man who destroyed my father?"

"Yes, dammit, with me." Riordan glowered at her, firelight flickering on his countenance, giving him a demonic look. Yet there was an aura of zest about him, of violent energy. "Unless you *want* to burn up."

"I don't—of course I don't!"

His fingers tightened painfully. "Look down there, look at the end of the street, at those buildings. The whole city is burning. This place is flaming up and we're all going with it!" He yanked at her, nearly pulling her off her feet. "I'm getting you out of here."

"And what about your strongbox?" she taunted. "Surely you're not going to abandon that in order to rescue two helpless women?"

"I'll take it with us. If necessary I'll abandon it, but I'm going to try to get my papers out. Now, are you coming or not?"

For a wild moment Alisa rebelled. She couldn't possibly accept help from her enemy, from this arrogant man who had hurt her father. And yet Riordan Daniels was right, she didn't want to die. She wanted to live, she wanted a chance to get even with him, she wanted so much, she wanted power, love, everything that life had to offer.

And this man could give it to her. She felt it instinctively. He was strong, a fighter; if anyone could get them out of this fire, it was he.

But she was a fighter, too. She stooped down and picked up one corner of the heavy box.

"No," he protested. "That's too heavy for you!"

"It isn't. I can carry anything *you* can."

He shrugged. "You'll tire soon enough. All right, then. Lift your end." They started off down State Street, a man and a woman carrying a strongbox, another woman hurrying beside them, cradling a green velvet hat.

They made their way east to the shore of Lake Michigan. Alisa carried her end of the strongbox until her back shrieked with agony and every muscle burned. She gritted her teeth, wishing she could drop it, that they could abandon the strongbox as so many other things were being abandoned by others as they grew too heavy—suitcases, boxes, puppies, paintings.

But she would not give Riordan Daniels the satisfaction of showing him her weakness. If he could carry the box, then so could she. She'd lug it miles if she had to. She'd go forever. . . .

She realized that she was slipping into a semi-trance, the reality of the fire fading for her. There was only the smoke and the billowing heat and the sparks that swirled in the air and bit at their legs, burning holes in their clothing. *Hell*, she thought. They were in hell. And Riordan was Satan.

"Come on, faster, hurry, Alisa!" He was merciless. He harried them on, shouting at Fifine when she sobbed and sank to her knees.

"I'm tired, too tired," she blubbered.

"We're all tired—all of Chicago is tired—*Keep going!*"

They skirted fires. Dodged burning debris. Cried out when sparks seared their skin, a rain of tiny, vicious fire-bits. A middle-aged man lay in the road, apparently dead of a heart attack. Riordan forced them on, refusing to allow them to stop.

Alisa lost all track of time, and never knew how long it took them to reach the lake, where the crowds of refugees had become dense, frantic, packed bodies with but a single purpose. To survive.

Some buried themselves shoulder-deep in the sand, to escape the torture of the burning sparks. Others waded out into the water, holding babies and small children high.

"We . . . we can't go any farther," Alisa gasped, surveying this terrible scene. Her capacity for horror seemed gone; she was beyond fright, beyond terror. She was so tired—her hands were raw from carrying the strongbox, her shoulders agonized.

She dropped her end of the box with a thump. They might as well bury it in the sand where it would be safe, and wade into the lake, as the others were doing.

But Riordan refused to let her. His face was the grim, carven mask of a stranger, scarred with lines of grief and tragedy. He pointed to the water. Already the dark heads of hundreds of people bobbed in the choppy waves, some of them terrorized, screaming, or dragging each other down.

"Those people are going tò drown each other. Come on. We'll dampen our clothes with water and then we'll walk south along the lake until we're away from the fire. We'll take as many others with us as will come."

"But—"

"Do as I say, Alisa. I intend to save us *and* the records of my business." Riordan stooped to heft up the heavy box, shouldering the entire thing himself. Shamed, she allowed it. Her entire body screamed for rest. He was male, he had been born physically stronger than she, this was a reality that had been forcefully brought to her attention tonight.

She staggered on through the sand behind him, pulling Fifine after her, experiencing an odd sense of calm in the midst of the raging fire, the frantic crowds. Riordan Daniels might be a ruthless predator, but his back was strong, and so was he. He would get them out.

And after that . . .

But beyond that point, she could not think.

*   *   *

Dawn was already breaking when they finally walked clear of the fire. Still burning, Chicago lay behind them, red and terrible, gray plumes of smoke billowing from it to stain all the sky. They had reached a part of the town untouched by the blaze. Here some of the residents of these streets were just waking up, and walked into their yards to stare at the smoke in astonishment. They hadn't known there was a fire at all.

Riordan commandeered a draper's wagon, pulling money out of his pocket to pay the startled driver, who helped him lift the strongbox into the bed of the wagon. They climbed in. Fifine sobbed softly, still cradling the sooty green velvet hat, which, amazingly, she had carried through all the horror of the fire.

A wave of exhaustion swept over Alisa, so strong that it was like opium, paralyzing her nerve ends, blotting out her senses. "We're alive," she heard herself say in a small, smoke-husky voice.

They sank onto leather-covered seats, and the conveyance started forward with a jolt. Alisa steadied herself, and then felt Riordan pull her to him, crushing his mouth down on hers. His lips took her mouth like a soldier seeking plunder after battle.

He pulled away. His eyes looked into hers, burning with triumph. "We did it!" he exulted. "We did it, we got out, and we even saved my records!"

"Please . . ."

It was crazy, brought on by their sudden jubilance at survival, it meant nothing but that. Weakly she tried to resist. But she was no match for him. This time his lips were softer, their pressure sweetly insistent. Dreamily Alisa let her own lips part, and felt a delicious lassitude melt through her.

The kiss seemed to last forever, long moments that were as frightening as they were rapturous. She was caught in him, lost in this electrical contact with him. The fire might never have happened, the jolting wagon and Fifine did not exist, there was only their clinging bodies, their mouths locked. . . .

He let her go. Alisa yanked herself away, her heart pounding thickly. She stared down at her lap, at her clenched hands, unable to look at him.

Dimly she heard Riordan give the driver some destination—she was too upset to hear what it was—and then the driver cracked his whip. They jolted along through shabby streets over which hung a thick, heavy pall of smoke.

Alisa felt her eyes close from exhaustion and her muscles sag under the regular jolting movements of the wagon. A strong, warm arm tightened around her. Mindlessly she gave herself up to its strength. She had reached the limit of her resources. She could not bear anything more; she wanted only to be held, cradled, comforted.

"That's it," he said softly. "Rest your head on me. You're a tough little creature, aren't you? Carrying your end of the box all those miles, defying me to stop you. . . . Rest, Alisa. Yes, that's it, rest. . . ."

She must have nodded off to sleep, for suddenly she was being carried into a house and up a huge flight of stairs embellished with porcelain balustrades. She blinked her eyes, feeling her body twitch with exhaustion. Riordan was carrying her, she was being cradled in the warm strength of his arms.

Had she slept all the way here? Where was Fifine? *Was this Riordan Daniels' house?*

Panic fluttered through her, and then seeped away, overpowered by weariness.

"You must be so tired," his voice murmured into her ear, its tone so soft that she knew she must be dreaming, for that rough tenderness could not be real. She hadn't experienced such tenderness since Papa had died. Her eyes fluttered shut and then opened briefly as she felt herself being carried into a room and laid down on an incredibly soft feather bed.

"There," Riordan said. She felt the mattress close about her body, and nothing had ever felt so good, so comfortable. "There, Alisa, you're here, you're safe, I've saved you."

Was it her imagination or did his voice break into a soft groan? "Your dress has been torn, and it's filthy. I'll call a maid to help you. Your Fifine is being taken care of now."

"No," she murmured, caught in the soft lassitude of this comfort after the hell of the fire she had fled. "No, I don't want a maid, I'll undress myself."

Her hands fluttered to her neck, and then to her side, where a row of pearl buttons fastened her bodice. They touched the buttons and gave up, falling limply to the mattress again.

"I'll call the maid," Riordan repeated. Then he

was gone and Alisa slept fitfully, half-awakening to feel hands easing the dress from her.

It was the maid, she thought sleepily. But when she forced her eyes open she saw that it was not a servant at all, but Riordan himself. Calmly he sponged her off, dipping a cloth into warm water and running it over her face, her arms, her soft breasts.

"Don't worry, I've seen women before, this is nothing new. The servants are exhausted, they wet down the roof of the house all night, saving it for me. I didn't have the heart to wake them, and you certainly can't sleep like this. Your arms, your legs—you've got dozens of tiny burns from sparks."

She moaned and attempted to cover herself, but finally gave up. He continued to bathe her, a tired, darkly handsome man with a husky voice and hands that were infinitely gentle.

"You are beautiful," he murmured. "Your body is so lovely, Alisa. And I don't think these burns will scar. Your clothing protected you somewhat."

It was wrong, and yet it was as if a spell had been cast on her, a soft, languorous spell created by her exhaustion, that held Alisa in hypnotized sway, erasing all sense of modesty or shame. His hands were so gentle, so healing. They extracted all the pain and tiredness from her body, leaving her feeling peaceful.

After he had washed her for what seemed like an endless, rapturous time, the cloth fell aside and Riordan lowered himself beside her on the bed, and recklessly Alisa pressed her body into his, knowing that she'd wanted this all along, and that he had, too.

His hands savored her skin, each touch lingering, as if to impress her curves forever on his mind. Then Riordan kissed the hollow of her throat, long, delicious kisses that sent shivers racing through her.

His mouth moved down, then, to her breast, and he tongued her nipples, at first gently and then with growing urgency, until Alisa found her whole body straining upward, her pelvis wanting only to arch into his, to find the very core of him.

"God . . . Alisa . . . oh, God," he groaned, gripping her buttocks in both of his hard hands to pull her to him. They rolled together fiercely, all of her languor gone now as she was possessed by a wild passion that matched his.

Hands kneaded flesh, caressing, and they groaned their pleasure and desire. His kisses burned up and down her body, searing her skin. Alisa cried out, and they rolled over again, pressed skin-to-skin, her thighs wide apart with the urgency that she felt and welcomed.

She had never before made love to a man. She experienced a moment of rough, hard pressure before he finally slid past the natural barrier of her virginity and was deep within her, claiming a core of her that she had not known existed. He thrust forward deeply and she met him with an answering push of her hips. They ground together, swept up in their frantic hunger.

He rode her powerfully, spreading her totally to him, and Alisa forgot everything in the joy of this union, the wild giving, the total abandonment. And when the pleasurable sensations grew, building like the very force of the fire they had just escaped, she did not try to stop it.

She let it happen, let it grow, until it was too big to stop and she did not want to stop it, she wanted it to burst, to explode. . . .

She heard Riordan's groan, felt him arch against her, shuddering in a spasm of pleasure. The sensation triggered her own explosion. She was flying, soaring in arc after arc of ecstasy, and she barely heard her own cry, screaming out her fulfillment.

They slept; for an hour, maybe longer, Alisa didn't know. She was wrapped deliciously close in his embrace, cradled next to the moist, silken smoothness of his skin. But something, perhaps another noise in the house, awakened her.

Out in the corridor—yes, wasn't that Fifine's voice, calling for her?

She stirred, feeling reality chill her with all the powerful force of a fire hose. She had made love to Riordan Daniels! She was lying here naked in his house, in his bed, in his arms.

She had betrayed her father. And in the worst way possible, with the very joy of her body.

She came to her senses. As if his flesh were a burning cloth, she jerked herself away from Riordan, sitting violently upright. *What had she done?* This was the very man who had driven her father to desperation and death, who had stopped at nothing to take his steel mill away. Alisa was furious at herself, and frightened at her own weakness. Her own exhaustion and fear, the madness of the fire, and the long, hellish night, had betrayed her.

Riordan stirred, his hold tightening on her. "Alisa, you're safe now. What are you—?"

"Don't touch me!" Desperation gave Alisa a renewed bitter strength, and she fought him off, jumping out of bed. She found the remains of her dress, which she threw on her body with violent movements.

"The fire is still burning; where do you think you're going?" Anger tinged Riordan's voice as he, too, flung himself off the bed, strikingly male in his nakedness.

"I'm getting out of here!" She twisted out of his grip and darted into the corridor. Fifine waited at the head of the stairs, her once-smart gray merino dress now sooty and torn beyond recognition. The Frenchwoman had put on the bonnet she had rescued from the fire, and filthy lace drooped over her eyes.

She babbled something that Alisa didn't catch. "Alisa! Where were you? I fell asleep for a while. Then I woke . . ." It was plain that Fifine was still fire-dazed.

"Sleeping," Alisa muttered. "Come on, Fifine, we can't stay here. We have to go."

"But—"

"We have to leave." Alisa grabbed her former maid and pulled her down the massive staircase, ignoring the sound of a door opening and Riordan's furious shout.

Where were they to go? What to do? As they left the luxurious area where Riordan Daniels lived and trudged through block after block of shabby houses, of factories and stockyards and shops,

Alisa's white-hot anger gradually faded to worry. All around them homeless people jostled. Hungry babies squalled, and tired children sagged in the arms of exhausted women. An elderly couple tried to carry an even older woman, emaciated with advanced age.

How much of the city had the fire destroyed? By the numbers of the refugees, Alisa guessed that it was a large area indeed, and it occurred to her that there were going to be thousands of people without homes. Already her belly was growling with hunger, and her mouth seemed as dry as cloth from thirst.

What had happened to her house near the court-house square? Alisa felt sure that it was gone, destroyed in the blaze, along with her shop. Malva, too, lived in an area that Alisa felt sure had been devastated by the fire. Where was Malva now? And what of the immigrant women who had worked in her shop, of Nella, and Billy, her delivery boy? Were they safe?

Alisa's thoughts became grimly practical. What of themselves? They needed a place to sleep, food to eat. She did not think she could huddle in the street, as she had seen one family do, and Fifine needed peace and calm and safety.

For the first time, she began to regret her hastiness in running out of Riordan Daniels' house. At least he would have taken care of them. Then savagely she pushed the thought out of her mind. She didn't want *his* help, *his* concern.

They paused to slake their thirst from an outdoor pump, and Alisa drank cool water from her cupped hands, thinking that she had never tasted anything so good in her life. She scrubbed her face, washing off, not soot, but layers of kisses.

With the wash, her thoughts grew clearer. They did have a place to go: Matt Eberley lived west of here. By looking at the dark, smoke-ravaged sky and gauging the smoke patterns, Alisa became convinced that Matt's home had not been touched by the fire.

Matt would surely take them in. All it meant was more walking, unless they were lucky enough to be able to commander a wagon, as Riordan had done.

"Alisa! Alisa . . . my God, I was worried sick about you," Matt said, taking one look at the two exhausted women who had arrived on his doorstep, footsore from miles of walking, their clothing burned with black holes from sparks that had landed on them sometime during the nightmarish hours of the fire.

Alisa managed a half-smile. "We couldn't catch a wagon that wasn't full of refugees. So we walked. Everything is gone, Matt. My house, the shop, all of it."

"Oh, darling . . . darling . . . I can't believe you got out of that fire all by yourself. Come in, come in. We've already taken in some other families. It's going to be crowded, but you'll stay with us, of course. My mother will be delighted to see that you're all right."

The Eberley house was typical of the day, with several drawing rooms full of heavy furniture, oak paneling, and a dark carved staircase that wound upstairs to a corridor lined with more rooms. As

Matt ushered them into the entrance hall, Alisa saw several pathetic piles of household goods, apparently belonging to the other refugees of whom Matt had spoken. Somewhere an infant was squalling, and she heard the chatter of older children.

"So you got out of the fire." Ida Eberley emerged from a downstairs door with a rather annoyed swish of black *moiré* skirts.

"Yes, we are safe," Alisa said simply.

The two women eyed each other. Ida Eberley was sixty-five, a tall, freckled woman with sandy hair faded to gray. She had at first approved of her son's interest in Alisa, but that was before Eben Amsell's downfall and the opening of the millinery shop.

"I think we still have a guestroom left," Ida said grudgingly. "It's small, and you'll have to share it with your maid, but I'm sure you won't mind that."

"We'll be very grateful," Alisa said. "But Fifine Desjardins is my employee, not my maid."

Ida's glance swept over Fifine, whose face was tear-streaked and who now held the velvet bonnet behind her, as if she had finally realized how incongruous it was that she should have chosen to rescue it from the fire.

"She *was* your employee, don't you mean? I'm sure now that your shop is gone, you'll have to settle into a more conventional life, Miss Amsell, as you should have done in the first place. The room is upstairs and down the hall to your right. I'll have a servant bring towels."

"Thank you," Alisa managed to say. Then she and Fifine were climbing the stairs. They found the room, which contained a feather bed and maple furniture and looked out on the brick-paved back service road. Numbly they pulled off their sooty dresses. Alisa collapsed onto the bed and fell instantly asleep.

∽᷾7᷾∾

Later, the fire would be blamed on a lamp upset by a cow in a barn belonging to Patrick and Catherine O'Leary, located on De Koven Street, a muddy tract near Halstead and Twelfth streets. Flames had quickly streaked out of the barn, and soon the wind tore away burning sticks and hurtled them into other barns and dwellings.

The bulk of the Great Chicago Fire burned for about twenty-nine hours, until rain finally fell Monday and doused most of the flames, except for burning coal piles, which were to smolder for days.

Alisa slept, deeply, drugged by exhaustion and the ordeal she had been through. She awoke at dawn the following day. Clothes had been laid out for both of them to wear, cast-off gowns of Ida Eberley's in slate gray, black, and lavender, all too large.

Alisa explored the corridor and found a large bathroom with a claw-footed porcelain tub. Gratefully she sank into the heaven of a bath, scrubbing at her skin until it felt pink and raw. She dressed in the least objectionable of Ida Eberley's gowns, making up her mind to have Fifine alter the dresses as soon as possible. Perhaps they wouldn't have to stay here for very long. Surely she'd think of something, some other alternative. . . .

She did the best she could with her hair, and descended the stairs to find a house swarming with restless refugee children. Four families had been taken in, and Henry and Julia, Matt's twins, raced among the newcomers, shouting loudly.

Already the children were playing "fire," and eight-year-old Henry told Alisa jubilantly that he didn't have school today, nor would he have to go for "weeks and weeks."

"That's one good thing the fire did!" he crowed. "Are you going to stay with us too, Miss Amsell? My grandmama says you're just a nuisance, she says you ought to earn your keep since you are just a shopkeeper anyway," he went on innocently. "Will you scrub our floors, Miss Amsell? I think you're far too pretty to be a housemaid."

Alisa forced a smile, feeling annoyed and humiliated; already she could see that her presence here was going to be difficult. Making her escape from the shouting children, she went to the small study, where a maidservant had told her she could find Matt.

"Matt!" She knocked on the door, at first gently, then with more vehemence. "Matt, are you in there?"

He pulled open the door and smiled at her. "Well. You look much better now, much more yourself, Alisa." He said this with satisfaction, as if he had engineered her transformation himself. "I

wouldn't let Mother wake you. You were so wild-
eyed last night that I confess I barely recognized
you."

"Matt." She walked into the room and closed its
door behind her. "Matt, your mother doesn't want
me here—I can't stay here, it's totally awkward."

He looked puzzled. "But of course Mother wants
you. Why wouldn't she? Alisa, darling, you must
face reality. This fire has been catastrophic, far
worse than anyone dreamed could ever happen.
They're saying that most of the major business
district is gone. The waterworks, the gasworks,
churches, homes, stores . . . It has been incredible.
Hundreds of insurance companies are going to go
bankrupt, among them my clients."

Was that all he could think of—insurance companies? Alisa stared at Matt, who had sunk into a
leather chair and was rubbing his forehead tiredly.

"I have to find out about Malva," she said. "And
the people who worked in my shop. Nella, Billy,
all of them."

"But the fire is still smoldering. Insurers have
been hit castastrophically—there's no way they can
begin to repay their subscribers."

At the remark, Alisa recovered her perspective.
Matt with his talk of insurance companies, she
with her petty objection to staying here under the
thumb of his mother—how small those concerns
were in the face of the huge disaster that had virtually leveled Chicago. She didn't even dare to think
how many people must have died.

"Anyway, I'm glad you're here," Matt went on.
"You're to have anything you want. Another room
if you wish it, clothes, whatever you need."

"I don't need much. And I'll stay here for a while, but I do plan to earn my keep. Your son informs me he has no school to go to. Well, I'll open a classroom here in your house. Fifine can busy herself with sewing; I'm sure there are dozens of things to be altered and repaired."

"That isn't necessary, Alisa."

"It is, for my own pride if nothing else. There's only one thing I ask of you, and that is that you take me back to visit my shop as soon as the fire has cooled enough to make that possible."

"But, darling, your shop is gone. I thought you knew that."

"Of course I know it!" Was it exhaustion that made her speak so sharply to Matt? "But my trimmers might come back to seek help there; I have to leave them a note, some way to contact me. I still have a little money, I must help them if I can."

"You don't need money as long as you are at my house. I want to take care of you, Alisa. I'd do anything for you. I'll help your women workers, I'll even offer them shelter here. But I won't allow you to go back into the fire area. I won't expose you to danger or ugliness. I'll go myself, and *I'll* leave the note."

It seemed to Alisa that Matt's attitude toward her had subtly changed. It was as if he had become more dominating now that she was a guest in his home, almost as if he rejoiced in her new and more helpless position.

"I'm coming too," she told him firmly.

"Nonsense! I've already heard, the rubble is frightfully dangerous, no place for a woman."

"I'm going."

"But, Alisa—"

"Matt, I was in that fire and I dodged burning debris and I had to run for my life. Do you think I'm afraid of ugliness or danger? Don't be silly!"

She had to leave the room to conceal her annoyance with Matt, and her unease. Surely it was a mistake for her to have sought shelter here, but with thousands of homeless refugees, housing was going to be at a premium now. Where else could she and Fifine possibly have gone?

Late that afternoon, Matt ordered the carriage and drove Alisa west into the raw, black, smoking destruction that had once been Chicago. By now, Matt had bought the *Evening Journal* extra, and everyone in the house had read and reread the horrifying headlines: "THE GREAT CALAMITY OF THE AGE!" "CHICAGO IN ASHES!" "ALL THE HOTELS, BANKS, PUBLIC BUILDINGS, NEWSPAPER OFFICES, AND GREAT BUSINESS BLOCKS SWEPT AWAY—FURY OF THE FLAMES . . ."

An area between six and seven miles in length and nearly a mile in width had been burned over, and one hundred and twenty bodies had already been recovered, although some estimated that the death toll would run as high as three hundred.

Three hundred. It was a number so large that Alisa's mind could barely encompass it. A horrible knot of worry tightened in her stomach as she wondered how many of the victims were her friends, her former servants, her employees.

But at least Cousin Malva was safe. Malva had sent a message to the Eberleys' that she was staying with friends and was already working at the orphanage, luckily untouched by flame, to open a soup kitchen for the refugees.

"You shouldn't have come, darling. You're not going to be able to stomach this," Matt said as they drove closer and closer to the burned city, from which emanated an acrid stink of smoke, ash, and death. Hundreds of plumes of black smoke still rose from coal piles in basements and coalyards, creating an eerie, hellish effect. "Shall I turn back?"

"No. Keep going. Please." Alisa clenched her hands tightly together in her lap as they neared the first burned-out area. Jagged brick walls rose out of rubble. Ashes and debris were everywhere, and a dead horse, half-burned, lay crushed under a charred beam. Alisa shuddered, looking around her with horror. The fire had been so powerful that it had virtually exploded these buildings. Steel beams had melted, stone had flaked, marble had been reduced to powder.

But now a few wagons rolled, already beginning to haul away debris, and people stood in front of a telegraph office, lining up to send telegrams to relatives in other cities. A peddler pushed a shabby cart, selling barrels of fresh water.

"Well, this is it, Alisa," Matt said, pulling up. "Here's your shop. Now, are you satisfied?"

Alisa stared, catching her breath in horror, for she hadn't even recognized the site. Where once her elegant little shop had been was now a gutted building collapsed into a heap of bricks. A few scraps of charred blue might once have been striped awnings, but there was no trace of the gilded eagle or of any of the contents of the building.

The harsh smell of melted cloth and ash filled her nostrils.

Alisa felt a wave of nausea sweep through her, and sat rigidly, gulping in an effort not to be sick.

"I told you," Matt said. "I told you it would be terrible. What good is it going to do to leave a note here among all this? Your sewing girls aren't going to come back here. No one with any sense would."

"I don't care, I still have to try."

She recovered herself, producing the handwritten placard she had written back at the Eberleys', instructing her employees where to go if they needed help. Before Matt could assist her, she swung down from the carriage and picked her way among pieces of brick that looked as if they had been exploded apart. At the back of the wreckage a small coal fire smoldered, black smoke twisting in the wind.

Breathing shallowly against the fire stench, she finally tied the placard, with wire she had brought with her, to the one section of the doorway that remained. It looked pathetic and brave.

"I hope some of them see this," she began.

"Get in," Matt ordered. "I'm taking you home now." He helped her into the carriage and then urged the horses, made skittish by the fire smells, back the way they had come. "Now that you've seen the ruins, you won't need to come back. It's gone, Alisa, your store is gone. Marry me. Surely you see it's the only solution for you now?"

She didn't look at her gutted shop as they drove away from it. "Matt, I don't want to marry you or anyone. I've already told you that. Why should the fire change my mind?"

He was angry, slapping at the reins. "Don't be a fool. What are you going to do, how are you going to support yourself?"

"Not by hiring myself out as someone's wife merely for food and shelter!" she snapped. "As long as I'm living at your house, I intend to work full-time for my keep. And if you won't allow me to do that, then I'll leave. I mean that, Matt. I won't take charity from anyone."

They rode the rest of the way back to Matt's house in strained silence. When they finally pulled into the back service road, he reached out to squeeze Alisa's hand.

"I'm sorry. It's just that I want you so much, I want to take care of you. I don't want you to have to worry about anything or to have to lift a finger, ever."

She tried to smile at him. "You're kind, Matt," she managed to say. But as he escorted her into the house, she felt uneasy and troubled.

In the days that followed, Alisa plunged into the hard work of earning her keep in a place where the lady of the house really did not want her presence.

She was given a large upstairs room, formerly a game room, to use as a school, and makeshift desks and chairs were moved in for her pupils. She had fifteen children in her class, ranging in age from four to sixteen. Several were neighbors of the Eberleys'. Two of the boys, Klaus and Peter, belonged to Nella, one of the bonnet trimmers, who had appeared three days after Alisa left the placard, begging for shelter.

"Miss Amsell, oh, miss!" Nella had wept, clinging to her. "When I saw your sign, I cried so . . . I can't thank you enough, you have saved all of us."

"Nonsense, Nella," Alisa protested, touched. "You would have managed."

"No, no. *Ach,* no!"

Helga, Alisa learned, was alive, but Nella knew nothing about any of the others. They could only hope that Billy and the rest were among the thousands who had either left the city or were camped out in refugee camps on the prairies.

Ida Eberley visited the schoolroom twice a day, frowning if the children became too boisterous.

"You are not really trained as a teacher," she told Alisa. "You haven't nearly enough history, and no Greek or Latin at all. Although," she added contemptuously, "I suppose your mathematics is excellent, since you have been involved in shopkeeping."

"Indeed it is," Alisa agreed evenly.

Ida nodded, not daring to voice her disapproval any stronger than this, for Matt had made his partisanship of Alisa clear. "Well, see that you keep the children quiet," she ordered. "At least they will be occupied, and that is better than having them racing about yelling and shouting. Since we now have two more children with us, thanks to that immigrant of yours who showed up."

Alisa struggled to keep her pupils under control, to devise lesson plans, and to oversee homework. Resolutely she pushed out of her mind disturbing thoughts of the man who had rescued her from the fire, whose strong arms and hard, seeking mouth had caused her to betray her father.

She was lucky to be at the Eberleys', she told herself. Didn't she have shelter—luxurious shelter—when thousands had to live in tents? She even had several new dresses that Matt had insisted on buying for her, claiming he didn't like to see her in his mother's cast-offs.

Matt went out daily, bringing back news. By some miracle of the capricious wind-blown flames, the house that had been Papa's survived, and the Amsell mill was also intact. Makeshift shops had been erected in the middle of the business district. W. D. Kerfoot, a real-estate dealer, had nailed up a sign over the door of his quickly built new shack: "ALL GONE BUT WIFE, CHILDREN, AND ENERGY."

Businessmen were beginning to recover safes from gutted stores. Sometimes, when the safes were opened too early, their overheated contents burst into flames as soon as the air hit them. Therefore, Matt told Alisa, many bankers poured water on the safes to cool them until the metal was chilled all the way through.

The city was under martial law, and signs announced that looters would be shot. Three laborers had been killed on South Water Street when a wall fell on them while they were trying to clear away debris. Other collapsing structures took more lives.

"You see?" Matt said. "It *is* dangerous, Alisa. You're much better off here at home and out of it all."

Alisa disagreed. She itched to get out of the house, to roam the city, to be a part of the courageous recovery that was going on there. Enterprising merchants peddled water throughout the town, and others did a rousing business selling souvenirs. Sightseers thronged to the city, many on special excursion trains that had been started on the Sunday after the Great Fire.

Ladies Relief Societies sprang into action. Trainloads of food and supplies rolled in from other cities, and President Grant himself sent a personal check for one thousand dollars.

"It's exciting, I must confess it, darling Alisa," Malva said when she paid a call on Alisa one afternoon in early November, bringing news of friends, survivals, disaster, and humor. Fluffy blond Cordelia Landsdowne was actually a heroine, pulling two younger sisters from their burning house, then returning for the family's large marmalade cat.

"These people—this wonderful city," Malva said. "Nothing can keep Chicago down for long. I've never seen anything like it. The rubble is being cleared away at an incredible rate. Did you know that the horse cars will be running soon?"

"What?"

"In the middle of chaos, we'll have regular transportation," Malva chortled. "Do you know, I feel good? Isn't it strange that a disaster should make a person feel stronger? But I do feel so useful. My soup kitchen has been feeding a thousand people a day. That's much more fun than giving parties, I must admit. What have you been doing?"

Alisa told her cousin about the makeshift school.

"Well, that's fine," Malva said. "But I wonder

that Matt allows it—why, you're not much more than a paid governess."

"That's exactly what I am, but it's at my own insistence. I can't take from him, Malva. He has become far too proprietary of me; he seems to assume that my presence here means much more than it does. Fortunately, I don't plan to stay here long."

"You really ought to consider marrying him," Malva remarked. "Matt Eberley is a good man and he does love you. Perhaps this fire might have worked some good, after all."

Alisa lifted her chin. Her day had been a long one, and Ida had been particularly irritating this afternoon, complaining about the noise of the children's boots on the wooden flooring. And she was tired of feeling like a prisoner, shut away from the excitement of the city's vibrant rebuilding.

"Malva, now really! Quit trying to marry me off! There isn't a man in this town I'd care to look at—and certainly not poor, dear, dull, persistent Matt."

But after Malva drove off, Alisa felt unaccountably restless. Leaving her pupils in the temporary care of the capable Nella, she put on a bonnet and mantle against the late chill and fled the house. She needed to think, and she'd had little time for that recently.

Taking long, preoccupied strides, she swung along the residential area, past large houses guarded by wrought-iron fencing, homes mercifully spared by the fire. She drew deep breaths of fresh air, savoring its autumn crispness.

It was the first opportunity she'd had to leave

Matt's house in several weeks. It was as if she'd deliberately buried herself in hard work in order to numb the thoughts that tormented her. Papa gone, her shop gone, and she herself pressing her body shamelessly against the man who had destroyed Eben Amsell, totally lost in the power of his lovemaking. Passion she'd wanted, needed, *enjoyed*.

Well, wasn't it true? If she were honest, she'd have to admit it to herself. She shook herself, quickening her stride, glancing up as a black buggy rattled past, driven by a man with the wide shoulders and erect posture that reminded her all too vividly of Riordan Daniels.

Riordan! She jerked her gaze away from the buggy as if it carried a load of vipers. In spite of herself, her heart started to pound sickeningly fast, as she wondered if the man she had glimpsed was indeed Daniels himself, on his way to or from an office.

But of course Riordan had no office now, she remembered. His business quarters had been located on State Street, which had been destroyed in the blaze. Therefore, if he had no office, he had to be working at home.

A chilly wind whipped along the sidewalk, picking up dead leaves and old ashes and spinning them around in tiny tornadoes. Alisa's thoughts, too, began to spin.

Yes, she had lost nearly everything in the fire. But she still possessed the few pieces of her mother's jewelry she'd pulled from the safe, and she still had herself, and her courage. What was she doing toiling as a governess, patronized by Matt and resented by his mother? What future could there possibly be for her at the Eberleys' but marriage to Matt?

Did she really want that?

A vegetable vendor drove his dilapidated wagon up the street, eyeing Alisa's tall good looks. Ignoring him, Alisa tightened her mantle about her shoulders, berating herself. She'd betrayed Papa— not just on the night of the fire, but even before that.

Oh, yes, it was true. Intimidated by all his power and riches, she'd been afraid to face Riordan Daniels. So she'd buried herself in the millinery shop as an excuse for not challenging him. Now here she was at Matt's, doing the same thing.

But today, with the November wind swirling up scraps of ash and debris from the Great Fire, she felt suddenly strong and free.

Get it back, if you can, Eben had begged her in his letter, the loss of which had been one of the many small tragedies of the fire. *Get the Amsell mill back, Alisa. And remember that I love you dearly. . . .*

She turned on her heel and started back, already planning in her mind what to do.

Alisa sank back in the leather seat of Matt's big phaeton as the driver drove the carriage along the edge of the city's burned-out area. Rubble. It was everywhere, monstrous, distorted heaps of it, along with jagged buildings and chimneys that stood raggedly alone. The few efforts that men had made to displace the ruin seemed pitifully small and futile.

Rebuilding Chicago was going to be a colossal

task, Alisa realized. And buildings could no longer be constructed of lumber, veneer, and stucco, but would have to be made of more fireproof materials, like brick and stone.

The surrey turned into the luxurious residential area where Riordan Daniels lived, located only blocks from the burned district. It rattled past big mansions, and at last pulled up in front of Daniels' house.

Alisa stared. The house seemed bigger than she remembered from the night of the fire, with only a few charred places on its shingled roof to mark where the servants had saved it from being ignited by sparks. Now its cream marble blocks caught the winter sunlight as it reigned over the street in arrogant majesty.

"Here it is, miss. Riordan Daniels' big house." Matt's coachman pulled up at a carriage stone and hopped down to help Alisa out. "Are you expected?"

For an instant of panic, Alisa felt her mouth go dry. No, she *wasn't* expected. For the first time since yesterday she was racked by doubt. Had it been a mistake to come here? To defy a man like Riordan, whom Matt had described as so rich that he could not even spend all his money? Who could buy anything he wished without restraint, and who must possess power beyond Alisa's wildest imagining?

What was she doing, defying such a man? She held her hands tightly together, feeling the cloth of her gloves press against her fingers.

"Miss?" The driver repeated it impatiently. "Shall I wait?"

"I . . . Yes, please do." It was as if he had made

the decision for her. She could hardly quail in fear in front of a servant, could she?

She allowed the driver to help her down, keeping her chin high with a courage that she did not feel.

~~∽∾ 8 ∽∾~~

Once again Alisa had to face the scrutiny of the suspicious butler, as he looked her up and down in her forest-green silk, its bodice trimmed in matching velvet bands.

"Mr. Daniels is busy, he is seeing no one," the man told her.

"Well, he'll see me. I have business to discuss with him."

"Ah?"

"Business," she repeated icily.

Finally she was shown inside, again to the library. As before, she paced the room while she waited.

"Well, well!" A moment later Riordan himself appeared in the door, leaning casually against the paneled frame to regard Alisa with gleaming dark eyes. Alisa couldn't help catching her breath. He was tall, lean, and infuriatingly good-looking. She'd forgotten just how craggy those high cheekbones were, how alluring that high-bridged nose, how full his mouth.

He smiled crookedly at her. "If it isn't little Miss Amsell, the refugee who rejected my shelter to dash away into the dawn."

She felt a wave of pink sweep up from her collar. "I . . . I felt it best."

"Oh, you did, did you? You'd rather join a herd of refugees and camp out on the plains than stay in my presence?"

She moistened her lips uneasily. To cover her confusion, she gazed around the opulent library. It had changed since last she was here. Now the furniture had been moved to the wall, replaced by disorderly stacks of boxes, dozens of them, piled everywhere. An untidy array of papers lay on a long table, most of them charred or smoke-stained. The room even smelled of ashes, she thought in disgust. Could he not organize his affairs any better than this?

"How do you find anything?" she asked him coolly.

He shrugged. "It isn't easy. My employees and I have been going back to the wreckage of my office for days, salvaging everything we could." Riordan frowned. "But enough of that. Why are you here, Miss Amsell? I assure you, I'm very busy."

She was an intruder; he could not have made that more plain. Alisa flushed again, forcing out the words she had come to say. "I assumed you'd be working hard. That's why I'm here. I can help."

Riordan Daniels stared at her, his eyes pinning her under intense scrutiny. "How?"

"Why . . . I can assist you in clearing away the mountains of work you must have accumulated since the fire," she said, feeling rattled. He did look so intimidating—no wonder people were afraid of him. "I came to ask you for a job."

"A job!"

"I'll work hard. Truly I will, harder than any man in similar circumstances. I want to learn as much as I can about business."

"You want a job. You want to learn about finance." He said each word as if her request were an incredible thing, scarcely believable.

She'd had enough of his arrogance. "And what's so wrong with that?" she flared. "Surely I'm not the first person who's come here to apply for work. I'm a graduate of Mrs. Soames's, and I've had a year's experience in business, as you surely are aware."

He lifted one eyebrow. "Selling hats?"

"Yes! What's wrong with that? It's a perfectly respectable occupation! It—"

But again that crooked smile touched Riordan's lips. "I'm sorry, I didn't mean to insult you. But you are the first woman who has ever come to ask me for a job, other than as a household servant. You can't blame me for being surprised. However, my answer is still no."

"But—"

He stepped away from the doorjamb against which he had been leaning, and gave her a small mock salute. "My assistant was killed in the fire. I have a staff of clerks and accountants who've all been working twenty hours a day along with me. We're buried in mountains of work. I'm sorry, but I don't have any more time to talk with you, Miss Amsell. I'll have my butler show you to the door."

Alisa couldn't believe it. He was dismissing her like an unwanted salesman. This man had pressed his naked skin against her own, had kissed almost every inch of her. Now he wanted to deny it had ever happened, get rid of her like an inconvenient alms-seeker.

She clenched her hands into fists, a wave of fury sweeping through her, almost singeing the nerve ends of her skin. "No," she snapped. "I won't go, not yet, not until you listen to me."

"I thought I had listened. As I told you, I'm swamped with work, and I have no more time. And so, I bid you good day."

She fixed him with a hard, blue, reckless look. "No! I can help you. I'm smart. I have an orderly mind, I know mathematics, I can think."

"So can the rest of my employees. And they have the advantage of being male."

"It doesn't matter, Mr. Daniels, whether I am male or female, because you owe me."

"Oh? For what?"

Fury spun through her. "You know for what! Mr. Daniels, in case you've forgotten, I was the one who helped you haul that miserable strongbox of yours out of the Chicago Fire, rescuing some of those very papers!" She pointed dramatically to the laden tables. "That in itself should make you consider me. But there are other things. The love we made. And my father."

Riordan Daniels' ruggedly carven features went suddenly cold. "I told you before, you're wrong if you think I deliberately caused harm to your father. As for the Fire, I saved *your* life, you little fool, or had you forgotten that? And *you* enjoyed our lovemaking every bit as much as I did. So I think we're even, don't you?"

Alisa wanted to smack Riordan, to pound both fists against that wide male chest, to make him wince with hurt. Instead she drew herself to her full proud height.

"Never mind about that. Your office is a disaster. Your papers are a burned, charred mess. This place *stinks!* You've been wasting time trying to deal with it. As your assistant, I'll give your time back to you."

She squared her chin, eyeing the manservant. "Besides, I'm not leaving here without a job. If you want me to go, you're going to have to tell *him* to drag me out. And I'll fight all the way."

"I believe you would."

They faced each other, their glances locked, as anger crackled between them. But grimly Alisa met Riordan's stare, refusing to look away. It was easier than she had thought, because she really didn't *care* if they hauled her bodily away. She had meant everything she told him. She'd say it all again. Damn him!

Gradually the look that locked them together began to change. Alisa felt herself subtly drawn into the depths of those dark, dark, compelling eyes. She fought for control, her color heightening. She could *not* look away first.

Suddenly he grinned, breaking the eye contact.

"My God, girl, not even Cyrus McCormick dares stare me down like that. Have you eyes made of steel? I've never seen anyone as stubborn as you. I think you *would* have let Smeede drag you out of here, wouldn't you? Kicking and screaming."

Shaking, she nodded.

"Well, see what you can make of this mess, then. I'm tired of looking at blackened papers that crumble in my hands."

"Then . . ." She stared at him incredulously. "I have the job?"

"If you relish the thought of working twenty hours a day, yes. But I warn you, I expect you to work as long and as hard as I do, and to be totally devoted to my business interests. The first time I hear you cry out fatigue, you're fired, Miss Amsell."

Alisa felt her knees start to sag from the suddenness of her victory. But, using all of her mental discipline, she managed a cool, competent smile. "Good. Then I'll start work immediately, Mr. Daniels. I only need to go and dismiss my driver, and then I can begin."

His nod was equally cool. "Very well. But I'm hard to work for, and I expect a lot. You'll find that out."

She dismissed her driver with a message that she would not be home until after midnight—let Ida Eberley teach her own school, Alisa thought defiantly. Immediately she went back into the house to begin work. She soon learned that there were several rooms stuffed with fire-damaged papers and boxes. A crew of clerks and accountants had been moved into an unused first-floor ballroom and sat perched at makeshift tables in a hubbub of confusion. There seemed to be little order to their activities, and Riordan Daniels stalked among them issuing orders to first one and then another, his expression harassed.

What was she to do? Where to start?

For an instant Alisa experienced a moment of sheer panic, her eyes watering with frustrated tears. She knew nothing about high finance. She was totally ignorant; she'd gotten this job under false pretenses. She'd reveal her ineptitude, and Riordan Daniels would laugh at her, dismissing her humiliatingly.

Darling Alisa, daughter of my heart. Papa's voice seemed to echo into her mind, full of warmth and love. *You can do it. I know you can; aren't you my girl? My own girl?*

She wiped away her tears, scolding herself. Where was her courage?

In the smoke-smelling library she sat down at the table littered with blackened papers. How could anyone find anything in such disorder? She decided that had to be her first step. She'd sort the papers, salvage what she could, order clerks to copy the damaged documents, and file everything so that it could be found at a second's notice.

It felt better to have some clear goals. Trembling with excitement, she reached out for a tattered, blackened ledger.

"Are you still working?" Riordan lounged in the door, his cravat loosened, his shock of black hair cascading over his forehead.

"Why, yes, I . . ." Surprised, Alisa glanced at the little chatelaine watch that she wore on a thin gold chain. To her shock, she saw that it was past midnight—she had worked for nine hours without stopping.

He went on casually. "I thought I'd stop for supper—I must confess my belly growls if I don't feed it. Does yours?"

As Alisa reacted to the word "belly," language unheard in fashionable, mannered drawing rooms,

Riordan grinned. "Never mind, I'm sure you're very prim and proper, Alisa."

She rose. Her muscles felt stiff from the long hours bent over the table, and she needed to use a bathroom. No one had thought to inform her of its location, and there had been no woman present whom she could ask.

She gazed at him calmly. "I prefer to be called Miss Amsell."

"Not Alisa? But it is a very pretty name. Almost musical. It rings on the tongue, reminding me of the trill of a beautiful small bird."

"Indeed I don't like to be compared to a . . . a *bird*, of all things, not when I am working for you in a business capacity," she began.

But he was smiling at her, brushing one hand through his glossy hair. As he moved toward her she could smell the heady male odors of soap, shirt starch, and tobacco. Alisa drew a breath in horror and tried to move away from his all-too-exciting proximity.

"We will have a relationship solely in a *business capacity*," he emphasized. "However, I must tell you that I dislike calling people by formal names. Therefore, as long as you work for me, I intend to call you Alisa."

She swallowed hard, and nodded. "Very well." She felt herself color. "I was wondering . . . that is, where the—?"

"Upstairs and to your right, the fourth door. I am sorry that no one informed you. If there is anything else you need, please ask."

"Very well."

"Good. Then, will you join me for supper? My

dining room is huge, and, frankly, I dislike eating alone in it. I do so as seldom as possible."

She hurried upstairs, primping herself and smoothing her thick hair with a feeling of strange, thick excitement. She was to sit at table with him, converse with him. What would she find to say? Her thoughts seemed to skitter in her head like the very wild bird he had compared her to.

Fifteen minutes later she joined him in a huge room with ceilings at least fifteen feet high, dominated by a twenty-foot mahogany table. There were chandeliers of shimmering crystal. A Gobelin tapestry, showing lords and ladies at a stag hunt, filled one entire wall. On a sideboard sat a collection of porcelain plates and figurines that dazzled the eye.

When she exclaimed aloud at one, a statuette of a fierce little dog done in bisque and turkey red, Riordan laughed.

"You picked my favorite, Alisa. This is a long-haired Bolognese hound made at Meissen for Augustus the Strong's Japanese Palace—it was fired about 1733. Don't you think it's a beauty? I confess animal motifs are my favorite."

"Tell me about yourself," she was emboldened to say after the fish course, when they had exhausted the conversational topics of porcelain, riding, and the fire.

"What do you want to know?"

She blushed. "I have read about you in the papers, of course. How you went West to make your money, then returned to double and quadruple it in the New York stock market, making that

your financial start. But surely there's more of a
. . . a personal nature."

He raised one dark eyebrow. "And you expect
me to talk of personal matters to you?"

She gazed back at him, speaking boldly. "Why
not? Since you insist on calling me by my first
name . . . *Riordan.*"

He laughed. Seated next to her at the long
burnished mahogany table, he seemed to emit a
restless energy that she found disturbing. "*Touché.*
All right, then. I suppose I should tell you that I
wasn't born to all this—"

He indicated the richly furnished room in which
they dined. "On the contrary, we lived in a little
log shack with one room and a dirt floor." Oddly,
he seemed to hesitate for a moment, his jawline
knotting, as if this were a story difficult to tell.
"My father was a tenant farmer near Petersburg,
Virginia. My mother had been the town school-
teacher.

"We were *poor,* Alisa, dirt-poor and proud. But
at least my mother had book-learning to give me,
and after I had worked hard all day in the fields,
she insisted I labor hard at night over my books
and sums."

"She must have been a wonderful person," Alisa
murmured, touched by some fierce quality in his
voice.

"She was. She died, finally, of consumption, a
lingering death." Again Riordan looked troubled,
and Alisa wondered about the things he was not
telling her. He went on. "Six weeks after my mother
died, my father cut himself on a plow blade and
died of tetanus. My two half-brothers hired them-

selves out to our landlord, and I left town and went West."

Alisa nodded. "Was it exciting? An adventure, to go among the gold fields? Did you find any nuggets?"

Riordan laughed dryly. "No, I did not find any nuggets, either of gold or of silver. I ended up selling water pumps and mine-shoring timbers to the miners in the ramshackle village of Telluride, Colorado." He grinned. "There I learned to appreciate the merits of a good cup of coffee and a hot bath. We didn't get either of them often, believe me. There were times when I stank, Alisa, and no wise man would have stood downwind of my sweating and greasy body."

"I . . . I see."

Again he smiled. "I've come a long way, haven't I? I'm clean, I use soap and imported pomades, and my clothes are tailored in New York and London."

A little silence lingered between them.

"I've heard all sorts of rumors about you," she probed, keeping her voice light. "That you've been jilted, that you fought a duel, that you . . . like actresses. Even that you keep an iced champagne tap in your kitchen, which you can turn on at any hour of the day or night to sip chilled champagne just as you please."

Riordan's rich laugh pealed out, echoing against the high carved ceilings of the enormous dining room. "So tongues are wagging about the champagne tap!"

"Well? Isn't it true?"

He sobered. "Most of the rumors about me are

true, Alisa. I'll be honest with you, I have not lived a prosaic life. I am not a 'gentleman' as people like you think of it. But, no, I don't keep a champagne tap in my kitchen. I prefer to order up a magnum or two, properly iced. When and if the occasion calls for it, and sometimes when it doesn't."

He had really denied nothing, she thought. "Then you really were jilted?"

"Yes, I really was."

"But . . . how? You?" Red-faced, she was suddenly floundering. "I mean . . . I can scarcely believe it."

He tossed his napkin down, rising to his feet. "Do believe it, because it's true. Come, Alisa, let's go walk off this heavy supper before I order up the carriage to send you home. I'll tell you about it, if you really want to hear."

They walked briskly around the block, which was dominated by the Daniels mansion. A November wind whistled through dead branches of chestnuts, oaks, elms, and apple trees, and everything seemed caught in a spell of night. A scatter of diamond stars glistened from behind a bank of clouds, as if flung there by some careless giant.

They walked apart, a fact for which Alisa was thankful. The deserted midnight street created an intimate feeling that she did not want.

"My fiancée was named Elizabeth," Riordan told her. "She was as tall as you are, Alisa, and as pretty. She had a dimpled smile and green eyes that could smolder with fire when she chose to let them."

"Oh . . ." Somehow this was more about the unknown Elizabeth than Alisa wished to hear.

But Riordan did not seem aware of her reluctance. He went on, "She was beautiful and rich, from one of New York's best families, and she moved in the most powerful circles of society. I met her while I was out riding one day—her horse had been lamed and I stopped to help her."

He paused, and they walked for a while in silence. "I didn't belong, Alisa. I was brash. Struggling to make my fortune, and beginning to succeed. Proud of my accomplishments. But *they* thought I was a fortune-hunter. They couldn't see that I wasn't interested in Elizabeth's money, only in her."

"But what happened?"

His voice tightened. "Elizabeth defied them, insisting on our engagement. We were happy at first, then one day we quarreled. I don't know about what—a party, I think. She criticized what I wore, and I hurled an answer back at her."

He darkened. "Our argument escalated, and Elizabeth referred to . . . something I'd told her in a moment of confidence. She told me to get out. Her parting words were that she'd made a terrible mistake—she'd be ashamed to be seen in public with a 'rough Southern clodhopper' who didn't even know what to wear."

Alisa did not know what to say. She sensed his deep pain, the grief that had obviously shaken him then, and still touched him with melancholy. As they walked in silence, she grew aware of the nearness of Riordan's wide shoulders, only inches away from hers, actually brushing her whenever the walk narrowed.

"What did you do then?" she finally asked in a low voice.

Riordan shrugged, the gesture tight, almost angry. "I visited the best tailor in New York. I polished myself, Alisa, I changed myself from a clodhopper to a man who *looked* as powerful as he was. Oh, I learned my lesson, all right."

They walked more long strides. Suddenly a carriage careened around a corner, full of the rollicking sound of young men's laughter, and was gone in a clatter of hooves.

"They have probably been to the gambling house," Riordan remarked, changing the subject. "The 'hairtrigger block' was destroyed in the fire, although they say that poker chips and portions of roulette tables are still being found. Some establishments are now being rebuilt on the ashes—can men exist without their faro and twenty-one? Come, Alisa. We had better get you back."

This time he did take her arm, and held it firmly. They walked the rest of the way back to the big mansion not speaking. As they reached the front, Riordan spoke huskily.

"I'm never going to love any woman again, Alisa. You heard the rumors about me. That I'm a womanizer, that I fought a duel over a woman, that I flit from one beautiful actress to another. Well, those things are true, and there's a reason for it. Love is only a trap for a man, a kind of humiliation. I don't intend to be humiliated ever again. I'm after power. Lots of it, all the power I can get. That's going to be enough for me."

He glared down at her, his expression fierce, and Alisa could only stare back at him, not knowing what to say.

9

They stood in the entrance hall and Alisa gathered her mantle about her, wondering how to hint to him that she wished he would summon the carriage now, as it was late and she was suddenly very, very tired. And she still had Matt and his mother to face when she arrived back at the Eberleys', not to mention Fifine.

But suddenly Riordan seemed reluctant to have her depart. "Would you like to see something?" he asked her abruptly.

"Couldn't it wait until tomorrow? I'm . . ." She chopped off the word "tired," remembering that he had told her that if she cried out fatigue she was fired. But surely he couldn't mean that she must be spinning with energy at the ungodly hour of . . . Yes . . . was it after two in the morning?

"Come," he said, taking her arm to urge her toward the ornate staircase.

"What?" She resisted, hot and cold shivers running all over her body. "Mr. Daniels! You really can't mean to pull me upstairs with you! I didn't hire out as your assistant to—"

"Don't be ridiculous." He dropped her arm almost violently, and started up the staircase without looking to see if she followed. "I didn't hire you to be my paramour. If I'd wanted one of those, I could have gone to any theater or dance hall. I assure you, there are plenty of women willing to sell themselves for a few elegant suppers and some jewels."

Not knowing what to do, she took a few tentative steps up the staircase, its rococo balustrades feeling smooth to the touch. Then she stopped.

"Well?" he demanded. "Are you coming or aren't you? But be still, for God's sake. She's asleep."

"She?"

Mystified, Alisa could not resist tiptoeing the rest of the way up the staircase and following Riordan down the corridor.

She had never seen a man move with such light care, and everything about Riordan Daniels' attitude had subtly changed. Gone was the arrogance, the standoffishness, the mockery, even the sad ness she had seen on his face when he had talked about his upbringing and the jilting.

He stopped in front of a room with a simple oak door. "In here."

"But—"

"Don't be foolish!" he snapped. He gestured to her and finally Alisa stepped behind him into the darkened room, holding her skirts so that they would not rustle. Gleaming in a dim shaft of moonlight, she saw the wooden bars of something that looked exactly like a . . .

A baby crib.

Riordan Daniels had a baby stashed away here in this huge, ornate mansion!

Not knowing whether to be amused, shocked, or angry, she followed him to the crib and looked down on the most beautiful infant girl that she had ever seen. The baby was about three months old, and slept on her stomach, her tiny rump thrust into the air. Her hair was dark curly wisps. Her little embroidered nightgown had ridden up, revealing tiny feet and enchanting dots of toes.

Alisa let out an involuntary sigh. The baby stirred her oddly. But who on earth could this child be? There hadn't been the slightest mention of a wife or a child in the newspapers, in the clippings that Alisa had collected, or even through gossip.

"Who . . . who is she?" Alisa managed to whisper.

"Shhh! You'll wake her." Riordan gazed down at the infant, his expression at once fierce and yearning.

"Well, do you want me to guess?" she said angrily as they went back downstairs again and Riordan signaled to the butler, who had appeared in the hall, clad in full livery despite the late hour. "Or are you going to tell me who she belongs to?"

"She belongs to me now."

"To you? But how . . . ? I mean . . ."

He gave her a long look and a smile flickered at the corner of his mouth. "No, I'm not going to talk about her. I just wanted you to see her. She's a beauty, isn't she?"

"Yes, she's lovely." Alisa felt exasperated, her chest tight with some emotion she couldn't quite identify. Why had he shown her this baby? What did he want her to say or do?

"Life is going to be golden for her, Alisa. In every way. She's never going to have to suffer as I did, ever. Since you're to be working in this house, you may occasionally hear her cries. Please ignore them; she has a capable nurse to care for her. I want her presence here to be kept a secret, do you understand?"

"A secret? Oh, surely you're jesting!"

"I am not. No one must know she's here until I am ready to reveal it. Any of my employees who disobey that edict will lose their jobs immediately, and with no severance pay. Do you understand that?"

Alisa managed a nod, saying little more as she waited for the carriage to be brought to the front of the mansion. She didn't understand this strange man—and she wasn't sure she wanted to! What a puzzle he was, with the secret infant he kept upstairs, the gossip that swirled around him like a summer storm, his open, hard declaration that power, not love, was to be enough for him.

As the carriage at last mercifully pulled away from the Daniels mansion, Alisa sank into its soft cushioned seat for the lengthy ride home.

Today already seemed a fantasy, scarcely real. Had she really gone to Riordan Daniels and demanded a job, told him she would not leave his house unless she was dragged away? The boldness of her move now stunned her. What if they had called her bluff? Could she really have fought and struggled against that muscular butler?

The dark city spun past, and they passed only one other carriage, a doctor's phaeton on the way to some late call. Frustrated questions spun in

Alisa's mind. Who was that baby's mother, and how had Riordan acquired the child? Was he the father? No doubt!

Then she pushed away the questions angrily. What business was it of hers?

Tiredly she leaned her head on the back of the seat, looking upward at the new moon, which had slid out from behind its cloud blanket and burned overhead like a curved silver flame. She focused her eyes on its improbable glow. It occurred to her that Riordan, too, was like a flame. Well, wasn't he? And she herself was a foolish moth, dipping, flying ever closer to the fire that could burn her.

"Where on earth have you been?" Matt demanded when she arrived back at the Eberleys', wanting nothing more than to crawl into bed for ten hours of solid sleep. But that wasn't going to be possible, for she would have to rise well before six in order to be at Riordan's by seven, the hour when he customarily began work. He had promised to send his carriage for her until she was able to find lodgings of her own in a more convenient location.

"Didn't you receive the message I sent with your driver?"

"Of course I did. What on earth could it mean, you have accepted a job? What job? You're busy here, Alisa—teaching my children and the others." Matt looked red-faced and tired, and she sensed the effort he was having to make to keep his voice even.

He did love her, she realized. And he really had thought that her presence in his home meant that she would eventually be his wife; in fact, he had already begun to think that he could dictate to her.

She stifled annoyance. "Matt. You knew that my being here was only temporary. You knew I couldn't continue to take help from you indefinitely."

"Why couldn't you?"

"Because . . . You know why, Matt. I don't feel the way toward you that you would like me to feel," she began, wearily fumbling for the right words, the kind ones.

"You will, someday."

"No, Matt."

They were in the entrance hall, and he paced the floor, his hands clasped behind him, his attitude exactly like an autocratic husband's. Alisa tried to explain the details of the job she had taken, only to be interrupted angrily. "What are you doing working for Riordan Daniels anyway? A man like him—and in his home! It's totally improper."

"Why? There are at least six accountants and clerks, and a whole staff of servants to chaperon us. I'm sure I'll be well protected from the advances of a 'man like him,' as you put it."

"You're being a fool, Alisa! You know why he's hired you, don't you? He consumes women like . . . like sugar-covered almonds! He wants to sleep with you, that's all, and you've fallen for his ploy, you've fallen straight into his trap."

"I'm not interested in Riordan Daniels and he's not interested in me—not in the low, sordid way that you imply," she managed to say calmly, although she was simmering inside. She gathered up her skirts, starting toward the stairs.

"Alisa! Come back here! Surely you owe me the courtesy of—"

"Enough, Matt. I have worked ten hours a day in your home, struggling to pacify boisterous children and the whims of your mother. I think I've paid back anything that I owe you. Now, please don't say anything more that you'll regret in the morning. I thank you for your hospitality. Fifine and I would have been desperate if you had not taken us in. But that doesn't mean that I owe you the rest of my life!"

She was aware, as she climbed the stairs and went to her room, of Matt's angry, disbelieving stare, but she was too tired to care, and she had already forgotten Matt as she pulled off her dress and climbed into bed, to sink into a deep, dreamless sleep.

Early the next morning Riordan's carriage was waiting for her. Ignoring Ida Eberley's look of displeasure and Matt's scowl, Alisa hurried out to it. She felt thankful that Matt did not try to stop her. He was becoming a problem—a sizable one—and the sooner she moved out of his home, the better it would be.

Although it was only seven o'clock in the morning, Riordan was already in the library when she arrived. Today he wore a gray morning coat woven with a subtle pinstripe that seemed to hug the lines of his well-made body, emphasizing the breadth of his shoulders, his maleness. His vest was of rich satin, his cravat equally fine.

"So you are on time," he said, pulling out his watch.

"Did you hope that I wouldn't be?"

"Hope?" He eyed her ironically, his gaze sweeping over the tailored russet silk she wore. "No, I merely expected promptness, as I do in all my employees, male or female."

Black eyes met hers.

"I . . . I see."

"I want to give you some instructions," he went on, "and then I have to leave—I'll be out of the office all day and I expect you to run the place in an orderly fashion."

She stared. "Me? Run it?"

His grin challenged her. "Aren't you capable of it? Your behavior yesterday seemed to indicate you could run the world single-handedly."

"I . . . of course I can do whatever you ask of me!"

"Well, then. Will Rice, my chief accountant, and my clerks will assist you as needed. Learn everything you can from them, especially from Will, who knows my affairs well and has been with me for years. Eventually you will be in full charge of my office."

At this alarming news, her heart contracted in surprise and alarm; she, in charge here? The men would hate her for it, they would rebel—he knew it as well as she did. Was that what Riordan secretly wanted, for her to be humiliated and driven away? To vanquish Eben Amsell's daughter as he had beaten her father?

Proudly she drew herself up. "Fine," she told him. "I'll see to it." She met his look, giving him a cool little nod. "You may trust me, Riordan, to look after your best interests—and by the end of the day I'll know a great deal more about them than I do now. Also, soon you won't have to trouble yourself sending a carriage for me, for I intend to move to a small house of my own as soon as I can."

She spent the day sorting through papers and meeting the clerks and accountants. Several, just as she had feared, made it clear to her that they resented her presence. One clerk, a middle-aged man named Bochert, even implied in a veiled way that she was only another of Riordan's mistresses, whom he had imported into his house in some fit of temporary madness, but of whom he would soon tire.

Alisa bristled. She had been seated at the long table absorbed in the sorting of the fragile charred papers. Abruptly she rose, feeling her cheeks sting red. "Mr. Bochert, let's get it all out in the open. What exactly do you mean?"

"I . . . Why, I . . ." The man had the grace to flush.

"Do you really believe that a man like Riordan Daniels, with his sharp business acumen, would bring in one of his paramours to help run his office? It seems to me that you are insulting your employer with such insinuations."

"I wasn't . . . I didn't mean that. I only meant . . ." He stared defiantly at her. "We don't want a woman here."

"I see." Her mouth was dry with tension; she knew if she could not face this man down, she was doomed here. Sooner or later these male clerks would force her out. "Well, I understand your feelings, but I have been hired by Mr. Daniels to do a job, and I intend to carry out my responsibilities. I'll help you whenever possible. But I intend to remain."

She focused her extraordinary blue eyes on him, filling her look with every ounce of power and forcefulness she possessed. Finally Bochert broke the eye contact and glanced away. She nodded sharply, dismissing the man.

Ducking his head, Bochert left the room. Alisa sank back into her chair, her heart pounding thickly.

He had implied she was Riordan's mistress! Her thoughts swirled in a jumble of guilty memories—Riordan's soft lips, his strong arms around her, the silky feel of his skin against her own. And even today, hadn't his eyes rested on her with unmistakable interest? Yes. Every time she was in the room with him, the air between them seemed highly charged, explosive with sexual tension.

For a moment she felt shaken, her confidence ebbing.

Then she ran her hands over her burning cheeks, smoothing away their high color. They had made love once; then she'd run away from him. But that certainly didn't make her Riordan's mistress. *It had only been a mistake, one she'd never make again.*

Anyway, what did it matter why she was here? She had managed it. She was in a perfect position to create for herself the opportunity to have her revenge on Riordan Daniels for what he had done to her father.

She didn't yet know how she'd accomplish this;

she only knew that it was going to happen. In the meanwhile she had gained a foothold here in Riordan's office, and it was where she intended to stay.

She spent several hours with Will Rice.

"I suppose I'd better brief you, or you'll never be able to sort those papers properly," the chief accountant sighed. He was in his thirties, a weedy man with thinning brown hair.

Alisa had been thinking the same thing. "Please. Go ahead, I want to know everything."

"Everything?" Rice raised a sandy eyebrow. "Even I don't know that. Mr. Daniels is closemouthed sometimes—he keeps his plans to himself."

"I can imagine," Alisa remarked wryly, thinking of the baby.

"Well, I suppose we'd better begin. But I warn you, I don't have time to answer questions, so if you don't understand anything, you're going to have to suffer."

Alisa tensed, knowing that Rice, too, must resent her here. But calmly she took out a pencil and a pad of paper. "Begin," she ordered. "If there is anything I don't understand, I'll find it out for myself later."

Rice gazed at her in surprise. Finally he began listing the interests that Riordan Daniels controlled. They were many and varied. He had ties with the Standard Oil Works at Cleveland, a firm run by two men named William and John Rockefeller. He owned four railroad lines in Illinois and Indiana, and a controlling share in the First National Bank of Chicago, whose vaults and safes had safely survived the fire.

There were three steel mills, a wrought-iron pipe mill, the Daniels Link-Belt Machinery Company, and several lumber and planing mills.

To Alisa the list seemed confusing and endless. And these were not even the main sources of Riordan's income, which came from investments, gold speculation, and dealing in the Chicago Board of Trade on Wall Street.

The Amsell mill was only a tiny part of Riordan's financial empire, just one more item on a long list.

Her cheeks burning, Alisa scribbled rapidly, praying that Will Rice wouldn't notice her total confusion about some things, especially specie notes and the mechanics of speculative investment. She didn't understand it now, but she'd learn. She'd stay up nights studying if she had to.

"Well, that's about it," Rice said at last, glancing at her pages of detailed notes. "I suppose I've only confused you."

"No, you've enlightened me. I thank you for your time."

"Oh, it's nothing. *He* asked that I do it," the accountant said neutrally, turning away. It was not much of a victory, but Alisa felt pleased with herself, feeling she had accomplished at least something today.

In the late afternoon Riordan Daniels breezed into the office, announcing to Alisa that he had found a house for her to rent nearby.

"What?" Startled, she dropped a folder she had been holding, to stare at him.

"I happened to hear of a house available. I

pulled some strings and grabbed it." He extracted a house key from his pocket and slid it across the tabletop toward her.

He hadn't had to do it, she thought in confusion. Why had he? Why was he looking at her like that, a light burning deep within his black eyes? He always seemed to set her on edge, to rattle her.

"It wasn't necessary," she began shortly. "I could have done it myself. I was intending to, later today."

He went on as if he had not heard her. "I paid the first month's rent, but you are responsible for making the rest of your rental payments out of the salary I pay you."

He had paid her rent—without even her permission! Remembering what Matt had said, and Bochert's insinuations, she felt her cheeks grow hot.

"I wish you hadn't done that! For you to rent a house for me . . . What will people think? Surely there will be gossip—"

His face tightened. "Nonsense, girl. I can't keep sending a carriage for you halfway across town—that *would* cause talk. Count yourself lucky that I got a house for you at all. Thousands are homeless. People are crammed sixteen to a room in some places, or are living in tents. Many have fled the city altogether."

It was all too true. She sighed, pocketing the key. "Very well, then. But I intend for Fifine to come with me—and perhaps Nella, too, as my maidservant."

"I don't care whom you hire as servants, or where you live, either. I just need your labor—

and that's *all* I need from you, Alisa Amsell. Do you understand that?"

Their gazes locked, the air between them thick. Alisa understood, all right: he was denying what had occurred between them, rejecting it, erasing it. She felt herself tremble, and fiercely she steadied herself. She could play that game too. She could be just as cold, just as implacable.

"Very well," she said icily. "But I intend to pay you back for the rent you've already paid. And for everything else I owe you as well."

"Fine." Riordan turned away, leaving Alisa to sink down in her chair, every muscle in her body quivering.

~10~

Two days later, Alisa moved out of the Eberleys' house. With her she took Fifine, Nella, and Nella's two children, boys of seven and thirteen. It was decided that Fifine would be her housekeeper and would start sewing a new wardrobe for Alisa, while Nella would act as maidservant. The two children could attend school nearby, and husky Klaus, Nella's thirteen-year-old, could carry coal and shovel snow.

The house was small, made of wood frame, a construction that Alisa now knew was definitely a fire hazard. But there was a tiny parlor filled with dark furniture and a bright Turkish rug, and enough bedrooms nestled under low eaves to provide space for all of them, in addition to a sewing room for Fifine.

Best of all, it was located only eight blocks away from Riordan Daniels', meaning that Alisa could walk to work and would not be dependent upon him for a ride.

"What sort of dresses do you wish me to make?" Fifine inquired grumpily. "And I suppose you

148

intend hats to go with them—in a sober style, as befits a woman of work?"

"Exactly," Alisa agreed. "Some of the dry-goods stores have reopened, and I want you to buy some bolts of silk and bring them home for my approval. Dove gray or a soft toast brown would be nice. Maybe some blue silk. Use your judgment, Fifine. I want to be fashionably but simply dressed."

"I know." Fifine looked sour, for she preferred bonnets laden with elaborate towers of ribbon and trim, and gowns heavy with the weight of flounces and trains. She set her mouth stubbornly. "It will come to no good, your employment with him."

"Oh? Why do you say that?"

"Pfah! Men! He will make you dance to his tune, whatever tune he wishes to play, you may be sure of that."

"It isn't so," Alisa began. "He—"

"He is a man," the Frenchwoman emphasized. "Men are the ones with the power and the money, and when they command, women jump. It is the way it has always been, and will always be. Women must combat the male sex with their beauty. It is all they have."

Later that day, as she directed Nella in the cleaning of the house, Alisa pondered what Fifine had said. She didn't want to battle Riordan Daniels with her beauty. She wanted to use her brains and guile, just as he did. And yet . . .

She *did* want him to think her beautiful. She'd be lying to herself if she said she didn't. She was female enough for that, female enough to respond to him, to . . .

Flushing, she pushed away the thought.

That night, Malva paid a call to deliver extra clothing for Nella and her boys and to see if there was anything that Alisa needed. Clad in a black merino visiting gown with a deep box-pleaded flounce and a long overjacket, Alisa's cousin looked far too imposing to be ladling out soup to refugees.

"Alisa, are you sure that all is well with you? Matt told me of your plan to work for Riordan Daniels, and I confess I was surprised."

So, Alisa thought. That was why Malva had really come—to dissuade her from working for Riordan. "But, Malva, why should you be surprised?" she heard herself ask.

"Why, my dear. After the way you snubbed the man at your father's funeral, the things you've said about him . . . and now you are at work in his very office. It seems strange, to say the least."

Alisa squared her chin. "I have a purpose in being there, and it's the *only* reason I'd work for him—ever. I'm going to get Papa's mill back. It should belong to me," she burst out. "He told me so in his letter, the one he left for me after he died."

"And you've been brooding about it all this time, I see," Malva remarked gently.

"I suppose I have. But why shouldn't I? He is responsible for Papa's death! Not directly, of course, but indirectly, and he should pay for it. He should!"

"Alisa." Malva's voice was soft, yet it held the firmness of a Victorian dowager. "Life isn't as cut-and-dried as you seem to think. People's actions aren't always so easy to read, either. There is much about your father that you didn't know. You adored him, as all young girls do, but—"

"Stop!" Alisa cried. "I don't want to hear! I know that Papa wasn't perfect, no one is. But that's no excuse for someone's using financial power to . . . to take a man and rend him apart, leaving him no pride and no recourse."

"Do you really think that's what happened, my dear?"

Alisa nodded.

"Oh, my dear girl." Malva looked troubled. "I worry about you. You should be like all the other girls in your debutante class—attending balls and parties, flirting with a dozen suitors, having fun."

"I am having fun," Alisa said stubbornly. "I do like working, Malva, it's oddly thrilling. I had no idea. To be a woman in such a different world, to hold your own in that world . . . There is nothing like it."

"I am sure you're right."

"Anyway, dear cousin, there *is* one advantage to my working for Riordan—I get a nice salary, and I can afford to rent this house. I don't have to take Matt's charity anymore, or anyone's."

The aftermath of the Great Fire had left most businesses in a state of chaos, and Riordan's interestes were no exception. But Chicago was definitely recovering fast. Within a week of the fire, nearly six thousand temporary buildings had been thrown up. Two enterprising merchants, Levi Leiter and Marshall Field, quickly set up quarters in a horse barn at State and Twentieth streets. Other businesses followed suit.

"Construction," Riordan said. "That's where the money is right now, Alisa. There are fortunes to be made in Chicago by those who step in quickly. Brick, marble, stone, steel—Chicago is hungry for everything it can get. And it will pay."

One morning in late November, Riordan briefed Alisa on her day's work. Sun glinted in the library windows, and they could hear a flock of Canadian geese as they flapped and honked their way south.

With a flourish, Riordan handed Alisa an envelope. It was sealed with red wax, yet there was no name or address. "What's this?" she asked, looking at it in puzzlement.

It contained, Riordan informed her, a graft payment.

"Graft!"

Riordan's smile was a bitter one, almost self-mocking. "In New York, where I come from, Tammany Hall politicians fight like hogs to get their noses in the public trough. Here in Chicago it's no better. Our beloved city councilmen have been accused of making fortunes from paving, bridge, and tunnel contracts." He shrugged. "But that's life, I'm afraid, distasteful as it may seem to you. Here is the payment. Take it to Gus Moriarty, at Conley's."

"But . . ." She stared at him in shock. "Conley's is a—"

"A gambling house, yes. Our councilman will no doubt receive his payoff and lose it, all within a few hours. But let him do as he pleased with it. *I* intend to get my building permits."

"One way or another?" she asked scornfully.

Riordan's face darkened. "This is the way the game is played here, and I don't like it any better than you do, especially when I heard of unscrupulous builders who put up buildings with a brick facade over a wooden interior. But I intend to build good fireproof buildings. Tall ones that Chicago can be proud of a hundred years from now. To do it, I have to get certain permits. *I* am honorable, even if Councilman Moriarty isn't."

She hesitated. "But . . ."

"Are you afraid to go to Conley's, Alisa?"

"No, oh, no!" she protested hastily, fearing he'd send someone else, or even fire her.

"Well, then, I suggest you order up the carriage and go. Didn't I give you a number of calls to make? You'd better get started."

Filled with trepidation, she set off. It was a crisp, cold day, dazzling with sunlight, the sky clean-washed and perfect. But as she neared the Amsell mill, her first call, she saw plumes of dark sooty smoke that marked the air like flags.

The carriage pulled into the mill driveway that led into a sprawling complex of red-brick structures bristling with smokestacks and surrounded by heaps of coal and slag. A small frame building flanked by twin fir trees contained the office, and she directed the driver to park here.

"Will you be long, Miss Amsell?"

"Probably an hour or so. There is a horse barn down the road to your left, where you can water the horse."

But she sat for a moment, pressing her hands tightly together within their kid gloves, her skin feeling alternately hot and clammy.

The Amsell mill. She'd forgotten the sheer impact of being here, of smelling the metallic odors of iron, coal, and dirty black smoke. From childhood she'd loved the gritty excitement of that unmistakable smell. "It's the stench of money," Papa had been fond of saying.

Now she looked at the office, remembering the day they'd planted the pines. A leggy eight-year-old, she'd begged to help the workmen dig the holes to sink the burlap-bagged tree roots in.

"You're too little," one of the men had teased.

"I'm not! I'm not!"

Grinning, the workman handed her a shovel, and Alisa had actually managed to heft up several shovelfuls of iron-hard Illinois earth. All the men applauded. Papa, laughing, hoisted her high in the air.

Now she saw that the trees were nearly ten feet tall, their needles glossy in spite of the soot and grime generated by the mill. Feeling a pang, she went inside.

"Alisa! How nice to see you! You're looking every bit the young lady, too big now for horehound drops or cinnamon sticks, I suppose!" Felix Morgan, the manager, greeted her like an old friend.

She smiled. "I haven't stopped loving them."

"Sit down, won't you?" He bustled around the office, brushing off a chair for her, straightening papers. "I'm afraid the office is a bit untidy—we've had a lot of new orders since Mr. Daniels took us over."

Alisa seated herself, glancing out of the window at the reddish glare flickering from a nearby blast furnace. "I'm Mr. Daniels' assistant now," she explained.

"You? Working for Mr. Daniels?" Morgan seemed confused.

"He was kind enough to employ me. But it's only temporary, I assure you. One day I'm going to buy this mill back and make it Amsell property again."

"I hope you will." A dubious note in the manager's voice revealed the fact that he thought this doubtful. "I'll look forward to that day, Alisa." He hesitated. "But now . . . you say you've come for . . . ?"

She got out the notebook she carried everywhere with her now. It was best, she had learned, simply to plunge into the business at hand, without encouraging objections.

"Here are the changes that Mr. Daniels wishes made," she began firmly.

An hour later, she was driving away again, her business accomplished. As the carriage pulled out of the mill gate, she saw steel rails being loaded onto wagons, dozens of workers sweating despite the chilly day. These were Riordan's men now, she thought. He employed more than five thousand in his mills.

She shivered, drawing her mantle snugly around her. Five thousand families dependent on him! Such power was hard to imagine. It cloaked the man with its aura, giving him a stature that she hated even as she was drawn to it. Damn Riordan Daniels! Damn him for the effect he had on her.

Her second errand was to Conley's. The gambling house was located in a row of frame buildings hastily rebuilt on Randolph Street on a rubble-cleared site. A dozen or so buggies and carriages were pulled up outside, their drivers squatted around a carriage block, playing poker.

As her driver helped her out of her carriage, Alisa was aware of the curious stares of the drivers.

"Don't stand on ceremony, missus, just go right in," one of the men called. "And when you can catch 'im, give yer husband hell!"

All the drivers guffawed. Flushing, Alisa pulled open the door and stepped inside. A small vestibule was carpeted in red plush and papered with velvet-flocked red wallpaper. From adjoining rooms drifted male laughter, along with the rippling of a piano and the rattle of dice. Alisa smelled the pungent mixture of cigar smoke, beer, whiskey, and hair pomade.

She stood, hesitating, wondering what to do. Then a man who had been sitting at a table selling some sort of tokens looked up. He whispered to an assistant, who took his place at the table.

"I am Seamus Conley," he said, coming over to her.

Alisa extended her hand, but the Irishman did not take it. He was spare of build, with ruddy cheeks and a drooping mustache that had been waxed at the tips to sharp points. His eyes swept over her, taking in the blue silk she wore, and the way it clung to her figure.

"We don't allow solicitation here, miss. This is a high-class gambling house, not a bordello."

Did he think her a prostitute? She drew back in confused indignation. "I haven't come here to . . . I'm not a—"

"Women aren't permitted to gamble here. And

if you've come to fetch your husband away from the roulette or the faro, to scold and berate him, we don't allow that either." Seamus Conley gave her a tight smile. "Once a gentleman enters our establishment, he is assured absolute privacy. Our customers like that, and we endeavor to protect them from any unwanted intrusion."

"Such as myself, do you mean?" Angrily Alisa reddened. This man thought her either a whore or a harridan, and when he sent her here, Riordan Daniels must have known full well the reception she would receive. But she controlled her fury; she had been ordered to deliver the envelope and she would do so.

"Very well," she told Conley, who grinned, as if pleased to see her discomfited. "I'll leave, then. I wouldn't want to sully your elegant establishment here with my female presence!"

On the way out, she took great satisfaction in slamming the door. Then she marched purposefully toward the group of drivers, still engrossed in their poker.

"Which of you drives Mr. Moriarty?" she demanded.

"Who wants to know?"

"I do. I have something I wish to deliver to him personally, and there is money in it for whoever will point him out to me when he leaves Conley's."

"If there's money . . . all right, miss." A grizzled man of fifty separated himself from the other drivers and approached her. Alisa arranged with him to sit inside her own carriage until Moriarty appeared, whereupon he would signal her with a cough.

It took two hours of waiting and fuming, during which Alisa cursed Riordan Daniels for his arrogance. But finally the sheepish councilman appeared, and she handed him the envelope.

"I thank you kindly, miss," the politician said, tucking the bribe into a waistcoat pocket. Alisa nodded and turned to get back into her carriage. This had been a test, she realized angrily. Riordan had known very well she would not be welcome at Conley's. He had wanted to see what she would do, how she would manage.

Well, she had managed very well, thank you. If he thought she could be frightened by the smell of liquor and the click of dice and ejection from a gambling establishment, he had much to learn about Miss Alisa Amsell.

At nine that evening she sat in her library-workroom struggling over a business letter to be sent to all of Riordan's mill managers. She had already done four laborious drafts, as the ink stains on her fingers attested. Her head throbbed with fatigue, and her stomach growled with unladylike hunger. Thanks to her two-hour delay at Conley's, she'd had to skip lunch, and it did not look as if she would get dinner either.

"Well, how are things coming here?" Riordan knocked briefly and then entered the room without further ado, his stride confident. "Did you get the envelope to Moriarty as I asked you to do?"

"I did." She said it coolly.

"Ah?"

"Oh, yes, I gave it to him *just* as you requested. Although I'm afraid he'll have to wait until tomorrow to gamble it all away, as I caught him outside Conley's, rather than inside its walls."

"Hmmm. I see."

Riordan looked as if he were stifling some private amusement, and Alisa could hold back no longer. "You knew it would be that way, didn't you? You *knew* they'd turn me away, that they'd treat me like a . . . a prostitute or a fishwife!"

He laughed. "You managed, however, I see."

Alisa was full of fury. "Oh, yes, I certainly did. I passed the little 'test' you set for me. Did you go there before I arrived, to pay that insolent Irishman to treat me like a denizen of a brothel? I wouldn't put it past you! Wouldn't it have been a lot easier just to have me deliver the envelope to some other location? I wasted two hours—two *hours*—on that foolish and unnecessary trip!"

Lazily, moving like a large, powerful jungle animal, Riordan Daniels straddled a chair, facing her. "Perhaps it wasn't time wasted," he said quietly.

"It wasn't . . . What do you mean?"

"Just what I said. You proved yourself to be resourceful, Alisa. You accomplished your task despite obstacles that would have caused many women to flee in humiliation. You proved your ability, and that certainly is no waste. Not in the long run."

She stared at him uncertainly, a wave of color beginning to flood her face. He had complimented her. Had implied that he might depend on her even more in the future, to do greater, more important tasks. . . .

She wrenched herself away from the warm glow of pride that suffused her. She wasn't here to receive compliments; she had to remember that. Riordan was her opponent, her enemy, the obstacle against which she must pit herself.

"Well?" He asked, changing the subject. "What about supper tonight? I assume that you're hungry; Will Rice told me you've been closeted in this room since six o'clock without respite."

Supper. Without warning, she felt a surging weakness melt her insides.

How could he do this to her? There'd been no repetition of that one meal they'd shared, or of their lovemaking, either, and that was just the way she wanted it. She'd made a mistake in giving in to him. She had no intention of repeating the experience. Let their relationship be cool. Separate, controlled. No matter how hard her heart pounded when he looked at her, as he was doing now.

"I . . . I'm not very hungry," she said faintly.

"Nonsense. Of course you are. And so am I. I've ordered salmon mousse and a fillet of beef with mushrooms. Does that strike your fancy? It does mine. Come on."

What was she to say without antagonizing him and risking her job? She rose from the table and felt him take her arm, his warm hands holding her firmly. She did not dare to twist away from him, although she wanted to do so very much.

~11~

Dark eyes challenged her. "So, Alisa, do you think that you will like working for me?"

She eyed him over the rim of a crystal goblet filled with deep-red burgundy, its dry bouquet impeccable. "What does 'like' have to do with it? I do work for you, and I work hard. That should be enough for both of us."

He raised a dark eyebrow, while Alisa felt herself go red, for she had not meant to sound quite so prickly.

As before, they sat at the long table in the huge dining room, waited on by servants, while Alisa tried to quell the strange, soft nervousness that had welled up in her. Was it her imagination, or did Riordan's eyes meet hers with ever-greater frequency?

Of course it wasn't her imagination, she told herself angrily. Riordan was a womanizer, his exploits with actresses, wives, and other, more common women general knowledge. And she was a woman dining alone with him at this late hour of the night, a woman who had already succumbed once to his seductions. Why shouldn't he be excited? He was probably expecting the same thing to happen again!

"Tell me about yourself, Alisa," he urged. "What do you like to do in your free time—assuming that I give you any, of course, since I'm such a hard taskmaster."

She wanted to laugh—there were times when she loved his wry sense of humor—but she also wanted to jump up from the table and run. How could he affect her like this? Trembles rippled up and down her skin whenever she was in the same room with him.

But she mustn't be attracted to him. There was the pouty little actress, Linette Marquis; there was the baby of mysterious origins upstairs; and there was the tragedy of Eben Amsell. She must never forget that.

She tried to think of a response to his question. "I . . . I love to drive, of course. When I have time, and a buggy or runabout at my disposal."

"Ah, yes. I remember. And you also like to race and win, as I well recall." His mouth formed one of the rare crooked, sweet smiles that meant he was in a good mood.

"Yes." She grew hot, remembering the first time she had seen him.

"Tell me more," he said, leaning forward. "Do you sing or play the harp? Sew, perhaps? Which of the gentle female arts do you enjoy most?"

"None," she admitted. "My needlework is only average. I can't abide fern-printing or pasting photos in albums, or painting silly designs on china.

As for singing, I'm about as gloriously musical as a frog."

He tipped his head back to laugh heartily. "Of all the animals I would have thought you might resemble, I don't believe it would be a frog. Would you make a pretty, shiny green tree frog? Or are you more of the lily-pad type of frog, slender and spotted, with a puffy throat?"

She giggled. "Oh, a tree frog, I think."

"And I'll be a big green croaker, and we'll serenade each other underneath the branches of some huge swamp tree until dawn reddens the sky."

Despite the humor, his eyes caressed her with irresistible warmth, as if he really meant it. Alisa's cheeks flamed; her giggles went into a higher key, and then nervously she cut them off, clasping her hands together in her lap.

Conversation between them died. Suddenly she was acutely aware of the breadth of his shoulders, the way his hair grew curly at his temples. The sweet cleft of his chin made her long to touch her fingertip to it. Once she had heard this called a "philanderer's cleft." Bleakly she wondered if this were a true sign.

He spoke into the silence that had fallen between them. "I would like you to attend the theater with me sometime. I promise you, you won't be required to sing, only to applaud politely at the end of each act."

"I . . . I seldom attend the theater."

"Why not?"

A maid entered the dining room to clear away their plates. Alisa waited painfully until the girl had left the room.

"I don't want to go to the theater with you." She tossed her napkin down and pushed her chair back. "I shouldn't have consented to have supper with you and I . . . I certainly don't want the kind of intimacies to which this evening is leading."

She gave the chair another frantic shove and fled for the door.

"Alisa!" In an instant he had overtaken her and had clasped both of his arms around her.

"Don't 'Alisa' me!" she cried, struggling. "What if your maid comes back and discovers us here like this? Or," she went on bitterly, "would it make any difference? I'm sure I'm not the first woman you've brought to this house—nor will I be the last. And what of that little baby you keep upstairs? What of her mother, what of—?"

"Enough, miss. You intrude." His voice was harsh.

She seized the opportunity to twist away from him. "I want you to leave me alone, Riordan, do you hear me? I'm not a pretty little creature whose sole function is to service your needs! I'm your employee. That's *all*, that's all I *want* to be, and—"

"I want you to be more." Suddenly he bent his mouth to hers. She moved her head wildly from side to side, trying to shake him free, but he would not allow it. He only scooped her closer, trapping her with his arms, forcing her to kiss him.

His tongue was strong and forceful and it probed deep within the recesses of her mouth, forcing her lips ever farther apart. Then, when he suddenly withdrew his tongue to the sensitive edge of her lips and ran its tip softly along her flesh, she thought she would scream out with the sudden deep pleasure this gave her.

"Alisa," he groaned. "I want you. I've wanted you in my bed ever since the fire—I have thought of nothing but you."

This was madness, she thought, utter and total. They were in his dining room, with servants lurking about and a maidservant due to return at any moment with a dessert course and coffee.

"Please," she begged. "Oh, please. Just . . . just stop. Please, Riordan, stop this right now."

"I don't want to stop, and you don't want me to. You know you want me as much as I want you, Alisa."

"I *don't,*" she breathed, knowing to her shame that it was a lie, that she did want him, as she had never wanted any man before. And it was wrong, *wrong.*

"You do. Alisa, don't lie to me, not now." His fingers loosened the placket of buttons that held her gown together, and she felt his hand slip inside, next to her skin. He cupped her nipples, kneading them erect into taut, sweet sensation.

"Alisa," he groaned, caressing her. "I want to kiss you . . . here, and here. . . . I want to hold you, to pleasure you as no woman has ever been pleasured before."

She struggled to keep the last tatters of her common sense. "The . . . the servants—"

"I've dismissed them. Come upstairs with me. No one will know . . . no one will care. I need to hold you. . . ."

* * *

He gripped her shoulders in his two strong hands and turned her, guiding her suddenly weakened body out into the main corridor. He urged her toward the wide staircase with the porcelain balustrades, the very staircase up which he had carried her on the night of the fire, the night when he had stripped her sooty, grimy dress from her body and made love to her with such tender violence.

"Please," Alisa whispered, but it was only a token protest now. She was lost, swept up in a fierce desire that could not be turned aside now.

They had just reached the top of the staircase when they heard a squalling infant wail. Then a door clicked and a tired-looking woman of about forty emerged from the baby's nursery, her expression worried.

"She's feverish, Mr. Daniels. I hoped for the best, and I didn't want to tell you until I knew for sure, but her little forehead is burning hot."

It was as if the infant's cry had sliced like a knife across their desire, cutting it away. Riordan's heavy breathing immediately changed. "How hot?"

"Hot, Mr. Daniels. I'm going to have to sponge her all night to bring the fever down."

"I'll sponge her."

"But, sir, she's a baby girl ... it is hardly proper—"

"I will take care of her this night, Fanny." Riordan leapt the two remaining steps, then paused, speaking to Alisa. "I'll send Fanny down to notify my driver that he's to drive you home, Alisa. I don't want you walking out this late at night by yourself."

"Please don't bother. I want to walk," Alisa managed to say, feeling physically shocked from the suddenness of the transition from lovemaking to worry over a child. "I . . . I hope the baby is better by morning."

Outside, she hurried down the bricked front walk, hearing the paper rattle of dead leaves being eddied by a night wind. She reached the heavy wrought-iron gate and threw it open.

No one followed her. She drew in deep breaths of cold city air, already moist with the promise of snow. Overhead floated a cold silver moon partly obscured by clouds, remote from human concerns.

Alisa walked as fast as she could, her thoughts pounding, refusing to give her peace. She and Riordan had almost made love. But it hadn't been only his fault. She had longed for him, too, had been on the verge of abandoning herself to him again, until the interruption of the sick child had brought them both back to their senses.

Thank God, she thought, that she had not given in to him. But as she continued to walk, hugging the mantle tightly about her shoulders, she was realistic enough to know that her escape might only be temporary. Something burned between them. As alive, as real, as the flames that only weeks ago had devoured half of Chicago. She could no longer deny it to herself.

Tonight a baby's fever had interrupted them. But there would be other nights, other occasions when Riordan's dark demanding eyes would seek hers. What was she going to do then, how would she combat it?

But she'd manage, she assured herself fiercely

as she turned a corner and entered the more modest neighborhood in which her own house was located. She would stay away from him as much as she could. She'd talk to him only of business. She'd never share another supper with him; she'd make sure they were always surrounded by servants, clerks, or accountants, a safe wall of other people to protect her.

She would push Riordan Daniels out of her heart at all costs.

The next day, all seemed as before when Alisa arrived to begin her work. Somewhere in the mansion she heard servants' chatter and a sharp slapping sound as someone beat a carpet. Inside their workroom, the accountants discussed some business matter. The interlude of passion last night, the sudden interruption, might only have been a dream or an episode in a novel, easily forgotten.

"How is the baby?" she asked Riordan as soon as she walked in.

"She is much better, thank God. Fever in an infant can be terrifying."

Terrifying? The word surprised her when used by a man as strong as Riordan. It implied vulnerability, tenderness, concern. She looked at him. Only a slight darkness under the eyes betrayed the fact that Riordan Daniels had been up most of the night with a sick infant. His dark hair was freshly washed, glistening in a shaft of morning sunlight, and his clean-shaven jaws were very smooth. Peversely, she caught herself wondering just *how* smooth. Then she pushed away the thought.

"I want you to go to Conley's again," he was saying.

She stared at him, jolted out of her thoughts. "*Conley's?* Surely it's foolish to send me there again, when it's already been made very plain that my presence isn't welcomed."

"But it is welcomed. I assure you, Alisa, Seamus Conley will treat you with every courtesy."

"As he did before?" she mocked.

"I paid him to test you," Riordan admitted. "Now I'm ordering him to give you the red-carpet treatment. He'll do as I tell him, since I own a controlling share in his establishment."

"Oh! I see!" Somehow this only irritated Alisa, but she tamped down a sharp reply.

Two hours later, at Conley's, she was greeted at the door by the mustached Irishman. Today, just as Riordan had predicted, Conley was all smiles and welcome. He eyed her dove-gray silk, recently made by Fifine, with black velvet rosettes and trim.

"Miss Amsell, you are looking lovely today. The very picture of vibrant, modern womanhood."

"I didn't think vibrant womanhood, or indeed *any* sort of womanhood, was welcome in your establishment," she could not resist remarking.

"Ah, well, you won't hold that against me, will you?" The Irishman grinned. "I was under orders, you know. When *he* wants something, he gets it."

"I'm sure of that!"

Conley took her into a cluttered, dusty office, where he rummaged on shelves and in drawers until he had found the books that Riordan had requested. All the while, he chatted on, complimenting Alisa outrageously and promising her eternal servitude.

After a few moments of it, Alisa lost her indignation and grew amused. "I suppose you are only blandishing me at his orders, too," she suggested, laughing.

The Irishman grimaced, touching one of the waxed tips of his mustache. "Sure, Miss Amsell, I'm a fine judge of women, and I assure you, all the compliments I gave you were sincerely meant. But I must admit, I do want to stay on Riordan Daniels' good side. Money talks, y'know, especially his."

The rest of the day Alisa was thoughtful, and it seemed to her that a hundred incidents that day illustrated Seamus Conley's point. A property owner was induced to sell his prime corner lot—with a huge money "sweetener." A brickyard owner was persuaded to devote his entire output to Riordan's interest.

Riordan grabbed a small lumber mill that was up for sale, beating out ten other eager contenders. He even donated a large sum to the relief of fire victims, for which he was duly praised in the *Tribune*. Money did talk, she thought uneasily, and what was its message? Riordan had already told her: power.

Late that afternoon, there was an unexpected caller. Linette Marquis arrived encased in a cloud of musky mignonette perfume, clad in an elaborate tea gown of plum velvet, on which row upon row of satin fringe shimmered whenever she moved. Her brunette curls were tucked under a bonnet trimmed with heath flowers and dried buttercups, draped with an ivory *crêpe lisse* scarf that tied around Linette's pouting, vain little chin.

"Good afternoon, Miss Marquis." As Riordan's assistant, Alisa greeted the petite actress politely. But inside she was rigid with surprise. She'd thought Linette safely in New York, starring in a musical there. Obviously, she wasn't. What did she want here with Riordan?

"Do I know you? You must be Riordan's new help." Linette gave a trilling theatrical giggle and started purposefully toward the closed door of the inner room, in which Riordan was closeted with Will Rice and another accountant.

"You can't go in now," Alisa began. "He's busy with—"

"But he'll see *me*, of course."

"I really—"

But, ignoring Alisa's protest, Linette sailed inside Riordan's office. A moment later, the two disgruntled accountants emerged and the door shut again.

Alisa sat in the outer work area, seething. How dare Linette Marquis treat her like some annoying servant, pretending she didn't even remember her? And to barge into Riordan's office like an imperious princess!

What did he see in her, anyway, with her dramatic throaty voice and her actressy airs?

Alisa snatched up a pen and dipped it into an inkwell, feeling her temples throb with disgust. How glad she was that she and Riordan hadn't made love last night! *Oh,* she hated him!

*　　*　　*

Linette finally emerged from Riordan's inner office, her hair slightly disheveled, her cheeks flushed with triumph. She did not even glance at Alisa as she swept out, leaving behind her a heavy cloud of musk.

Alisa tried not to breathe it; did actresses consider it necessary to *bathe* in scent! But she knew deep in her heart that Linette's scent was far more subtle than that which could have been applied from a stoppered bottle. Her fragrance was all herself, feline, totally sexual.

"All right, get me the accountants again," Riordan said, emerging. "I've just wasted an hour and I'd like to catch up as much as I can."

Alisa stared at him. For the past hour she'd tortured herself imagining the worst, but he looked tired and angry, his expression glowering, his brows knit together in a scowl.

She could not understand. Surely Linette was his mistress. Had they quarreled? But swiftly she pushed the questions away. It wasn't her business what Riordan did, or with whom.

"I'll get them, of course. But . . ." To her horror, she heard her voice pause in an unspoken query.

"But what, Alisa?"

She faltered. "I . . . I only wondered . . . You look angry. Why would you allow such an interruption if it was unwelcome to you?"

"Did I say it was unwelcome?"

"No. You didn't. But I thought—"

His tone froze her. "I'm not paying you to think, Alisa, I'm paying you to work. So I would suggest that you do that very thing. Please give me an up-to-date list of all my properties in the burned-out area, along with your suggestions for possible rebuilding on each site."

"Yes, sir!" she snapped, her patience at an end. He was impossible! She didn't know why anyone would want to work for such a man; she certainly didn't. She sat down to begin the latest task he had set her, too angry to realize that it was thus far the most creative job he had given her, that he was asking for her opinions, her ideas, her advice.

A few days later, Alisa encountered Fanny, the baby's nurse, in the upstairs corridor. The woman nodded, and Alisa seized the opportunity to question her.

"The baby . . . how is she? Is her fever gone?"

"She is fine," the nurse replied briefly, smoothing her hands on her apron and preparing to reenter the infant's nursery. She had brown hair pulled back into a roll, a careworn face, and permanent circles of exhaustion smudged under her eyes.

Some demon made Alisa persist. "Do you know who her mother is? Why is Mr. Daniels keeping her a secret?"

The woman shrugged. "I don't know. I didn't ask him and I guess he pays me enough not to ask. All I know is that he brought her here about three weeks before the fire."

Then Fanny disappeared into the child's room, leaving Alisa filled with a burst of frustrating questions to which she could find no answers.

Days passed, merging into weeks of hard work as Alisa struggled to assess the many properties that Riordan Daniels possessed, examining each in the light of possible new construction. She made many trips to the burned-out areas, where wagonloads of rubble were being hauled away and scaffolding bristled on new buildings that were going up.

Despite her anger at Riordan, Alisa grew absorbed in her task. She filled sheet after sheet with her recommendations. To have a say in the Chicago of tomorrow, to make plans for buildings that might be used by her grandchildren or great-grandchildren—it was a heady feeling, and she gave herself up to the pleasure of this work.

One day an unexpected caller arrived at the mansion, insisting that he be allowed to see Riordan Daniels at once. Alisa, whose job it now was to screen such callers, hesitated. Riordan was out, at a bank directors' meeting.

But even if he were not, "Pots" Ogden did not look like the type of businessman with whom her employer usually dealt. He was a small man, barely five feet tall even with his shoes on, and his black frock coat stretched perilously over his full belly. His cravat was soiled with spilled food, and, to Alisa's consternation, there seemed to be more bits of food caught in his crinkly brown beard. His ruddy cheeks bespoke a life spent mostly out-of-doors.

Sneaking looks at the rococo splendor of the library, into which he had been shown, Pots informed Alisa that he was the owner of a small brickyard near Fort Wayne, Indiana. He had come here by train, he explained, to urge Riordan to buy the entire contents of his brickyard.

"Seein' as how I hear he is into the building

trade and might just possibly be interested." Pots
grinned at Alisa, his blue eyes round and friendly.
"Besides which, *I* aim to get married again—my
third wife, don't you know—and she wants me to
build us a big house. Mebbe like this one," he
added, looking admiringly at the canopied couch,
the velvet lambrequins above the doors that led to
Riordan's office.

"I see." Alisa studied him, feeling her interest
quicken. She asked him questions about his brickyard, its capacity, and the types of bricks he made.

"Oh . . . a little of this, and a tad of that. Common brick, naturally, and obsidian brick and
metallic-dressed brick, all of it fireproof, miss, and
I believe that fireproof is all the rage here in
Chicago, is it not?"

"Yes," Alisa agreed, her mind running over the
figures Ogden had given her. The brickyard was
very small, of course, almost too small for Riordan
to be interested in.

Pots Ogden had brought a shabby leather suit-
case, and now he pulled some sample bricks from
it to show her. Alisa examined them, enjoying the
feel of their rough texture, somehow reluctant to
let this strange little man go.

"If you buy all I got, I'll give you a good sharp
rate," Pots promised. "The woman I got in mind—
she has her heart set on a fancy house and won't
marry me unless I give it to her. She thinks I'm
richer than I am, if you take my meaning."

"What kind of price are you talking about for
your bricks?"

Pots named a figure, surprisingly low, and Alisa
tried not to show her startled reaction. It *was* a

bargain rate. Better than what they'd been getting at local yards.

"Includes shipping," he went on. "I got to, you see. I . . . well, I already told the lady we'd break ground on the house."

Alisa nodded, her mind not on Pots's marital problems, but on the deal he offered. Riordan was out for most of the day, would not return until after seven. He did not expect Ogden, had undertaken no correspondence with the small brickyard located a state away. If she herself didn't tell him of today's caller, he would never know.

Bricks, she thought, her mouth going suddenly dry. A small brickyard full of them, being offered at a bargain rate. And hadn't Riordan himself told her that Chicago was open right now for fortunes to be made?

Why should he make all the money?

The thought seemed to sneak in through some secret back entrance of her mind, but once it had arrived, it would not depart. It teased and taunted, causing Alisa's heart to race with excitement.

She could buy the contents of Pots's brickyard. She still had the pieces of her mother's jewelry that she had rescued from the fire, and if she were to sell them . . .

Tempted, Alisa rose from her chair to pace the ornate room, utterly unaware of the elaborate furnishings, gilded and carved, at which Pots Ogden kept staring.

Excitement charged through her like bright, sparkling champagne. This was her chance. She felt sure of it.

Get it back, if you can, Papa had begged. *Get the mill back, Alisa.*

Yes. A sick, excited nervousness was taking possession of her. She could do it, she could. It had been meant to happen—otherwise why would Ogden have shown up like this, totally unexpectedly, like a signal from heaven?

Of course, if Riordan were to discover what she'd done . . .

Her mood of exhilaration faded a bit. She'd be keeping a secret from her employer, and she knew that Riordan would be angry if he learned about it; hadn't he told her that he expected her to be totally devoted to his business interests? Still, she wouldn't be cheating him, she assured herself, for she'd be paying for the bricks with her own money, not his. And he never would have dealt with such a small factory anyway.

She turned, her long skirts rustling, and smiled calmly at Pots Ogden. "I think I can speak for Mr. Riordan when I say he may be interested in your bricks. However, the price you mention is much too high."

"Too high!" Pots sputtered. "Why, Miss Amsell, it's shamefully low and you know it. It's a distress sale."

Alisa bargained, finally bringing him down to achieve a buy that was truly extraordinary. She could hardly hide her elation. "If you'll come back in four hours, Mr. Ogden, I will have your money for you."

"But am I not to meet Mr. Daniels himself? I thought—"

"He is otherwise engaged, and will not be available for a week," she explained hastily. "I have been authorized to make purchases for him."

After Ogden had left, casting one last longing stare about him at the rich furnishings of the Riordan mansion, Alisa went back into the library and sank into an upholstered chair. Her heart was pounding, and she felt giddy, almost sick with the realization of what she had just done.

Had she really spent the last of her assets, nearly every penny in the world that she still possessed, risking even her job, on a factory full of bricks?

But then Alisa wrenched herself away from her doubts and hurried to the small closet where she kept her bonnet and mantle. There was much to do. She had to go home, get the jewels out of their temporary hiding place behind the drawing-room fireplace mantel, and sell them.

Fortunes were to be made here in Chicago— Riordan himself had told her that. She intended to make it happen for herself. This was her start, and she must seize it.

~12~

"Well? What about the theater tomorrow night?" Riordan broached the topic abruptly a few days later. It was a morning in early December, a few hard flakes of snow dotting the air and making tiny taps against the windows. A fire crackled in the fireplace, pine knots snapping.

Outwardly, a cozy scene, Alisa thought. But the table loaded with wooden file drawers and stacks of papers was businesslike, and she and Riordan were all business, too, discussing details of five more blast furnaces he wished to add to the Amsell mill.

"What?" At the suggestion, totally out of line with what they had been discussing, she could only look at him.

"You put in as long hours as I do, without complaint. You've virtually turned into a work machine, Alisa. Don't you ever desire to take some time off?"

The remark caused spasms of guilt to tighten in her throat, for only the previous day she had sold the bricks she had bought from Pots Ogden, pocketing what seemed to her like a tiny fortune.

179

"Nonsense, I don't really work that hard," she mumbled, reddening.

"On the contrary, you're the best assistant I've ever had. And to celebrate it, tomorrow night I'm taking you to see *Seven Sisters*. It's opening at the opera house."

Alisa drew a knife-sharp breath. The *Tribune* had been full of accounts of the musical, which had been called an "operatic, spectacular, diabolic, musical, terpsichorean, farcical burletta." Starring in it were Linette Marquis, Bijou Heron, and Charlotte Thompson, all well-known actresses from the New York stage.

She searched for an excuse. "I'm sorry, but I don't have anything suitable to wear. As you know, my clothes were burned in the fire, and what I do own are either Ida Eberley's cast-offs or suitable for work only."

He shrugged, as if this were of little importance. "Then I'll buy you something grand, and you can wear that."

"No!" Color suffused her face. "I couldn't possibly take anything of that sort from you, and there isn't time for Fifine to sew me a gown, not if we're to attend tomorrow night."

"There is a woman who often sews for actresses, and she has a staff of seamstresses who can work around the clock to complete a garment within twenty-four hours, if that is required." Riordan pulled out his watch. "I think we just have about that much time. Let's go, Alisa."

"No! I won't!" She held back as he tried to take her elbow, and there was a brief, ludicrous struggle that ended with her being pinned by his large, strong hands, trembling angrily in his grip.

"Who do you think you are, Riordan Daniels? I am not a domestic animal, a sheep that you can stampede into doing what you wish me to do!"

"I know very well you're not. Has it occurred to you that you might *enjoy* going out? That it might be a pleasant change from ledgers and accountants and endless correspondence? Dammit, don't be such a stubborn little bulldog. I *am* your employer, if you remember."

"And what's that supposed to mean?" She was incredulous. "That you'd fire me if I refused your invitation?"

He shrugged. "Stop being silly. I'll summon up the carriage, and let that be an end to arguing."

Rebelliously Alisa sat beside Riordan as he drove his smart little runabout to a business street at the edge of the burned area. Here, in a busy, shabby street, pawnshops did a rousing business, and sidewalk peddlers hawked Lake Michigan whitefish.

He had no right, no *right*, to make her do this, she thought angrily. She was fine, she enjoyed working, she needed no recreation. What arrogance, to imply that he'd fire her if she didn't obey! And what if he expected her to wear jewels at her throat and wrists?

Her heart sank. She didn't own any, not anymore. Except for a little garnet ring she'd kept for sentimental reasons, she had sold Mama's jewels to buy the bricks.

Riordan pulled up to a corner building, where a draper occupied the first floor, signs advertising flannels, sheeting, and damasks.

"This isn't Mrs. Capeziano's usual shop, but she was burned out and has taken temporary quarters here," he explained as he helped Alisa down from the buggy, his hand firm on her elbow. He escorted her toward a door that led to a flight of stairs, seeming to know the way very well indeed.

As she climbed the stairs, Alisa seethed, her black mood increasing. Was this dressmaker the one who sewed for Riordan's other women? She squared her chin, deciding to wear the gown only once, then return it.

Mrs. Capeziano turned out to be a pretty young widow with flashing dark eyes, shiny jet-black hair pulled back into a knot, and an infectious smile. Black crepe hugged her generously curved figure, and like those of her trade, around her left wrist she wore a band with a pincushion attached, bristling with stuck-in pins and needles.

When Riordan told the dressmaker they needed an evening dress on twenty-four hours' notice, she didn't even quail.

"Actresses often demand dresses on short order," Maria Capeziano explained. "So I keep a few things partly made up. That way all I do is complete the finishing touches. Would you like to see what I have?"

It was a resourceful idea—ready-made dresses were usually of poor quality, and few wore them. But Alisa was in no mood to be accommodated, or to love the gowns she was shown. Why did Riordan insist on this? And worse, why did he stride around the shop with such obvious familiarity? By the way he bantered back and forth with the pretty dressmaker, the two were old friends.

A horrible thought occurred to her. Could Maria Capeziano be the mother of the child Riordan kept upstairs in his house? Her heart pounding, Alisa searched the woman's features for signs of possible resemblance. Like the dressmaker, the infant girl also had dark hair and eyes. But then, so did Riordan.

Stop, she told herself finally. She was only torturing herself with such speculations.

Now Mrs. Capeziano was showing her a succession of ball dresses. Mauve silk. Amber satin. A deep cream gown with a dramatic square neckline, its overdress gathered in graceful folds over an underskirt of changeable celery-colored silk that flashed lush shimmers as the pretty seamstress held it up to view.

Alisa caught her breath. The deep, square neckline, trimmed with intricate pleatlike ruching, was striking in its design and would show off the porcelain quality of her skin, hinting at curves.

"Oh!" she cried involuntarily. "It's lovely!"

"We'll take that one," Riordan commanded.

"But I can't," Alisa began. "Really, I—"

"Fit it to her, please, and I'll send someone to pick it up tomorrow evening at five. I want her to be outfitted with everything to go with it. Slippers. Gloves. Some doodads for her hair. And whatever evening wrap is appropriate. Perhaps something lined with fur."

"I *can't* . . ." But Alisa's protest went unheard as the dressmaker ushered her into a fitting room and began to tuck, pin, and baste.

"You are very pretty," Maria Capeziano mur-

mured as she worked. "This gown will look splendid on you."

"I . . . that is," Alisa said, swallowing, "has Mr.
Daniels come to you before?"

The woman paused in her even stitching. "I
made a full layette and wardrobe for a child, at
his request. He said that it was a gift to a godchild."

"Of course." Was it literal truth, or had Riordan
come to this woman for more than a layette? Alisa
bit her lip and said no more.

Half an hour later, they left the dressmaker's,
but Riordan was not finished with her. "You must
have jewels."

"*Jewels?*" She said it in horror. This was it, she
thought. He'd remembered her mother's legacy;
surely she'd mentioned it to him on the night of
the fire. Now—it was natural enough—he was going
to ask her to wear the gems.

She fumbled for an excuse to explain their
absence. "I . . . I prefer a plain neckline. That
dress is so laden with decoration already, jewelry
will spoil the effect."

"Nonsense. You'd look naked without something
to glitter at your throat."

Alisa bit her lip as they jolted along in the
carriage. She'd borrow a necklace and tiara from
Malva, she decided frantically. Tell Riordan it was
her own. Oh, why did one lie have to lead so
irresistibly into another?

But before she could calm herself, Riordan pulled
up in front of a small frame home, where a discreet sign, "JEWELER AND GOLDSMITH," announced that
one of Chicago's merchants had taken temporary

quarters until his store on Lake Street could be rebuilt.

Again, the jeweler seemed to know Riordan, greeting him effusively.

"I want her in diamonds," Riordan ordered as soon as they were seated in a small parlor.

The man nodded. "What sort of stones did you wish, Mr. Daniels? I have many beautiful gems I can show you."

Alisa lost her temper. "I don't want to look at anything!" She jumped to her feet, heedless of the jeweler's startled stare. She glared at Riordan. "You might have bought me a dress, but you are *not* going to buy me diamonds! Do you think I am a kept woman? Well, I'm not! I'll never be one!"

"Hush." Riordan pulled her aside while the merchant tactfully busied himself laying out a selection of his wares in velvet-lined boxes. "Get it through your head, Alisa, I can afford anything this man has in his shop. I can deck you in jewels from the top of your stubborn head to the toes of your pretty feet, I can *swathe* you in them."

"Don't be so proud of it!" she snapped.

"I'm merely stating fact."

"Well, that may be so—I'm not doubting that you are one of the richest men in the country. But it's uncouth and rude to boast about it!"

As Riordan reddened, she went on. "The phrase is *nouveau riche*," she taunted. "In French, it means 'new rich,' and it applies to brash, upstart people who have just recently made large amounts of money and are too ill-bred to know how to spend it gracefully."

She stopped, afraid she had said too much, for

Riordan's mouth had twisted angrily, his cheekbones darkened. "Do you really think that your insults make any difference to me, Alisa?"

"I—"

"I have received far more cutting insults in my lifetime than being called *nouveau riche*, I assure you." He strode over to the jeweler's display cases and pointed, seemingly at random, to one of the necklaces displayed therein. "I'll take that one."

"But, sir . . . the lady . . . that is, she should try on the creation first, to see if it—"

"I said that's the one I want."

Bewildered, the man held up the necklace, a triple rope of pearls the color of dawn, set with circles of diamonds that flashed with prisms of light.

Shocked in spite of herself, Alisa drew in her breath. The expense! She felt sure that the necklace must cost thousands of dollars, more money than Pots Ogden's entire brickyard.

But she knew instinctively that the necklace would look just right with the cream gown, the pale pearls setting off its luster, the diamonds glorious.

"This is very lovely, and I will be delighted to wear it tomorrow night," she told the jeweler, amazed at the calm words that emerged from her lips. "But I can't accept it as a gift; no lady could. Therefore I will wear this and return it to you the following morning."

"But . . . but . . ." The man could not hide his dismay at losing a sale.

However, Riordan nodded to him, arranging a rental fee, and tipping the man several large bills. The merchant smiled, seemingly placated.

They waited while the necklace was packed in a velvet-lined box.

"You are a stubborn, prideful woman, Alisa Amsell," Riordan remarked when they were in the buggy again.

"I'm a *lady*," she told him. And sat for the rest of the ride in silence, for, to satisfy her honor, she had just refused a gift that would have helped to buy back her father's mill. Where was her fine urge for revenge? Where was her *sense*?

There had been rain earlier in the evening, but it had cleared, leaving a fine, almost opaque mist in the air. The reflected gleam of windows and carriage lamps gave the city a jeweled glamor. If you did not glance toward the burned-out areas, you would never know the town had been damaged, and there was no longer the heavy smell of smoke and ashes that had lingered here for so many weeks.

Sighing with anticipation and nervousness, Alisa settled back in the seat of Riordan's luxurious, shiny landau. One of six equipages that he owned, this one was pulled by two bay geldings, perfectly matched both to color and size, their trappings decorated by silver shields that bore Riordan's initials. A liveried coachman sat stiffly on his perch, wielding a silver-handled buggy whip that also bore the Daniels emblem.

The play was being staged in a disused old opera house located adjacent to the burned area. Previously it had been scheduled to be torn down. Now, however, it had been pressed into service again, and gas lamps blazed from its entrance, where playbills announced coming performances.

Riordan himself helped Alisa from the carriage. He nodded in dismissal to his coachman, who would wait with the other drivers until the performance was over.

As they entered the theater, joining the throngs of well-dressed men and women in the lobby, Alisa felt a spurt of unwilling excitement.

Riordan checked her evening wrap, a mantle lined on the inside with soft rabbit fur, and his own satin-lined opera cape and tall hat. He leaned toward her, his eyes full of warm admiration.

"You may have fought like a tiger not to accept that dress from me, but you look beautiful in it, Alisa. You are by far the prettiest woman here."

"Nonsense," she said evenly. "We've barely arrived, and there will be many women far more striking than I." Still, she felt a blush surge up from the creamy silken ruches of the gown.

She looked around eagerly, for she had not been out socially since the fire, and had almost forgotten what it felt like to wear a glorious gown, to move among people bent only on pleasure.

The redecorated lobby glittered with crystal chandeliers and gold leaf, and they could hear the dissonant notes of the orchestra tuning.

"Alisa, you look beautiful. We never see you anymore," murmured Philip Armour, a pudgy, balding man with muttonchop sideburns that descended into his high collar. He had made millions in livestock and grain. He nodded coolly to Riordan, barely acknowledging him, although they were business associates.

"I have been busy," Alisa began.

They were interrupted by Cordelia Landsdowne,

in pink silk. "Oooo! Alisa! Your necklace! It is splendid. Wherever did you get it?" Cordelia gazed at the necklace, and then, curiously, at Riordan.

"They are only on loan and I must return them tomorrow," Alisa responded hastily, for she did not wish anyone to think Riordan had bought the necklace for her. She introduced her escort to Cordelia, who eyed him and giggled.

"Are you going to Glenda Forbes's tea dance?" Cordelia wanted to know.

"No, I can't attend. I have work to do—it's a necessity now, you know," Alisa explained lightly.

She greeted others. The Potter Palmers. Cyrus McCormick, Chicago's "Reaper King."

"Alisa, how are you?" Matt Eberley came up to greet her, with two women on his arms. His mother, Ida, was clad in gray brocade and sapphires, and there was also a small, pretty blond in lilac satin. "I'd like you to meet Charity Palmer. She is a third cousin, once removed, visiting the Palmers from Philadelphia."

"So pleasant to meet you, Miss Amsell. I have seen the fire damage here with my own eyes—isn't it appalling?" Warily the women chatted, Charity gazing at Alisa's honey-gold hair and the opulent necklace while clinging possessively to Matt's arm.

Alisa felt relieved when Malva swept through the crowd just as a discreet chiming bell announced that the performance was about to begin.

"Alisa, my darling cousin, what a surprise to see you here!" Malva's escort, a widower much in demand for social events, stood waiting nearby.

"Malva, have you met Riordan Daniels?" Alisa turned to introduce her employer.

Malva took Riordan's proffered hand and the two sized each other up, the energetic dowager in flowing black, wearing a diamond parure, and the tall, handsome black-haired financier.

"I have heard much about you." Riordan gave Malva his most charming smile. "You are the formidable person who runs a soup kitchen single-handedly, cares for twenty orphan girls, and still has time to look utterly elegant."

Malva acknowledged the compliment with a twinkling smile. "I'm glad to see you've brought Alisa out for some enjoyment. My young cousin works entirely too hard."

"She certainly does," Riordan agreed.

"Malva—" Alisa began, annoyed.

"No, I'm not going to scold you, dear, you know me better than that. I am your friend, not just a stodgy relative to whom you must be polite. I wish only the best for Alisa," she added, fixing Riordan with a steely eye. "And if anyone were ever to harm her, I think I would tear his eyes out."

Riordan looked startled; then he threw back his head and laughed, the sound rich. "Ah, you are a fierce one, Malva Eames! But I assure you it won't be necessary for you to maim me. Your cousin is quite safe with me."

Later, as they were settling into their seats, Riordan leaned over to whisper, "Malva is a great lady. In fact, all of these people seem to like you," he added thoughtfully, as the orchestra began its overture. "Why wouldn't you go to that tea dance?"

"I just don't want to. What would I talk to those girls about? Balls? Afternoon teas? Ice-skating expeditions? Those topics would just bore me!

And I'm sure my talk of contracts and bills of lading and ledgers would bore them, too."

"Perhaps. But you could still move socially among those people if you chose."

"I could, yes."

Still Riordan looked thoughtful. "These people barely acknowledged me, but you are the center of attention, and even the fact that you were 'in trade' has not seemed to quell their admiration for you one whit. Why do you work, when you could still be a part of this elegant, pampered crowd?"

Alisa turned her face toward the stage, feeling the telltale blush spread over her neck and shoulders.

I work because I want to avenge my father, she longed to say to him. *Because I don't wish to be dependent, even on Malva, nor do I wish to marry dear, dull Matt. And because I want to play your game, Riordan Daniels. Yes, that, too.*

But perhaps there was more to it than that, she admitted to herself as the bejeweled audience began an anticipatory stir, and the heavy velvet curtain rustled up on a painted set of a drawing room.

As Scene I began, Alisa was achingly aware of the presence of the man beside her. His thighs encased in excellent broadcloth, wide and muscular. His shoulders, his big, gentle hands. Electricity seemed always to arc between them, charging every particle of air.

She worked to be near Riordan Daniels. Well, if she were to be utterly honest with herself, wasn't that part of it? She loved being near him, close enough to touch him; she lived to be able to walk into his office each morning, to see his smiles, laugh at his wry jokes. She didn't even mind his sudden black moods that could evaporate into good humor within minutes.

My God, she thought in a sudden soaring wave of despair, she was falling in love with Riordan.

But maybe it wasn't too late—maybe she could still stop the feelings, push them away, relegating them to some unused back room of her mind, where she could slam the door on them.

Papa. She owed her father, and all that he had been, and she could not betray him now.

✄13✄

Linette Marquis, as the third sister, with a thick, glossy braid hanging down the middle of her back, made a charming imp, garnering a full response from the opening-night audience.

How, Alisa wondered, could a woman own such a fractured personality? Offstage, Linette was flamboyant, petulant, pouting, and greedy. But onstage, she exuded joy and innocence.

However, at the first interval, when it was customary for the performers to take bows and receive their first bouquets, the curtsying Linette cast such a heavy-lidded, sultry look over the footlights that Alisa started. Surely the actress's questing glance, fixed on the dress circle, had Riordan as its target.

He seemed to sense it too, for beside her she felt him shift uneasily.

When the last huge set piece of roses and lilies had been delivered onstage, and the curtain dropped for the final time, Alisa rose with the others. Abruptly she felt tired and dispirited. She had tried to enjoy the stage performance but had not succeeded. Now she longed to get home, to rip off the cream gown, to deposit the pearl-and-diamond rope back in its box, ready to be returned to the jeweler.

"Come," Riordan said, taking her arm. "We'll go backstage."

"Backstage!" It was the very last thing that Alisa wanted to do.

"Yes, I'm sure you would enjoy meeting the actresses—they were charming, didn't you think?"

Before Alisa could voice a protest, Riordan took her arm and led her toward the pass-through door.

Backstage, the old opera house had not yet received the benefits of refurbishing. It smelled pungently of dust, mold, animal glue, powder, and generations of human perspiration. The green room, located under the stage, was a shabby room with exposed steam pipes, paint peeling from its much-initialed walls.

Yet the glittering crowd of well-wishers who had flocked here seemed unaware of the tawdriness of their surroundings. They crowded around the leading actresses, jostling for position.

Bijou Heron, who in her *Sisters* costume looked barely fourteen years old, scribbled autographs, while dark-haired Charlotte Thompson, laughing huskily, embraced some male admirer. A theatrical columnist crowded close, taking notes on the costumes each actress wore. College students and foppish young dandies begged for supper dates.

A waiter pushed a cart into the room on which reposed a large barrel filled with cracked ice and magnums of champagne. He could barely move through the close-packed crowd.

"Well? What did you think?" a throaty voice demanded. "What did you think of me? Was I wonderful?"

The opening-night fans parted to make a path for Linette Marquis. The actress's thick, dark hair had been unplaited, to stream wantonly about her shoulders, a single pink rosebud tucked among her curls. The effect was striking, as if a child had suddenly taken on courtesan qualities, and Alisa was not the only one who turned to stare.

Linette swept up to Riordan and took his arm, ignoring Alisa. "Darling, I want to know what did you *think?*"

Riordan looked down at the petite actress. "You were wonderful, of course, Linette. You always are."

She preened. "I *was* good, wasn't I? I got loads and loads of flowers . . . and the ones you sent were beautiful! A huge, huge basket of roses," she gloated, speaking for the first time to Alisa. "He knows how much I love them, pink roses are my favorite. That's what he always sends me."

Alisa stood rigid, loathing the triumphant, cloying quality of Linette's words, her possessiveness. And beside her even Riordan seemed taken aback, his expression angry, although she wondered why it should be. He knew Linette, knew her behavior. Why had he brought her backstage to subject her to this? She should never have come to the theater with him!

But the worst was yet to come, for Linette suddenly slid her slender white arms around Riordan, planting a long kiss directly on his lips. The picture they made would remain burned on Alisa's mind for years: the tall man, the petite girl melting into his embrace, her body arched to his.

Alisa could stand no more. She turned and pushed her way blindly out of the green room, stumbling down dark, drafty, unfamiliar corridors, and up a narrow staircase barely wide enough for her skirts, until she found her way into the empty auditorium. She sank into one of the front-row seats, unable to propel herself further.

Miserably she castigated herself. She shouldn't have come here! And she should not have accepted Riordan's dress, his jewelry. She'd been a fool to do so.

Jealousy stabbed at her. She'd hated it when Linette's glance had singled out Riordan from onstage. And then, when she'd seen those pretty arms slide around him, she'd thought she would be sick with the unfamiliar emotions that surged through her like acid.

He had sent Linette roses. Pink ones, a bud of which she had put in her unbound hair.

Decisively Alisa rose, smoothing down the folds of the cream silk. She felt the weight of the borrowed necklace drag around her throat like a chain.

She had no cause to feel jealous, she scolded herself. She had no claim on Riordan. She'd only come to the theater because he had insisted on it; no doubt he had needed a respectable companion and she was the answer to that need. What did it matter to her if he had a mistress—or ten thousand of them?

Riordan found her standing alone in the refurbished theater lobby, restlessly pacing the red carpet.

"Where were you, Alisa? Why did you go, leaving me like that?" His expression was black, and savagely he took her arm, pulling her along as if she had committed some crime.

She moved with as much dignity as she could, refusing to allow herself to be ruffled by him. "I didn't care to stand about while you and your mistress publicly embraced."

"My . . ." Then the savagery of Riordan's expression faded. His dark eyes searched hers. "I'm sorry. My behavior was uncalled for. I'm afraid Linette is far more possessive than she has any right to be, and I apologize for offending your sensibilities in any way. Please wait while I get our coats and have our carriage called up. I'll be right back."

In a few moments he returned to escort Alisa to the carriage. He helped her into her wrap, his hands brushing her shoulders as he did so. Alisa thought she would scream from his touch, his smell, the nearness of him.

Angrily she refused his attempt to help her into the carriage, and managed it herself, climbing lightly up despite the encumbrances of the heavy gown and its many layers of lace-trimmed petticoats and stiffening.

He murmured something to his driver and they set off, bypassing the carriage line, now shortened so that it contained only the vehicles of those still gathered backstage. A fine, light moisture danced in the gaslights, creating a fairy world of light and mysterious, glowing shadows.

"I want to be taken straight home," Alisa announced.

"Why? I'd like to escort you to supper."

"I don't *want* to have supper with you, I don't want to have anything to do with you. It was inexcusable for you to take me to that play as you did, exposing me to the ridicule of your mistress."

"Alisa . . ."

But she refused to listen. She didn't want to hear his excuses. She had never been so coldly furious; if it had not been after midnight and the streets dangerous at this hour, she would have jumped down from the carriage and walked home. As it was, fuming, she leaned forward to tap the coachman on his shoulder.

"Oneida Street, please."

Riordan immediately leaned forward and countermanded the order, naming his own address.

It was like a comedic charade, and if Alisa had not been so incensed, she might even have laughed.

"No! I *won't* go there. I want to go to my home. Ten Oneida Street, please, and here is something for your trouble." She repeated her address to the driver, fishing out a coin from her evening purse and handing it to him.

Then, satisifed, she unclasped the pearl-and-diamond necklace and placed it in Riordan's hand. It gleamed lustrously in the lamplight, the glimmer of the diamonds like tears.

"There! There is your necklace back. I'm sorry I ever borrowed it. And I don't want your dress, either. I regret that I consented to attend the theater with you, and I can assure you it will never happen again."

"Very well." Calmly, as if he accepted the return of gorgeous necklaces every day of his life, Riordan wound the pearls around his hand and thrust them inside his jacket. Then he leaned back in the carriage, his arms folded across his chest, and said not another word.

They rode in simmering silence through the mist-shrouded streets, where every sound seemed magnified, hollow and echoing. He didn't speak to her again, and perversely, Alisa didn't speak to him. She, too, could use the weapon of silence!

She could hardly wait to be home, away from him.

The ride seemed to stretch out forever. She listened to the noises of bridle jingle, the hollow clop-clop of horses' hooves. An occasional jolt of the carriage would toss her into Riordan's shoulder, and even through the layers of fur and satin that separated them, she felt the burning contact of their bodies.

She shuddered lightly. What was happening to her? She wanted to slide her arms around him, exactly as Linette had done. She wanted to open her mouth to his, to feel his warm, seeking, demanding tongue. . . . Alisa shivered like a wild animal, praying for the ride to be over soon, her torture finished.

The carriage turned down an unfamiliar street, then another. Alisa turned to her companion. "Riordan, this isn't the way to my house. We should have turned south."

He grinned, his teeth very white in a sudden

glare of a corner gaslight. "We're not going to your house."

"But, I gave your driver money."

"I give him more, every week. He is *my* servant and he does as I wish."

"I see! And when you wish to kidnap a lady, he goes along with that?" she demanded.

"Absolutely. Especially when he knows, as I do, that the lady indeed wishes to come home with me, that all of her protests are entirely too vehement. You are mine, Alisa. Mine, and I'm going to make you admit it."

Before she could utter a protest, Riordan scooped her into his arms, his mouth possessing hers with such consuming male vigor that Alisa was incapable of fighting back.

And maybe she didn't want to fight back, she realized, as she opened her lips to the sweet thrusts of his tongue. Maybe this, deep in her heart, was what she had wanted all along.

Back at Riordan's mansion, only a few gaslights glowed, highlighting the rich patina of woodwork. Alisa breathed the spicy fragrance of the lemon oil used on the furniture. There were no servants in evidence, the place seemingly deserted. She felt totally under the spell of her senses and the magnetism of this compelling man.

By the time Riordan escorted her up the wide staircase with its porcelain balusters, Alisa was weak from desire and from the exciting, terrifying, overwhelming feeling that she was burning her bridges behind her. Riordan was wonderful—but he was her father's betrayer. He had a mistress, and possibly other women as well, and he had warned her that he would never love her.

Those things were reality.

But tonight . . . oh, tonight Alisa didn't want to listen to reality. In Riordan's big bed she lay naked while he stripped the fashionable dress and petticoats from her, his mouth kissing each portion of her flesh as he removed the cloth that bound it.

"Beautiful," he murmured. "Your skin . . . it's like silk, warm, glowing silk."

As he pulled off his own clothes, Alisa stared tranfixed at his nakedness. He was as different from her softness as granite was from silk. He had broad, hard shoulders. His chest was wide and strong, curved with muscle, adorned by a thatch of curls fragrant with male musk. His torso tapered down to a flat belly that was also corded with muscle. Here the silken hair began again in a V that continued to the groin.

Alisa's breath caught as she followed that V to its source.

He, too, seemed equally enthralled by her. He groaned, his eyes glittering at her, seeming almost to burn with desire. "Oh, Alisa, Alisa, Alisa." It was if he could not say her name enough, could not kiss her enough.

He kissed every part of her, and this took an exquisitely long time, during which his mouth nuzzled her, his tongue teased, his lips found every secret curve and crevice, bringing Alisa to spasms of hot delight.

But still he was not finished with her. His hands stroked her, his mouth drank her, his hips arched into hers, urging her along a river of sensation that was beginning to sweep her away.

Then, when she thought she could bear no more, he lifted her up and placed her on top of him, positioning her so that her spread thighs straddled his hardness. At first gently, then with growing ardor, he began to thrust, showing her how to ride him. They merged together in an undulating dance of love, she arched above him, he cupping her breasts, caressing them urgently.

The strokes within her grew deeper, more frenzied. Alisa responded fully, totally. She heard Riordan's hoarse groan, and felt him grip her and roll her over yet again, still not leaving her body. Their passion mounted unbridled now until at last she heard his cry and felt herself go, exploding, breaking apart into a thousand diamond-hard shudders of ecstasy.

They lay together, spent, their bodies moist, their breathing gradually calming. Alisa felt suffused with an exhausted joy. There was no room in her mind for thoughts of Linette Marquis, or of Papa, for anything except the man who held her tightly in his arms. She wanted to cradle herself inside Riordan's strength, to be forever encircled by his arms.

They slept, entwined in each other's arms, the peace so deep that Alisa could have cried from happiness. Then they woke to new, slow caresses. He made love to her again, this time with sure knowledge of her body. She climaxed again and again, spasming in swift, exquisite bursts of rapture. At last she lay exhausted and laughing, begging him to leave her alone—she could not stand such joy, he would drive her mad, insane. . . .

But Riordan only laughed and entered her again. This time she was pinned beneath him at his mercy, and his movements were slow, deep, and inexorable. She had nothing left to hold back from him, no defenses he had not breached.

Her final explosion was almost a sob, for he had taken her, marked her, made her his, and she knew that for the rest of her life she would never again be the same.

Near dawn, reluctantly, Riordan hitched up his buggy and drove her home himself. Outside her darkened house, he held her in his arms. The fog had turned to rain and Alisa was tired, some of her joy seeping away now.

"Good night, my darling, you were beautiful and loving and perfect. You're wonderful, Alisa."

"No. No, I'm not. To have gone to your house as I did . . . What would all those people we saw at the theater think if they knew? Oh, Riordan, what if your driver were to gossip?"

She rubbed her eyes tiredly, feeling reality flood her like a wash of chilly rain. The faces of everyone she knew seemed to range about the buggy in an accusing circle. Matt, Ida Eberley, Papa . . .

"People won't think anything, because they aren't going to know," Riordan said. "As for my driver and my other servants, I pay them all handsome salaries. They keep my secrets, you may be sure of it." He gave her a soft, tender kiss that threatened to turn into something much more incendiary.

"My God, Alisa. You make a man think thoughts, you cause him to lose control . . ."

Hastily Alisa pulled away. "I . . . I must go. I'll see you in the morning for work as usual."

She fled up the walk, away from him, and let herself into the house. A single gasolier burned in the hall. With shaking hands Alisa turned up the flame, going to the mirror that hung on the wall to stare at herself in numb dismay.

Her own face gazed back at her, her lips reddened, bruised, crushed from endless kissing. Her cheeks were flushed from lovemaking, too, and her eyes held a wanton look that Alisa knew had never been there before. Even her hair was a honey-colored tangle, reeking of the scents of love.

Guiltily she doused the light and started up the staircase.

"Well, well! *Amour* suits you, *n'est-ce pas*?" It was Fifine, wrapped in a dressing gown, her hair in curl papers, her expression knowing.

"Fifine!" Alisa jumped. "You . . . you startled me."

"Come into my sewing room, for there are some things I must tell you about the ways of a man with a woman, and how a woman can protect herself."

"Really, I'm so tired . . ."

"This will not take long, *chérie*. Men! Pfah! They take their pleasure and use us as pretty toys, but when they are finished with us, what happens, eh? They forget about us. But *we* do not forget about them."

There could not have been anything more calculated to ruin the rapture and joy of the night she had just spent with Riordan. But Alisa felt so guilty and ashamed that she followed Fifine into her cluttered little sewing room.

There, amid dress forms and cards of point-rose and Mechlin lace, Fifine lectured her on the use of the vaginal sponge and certain creams and unguents.

"American women don't wish to know such things, they are perilously uninformed, trusting to chance or to God to protect them," Fifine declared. "He is a rich man, you are poor, and that is the way it is, that is the way of it." Her eyes glittered, as if she were amused at some irony. "I know. I, too, was used by someone. Did he make me his wife and the mistress of his fine large house? No, he did not."

Alisa stirred uneasily, wishing she had not come. Fifine had been with the Amsells since Alisa was a child; Alisa knew there had been male admirers on her days off, for Fifine, in her dark, sallow way, was attractive to men. But these men had all been draymen or mill workers, certainly not rich.

Alisa swallowed hard, suddenly afraid of what Fifine might reveal. Hastily she spoke up, cutting off the other woman's rambling. "I . . . I'll protect myself, just as you say, but now I must go to bed. I'm so tired, I think I could sleep for a week, but I have to get up in a few hours and go to work."

"Ah? Yes, that is the way of it, too. He will accept your labors willingly enough. But he has no intention of marrying you. Ah, *non,* not in a thousand years of Sundays! He merely wishes to—"

Alisa had had enough. "I won't listen! I won't

listen to any more! I ... I just don't want to hear!"

She pushed past Fifine and ran to her room. Inside, she flung herself on the bed, not bothering to take off her gown. She pounded her fists into the pillow, allowing wave after wave of pain to sweep through her.

He will accept your labors but he has no intention of marrying you. The Frenchwoman's words punished her. And Alisa knew they were probably very true, for hadn't Riordan himself warned her he would never love anyone? Didn't he keep a succession of mistresses and other women, marrying none of them?

But it was too late, too late now for her to change her feelings.

"Miss Amsell? Miss Amsell! You must wake up— you'll be late." It was Nella's anxious voice as she rapped on Alisa's door repeatedly, finally pushing open the door to peer inside.

Alisa stirred, her eyelids feeling heavy, her body sluggish and unwilling to leave the warm quilts.

"Miss, are you all right, are you ill? *Ach,* usually you bound out of bed."

"I ... I'm just sleepy, Nella."

Alisa dragged herself out of bed. The room was dark and chilly, and when she lit the gasolier the cream-colored gown, hastily flung over a chair, mocked her with its presence.

She dressed quickly, and then packed the gown into a box, tying its strings in a firm, tight knot. *There,* she thought, trembling. She would return it to Riordan today. She might have allowed him to make love to her—that had happened, and could never be erased.

But it did not have to occur again. She wasn't a helpless moth, drawn willy-nilly to a powerful and dangerous flame. She had willpower, she possessed choices.

Feeling better, she remembered a day several years ago when Papa had taken her out in his buggy for instructions on how to control a spirited horse.

"You're the master, Alisa," he'd told her. "Handle the reins with authority and let him know you are worthy of commanding him."

"Like this, Papa?" She'd tried to do as he did.

"Yes . . . ah, that's better, much better. Ah, you're a competitor, aren't you? You're just like me. You're going to win out over all of them, aren't you? Someday, my darling girl."

Abruptly her eyes moistened with tears.

An hour later she was with Riordan, the dress box lying on the table between them like an accusation.

"It's yours. I want you to keep it, Alisa. Why else would I have had it made to your measurements?"

"I don't want it. I never wanted it. And I . . . I don't want what is happening between us, Riordan."

His eyes, so dark, seemed to sear her with their hot look. "Then you're lying to yourself, and to me."

"No." She stood to her full height, fixing him with a long, determined look. "I'm not lying to myself, Riordan, I'm telling myself the truth, and I don't like that truth. I am your employee, not your mistress. I don't want to be in that anomalous position, and I don't wish to be the butt of gossip or conjecture."

"But, my darling, gossip will happen whether you wish it or not, and whether you sleep with me or not." Riordan's laugh was harsh.

She lifted her chin. "I don't think so, because if I am free of guilt then I'll carry myself differently and I'll have more confidence. *I'm not going to sleep with you again, Riordan.* If you can't abide by that, if you can't agree to . . ." She faltered, then recovered herself. "If you can't agree to leave me alone, then I must leave your employ now, today."

For a long moment they gazed at each other, and then finally Riordan nodded. "If that's what you want."

"Yes. It is."

"We will be employer and employee, nothing more," he went on, savagely repeating her desires. "That *is* what you wish, isn't it? Let's get it very clear, for there should be no misunderstanding between us, none at all."

"It . . . it is what I want." Why did her throat choose that very moment to close up so that she could barely force the words out? "I . . . I would like you to give me my work assignments for the day, Riordan. I want to get to work."

He lifted an ironic eyebrow, then slid a stack of ledgers in her direction. "Good. So do I. We'll start with these. Work, Alisa—it's marvelous for the spirit, don't you agree? Of course, you must not object to my continuing to live my life as I see fit; after all, I am a man, with a man's needs."

"I'm aware of that!" she snapped.

His tone was equally savage. "Good. Then we understand each other."

That day Alisa toiled until nearly midnight, punishing herself with hard labor, unwilling to give up until her eyes burned with fatigue and her head throbbed with exhaustion. But in the inner room that opened off the library, she knew full well that Riordan worked just as hard, and she was determined not to quit before he did.

He had hurt her—deeply, cruelly—with his talk of a "man's needs," and he had known that he was doing so. But never, by look or word, would she let him know it.

∽ 14 ∾

December and January passed, the winter bringing heavy snows to Chicago. Windblown flakes swirled across Lake Michigan to block the streets with drifts, some of which had to be broken out with oxen when men with shovels could not do the job. Slow as they were, oxen were far better than horses for getting through snowdrifts, for horses were apt to flounder in deep snow.

In the burned area, ragged chimneys and half-fallen walls wore white caps, taking on an eerie beauty, and where new buildings were under construction, piles of brick and marble acquired a pristine, snowy frosting.

Alisa loved the winter, and was especially proud of the new Chamber of Commerce building that was going up at Washington and LaSalle streets. The first stone had been laid on November 6, and bricklayers were already at work, using, to Alisa's overwhelming pride, some of the bricks from Pots Ogden's yard.

Several times, in wary truce with her, Riordan took her out for an afternoon of cutter racing.

Sleighs spun down a snowy roadway, steam puffing out of the horses' nostrils, snow flying from their feet.

The racers wore sealskin caps and dogskin gloves, some of them coachmen who, unknown to their employers, had slipped out to the speedway. The prize was usually a fine horsewhip, the competition keen.

She felt light-headed, giddy, infected with the cold clarity of the winter air, the excitement of the gathered crowds who paced about, stamping their feet and rubbing their hands to stay warm against a frigid wind. A chestnut vendor moved among them with his cart.

"I'll bet a week's pay I can beat you, Riordan," Alisa challenged, unable to resist.

"And I'll double that wager." He grinned at her, wearing a woolen cap that tilted rakishly over his forehead. "There is only one problem," he pointed out. "We rode here in the same cutter—so how are we going to race each other?"

"Simple. I'll borrow a sleigh from one of these gentlemen. I'm sure one can be found who will oblige for a fee."

Riordan raised his eyebrows. "But that would give you the disadvantage. An unfamiliar vehicle, a new horse . . . No. I'll do the borrowing."

"*I* will." Their eyes locked and Alisa hardened her chin, determined not to be overridden. "My victory will be all the sweeter if I beat you against the odds," she finished.

"Very well, then. What about that cutter over there, by the feed store? That chestnut gelding looks spirited. What do you say?"

Fifteen minutes later, money had changed hands and Alisa found herself seated in an elegant little cutter equipped with brass sleigh bells and piles of warm woolen lap rugs. The horse, a tall gelding with white markings on his muzzle, stamped the snow. A crowd of onlookers, attracted by the novelty of a woman racing a man, had gathered to watch. Many were placing bets.

"I'm warning you," Riordan called. "I give no quarter—and today the roadway is clear. There won't be any newsboys wandering into the road to cause me to swerve."

"Good," she snapped. "Are we ready? Where is the starter?"

A pistol shot echoed in the thin winter air and both cutters surged forward, the runners whistling over smooth-packed snow. Eagerly Alisa leaned forward, totally caught up in the race. It was as if everything else in her life had temporarily evaporated, leaving only *now*. The crunch of horses' hooves in snow, the whir of runners, Riordan's husky shout, the cries of the crowd.

She concentrated all her efforts on winning, her eyes assessing the road, which curved past a livery stable and then ran straight past a farmer's open field. A fence was lined with farmhands and cheering spectators, many waving hats.

Excitement tightened in her. This was what she loved, challenge, adventure! She breathed in great gulps of cold hair, her heart pounding. This time—this time—it would not be a standoff, a draw. She would win fully, and she would do it in a borrowed cutter and with an unfamiliar horse.

"Come on! Come on!" she screamed at the gelding, exhilarating in the strength of the animal as it surged ahead, responding to her surging.

Faster they went, the runners flying. She was neck and neck with Riordan now, and from the corner of her eye she glimpsed his taut stance, his skillful command of his horse.

But she was more skillful. She . . .

They hit the curve. Suddenly Alisa felt the skewing slide of her cutter. She screamed at the horse, shifting her weight to avoid tipping. But Riordan's sleigh was too close to her own, and the borrowed gelding seemed suddenly to panic, jerking his body sideways.

Alisa went flying in a welter of snow and loose reins. She hit snow and felt herself slide, slamming into a snowdrift that had piled against the fence. Icy snow crystals were jammed up against her face, filling her nostrils.

She heard laughter, jeering.

Angrily she struggled to sit up. Two men climbed the fence from the crowd and Alisa fought to be free of their grip, aware of the sharp stab of disappointment that filled her. She hadn't been injured, but she was covered with snow from head to foot. Humiliatingly, there was even snow in her eyes and mouth.

She spat it out, rubbing at her eyes.

"Alisa, are you hurt?" Riordan had stopped his cutter and run back to her. He grabbed her away from the two good samaritans, slapping at the snow on her coat.

"I'm fine! I can take care of myself!" She dabbed at the achingly cold snow on her face, which the frigid wind had begun to freeze there. She had begun to shiver violently.

"You're not all right, and in this cold wind you're likely to have frostbite." As he spoke, Riordan gently wiped the snow off Alisa's face with his scarf. "Come on. Thank God your horse isn't injured. We'll take care of everything here, and then I'm getting you home. Some hot chocolate wouldn't hurt you either."

"I don't need hot chocolate like a child who's taken a nasty tumble!" she protested indignantly.

"Don't be so ungrateful. *I* want some, even if you don't, and I intend to have it."

They drove back to Riordan's, Alisa wrapped in layers of blankets, another scarf pulled over her cheeks to protect her from the worst of the wind.

"I will beat you," she muttered defiantly. "One day."

"One day I'm sure you will. But not today. I have no intention of allowing you to catch pneumonia."

Back at his mansion, Riordan ordered a feast of hot chocolate, roast beef, breads, and cheeses. They sat on the floor in the library in front of a huge fire, feasting like children. Alisa, bundled in comforters and quilts, was pleasantly aware of the crackle of applewood, the sweet scent of its burning.

"Here." Riordan laughed when a corner of the comforter slipped as she tried to take a bite of her sandwich. "You'll drop everything and chill yourself. Open your mouth."

"I can feed myself."

"No, you can't. Not with six layers of eiderdown wrapped around you. Do as I tell you, woman."

They laughed and talked in a companionable way, the fire burning lower. Alisa was thankful that their mood was light and that Riordan did not touch her again, scrupulously adhering to their agreement.

Gradually the talk turned to business, for Riordan's mind was never far from his work, and he took keen interest in the ups and downs of the stock exchanges. As he talked of a recent coup in the market, Alisa's mind turned to Pots Ogden and his brickyard.

For weeks now she'd been thinking of buying a limited partnership in the yard and helping Pots to finance some enlargements there. But it was growing increasingly hard to deal with a brickworks she'd never seen, relying on laconic letters from Pots.

Since she was in charge of all Riordan's mail, she had managed to conceal her relationship with the brickyard owner; nevertheless, it was time she visited the yard. She had already thought of a reason to absent herself for several days, and today Riordan's mellow mood was granting her the ideal opportunity to make her request.

Now, as she poured them each a third cup of chocolate, Alisa drew a deep breath and told him that she needed to go to Detroit to visit an ailing relative.

"Someone close?" he inquired.

"An aunt," she lied. "She has been ill with heart failure for some time, and I'm afraid she . . ." She managed to force the falsehood out. ". . . she has not long to live."

Did Riordan look at her strangely, as if he doubted her story? But Alisa decided he was only giving her the same sharp scrutiny that he always did.

"Then I'll order up some hothouse flowers and you can take them with you," he said. "What would she prefer? Roses or lilies?"

Alisa thought her wind-reddened cheeks would burn crimson with guilt. "Oh, that's kind, but it isn't necessary."

"Nonsense. Flowers always cheer an invalid. Order five dozen pink rosebuds from Thompsen's and have them billed to my account. They will know how to pack them for the journey."

Pink rosebuds. Those were what Riordan had given to Linette. Alisa knew Linette Marquis had returned to New York for a play, but according to the theatrical columns of the *Tribune*, had reappeared in Chicago several times.

She rose, letting the quilts drop, and told Riordan that she felt well enough to go back to work.

The following day, her heart shrinking, Alisa was forced to order flowers for a nonexistent aunt and to arrange for their shipping. She hated lying like this. But she was not harming Riordan Daniels, she assured herself. Eventually, when she'd saved enough to get the Amsell mill back, she could confess everything to him.

Then let him do what he wished—punish her as he saw fit. It wouldn't matter then, for she would have achieved victory—a victory, she realized, far sweeter than merely winning a cutter race.

*   *   *

Fort Wayne was a sooty, smoky little city, abounding in manufactories and railroads, and Alisa liked it at once, with its atmosphere of important business being transacted. At the railway depot she made arrangements to have the roses delivered to a hospital, and then hired a driver to take her to Pots Ogden's brickyard.

"Miss Amsell! Why . . . why, hello!" Pots seemed startled to see her, hurrying into his office wearing the same food-stained frock coat he had worn when he had first visited Riordan's office.

"Mr. Daniels asked me to come and look your place over," she told him, smiling. "Would you show it to me?"

Pots looked dubious. "It isn't any place for a woman," he muttered. "It's mucky, and the men will stare—"

"But I am Mr. Daniels' employee, with full authority to act on his behalf. And I'm not afraid of getting dirty; I brought a heavy coat and boots to wear."

"Well." Plainly the brickyard owner was torn between his sense of propriety and his realization that Alisa represented a business contact. Finally business won out. "Oh, very well. If Mr. Daniels really wants you to see it . . ."

As they both donned outdoor gear, Alisa wondered what Ogden would say if he knew that he had never dealt with Riordan, but always with her. But she forgot these misgivings in the exhilaration of seeing the yard. It covered twenty acres, an expanse of untidiness and activity.

Everywhere swarmed laborers in muddy work garb, amid a confusion of horse-drawn wagons, wheelbarrows, and carts. A spur railroad line ran through the yard, and more workmen loaded cars, sweating profusely despite the cold. There were huge heaps of clay, rows of pallets of stored bricks, and black piles of the coal that was used as fuel.

Alisa breathed deeply of the smell of coal, mud, horse droppings, and burned clay. The odor was pungent, and not unpleasant. As always around a manufactory, she felt an odd, singing thrill, as if she'd been let into some hard, powerful male world usually barred to women.

Pots escorted her to a long shedlike building bristling with three smokestacks, from which gray smoke billowed.

"Here's where we make the bricks from clay." Inside, Alisa inspected the wooden tublike device that Pots called a "pugmill." As the column of clay emerged from the pugmill, it was cut off to brick size by a wire, like a grocer cutting cheese.

"Then," Pots explained, "we age the bricks for a while, air 'em out, let the elements take hold." He showed her a device he called a "hot floor," made of cast iron, under which a coal fire glowed, stoked by bare-chested, muscular immigrant workers.

"Step back, honey, or you'll get run over," he cautioned as a burly Italian pushed a wheelbarrow piled with green bricks past them. "It's a wonder Mr. Daniels let you come here. Why, you're just a girl! And look—the hem of your dress is filthy."

Both of them looked down at the hem of Alisa's black traveling dress, which, indeed, was caked with sticky gobbets of clay.

"It's all right," Alisa said quickly.

"It is? My Etta, now, she'd shriek and wail at the very idea of getting her precious skirts soiled. She won't even set foot in the yards. Says no decent woman would dirty herself here."

They entered the kiln building, with its dense, smoky odor and its heat that fell upon them like a hot cloth as soon as they walked in. Pots showed her a long brick structure that he called a "tunnel kiln."

"Kiln cars go in this end," he shouted above the churning noise of engines and screws. "And the bricks come out baked."

Alisa was fascinated. The cars of green brick slowly moved along the tunnel, absorbing heat from other carloads already heated red-hot. Glowing gradually cherry-red, they moved over the main fires to bake, then were pushed slowly on, in their turn yielding heat to the new, incoming cars of raw brick. No heat was wasted.

"We load 'em from here onto railroad cars. From there they go to you," Pots said, leading Alisa out of the huge shed, with its clanging noise and heat. "Or, rather, to Mr. Daniels."

That night the brickyard owner invited Alisa for dinner, and she met the plump, snobbish Etta, who fawned over the Amsell name and insisted on showing Alisa the plans for the elaborate mansion she insisted her husband build, on which construction had already begun.

"We're not going to have brick, though," Etta Ogden announced. "They're too common, too ugly. *I* want marble. White Italianate marble, nothing less."

Thoughtfully Alisa went back to her hotel, her mind focused on the brickyard and the gritty power of it that had so fascinated her.

She allowed her mind to drift into dreams of

ownership and riches. Etta was wrong. Bricks
weren't ugly, they were beautiful, their colors rich
and earthy. They would help build a new Chicago,
and would help her get back the Amsell mill, and
more. . . .

She returned to Chicago filled with new plans,
having contracted with Pots for another large order
of bricks, and negotiated the purchase of a small
share of the business. It was a start, she told herself.
Later, she might try to buy Pots out, or at least
another brickyard like his.

All through a snowy February, Alisa worked
hard for Riordan, but also spent increasingly long
hours at home, seated at a small pigeonhole desk
she had bought, working on the books of her
growing construction business. She was growing
expert at juggling her responsiblities, she told herself wryly, wondering what she would do later,
when the work grew too much.

But for now there were orders to fill, calls to make
on the smaller builders, who, like Ogden, thought
she was transacting business in Riordan's name.

One February afternoon, the chiming sound of
sleighbells announced the arrival of a visitor at the
Daniels mansion. A few minutes later, Linette Marquis again swept into Riordan's private office. It
was an eerie repeat of her earlier visit.

"I must see Riordan," the actress announced
imperiously. Today she wore deep wine velvet
with endless, heavily fringed flounces, a sable
mantle, and matching fur bonnet. Snowflakes glistened like diamonds in Linette's dark curls, and
another glitter of light at her earlobes indicated
she was wearing real diamonds in her ears.

"I'm sorry, but he is working and has asked that he not be disturbed," Alisa responded as smoothly as she could. Her stomach had tightened into a hard knot. Was Linette here in Chicago to reopen another play?

"But of course he'll see *me*."

"He isn't seeing anyone. He made that very clear to me this morning when he arrived."

But Linette sailed on past as if she had not heard a single word, sweeping into Riordan's private inner office and swinging its heavy door shut behind her.

Grimly Alisa tried to concentrate on her work, furious at herself when she dipped her pen into its crystal inkwell and splashed two ugly, spreading blots on the letter she was writing. She crumpled it and started another, straining to hear what was going on behind those doors.

Was Riordan kissing Linette? Holding her in his arms, telling her how glad he was to see her, how much he'd missed her? Was he making arrangements to take her to supper, to see her later? During these long months Alisa had been aware that Riordan did continue to see women occasionally. There had been a few perfumed notes, and once she had glimpsed Riordan leaving the house in evening wear.

So why should it surprise her when Linette called here? Nothing surprised her, she told herself as she penned line after line of looping, even script, determined not to betray herself with another blot.

A long forty minutes passed. But finally Linette emerged, shrugging on her furs again, her triumphant smile flashing. A second later, Riordan himself appeared. Scowling, he strode out to the table where Alisa sat.

"Here," he said, tossing some papers in front of her. "Please pay these, if you would."

Furiously Alisa leafed through a stack of bills—from Mrs. Capeziano, from a jeweler, a milliner, a draper, and a furrier. Apparently Linette had been in town for several weeks, Alisa realized furiously. How had she missed it in the theatrical columns? The jeweler's bill alone would have fed several families for years.

Her anger surprised her.

"Pay them yourself!" she snapped, slapping them down on the tabletop.

"I asked you to do it."

"Don't involve me in your sordid affairs. I'm your employee, not your . . . your . . ." She searched for a word strong enough, insulting enough. "Your . . . panderer!" she finished, spitting the word out.

"Panderer?" Riordan laughed harshly. "A go-between in sexual intrigues? Don't be ridiculous, Alisa."

They glared at each other, electricity crackling between them. Riordan's full mouth twisted as he scooped up the bills. "Damn it, I hired you as my assistant, to take such onerous duties off my hands. My previous assistant always paid this sort of bill. He was quite willing to . . ."

Tears brimmed in her eyes, and she knew she'd cry later, but right now she hated him too much. How dare he ask her to pay his mistress's bills? How dare he flaunt his relationship with greedy, lovely, arrogant little Linette in front of her? She hated it, she hated the idea of all his women.

"Very well!" She snatched the bills back from him. "If that's part of the job, I'll do it. I'll pay your mistress's bills. Are you sure these are all? Do you have any from other women? More actresses, a married woman or two?" Her words lashed out, beyond her power to bite them back. "Or maybe even from Mrs. Capeziano? She is very, very pretty. Or—"

"Stop it, Alisa. You're demeaning yourself and you're interfering in something you don't understand."

"Oh, I understand all right! You're a womanizer, aren't you? Never happy unless you have a dozen or two at your disposal! Does it give you pleasure to parade them in front of me? To make a fool of me?"

"You haven't any right to talk that way to me," Riordan said heavily. "Didn't you make it clear to me several months ago that the relationship we had enjoyed was to end, that you no longer wished to share a bed with me? That you wanted only to work? I remember your emphasizing that very word."

She swallowed back her hurt, wondering if her cheeks looked as red as they felt. "I . . . I'm sorry. I had no right to be upset. I . . . I don't know what came over me."

Again Riordan frowned, and then firmly he pried the bills out of her hands. "I'll take these. I'll pay them myself. You're right, I should not have asked you."

He looked troubled, his lips pressed into a hard line, and Alisa fought the urge to reach up and smooth his upper lip, to erase the tension from it with her fingertips. To her horror, she realized that her hand had actually lifted, that she *was* on the verge of touching him.

She jerked her hand away as if she had nearly touched a gas flame.

Something sang between them.

"Alisa. Dear God ..." Riordan's voice was a husky, agonized cry. Then, before Alisa could react, he pulled her into his arms. She tried to fight him, but her resistance lasted only a few seconds. Then, helplessly, she curved herself to him, giving herself up to his demanding mouth.

She loved him. Needed him, his kisses, his arms, the feel of him, the smell of him, all of him. No matter how many other women he had.

Oh, God, she thought in despair. Was she cursed, damned? How could this have happened to her, where could it possibly lead? She mustn't give in to this, *must not.*

"Alisa, Alisa, Alisa," he muttered. "Love isn't for me. I have obligations you can't understand. God, how I wish you could."

She shook her head, hating the difference between the sexes, the double standards that allowed men to rove among women like a bee in blossoms, while a woman must struggle with honor and propriety. "No, Riordan, I don't understand. I can't."

∽❦15❦∽

Alisa brushed a hand tiredly through her thick hair, pushing a stray curl away from her forehead. It was nearly May, the day unseasonably humid. Gusts of warm, moist Lake Michigan air blew in through the mansion's open windows, teasing the papers that lay on Alisa's long table. She'd spent most of the day writing letters and she felt smudgy and sticky with ink.

Seven months had passed since the Great Fire, but Riordan had never moved his offices. He seemed content to work at home, insisting that the capacious house was far more comfortable than any office, and it saved him time to have his work so close at hand. Often he worked until midnight or later, the despair of the burly butler, Smeede, whose job it was to bring him the endless cups of coffee that Riordan demanded to sustain his energy.

Gradually, under Alisa's direction, the once-haphazard offices had assumed new efficiency. Each clerk now had his own comfortable cubicle in the former ballroom, and Will Rice a small office. Alisa's own library quarters held wooden file cabinets and shelves where she stored books and ledgers, and could find them at a moment's notice.

Riordan's inner room, with its bright Persian rugs, was a haven of leather chairs and dark paneling. In a glass-enclosed cabinet he had placed several new acquisitions: a rare edition of the *Histoire Heliodore* worth six thousand dollars, and an illuminated Byzantine manuscript of the New Testament in Greek valued at fourteen thousand dollars.

Alisa had been surprised when Riordan had purchased these treasures. But then, she always found her employer surprising. He was aggressive, proud, demanding, thoughtful, serious. Wry, with a bitter tinge to his humor sometimes, as if he had suffered some deep pain in the past.

Now she rose from her table, smoothing the folds of her blue poplin dress. Fifine had designed it, restraining her usual penchant for ornamentation to produce a simple, flattering gown. With Alisa as her first customer, the Frenchwoman had begun a small dressmaking and millinery business, working out of Alisa's home.

The arrangement worked out well. Alisa needed Fifine's presence for respectability, and Fifine needed a place to live, as well as work space.

But there were times when the autocratic Fifine sorely tried Alisa's patience.

"So he has a mistress, eh?" the Frenchwoman was fond of saying. "And probably more than one, if the truth were known! A fluffy little actress, pfah, it's so typical of men! He keeps her, and he'll keep you, too, Alisa, if he can. Until he tires of you."

"He ... he isn't ... I'm not ... I'm his employee, no more," Alisa had sputtered.

Fifine had shrugged, her gesture maddeningly French. "Some men like to find their lovemaking close to them, so they do not have to leave the comfort of their homes."

Alisa had bitten back an angry reply. Was Fifine hinting again about her relationship with Alisa's father? But Alisa didn't want to picture her adored father as having a mistress, especially not one like Fifine, and she had struggled to block this out of her mind. Just as she had also blocked away thoughts of Riordan and his women, and the troubling presence of the baby in the upstairs nursery.

"Did you go through those ledgers as I requested?" Will Rice greeted her in the hallway.

"I did, and Riordan has them now," she told the lanky accountant, displaying her hands, her right palm and forefinger stained with ink. "Look at my smudges. I feel like a chimney sweep."

As Will grinned and disappeared into the clerks' room, Alisa continued up the wide staircase, intending to freshen up. A bubbling ripple of baby laughter stopped her at the top of the stairs.

Alisa stopped. At the far end of the long corridor, where small-paned windows created oblong patterns of May light, a woman played with a small child.

It was a pretty picture, the dark-haired baby holding up chubby hands to her nurse, giggling in delight. Alisa caught her breath, knowing that this was the little girl that Riordan had shown her months ago, when she had first come to the mansion.

Several times since then Alisa had heard the crying of a baby, and once, the soft crooning of the nurse. But the child was apparently a contented one, her noises few, and Riordan had made it clear he did not wish her to interfere.

Now, however, Alisa watched as the nurse put the nine-month-old baby down and helped her to toddle a few steps. The little girl gurgled in triumph, and the nurse encouraged her with soft laughs. It was early for a baby to be toddling, and Alisa felt her heart squeeze hard.

She could not longer deny it. This was Riordan's daughter, she felt sure of it. Why else would he go to all this trouble to provide a home for an infant? But who was the baby's mother? Linette Marquis? One of the other women who sent Riordan perfumed notes?

Alisa's thoughts blackened for a moment. She found that she had started toward the nurse, who was the same worn-looking woman named Fanny that she had encountered before.

"What a beautiful baby," she remarked.

Fanny smiled and stooped to pick up the child. From the woman's arms, the baby stared at Alisa with bright, unafraid eyes. Black eyes like Riordan's, Alisa saw with another strange trembling thrill. The child's silken hair was as dark as her father's, and her chin, feminine and delicate, had Riordan's cleft. But was there anything of Linette?

Anxiously Alisa searched the baby's immature features.

"Beautiful? Oh, yes, and so good," Fanny boasted. "Baby hardly ever cries."

"I've noticed that." They shared a smiling moment, two women drawn together in admiration of a pretty baby. Suddenly the child reached out both hands, begging to be held.

Alisa took the little girl into her arms. The child's hair had been freshly washed, and there was a sweet, sunny, milky odor about her that gave Alisa another wrenching twist of the heart.

"What is her name?"

Fanny looked bewildered. "Why, we just call her Baby."

"Baby?" Holding the firm, solid infant, Alisa felt her mouth drop open. "Surely she has a name!"

The woman shrugged. "None that he ever told us, anyway. She's Baby to us."

Alisa felt stunned at the cold carelessness of a man who could keep a child all these months without naming her. As Fanny reached out to take the baby back, she pleaded, "Please, could I walk her for a bit, visit with her? Surely you must be very busy, and it would give you a chance to sit down for a while and take a break."

Fanny hesitated. "He might not like it. He's fussy about her, he wants everything just so."

"Except her name," Alisa remarked angrily. "I'll take excellent care of her, I promise. I'll have her back in fifteen minutes if you like."

"Oh, all right. Bring her to the nursery, then, when you're done. But mind you don't let Mr. Daniels see you. He told us not to show her about, not until he decides what to do about her."

Thoughtfully Alisa took the baby and walked to

the end of the hall. Holding her, she stood at the mullioned window and looked down on a back garden, where hedges and flowering cherry trees surrounded a marble fountain.

Statues of plump, half-naked nymphs played about a splashing column of water. As always, in this extravagant mansion, there were too many nymphs, and they were too ornate, but the total effect, Alisa decided, was gentle and pleasing.

The baby saw the silvery motion of the water and crowed in delight, waving small fists.

Charmed, Alisa hugged her. "Do you like the fountain? Oh, Baby . . ." She stopped. "I can't keep calling you Baby, it's a ridiculous name, like calling a cat 'Cat.' You ought to have something prettier."

As if in agreement, the child gurgled.

Alisa laughed. "Oh, you *want* a name, do you? Well, I'm going to give you one. Let's see . . . what should it be? It must sound beautiful, of course, because you are. Eleanor? No. Victoria? Julia? No, none of those are right."

She gazed out of the window at the gentle nymphs, lost in thought, her mind taking her to a marble boy, a remembered soft voice. Finally she said, "My mother was named Tessa. Yes, that sounds as if it could be you. Anyway, why not?"

The little girl laughed, and Alisa hugged her. "Tessa, I think you and I are going to get along together wonderfully."

She put the child down and walked her for a few minutes as the nurse had done, the tiny fists clinging trustfully to Alisa's fingers. But a cloud marred Alisa's pleasure in this simple, loving act.

Who *was* Tessa? How had she come here, what was her story? But there were no answers. Finally, reluctantly, she delivered her back to the nursery.

"I'm going to come back tomorrow for a while," she announced to the surprised Fanny. "That will give you a rest. I'm sure you won't object."

The woman nodded.

"And she isn't to be called Baby anymore. Her name is Tessa."

"Tessa?"

"That's right. And if he objects to it, then let him talk to me."

Later that afternoon, back in the library-office, Alisa dealt with a steady stream of visitors. One was an architect who wished to consult with Riordan concerning design details on a new bank building that Riordan was putting up.

Carter LaRiviere, born in New Orleans, was a fashionable architect who had designed homes for many of Chicago's leading citizens, including Cousin Malva. He had studied his art in Paris, and was renowned for the serene, tasteful elegance of his designs.

Now, exploding from behind the closed door of Riordan's private office, Alisa heard familiar, angry shouts—many of Riordan's callers, it seemed, lost their tempers. Then the architect himself hurtled out of the door. He was about forty, a dapper, dark-haired man now red-faced with fury.

"You have no taste!" he shouted back at Riordan. "You are . . . Pfah! *Nouveau, nouveau riche!* The bigger and more ostentatious, the more expensive, the more dripping with gilt, the better you like it.

Like this overdone mansion. It's atrocious! Have you never heard of good taste? Refinement? Art?"

"The hell with art," Riordan's voice came coldly. "My building is going to house a bank and I want it to impress the depositors."

"Impress! Impress!" The tempermental architect beseeched Alisa. "Am I right, Miss Amsell? Is he not just impossible?"

"Why . . . I am sure . . ."

Riordan himself appeared in the door of his office, his brows beetled together. Plainly he was not pleased to have his home insulted and his taste called *nouveau riche*. "I don't think we have anything more to discuss, Mr. LaRiviere. Obviously I made a mistake in hiring you to work on my projects. I'm certain you'll be as happy as I when I tell you that I'm going to replace you with someone else. Good day, Mr. LaRiviere."

The architect cursed under his breath and walked quickly out. Riordan glared after him. "Well?" he snapped to Alisa. "I suppose you agree with him?"

Alisa privately did consider the mansion to be far too showy and ornate, and she herself had once called Riordan *nouveau riche,* a fact of which she was uncomfortably aware. Indeed, today she had also intended to confront Riordan for his arrogance in keeping an unnamed baby in his home.

Now quietly she held her tongue. She would discuss Tessa with Riordan when he was in a calmer, more tractable mood. Meanwhile, she intended to find out for herself who the baby's mother was. She'd put off thinking about it long enough, and now it was time to find out.

* * *

The following afternoon, Alisa stepped across the threshold of Mrs. Capeziano's dressmaking shop, causing a cheerful little bell to tinkle. She stood waiting to be noticed. A tiny waiting room held issues of *Godey's Lady's Book* and pictures of fashionable gowns that had been clipped from that publication and pasted to the walls. A doorway revealed a workroom where seamstresses worked on separate panels of a yellow ball gown, one applying velvet ribbon, two others adding beadwork and embroidery.

Maria Capeziano came hurrying out of a fitting room to greet her caller.

"Miss ... Amsell, is it? Ah, yes, the lady for whom I provided the theater dress at short notice last fall. It is nice to see you again, and I hope that we will be able to please you."

The dark-haired widow, now clad in dove-gray "half-mourning," ushered Alisa into a tiny office littered with paper patterns, dress forms, and scraps of material and ribbons. Her jet hair glistened like a bird's wing, pulled into a knot at the nape of her neck.

If anything, Maria Capeziano seemed more attractive than Alisa remembered, and she felt a red flush creep up from her neckline as she wondered if Riordan, too, had noticed this. Had he taken the pins out of that black, black hair, allowing it to stream over white shoulders? ...

With a shudder, she chopped away the thought.

"Would you like tea? Cake? Perhaps some lemonade?" the dressmaker asked.

"No, thank you, I haven't come here to buy a

dress. I need information, and, frankly, I didn't know where else to turn."

"Information? What do you want to know?"

Alisa bit her lip, wondering how to begin, how it could possibly be said. "I want to know who is the mother of . . . of a certain infant."

"Yes?" Did Maria Capeziano seem to freeze slightly, or was it only Alisa's imagination? "What makes you think that *I* might know?"

Oh, Alisa thought, her throat squeezing, there was no way to say this tactfully. Still, an impulse too strong to be merely curiosity drove her, and she struggled to find words.

"I thought perhaps . . . sometimes when a woman gives birth to a child she does not wish to keep it for . . . for economic reasons, or perhaps because she has no husband . . ."

Maria Capeziano drew herself tall, fixing Alisa with a steely look. "Such things do happen, yes. But not to those who are prudent. I personally have never been able to bear a child, so I do not know the problems involved. Now, Miss Amsell, if you are quite finished with your questions—"

"No!" Alisa spoke hastily. "I'm not. I mean . . . I was hoping you could tell me about Linette Marquis."

"Linette *Marquis?*"

"Yes. I . . . I know Linette comes to you, that you sew regularly for her, that you might know something of her history, or be able to direct me to others who do. People who . . . who are aware of gossip."

"Gossip!" Her patience clearly at an end, Maria Capeziano tightened her lips. Her black eyes flashed. "Miss Amsell, I'm sure you meant well in coming to me, but I assure you, I know nothing about Linette Marquis' personal affairs, nor do I wish to. I have made her a number of gowns. She is a good customer. I don't ask any questions. As far as I know, she does not have a child and never has had. If you want to find out more, I suggest that you go somewhere else."

She rose, plainly dismissing Alisa.

"But . . where? Whom should I talk to?"

"You ask me to recommend a person who knows gossip, but I know of no such person. I'm only a common dressmaker, while you have access to far more powerful persons."

She meant, of course, Riordan Daniels. The women eyed each other, and it was plain that Mrs. Capeziano was offended, but Alisa did not intend to be intimidated. She fixed her intensely blue eyes on the young dressmaker.

"I cannot go to Mr. Daniels. Who else could talk to me about Linette Marquis?"

"Try the stage manager then," Mrs. Capeziano said unwillingly. "At the theater where she works. He may talk to you if you pay him. But I'd advise you not to let Miss Marquis know you're inquiring about her. She has a nasty temper—I do know that much about her. And, please, Miss Amsell, do not come back here asking me such things again."

Alisa left the shop. On the street, shoppers hurried back and forth, and a sausage vendor and peanut girl cried out their wares, competing for customers.

She turned and quickly walked the ten blocks to the old opera house, where playbills announced a production of *Forty Thieves* and a performance of *Macbeth*. The front doors of the theater were locked, for there was no matinee today, but a carriage alley ran behind the building. Here the stage door opened on an untidy brick courtyard.

Alisa walked boldly in, ignoring the stares of two scene painters who were perched on a scaffolding at the back of the theater. As she had observed before, the old opera house was shabby beyond measure, its back walls composed of crumbling, moldy brick. Despite the warm May afternoon, chilly shadows lurked in the corners. Alisa was almost certain she saw a rat scurry across the wings and disappear behind a sandbag.

She shuddered, thinking of the sharp contrast between the glamour of the performance and the gritty reality of backstage. It was hard to imagine the imperious Linette working in such sordid surroundings.

"Could you tell me where I can find the stage manager?" She called the question to one of the scene painters.

"Mr. Henkel? He's in his office—thatta way." The man grinned and pointed. Alisa followed his directions to a scruffy little office in which an ancient hole had been knocked through plaster, giving the room's occupant a peephole view of backstage. A battered desk held piles of scripts, old playbills, and rolls of printed tickets.

"Well, hel*lo*! Who have we here? A pretty creature here to apply for a role?" Henkel had a bony, handsome face, a mane of wavy blond hair heavily combed with pomade, and the deep, resonant voice of a male thespian. He eyed Alisa with consider-able interest.

"I'm not here for a job." Alisa reached into her purse to extract an envelope which she laid down on the desk, a few bills peeking discreetly from its flap. Not for nothing had she pressed out bribes to councilmen at Conley's gambling house. "I want information."

"Yes?" Henkel pocketed the envelope. He closed his office door and leaned against it, waiting.

Alisa began, "There is a child, a baby—I am trying to learn who her mother is."

"Yes?"

"I . . . I wonder if . . . that is, there is an actress playing here . . . Linette Marquis . . ."

"Linette?" As Mrs. Capeziano had done, Henkel also looked incredulous. "Oh, ho! Our Linette, she's a lot of things, but Mama isn't one of 'em!" To Alisa's dismay, he began to laugh, running one hand through his mane of hair.

"But . . . couldn't it be possible somehow?"

"You have to be joshing me. Linette, pregnant? That woman is too careful! As far as I know, she's never missed a performance, and she certainly doesn't have a kid—not unless she's got it hidden in her stage trunk!"

"But the child wouldn't be living with her."

The manager shrugged. He leaned toward Alisa. "Hey. Do you know what it'd be like for an actress to try to raise a baby? Trying to wash out diapers in hotel rooms and do God knows what other motherhood chores in railway cars and dressing rooms? Oh, no. Our Linette is too ambitious to be stuck like that."

"I . . . I see."

Henkel grinned, pulling out a pocket watch to glance at it. "Sorry I can't talk longer, but I have costume fittings. Thanks for the funds, they'll come in real handy. And come on back sometime, if you want more 'information.' Or even a job. Yes, you'd do as a chorus girl, honey."

Alisa left the theater and took a horse car home, feeling frustrated and uneasy. Linette Marquis had never had a child, nor, apparently, had Maria Capeziano. Did Tessa belong to someone Alisa didn't know about?

And what business is it of yours anyway? she asked herself. But she knew that she still wanted to know.

That Sunday, Alisa went riding with Matt, who had sent her a message saying that he wanted to talk with her. She reread the note, wondering what her former suitor wanted to discuss. She'd seen little of him since she had encountered him at the theater. She'd presumed he was now interested in Charity Palmer, and that was fine with her.

"You're looking as beautiful as ever, Alisa," Matt said, handing her into his runabout, then swinging up himself. "Work hasn't spoiled your looks, it appears. When are you going to forget this foolishness and settle down?"

"Never," she told him lightly, settling her skirts on the soft leather seat and breathing deeply of the May afternoon.

They drove toward Lake Michigan. The windy spring day was beguiling, the rural fringes of the

city fragrant with daffodils, new grass, and forsythia.

For a while they exchanged small talk, and Alisa
asked about some of Matt's insurance clients who
had gone bankrupt because of the fire, a topic
that interested her. They talked of Matt's ambition to enlarge his practice, catering only to a few
rich clients.

However, finally Matt sighed. "I thought it necessary to talk to you, Alisa." He had pulled the
carriage toward a view of docks, Illinois Central
railway tracks, blue lake, and rolling whitecaps.
On the horizon, a flotilla of white-sailed schooners,
looking like tiny toys, inched toward the state of
Michigan. A breeze spanked at the rim of Alisa's
hat, so that she had to hold it with both hands.

"Oh," she said flatly. She wasn't sure she wanted
a talking-to from Matt.

"Your behavior, Alisa, is beginning to cause
whispers. You are employed by that renegade
Riordan Daniels, and you work all day at his house,
and have been seen leaving it at shockingly late
hours."

"We work late."

"Well, it isn't seemly. Not for a lady, a woman of
your name and position! Thank God the gossip
isn't widespread yet, and people still seem to regard you kindly. But I have heard that you went
to the opera house and applied for a job as an
actress!"

"*What!*" Alisa threw back her head and laughed,
merriment rippling out of her in great, healing
waves. "Oh, Matt, Matt. That wasn't it at all. I

merely went to the theater on another errand, and—"

"Well, it isn't the only strange place you've been seen. What about Conley's gambling house? And you've traveled alone, more than once, to Indiana. What do you do there? And that's not all. I've heard that you are now in the construction business. The *construction business!*" Matt looked indignant. "One of my clients tells me that you actually deal with builders."

"And what's wrong with that? It happens to be part of Riordan's business."

Matt threw out his hands impatiently. "Perhaps. Alisa, I was your father's attorney as well as his friend, and I am still your suitor. I would marry you tomorrow, and I think you know that."

As the wind gusted a little whirlwind of sand toward them, Alisa felt a spurt of irritation. How possessive Matt could be sometimes! She reached out to touch his arm, feeling the tenseness of his muscles beneath the fabric of his coat.

"Matt, I thank you for your . . . your concern. But you don't need to worry about me. I have had dealings with a brickyard in Fort Wayne, Indiana. That's why I go there. I'm selling the bricks here in Chicago and making a nice profit from them. I intend to go on doing so until I earn enough to get my father's mill back."

Matt pulled away to stare at her incredulously. "Alisa!"

"Well, I told you I was going to do it."

"Yes, but . . . it's foolish, it's stupid. You're only a girl. You don't know anything about—"

"About business?" she mocked. "But I'm learning a lot. And I've already begun to make money."

"And what does Riordan Daniels think of this fine ambition of yours?"

"He doesn't know," she admitted shamefacedly.

"Ah! Alisa, do you realize what you're doing? Do you realize . . . ?" Matt's freckled complexion grew ruddy with anger. "That man is no one to fool with. He has dealt mercilessly with his business enemies, giving them no quarter. Can't you understand that?"

She lifted her chin. "I understand it, all right, but I haven't done anything to wrong Riordan Daniels. I bought every brick with my own money and I have made all arrangements on my own personal time, so that he cannot claim I've slacked off on my job."

"But you're doing it in secret."

"Yes, but . . ."

Matt shook his head. "I can tell you this. Riordan Daniels is a man who doesn't enjoy being fooled. He doesn't like things going on behind his back. Sooner or later he's going to find out what you're doing, and when he does . . ."

"I don't want to talk about it," Alisa said, feeling suddenly chilly. She gripped her bonnet against a new onslaught of gusty spring wind. Was Matt right? Was she treading into dangerous territory?

But it was too late now to stop, and she knew she didn't want to.

⚌16⚌

Summer passed in a blaze of heat, filled for Alisa with grindingly hard work. Using the pretext of her "sick aunt," she managed two more trips to the brickyard, and encouraged Pots to add another tunnel-kiln to increase their output.

At home, she converted a corner of her bedroom into a tiny office, and sat there every night bent over ledgers until exhaustion finally drove her to sleep. But already her profits were growing. Taking Riordan's example, she invested some of them in livestock and grain, making sharp gains.

Time, Alisa reflected. She had too little of it, constantly forced to juggle her responsibilities, living in the terror that Riordan would discover what she did.

But Riordan did not seem to notice the circles beneath her eyes from lack of sleep, only demanding more of her, working her as mercilessly as he did himself.

One afternoon in early October 1872, Will Rice, the chief accountant, peered around the corner of Alisa's work area, frowning.

"Miss Amsell? Are you finished with those letters yet?"

Alisa looked up. "Why, no, Will, I'll probably be at them for the rest of the day. I'm to write more than fifty of them."

"Then you must just leave them. I want to talk to you."

"I told you, Mr. Daniels has asked me to finish this series of letters; he wishes to contact each of his investors for a—"

"Nonetheless, I must talk to you." The usually taciturn accountant seemed insistent, and finally Alisa sighed, putting aside the pile of correspondence. She rose and followed Will into the corridor.

"He has gone out to a meeting of the bank directors," Will told Alisa unnecessarily, for she was privy to all of her employer's activities. "But I would still like privacy for this conversation, so I have ordered up a buggy. I thought we would go for a drive."

A drive? In the middle of a hectic working day? Alisa felt her heart sink, the more so when she glanced at Will Rice's sober face, his lips pressed together in a tight line. A knot of guilty apprehension clenched her stomach, but she forced herself to go to the cupboard where she kept her outdoor clothing, and slipped into a semifitted jacket.

She had pasted a small mirror to the inside of the cupboard and she stared at her pale face in its glass before closing the door again. Will knew. That had to be the reason he wanted to talk to her in privacy. Somehow she'd have to deal with him.

The buggy had already been driven up in front of the mansion, and a stableboy stood by to hand

Will the buggy whip and to help Alisa in. In a rustle of petticoats, she settled herself in the passenger seat, thinking that this was the way it always was. The man drove, while the woman was a pampered and subservient rider.

Impulsively, before Will could swing up, she slid over, taking the whip and reins. "I'll drive."

"But—"

"Since this buggy belongs to our employer, rather than to you or to me, it doesn't matter which of us drives, does it? And I prefer to do so."

Will looked as if he would protest, but Alisa lifted the reins and smiled at him, well pleased with her victory. As driver, she held a subtle advantage, for she would be in control of their route and speed.

They started toward the wrought-iron gate, which the boy held open until they had passed through in a rattle of buggy wheels. It was a cool October morning, the sky brilliant aquamarine, piled to the east with massed cumulus clouds. Red maples formed a vivid burst of fall color, and a hedge of flame bushes added to the autumn palette.

Alisa slapped the reins, urging the horse to a brisk trot that took them quickly out of the residential neighborhood. Instinctively she turned east, toward the burned area.

It always cheered Alisa to look at the extensive rebuilding that was going on in the fire-scarred city, some of it through her own efforts. They drove past half-finished buildings studded with scaffolding, on which carpenters and bricklayers swarmed. Most of the rubble had now been carted away, and piles of marble and brick were stored everywhere, symbolic of a new beginning.

A new block of saloons and small shops had gone up, and they saw a sign painter who teetered on a ladder to nail up a sign announcing the opening of a place called Peck's. As the *Tribune* had morosely reported, a year after the Great Fire, Chicago could count precisely 2,218 saloons, one for every 150 inhabitants. And the bricks for this particular one were Pots's—or, she amended quickly, hers.

A brewery wagon swerved toward them, and Alisa deftly avoided it, jouncing both of them to the left.

"All right," Will sighed, grabbing the buggy's side for support. "You've proved your point, Miss Amsell, you've certainly taken the reins today— literally as well as figuratively. But that still doesn't excuse the fact that you have been using Riordan Daniels' influence to feather your own nest."

Alisa's heart lurched. "Whatever are you talking about?"

"Don't try to bluff me, I know all about it. You've bought a brickyard, haven't you? You're selling your bricks all over town, making a pretty penny at it, I've no doubt."

In the space of a few seconds, Alisa's mind advanced and rejected a dozen defenses. To cover her confusion and give herself extra time, she turned the buggy to cross a newly rebuilt drawbridge over the South Branch of the Chicago River. But for once she was unable to savor the brawny confusion of barges, boats, lumber schooners, and warehouses that usually drew her eye.

"Well?" the accountant demanded. "What have you to say for yourself "

Despite the crisp fall air, Alisa felt perspiration spring out on her skin, trickling down her sides. How much did Will know of her activities? What did he want? But she mustn't let him suspect her fright, not if she hoped to deal with him.

Quickly she decided to tell the truth, sensing that here lay her only real defense.

"I can't deny the facts, Mr. Rice," she said evenly. "Yes, I've been dealing for some months with Mr. Pots Ogden's brickyard in Indiana, and I've bought sizable shipments of bricks, which I did sell here in Chicago for an excellent profit. I don't own the yard yet, only a small share, but my ambition is to take it over one day."

"Go on," Will said.

"I need help, Mr. Rice, with my construction business. It has grown too big for one person to handle. In fact, I was thinking of taking on a partner."

"Indeed?"

"Would you be interested?" As she said this, Alisa tried not to betray her tenseness. What she was proposing was, of course, treachery for Will as well as for herself. They were both Riordan Daniels' employees, and as such were expected to cleave only to him, putting his interests first.

Will's expression looked unyielding. "Do you realize just what you're asking of me, Miss Amsell? Riordan Daniels demands and gets the full devotion of every person who works for him. If he doesn't . . ." The accountant's shrug was eloquent. "On the other hand, I do have a family, you know, and my wife has been ill with consumption. Her physician has recommended an extended cruise and the hiring of extra servants."

"I . . . I see." Alisa swallowed hard. Will must intend to blackmail her, then. Oh, she'd been afraid of this! For the first time her courage faltered, and her fingers tightened on the reins, her flesh hurting with the desperate strength of her grip.

"I will allow no one to blackmail me, Mr. Rice."

"Ah? And did I suggest such a thing?"

"No, but you implied it. Legally I have done nothing wrong. I give Riordan twelve hours a day of hard work. I am *not* a criminal or a wrongdoer, and the worst you can do is to cause me to lose my job. I assure you, I'll get another one easily."

Rice's expression changed. "I know that, Miss Amsell. I have been watching you since you came to work for Mr. Daniels, and you work as hard as he does. I suspect that you are nearly as bold. I like that. I had you followed last week when you went to Indiana, that's how I know about the Ogden brickyard. I want in. I have some savings . . ."

Wanting to laugh aloud with sheer relief, Alisa pulled the buggy to a halt. She stared at the lanky accountant. He wanted to be her partner, not her blackmailer. He even wanted to add to her capital base. With two of them, and with Will's money and further contacts, she could accomplish so much more.

"Very well, then," she told him cautiously. "Perhaps we can work something out. But *I* will be the one in charge. Understand that now, and we will be able to work together."

* * *

Late that night, exhaustion pulling at her shoulders and neck, Alisa climbed the stairs to her bedroom. It has been a long, tiring day. After her confrontation with Will Rice, there had been an argument with the surly clerk, Bochert, over an assignment she had given him. As if that weren't enough, even Riordan had been short-tempered, sunk deep into one of the black moods that periodically plagued him for no apparent reason.

As she climbed the stairs, tiredly she began unbuttoning her dress. There were still entries to make in her ledgers, and a letter to compose to Pots Ogden.

She reached her room and, sighing, allowed the familiar setting to surround her like balm. In one corner was her desk, its pigeonholes bristling with papers. On the wall, looking down at her with serious eyes, hung a daguerreotype of her father. A few months ago Alisa had found it in a shop, saved from the Great Fire by a photographer who had tossed his phtographic plates into a wagon and battled his way across the State Street Bridge.

Glancing, as always, at the picture, she stripped off her dress and tossed it onto a chair. As she did so, she became aware of something amiss.

A musky odor seemed to float in the room like a memory of frangipani, barely perceptible to the senses. Alisa paused to sniff, a little shiver of unease running through her. Fifine wore a flowery home-made cologne, and her maid, Nella, wore no perfume at all. And was she mistaken, or did the portrait of her father hang an inch crookedly?

Another woman had been in her room.

Drawing another deep breath, she felt even more

sure of it. In her petticoats, Alisa strode barefoot down the corridor to Fifine's workroom, from which she had seen a light when she first entered the house.

"*Oui?*" Despite the lateness of the hour, Fifine responded to her knock.

Alisa burst into the room. "Has one of your customers been in my bedroom? Because I can smell her scent in the air, it's very disturbing."

She stopped, startled. There were two women wedged into the crowded work space. One, of course, was Fifine, perched on a high stool, draping red velvet around a hat brim. The other was her plump maidservant. "Nella! What are you doing here?"

The woman started guiltily. "I . . . She needed extra help, and I . . ."

Alisa looked at Fifine. "But Nella already has a job, she is my maid. I didn't give her permission to trim hats for you."

"She was in the kitchen drinking coffee—at *your* expense," Fifine said defiantly. "And I had a rush job for one of the actresses at the opera house. So I thought, why not put Nella to work? So I did. I am going to give her a new bonnet for herself and perhaps a dress, too."

It had been a long, frustrating day. Alisa's temper flared. "But she isn't your employee, Fifine, she is mine. I pay her, I give *you* work space in my home!"

Fifine shrugged, her eyes dark, unreadable. "For which I am grateful. Ah, you are most generous, Alisa, just as your father was, and I appreciate it." Fifine lifted up the bonnet she was trimming. "Do you not think this is lovely? It is for Linette Marquis."

"Linette!" Alisa started. "Is she the one who was prowling about in my bedroom?"

"*Non.* Ah, *non,* she did not come here at all this week, did she, Nella?" Fifine looked at the German woman for confirmation, but Nella blushed hotly and looked downward at her lap.

Alisa sighed. "Nella, I must ask you to resume your regular duties in my house. If you don't wish to do so, then you're fired."

"Y-yes, miss." Looking frightened, Nella scurried out of the workroom. Fifine concentrated on the bonnet she was trimming, her lower lip set mutinously.

"I don't want Linette Marquis here again," Alisa told her.

"But she is my customer, *chérie.* Where else would she come, since my shop is here in your house?"

"I tell you, I don't want her here."

"But they all come when you are not here, what can that matter? They touch nothing of yours. As for Linette, she has said that she will talk up my hats among her actress friends. All I have to do is make her a new bonnet now and again. Surely you do not begrudge me such good fortune."

"I do not begrudge you anything, Fifine. But this is my home."

"Very well, then." Fifine's eyes flashed. "I will go to her, since you are being so foolish."

Alisa turned and left, feeling abruptly disgusted with herself. She had smelled perfume in her bedroom, and had lashed out at both Fifine and

Nella. But wasn't the real source of her anger elsewhere?

She knew she was really angry at Riordan, for his dalliances with Linette and other women, for forcing her into subterfuge and lies.

And for causing her to love him, she added to herself bleakly. That, too.

The grand opening of the new Chamber of Commerce building was to be held October 9. There would be a huge parade, ceremonies, and speeches, including one by Mayor Medill, who had achieved election on a "fireproof" ticket.

As one of the building's main backers, Riordan also would speak, and Alisa decided to ask Malva to attend the dedication with her.

"I wouldn't miss a parade for anything," Malva declared. "And neither would my girls. Do you mind if I bring them too?"

It took a train of six carriages to transport the giggling and excited little girls, who ranged in age from three to fourteen, all of them agog at the prospect of the festivities. Malva seemed in her element, teasing, scolding, directing, kissing the top of one curly red head.

At Malva's suggestion, they stopped in a tearoom before the parade was to begin, and ordered plates full of tea cakes, and tea watered down with milk for the children. While the girls chattered, Alisa allowed her mind to stray to the opening-day ceremonies.

Her own part in this building was tiny in comparison to Riordan's, and no one knew about it save for Will. Still, her bricks had been used too, mostly in the interior, and it gave Alisa a feeling of pride. Alisa Amsell, a woman of barely twenty-one, was part of this important building.

And yet, what would Riordan say if he knew that, if he knew her trip here was more than a morning of fun with Malva's girls, or to hear his speech?

Finally Malva beckoned to the headwaiter and settled the bill. They left, the girls parading behind Malva in orderly pairs, Alisa bringing up the rear. It was a beguiling day with soft, moist lake breezes that smelled of burning leaves.

From somewhere could be heard drumrolls and the practice ripple of clarinets, while a crew of policemen hurried back and forth, attempting without success to clear the street of traffic so that the parade could begin. A popcorn man wheeled his wagon near the orphans, and Malva grandly bought up his entire wares for her charges.

They found places on the reviewing stands. "There is your employer," Malva pointed out. "My, what a good-looking man."

Craning her neck, Alisa spotted Riordan, sitting slightly aloof from the other dignitaries. His expression seemed brooding and remote and she wondered what dark thoughts occupied him.

Then he turned and saw her. A sweet half-smile curved his mouth, banishing the brooding look. Their eyes met in a brief moment of intimacy, despite the chattering orphan girls.

Alisa flushed and looked away. Riordan thought she was here to listen to his speech. He had no idea that she, too, had a stake in this building. . . .

The parade began with the stirring drumrolls

of a military band, the Chicago Dragoons. Others followed: the Highland Guards with their skirling bagpipes, the Zouaves with their gaudy Algerian uniforms and eccentric drill. Then came the fire companies, each flaunting their newest, shiniest steam engines and hook-and-ladder wagons, gloriously oblivious of the fact that this equipment had not been able to stem last year's Great Fire.

Alisa's attention lapsed, her eyes once more going to the back of Riordan's head. Yes, she thought, he was handsome. Next to him, the other dignitaries looked flabby and soft. She swallowed thickly. She knew she loved Riordan, deeply, helplessly, in a way she had never dreamed possible.

The thought frightened her. Where could such love lead? And what would happen when Riordan learned of her rising fortune, her part-ownership of a brickyard, her plans to buy back Papa's mill?

"Alisa!" Malva nudged her. "I declare, you might be staring at those fire wagons, but your thoughts are ten thousand miles away."

"I . . . I'm sorry."

"Are you sure everything is all right with you? Until today, I've seen hardly anything of you for months. You have utterly withdrawn from society. All you do, it seems, is work."

Alisa forced a smile. She loved Malva, but she couldn't talk to her now, not with the girls giggling and applauding, and Riordan seated only a few yards away, dominating the entire day with his presence. "I like to work," she finally said. "I thrive on it."

"Mmmmm. I wonder. Matt Eberley tells me you still have ideas of revenge in your head. He says—"

"Matt?" Alisa felt a spurt of annoyance. "When did you talk to him?"

"I saw him at the McCormicks' last week. He seemed worried about you."

"Well, he has no right to be!" Alisa snapped. "I'm getting along just fine, I'm doing what I want to do, and I'm happy." It was a rebuke meant for Malva as well.

"I see," Malva said stiffly. "Well, Alisa, I just hope you'll not allow yourself to become obsessed with something that should be let go and forgotten. Your father died by his own hand. It was tragic, but it happened nearly two years ago. Surely it's time for you to move on, and to think of other things."

The last of the fire companies had marched past in a jingle of music and noise, and Riordan rose to begin his talk, his deep voice projecting well into the bleachers. Alisa turned with relief to hear his speech. She wasn't obsessed—at least not in the way that Malva meant.

"Ladies and gentlemen," Riordan began. His broad, good-looking face was earnest with belief. "Chicago is going to rise again. Out of its ashes of despair, its debris of desolation . . ."

Forgetting her distress at the little quarrel with Malva, Alisa listened, stirred by the powerful and encouraging word pictures that Riordan drew. Of a vibrant waterfront city booming with industry, where fortunes waited to be made and life waited to be lived.

Afterward, while Malva shepherded her girls back toward their waiting carriages, Alisa sought out Riordan and told him how much she had enjoyed his speech.

"I suppose a good deal of it was exaggeration and hyperbole," he said thoughtfully. "But I meant what I said."

"I know you did. And it was inspiring—I know it filled me with enthusiasm."

"Good." Riordan cleared his throat. "I take it that you and Malva have some sort of plans for the little girls today? Why don't you take the rest of the day off so you can enjoy them?"

It was an unexpected kindness—often Riordan forgot that his employees, unlike himself, could grow tired. But a sudden mood of melancholy had swept through Alisa like a bleak autumn cloud. "I . . . I believe that Malva intends to take them back to her house so the littlest girls can take naps," she demurred. "As for myself, I think I'll go back to work."

"Work?" He gave her a look of respect. "Do you never take a break?"

"Seldom," she managed to say, mumbling an excuse and then hurrying off to take her farewells of Malva and the girls. Guilt seesawed within her. Riordan had given her a look of respect that she didn't deserve.

She was betraying him—well, wasn't that true? In fact, she had betrayed both men she loved, Papa by falling in love with Riordan, and Riordan by trying to avenge Papa.

She took a crowded horse car back to Riordan's mansion and walked into the library-office, shedding her outdoor garments almost with relief.

Work, she thought. No matter what else happened in her life, at least she had that.

But an hour later, Riordan still had not returned to the office and Alisa felt restless, pushing aside the long report on which she had been working. She decided to go upstairs and see Tessa.

"Yes? Oh, it's you, Miss Amsell. Come in." Fanny gave Alisa a tired smile. The nurse suffered from varicose veins, a fact she had concealed from her employer, and treasured Alisa's visits for the chance to put her feet up.

Already beginning to relax, Alisa let her gaze travel around the nursery. The baby's rooms were furnished lavishly in white and gold, with a crib adorned by an angel canopy, ornamented by silk roses. White-painted paneling was carved with designs picked out in gold leaf, and more gold leaf adorned the white furniture. Against one wall stood a glass case stuffed with rows of procelain-faced dolls.

It was a gilded prison, Alisa often thought, for Tessa rarely left these rooms except to go into the garden.

"Where's my Tessa? Where's my Tessa?" Alisa called out gaily, and was answered by a silvery baby giggle from the interior room. Then Tessa appeared in the doorway, stark naked. Her long white dress and an infant corset, with which little girls of good family were often fitted as early as nine months of age, dragged from one chubby hand.

"Oh, mercy!" Fanny cried out in shock at the child's nudity.

"Sa! Sa!" Tessa crowed in a baby approximation

of "Alisa," and toddled toward her visitor, her skin flawless peach, her body appealingly round, her tiny pink cleft adorable. As she came, Tessa tripped over the dress, sitting down on her rump.

Alisa darted forward to scoop up the naked baby girl. Holding Tessa, she bent to pick up the corset.

"Who put this on her?" She held up the satin garment, which had shirred ruffles along its sides and laces up the back. It was not boned, as it would be for an adult woman, but still the device looked uncomfortable, and Alisa saw a reddened, chafed area around the baby's midriff.

"Why . . . I did," Fanny said.

"But who told you to do it?"

The woman shrugged. "He did."

"Mr. Daniels told you to put a snug and confining corset on this little girl only a year old?"

Fanny sighed. "No, not exactly. But all her clothes were getting small and he told me to go out and buy her what she needed. So I went to Mr. Marshall Field's store and the salesclerk said this was proper, so I—"

"Never mind." Alisa took the offending garment and dropped it into a nearby wastebasket. "Tomorrow just dress her as usual in her little gowns—I'll do it today—and don't tell Mr. Daniels that you've left off the corset. I guarantee you he'll never even notice the difference, and she'll be much more comfortable."

"All right." Fanny nodded, and leaving Tessa in Alisa's care, went off down the back staircase to the kitchen, where she could put her feet up and sip tea.

Alisa was glad to see the nurse go. She enjoyed the task of redressing the wiggly, active little girl, who bounced up and down on her lap, making the job a challenge. But finally Tessa was dressed again, and Alisa brushed the child's soft, dark curls, taking her time, for she truly enjoyed her hours with Tessa, and stole up to the nursery nearly every day if she could.

She was seated in the inner room of the nursery suite telling Tessa a story, when she heard the sudden click of a door opening. Footsteps strode across flooring, and even before the inner door swung open, Alisa's heart had already squeezed into a hard, tight ball of apprehension. *Riordan.*

"What the . . . !"

He was as surprised to see her as she was to see him. They stared at each other blankly before Tessa finally broke the tension by crowing out a delighted "Da!"

"Did you hear that?" Alisa blurted the first words that popped into her head. "She says 'Daddy.' "

"What are *you* doing here?" Riordan demanded. He shouldered his way into the gold-and-white room, his maleness instantly making the space seem cramped and confined. "Who gave you permission to visit Baby?"

Alisa had treasured her brief moments of tranquillity, which now had been so roughly shattered. Further, she resented being treated as an intruder.

" 'Baby'?" she mocked.

"Yes, Baby. What's wrong with you, Alisa? I don't understand you. I gave you the afternoon off, but you refused to take it, insisting that you had to work. But instead of working I find you up here in the nursery—without invitation. If I had wanted you to visit, don't you think I would have requested it?"

Alisa lifted up the baby and put her back in her ornate crib, where Tessa immediately began to jump up and down, gripping the bars and squalling in protest.

Alisa drew herself up, fixing Riordan with a sweeping look. "I'm sorry I visited Tessa without your permission, but it seemed to me that the poor mite deserved some company. She's shut away here in your big mansion with no one to attend her but a nurse!"

Riordan's eyebrows flashed upward satanically. *"Tessa?"*

"Yes! I gave her a name, Riordan, since *you* didn't."

He looked startled, and Alisa's indignation gathered momentum. "I could hardly believe it when I first came and found that you were keeping a little human being here, without a name. The nurses were calling her Baby. Baby! Like Dog, or Cat. Riordan, it's scandalous. You treat her as less than a pet. At least a dog or a cat is allowed to go out in public, and isn't concealed upstairs like a criminal!"

"Enough!" Riordan commanded. A muscle in his jaw flickered. "Tessa," he added more quietly. "It sounds pleasant enough, even pretty."

"It's a lovely name! Tessa is a far nicer name than . . ." But Alisa refused even to repeat the word Baby. She stood glaring at Riordan, who finally nodded.

"Very well, then. I was derelict in that. Tessa it

will be." His sudden lopsided smile was unexpectedly sweet. Alisa fought a traitorous squeeze of her heart, and looked at the object of this discussion, who had plumped down in her bed and now was trying to suck on her own toes.

"Who *is* Tessa, Riordan? Is she your daughter? Why won't you acknowledge her, bring her out into the open and admit that you're keeping her here?"

Riordan's smile vanished. "I don't wish to discuss it."

"But you have to discuss it. Tessa is a person. She deserves decent treatment."

"She's getting decent treatment! Look around you, look at these rooms. Everything is here. Dolls. Toys. She has a capable nurse, who loves her. Clothes. All the food she can eat. She has—"

"Everything," Alisa interrupted recklessly, "except a mother and a father and playmates and fun and a normal life. Who is Tessa, Riordan? Is she your illegitimate—"

"Stop!" His words were a savage lash. "Stop before you say something you'll deeply regret. Yes, Tessa is illegitimate. That fact should be obvious."

Alisa faltered. "But . . . her mother . . ."

"Don't *press*, Alisa." Riordan's jaw gritted and for a quivering, awful moment she feared he would strike her. Yet she sensed that his anger was directed not toward her, but toward another.

"The 'mother,' if you can call her that, would have abandoned the child, wanting to use her only for her own purposes. I got there first and took her."

"I see. But then why—?"

"Because I'm waiting for the chance to establish her. Tessa, as you have named her, is a wonderful child, a beauty. Do you think that I don't appreciate that? That I don't love her and want the best for her? I do!"

"You certainly don't show it."

Riordan slammed a fist down on the dresser, the noise causing the child to wail. "Don't interfere, Alisa! I want things to go right for Tessa. *I* was illegitimate, and I know what it can mean."

"You?" She stared at him in stunned surprise.

"Are you so shocked? It's something that I rarely talk about, a fact I wish to forget. But it's certainly very true."

"But . . . how?" Alisa breathed.

"My mother was seduced by the son of a local banker, a man who happened to be married. She was a proud and sensitive woman, and when her condition became obvious, she tried to kill herself by slitting her wrists. She was saved in time from bleeding to death, but the scandal had already spread throughout our little town.

"Six months after I was born, she married my father, a poor farmer, the only man who would accept a 'by-blow,' a 'woods colt,' as such babies are called. He was good to me, but the town never forgot."

His voice lowered to a husky whisper. "Often I fought savagely against my tormentors. I bloodied plenty of noses, and did worse, too. Grown men were wary of me." Riordan shook his head from side to side like an angry bull. "I won't have that for Tessa. I will not. I'll kill anyone who hurts my baby!"

Riordan clenched his jaws and drew his brows together in a black glower, and Alisa realized that he meant exactly what he said. Sympathy flooded her and instinctively she reached out to touch his hand.

Her jerked his hand away as if she had offered him the flaming end of a candle. Then he turned on his heel and paced toward the ornately draped window, where he stood staring downward through the panes. When he turned, she saw the torment on his face.

"I'll solve everything for her—that was a promise I made to her the day I first saw her, so small and pretty and helpless. Now, let there be an end to your questions. I would like to finish my visit with my daughter, and I am sure you have work to finish downstairs."

It was dismissal. She was being sent away exactly like a servant, an employee, an underling. Or worse, an intruder into a situation where she did not belong. Hurt flooded Alisa, as sharp as thorny needles.

"Yes," she snapped, unable to help herself. "I do have work. I'm sorry I intruded here, and I won't do so again. My humble apologies," she flung out in a way that was not humble at all.

"Oh, Alisa . . ." For a moment it seemed that Riordan might reach out for her and fold her into his arms. But Alisa whirled away from him before that could happen, and left the nursery, stalking downstairs.

Restlessly she tried to work, but was unable to

concentrate. She pictured Riordan as a small, defiant boy fighting against taunts and ridicule. Was it that tough, sad background that had made him such a fighter, struggling against odds?

It was noble of him to want a better life for his child. But she wished he hadn't sent her from the nursery like an interloper. Hadn't he himself, when she first came to the mansion, taken her upstairs to see the baby? How could he be so cruel as to allow the child no visitors at all? What did he intend to *do* about Tessa?

Finally she rubbed both of her throbbing temples. Riordan Daniels was an enigma, a puzzling and contradictory man. But his life was not her concern, nor was his child.

If he chose to keep one mistress or ten, if he elected to keep fifteen babies imprisoned in the upper reaches of his big house, what business was it of hers? None. He had made that abundantly clear.

∽17∾

"Your luncheon guest has arrived, miss." A head-waiter, clad in spotless black and white, bowed to Alisa.

Alisa, on a tour of Riordan's stamping mills and the Amsell mill, had stopped in a small hotel dining room for a bite of lunch. She looked up startled. "My guest? I'm not expecting . . ."

"Hello, dearie. I'm sorry I was late, but that ill-tempered stage manager called an extra rehearsal and I couldn't get out of it." Linette Marquis bore down on her, flamboyant in green silk trimmed with frogged braid and silk roses, her skirt tiered and elaborate. She wore a velvet-trimmed hat that showed evidence of Fifine's handiwork.

"But I . . ." Alisa half-rose in dismay.

However, Linette seated herself and nodded at the headwaiter, indicating that he was to set another place. Diners were turning to stare at the actress, whose dark hair curled charmingly from beneath her bonnet and whose cheeks were delicately tinted with rouge, giving her the stylized prettiness of a drawing from *Godey's Lady's Book*.

"I happened to see you walk in, Miss Amsell. Or are you too fine, too *high society* to dine with me?"

"I had intended to eat alone."

Ignoring her lack of welcome, Linette leaned over to peer at Alisa's plate. "What are you having? Lamb chops? I might get those myself. And some French wine." She waved imperiously to the waiter. "Waiter! The wine list, please."

Alisa sighed, for Linette plainly intended to thrust her presence on her, and there was little that could be done about it without causing a public spectacle. And, she reflected grimly, Linette would probably enjoy that. What did the woman want? She supposed there was only one way to find out, and that was to endure this charade of a luncheon.

As the waiter poured them first one glass of wine, then another, Linette chattered volubly. Alisa found herself growing interested in the racy theater gossip and backstage intrigues laced with the names of celebrated actors such as Otis Skinner, Maurice Barrymore, and Fanny Davenport. The theater was obviously Linette's world. She had played her first role at six, in *Uncle Tom's Cabin*, under the tutelage of her parents.

"I'm a backstage rat," Linette said, shrugging. "It's the only thing I know, really."

As the actress talked, Alisa searched her face, trying to find a resemblance in it to Tessa. Surely there was a similarity in the eyes, the sweep of brow, the small, firm chin. . . . Or was there? Tessa was still a baby, too immature for any real resemblance to show itself yet. Besides, hadn't both Maria Capeziano and the stage manager told her that Linette had never borne a child?

Their plates were cleared away and coffee and dessert were brought. At last Linette came to the point. "I don't like you, you know."

Alisa started. "I concluded that."

The actress giggled. She was now on her third glass of wine, and the sound was so trilling and stagy that two men at an adjoining table gave her a curious look. "You know why, Miss Amsell, you're not stupid. It's him."

"Him?"

"Riordan, of course!" Linette leaned forward, her eyes narrowing. "He talks about you all the time. Talks about the bold Alisa Amsell, who is such a paragon at business, who can do the work of four men and still look sweet and charming and pretty. Who can even race a cutter against him, nearly injuring herself in her desire to win."

Linette spoke with such venom that Alisa nearly dropped her dessert fork. Riordan, talking about her at great length to this other woman? She could scarcely believe it.

She began to say so, but Linette was going on. "He has told me all about your family background . . . *blue-blooded* to the core," Linette mocked. "John Adams! Abigail Adams! Nicholas Biddle! Oh, you come from snobbish stock, don't you? Far from the likes of me. My great-grandmother was a London whore."

Alisa did not know what to say.

Linette lifted her wineglass and drained its contents, motioning to the waiter to pour more. "Why do you work for him, anyway? When you could be out hobnobbing with a bunch of fat, diamond-decked millionaires?"

Alisa flushed. "I am no millionaire. I work for Riordan because I need the money. Further, I'm lucky to be under his tutelage. He is—"

"He is rich," Linette interrupted. "That's what you mean. Rich, rich, *rich!* That's what you're really interested in, aren't you? His money."

Alisa pushed away her untouched pie. "I'm late, I really must leave—"

Linette's strong, trained voice held her like a cord. "Don't lie to me. *I* know what you are. You've got background but no money. Your father's suicide turned you into a pauper. Now you think you're going to marry him and take everything he has, don't you? Well, I have news for you. You're not."

"I don't want to marry him," Alisa insisted over the clink of cutlery and decorous restaurant chatter.

Linette's lips twisted. "He said that about me once. Can you imagine? 'We are too different,'" she mocked viciously. "No one says that about me. No one!"

As Alisa shifted uncomfortably, Linette grinned. "But now that's over with. I have the beginning of what I want with Riordan, and I intend to get more. I have plans. Do you hear me? *I have plans.*"

"What do you mean?"

But grandly and with expert timing, Linette rose from the table. From a brocaded, bead-embroidered purse she pulled out a handful of bills and dropped several on the table, a payment far in excess of the value of their lunch and the tip.

"Why should I tell you? You're only his employee," Linette sneered. "His sweet little society assistant, playing at work, impressing him with your prettiness and your courage and your *name*." Each word was like a slap. "Well, play all you want, Miss Amsell. *I* have him now. I intend to keep him. No matter what you do."

She was gone, sweeping away from the table with as much drama as her entrance, leaving Alisa to stare after her. What a bizarre conversation it had been! Had Riordan really told Linette that he would not marry her? Alisa tried to imagine such a conversation and failed.

A sudden shiver overtook her, rippling across the pores of Alisa's skin like a fingernail across silk. *I have plans.* The actress's words echoed unpleasantly in her head.

As several weeks passed, Alisa pondered her conversation with Linette, going over and over it in her thoughts, to put it aside at last in frustration. Linette was surely a spiteful, jealous woman, but the actress's relationship with Riordan, whatever it was, was not Alisa's concern. Riordan was no longer her lover. He had the right to do as he pleased. And if thoughts of him tormented her in the night, causing her to toss and turn restlessly, that was no one's fault but her own.

As for Tessa, Riordan had made it clear where she stood there: she had no right to visit the baby, was an interloper in the nursery, unwelcome there.

Proudly Alisa forced her mind back to plans for her own business. Her partnership with Will Rice looked as it if would be profitable. While on other errands for Riordan, Will had managed to make several important sales for the brickyard. He returned one afternoon in triumph to tell Alisa that he had gotten a lead on another brickworks that had just gone up for sale.

"It's ours, Miss Amsell, if we can raise the capital. And I think we should grab it. Chicago is exploding with new construction, it needs all the building materials it can get. Why shouldn't we provide them?"

Alisa couldn't have agreed more. Besides, to own a second brickyard would be that much more victory over Riordan. Damn him for the way he made her feel! "How much capital can we raise?"

"I have a small inheritance and my wife has some money set aside, as well. We'd like to put in as much as we can." Will named a figure.

"But, Will," Alisa couldn't help saying, "you said your wife has been ill. You know this is risky. If he should find out, I can't guarantee your job."

The man shrugged. "I know too much about his business, I'm too valuable to him. He'll never fire me."

Remembering Riordan's quick temper, Alisa wondered. But she needed Will Rice, and with the money the Rices could put in, her own fortune would grow that much faster. Her mind quickly assessed her own assets. Although many these days were speculating heavily in railroads and bank notes, Riordan said that such practices were risky. He preferred to keep his own holdings in tangible items such as factories, livestock, and grain. Alisa had imitated him, and would have to sell some of these in order to buy the brickworks.

"Very well, then," she said to Will, agreeing to the purchase.

"Good. I'll go to the owner and make an offer. You won't regret it, Miss Amsell."

"I'm sure I won't." Alisa watched the chief accountant go back into his office, a tall, weedy man who looked as if life's vital juices had long ago been drained out of him. However, he was sharp at business, and she was well pleased with Will Rice. Ambitious and careful, Will had been waiting years for this opportunity, and thus far his suggestions had proved excellent. He could not betray her now without implicating himself. Further, she had protected herself by maintaining a sixty-percent share in any joint venture, and was convinced that in five years both of them would be rich beyond their wildest dreams.

She turned into her own work area, hurrying toward the cupboard where she kept her mantle and bonnet. Encountering the clerk, Bochert, she nodded to him.

"Off on errands, Miss Amsell?"

"Yes, I have some envelopes to deliver, and I must see the manager of the Amsell mill."

"How long will you be gone?" the clerk asked sourly.

"All day, I presume. Please finish all of those letters I gave you, and begin the ledger entries for the pipe mill," she instructed.

She paced impatiently while the boy brought the buggy up. October was sliding into November, and the wind had denuded the oaks and elms in front of the mansion, leaving skeleton branches. Leaves blew along the street, their dry odor fusty with autumn. Alisa smelled the blue, acrid drift of smoke, and shivered. No doubt it was only burning leaves, but she would never again be able to smell smoke without thinking of the fiery night on which she, Fifine, and Riordan had fled for their lives.

At Conley's, Seamus Conley greeted her at a discreet side entrance. "Miss Amsell, it's nice to see you. You're looking lovely ... but, then, you always do. What do you have for me today?"

Alisa reached into her reticule and withdrew six identical envelopes. In the past year, her presence at Conley's had become accepted, and Seamus even took the envelopes from her, personally delivering them so that Alisa would not have to walk openly through the gambling rooms.

Today, however, only four of the envelopes were Riordan's. Two were her own, bribes that she and Will had decided to pay to several councilmen in order to be recognized as low bidder on a city building project.

As Alisa waited in a small anteroom, she listened idly to the bursts of male laughter and the rattle of chips and dice that drifted from the gaming rooms. The sounds teased her with the sense of a lost memory. Alisa thought of Papa. She was a small girl, being lifted by him far into the air and tossed high, high toward the ceiling.

"We did it, sweetheart, we did it!" he had crowed, tossing her up again and again, while she screamed in pleasurable terror. She loved it when Papa played with her; to Alisa he was the most wonderful man in the universe—she wanted nothing more than to be with him. But why he had been so jubilant that long-ago day, she no longer remembered.

Alisa was abruptly plunged into melancholy, feeling tears prick at her lashes. *Papa*. He was a ghost that haunted her, sometimes with piercing grief, and at other times with a dim, dull ache.

"There, Miss Amsell. Your deliveries are all finished. And I have a small packet for you to take back to your employer. He was kind enough to do some investing for me, allowing me to purchase some shares in his mill."

Alisa took the packet he gave her. "Which mill?"

Seamus Conley looked away, not meeting her eyes. "Why, the Amsell mill. It's doing very well under Mr. Daniels' lead, I'm told. They say he saved the place from bankruptcy. He's quite the bold entrepreneur. Much more so than your father, no offense intended."

But Alisa did feel offended. "My father was an astute businessman!" she protested.

But Conley only shrugged. "Astute at the faro table, don't you mean?"

Nearly all men of Eben Amsell's class spent some time at gaming tables, and Alisa had no intention of discussing her beloved father with the owner of a gambling establishment. She swallowed a sharp reply and hastily paid Conley the tip that he always expected. Then she left, driving down new business streets where mortar was barely dry between the bricks.

How dare Conley speak disparagingly of Papa? She loathed the idea of his possessing shares of *her* mill—for she already thought of the Amsell mill in those terms.

For a while she seethed, but gradually her mood lifted. She gazed with interest at these new buildings, taking a proprietary interest in them. Many had been built by Riordan, and she had helped with plans, or provided shipments of bricks.

Just as Riordan had said in his speech, Chicago was forging ahead. Only a year after the Great Fire, thirty-four million dollars' worth of new construction had gone up on the South Side, nearly four million on the North Side, and two million on the West. In the 1870's, these were huge amounts of money. On streets that last year had been blackened and smoking, young saplings now swayed in the wind, and by spring there would be patches of new green parks.

The notion of new growth cheered Alisa. She was like those slender new trees. She would dig in her roots, put out leaves, and one day she'd grow tall.

She drove to the Amsell mill, where the sight of the smokestacks and the flaming glow of steel being poured drove her mood downward again. To her annoyance, Felix Morgan, the manager, had forgotten his appointment with her and had gone out on some other business. Alisa felt sure that she had slipped his mind because he discounted her, never believing she could win back the mill as she had told him she intended to do.

"Inform him that I'll be back at nine o'clock in the morning," she told his clerk sharply. "I will expect to find him in his office."

"Yes, ma'am."

She returned to the Riordan mansion and drove the buggy around to the back stable, jumping out before the boy could help her. She walked quickly into a side entrance of the house, pulling off her bonnet and mantle as she went.

In her office she saw that Riordan's inner door was closed. A faint scent lingered in the air, and Alisa looked around for its source, her eyes finally settling on a bouquet of yellow hothouse roses arranged on a table. The house was regularly supplied with fresh flowers, and the bouquets were changed every three days.

She put the packet from Conley on the worktable, and sat down, reaching for a stack of ledgers. She took up her pen and was about to open the first one, when she heard a muffled noise coming from the inner office. Riordan was working there, she realized.

She did not feel like greeting him, and worked steadily, concentrating on the figures penned in Henry Bochert's somewhat crabbed handwriting. Then she heard the sound again, and lifted her head. It hadn't been Riordan's irritated sigh, or his under-the-breath curse as he encountered something in frustrating in his work. She was very familiar with those. No, this noise had been different.

Louder, it came again, a low, throaty, purring laugh. Its quality was redolent with a deep sexuality as cloying as the musky flower perfume she'd just breathed. In fact . . .

Alisa's pen dropped from her fingers and rolled to the edge of the table. She stared at it, her throat squeezed tight, as if unseen hands strangled her. A woman was in Riordan's office, and she felt certain she knew who it was.

Alisa rose, her heart seeming to flame within her like one of the cherry-hot bricks in Pots Ogden's kiln-tunnel. Swiftly she reached out for the package that Seamus Conley had given her to deliver, and started toward the door of the inner room. The packet would be her excuse for knocking. Because she had to knock on that door, had to see . . .

But when she faced that closed oak door and heard, drifting from beneath it, a trilling, intimate giggle, Alisa forgot to knock. She simply grabbed the door handle and pushed the door inward.

At first they did not see her. They lay on the leather couch that Riordan kept for visitors, wrapped deep in greedy embrace, Riordan clothed but disheveled, Linette half-naked. On a nearby table stood a bottle of wine and two crystal goblets.

Alisa stood riveted, clutching Seamus Conley's package to her chest. They'd thought she was gone for the day. Hadn't she told Henry Bochert that she would be?

In the space of only a few seconds, her shocked eyes took in everything. The lacy chemise that slid from Linette's naked shoulders to reveal most of a full breast, and even a dark, pouting nipple. And the chemise was all that Linette wore. As the actress ground her naked hips seductively against Riordan's clothing, Alisa thought she would scream.

Riordan finally lifted his head and saw her. Alisa watched his face drain of color. "Alisa. Oh, my God."

He pushed Linette away and sprang off the couch, reaching downward to where a froth of lace and pink velvet lay in a heap on the floor. He grabbed one of Linette's petticoats and pulled it up to cover her.

"Why, Riordan," Linette drawled, "it's your sweet

little assistant. Back a bit early, aren't you, dear?" Linette shrugged the lace around herself as if being found in such compromising situations happened to her every day.

Alisa's lips felt so thick she could scarcely speak. "I certainly do seem to be early, don't I?"

"Do you always burst in without knocking?" Riordan slapped at the buttons of his shirt, almost smacking them closed. His face was dark with fury; he could not have looked more formidable if he had been about to kill someone. "What do you want, Alisa?"

Wordlessly she held up the package from Conley.

He grabbed it from her and threw it on a table.

Why? Alisa wondered, tormented by her own folly. Why had she pushed open that door? Hadn't she known what to expect? Pinned under her employer's angry scrutiny, she took a backward step, then another.

"I didn't mean . . ." she began.

"You 'didn't mean,'" he mocked. "I thought you were a lady, Alisa, born and bred to the gentry, your lineage going back to the founding of this country. Instead, you peek through keyholes like a spy."

Linette smirked, plainly pleased to see Alisa thus humiliated.

Alisa was furious. "I didn't *peep,* I walked in. After all, I do work here and I'm no spy. How dare you degrade me in front of your mistress? I *am* a lady, more so than she could ever manage if she were to study a script for a hundred years. I hate you, Riordan Daniels. *Oh, I hate you!*"

The color ebbed from Riordan's cheeks, then

surged back again. "You have no right to judge me. Or to hate me either. You don't know me, you don't know the facts."

"I know that I found you with her," Alisa shouted, past ladyhood now, or anything but her own surging, powerful emotions. "You ... you womanizer, you shameless philanderer! How dare you berate me because I walked in to discover you?"

Horribly aware of Linette's mocking laughter, Alisa stooped to snatch up a handful of pink velvet gown. She flung the dress at Linette. "Take your clothes and get out of here."

"Alisa—" Riordan growled warningly.

She whirled on him. "Oh! You want to keep her here, do you? You want to roll around with her on the couch in your office like any roué. Well, you might be rich, Riordan Daniels, you might be as rich as Croesus, but inside you are as common as dirt!"

She had not called him "bastard," but Riordan reacted as if she had. In one stride he seemed to envelop her like a cyclone, his fingers digging into her forearms. "I am what I am, but *you* certainly enjoyed falling into bed with me yourself, once upon a time."

She wrenched at him, her fists pounding him. "I didn't! I hated it! I hated every minute with you!"

"Oh?" Riordan taunted. "What a little liar you are. You adored my lovemaking and you know it. You writhed under my touch, you—"

Linette's laughter pealed. Alisa could stand no more. She gave a powerful lunge backward, at the same time giving Riordan a sharp kick in the shins.

He uttered an angry cry. She seized the opportunity to twist away from him, gathering her skirts to whirl through the doorway in flight.

She fled upstairs, nearly knocking over a housemaid carrying an armload of bed linens. As the girl stared, Alisa ran into the only private haven she could think of, the washroom. There was a key kept permanently in the lock and Alisa gave it a cranking turn, sinking against the door with knees that had suddenly buckled. She gave way to racking sobs.

She cried uncontrollably for several minutes, the emotions so violent that she could not think, but could only give way to the rocking spasms of her torment. But finally the sobs lessened. She had known, even before she had walked into Riordan's office, exactly what she would see. Well, hadn't she? It took no fancy guessing to realize that Linette Marquis would be the one in Riordan's arms.

But to see Linette's nakedness somehow brought home to Alisa the reality of his relationship with his mistress as nothing else could. He slept with Linette, made love to her, allowed her to do as she pleased, even if it meant interrupting his precious workday. Worse, he had humiliated Alisa in front of his paramour. . . .

Alisa's thoughts again disintegrated in a burst of agony. Miserably she sank down on the marble floor of the bathroom and bent her head on her knees.

*   *   *

An hour later, she had cried herself dry. Alisa pulled herself to her feet, her body aching. Her upper arms throbbed where Riordan had gripped her. Her tear-swollen eyes burned and her throat felt as if it were lined with flannel cloth.

She ran water in the basin, and, cupping her hands, drank some. Fiercely she scrubbed her face, soaking a towel with water and holding it to her puffy eyelids.

Now she knew Riordan for what he was—despicable! A philanderer, a predator who used women, who humiliated them mercilessly, who had the instincts of a stallion, not a gentleman.

Proudly Alisa went downstairs, holding herself to her full height, intending to find her mantle and hat and go home. To her relief, she saw that the library's inner room was empty. The couch had been straightened from the imprint of two bodies, and the wine bottle and goblets had been cleared away. The only remnant of the scene that Alisa had witnessed was the faint lingering odor of Linette's perfume.

Alisa shuddered and slammed the door shut.

"Well?" Riordan stepped into the library from the corridor. "Have you had your cry?"

She went rigid. "I don't want to talk to you. I'm going home."

He raised an eyebrow. "At this early hour? Didn't I give you enough work to do?"

Surely he could not believe that she would stay here after what had happened. She stared at him, at his clothing, now ordered, the expensive silk cravat tied flawlessly. Riordan's full mouth, which only an hour before had been twisted in anger, now held a mocking half-smile. He looked at ease, as if his outburst of fury had only refreshed him.

"I can't believe that you would insist on keeping her here after—" she began coldly.

"Why not? Aren't you the woman who once demanded to work for me, who told me that she would have to be dragged out of here if I did not give her the job that she wanted?"

The glances met and challenged, steely-hard. Alisa shivered like a wild animal. He wanted to break her, she thought, to push her to the limits of what she could bear. Well, she didn't have to bear anything. All she need do was to hurry a few steps to the cupboard and take out her mantle, leave this place, and never come back.

Yet she knew with a sick feeling that she didn't want to leave. And if Riordan were to touch her again, as he had done earlier in front of Linette, if he were to push her toward that very sofa . . . She felt violent desire, a weakening of her thighs, and wrenched her thoughts away from Riordan's lovemaking.

"Yes," she whispered. "I am still that woman. Unless you've decided to fire me."

They eyed each other, tension alive between them.

"Why should I do that? You work twice as hard as any male assistant I've ever had. For the same pay."

He was toying with her, Alisa thought, as a lion might paw some helpless jungle creature, enjoying his mastery over it. But she wasn't helpless; she refused to be! She said defiantly, "I stay here on one condition only."

"Yes? And what is that?"

"That is that my sensibilities are not offended by the sight of you carousing with your mistress."

Riordan's face went stony. "I'm a single man, I have no wife to whom I owe loyalty."

"Indeed!" she snapped. "So I've noticed! Do whatever you want, then—but don't force me to witness it, *ever again*. Or I'll leave your employ, and I'll do everything I can to make you as sorry as possible."

"Ah?" Riordan raised one black, ironic eyebrow. "I doubt there is much that you can do to me, Alisa, even if you tried. And I don't think you will try."

She glared at him, speechless. Riordan gave her a victorious grin and left, the sounds of his footsteps firm in the corridor. Alisa slammed the door shut, taking satisfaction in the loud, echoing crash it made. She sank into the nearest chair, shaking.

How arrogant he was! She hated him, she did! And he was wrong if he thought that he was invulnerable to her, for she knew one way to hurt him.

With trembling hands she took out a sheet of fine vellum and reached for the pen she kept in an elegant silver holder. She sat drawing deep breaths, bringing herself under stern control. Finally, when her body was calm again, and her breathing normal, she began to write a letter to Matt Eberley.

ᘓ18ᘓ

November rain drummed down on Alisa's house, sending its chilly damp through shingles and framing so that even her bones felt cold.

"Alisa. Is anything wrong? I was in meetings all day with important clients. Why would you send for me with such urgency? Has anything happened? Are you ill?" Matt's face held a mixture of anxiety and irritation as he strode through her front door that evening, droplets of water clinging to his hat and shoulders.

"No, I'm not ill, Matt, I just wanted to talk to you." As soon as she had composed the letter to Matt, Alisa had left Riordan's and gone home, where she had dispatched the message with Nella's son. Now Nella, Klaus, and Peter were visiting relatives, and Fifine was out with her cronies, leaving the house empty.

Alisa took Matt's coat and hat and hung them in the small hall closet, wondering what she would say to him. For hours, the scene with Riordan and Linette had haunted her thoughts, vivid and alive, refusing to leave her alone. Her eyes felt raw and red, and her throat ached, her chest tight with held-back sobs.

Riordan, she thought dully—how could she have given him the power to hurt her like this?

Matt said, "Well, I came just as soon as I could. I was meeting with some insurance clients—things have been all up in the air since the fire, you know. Many insurers have gone bankrupt or have been able to pay only pennies on the dollar. It's been terribly hectic."

She nodded. "We have been reading about it in the *Tribune*. And of course some of our . . . some of Riordan's companies are involved in litigation, too. It's a constant thing with him."

We. Our. With a pang she heard the proprietary words emerge from her lips. She ushered Matt into the small, well-furnished parlor and waited while he sank into a chair. Forcing a smile, she looked at her former suitor. Matt seemed harassed and tired, his sandy hair rumpled.

"Would you like coffee?" she offered.

"Not really." Matt shifted his feet. "But it's been a long day. If you have something stronger . . . Oh, I'm sorry. Of course, it isn't proper for a lady to serve a gentleman brandy at this late hour."

"Don't be silly." Brandy, Alisa decided, would make her own task easier. She went to a sideboard where she kept a bottle of medicinal brandy that she had bought the previous spring when Nella's younger boy had had bronchitis. She found two glasses and poured them each generous drinks.

"Ah." Matt took a swallow and sighed. "That's better. It's a raw night, Alisa. But good to be with you," he added. "I confess I was surprised to get the note from you. Or perhaps 'stunned' is a better word. I haven't heard from you in months."

"I . . . missed you," she responded faintly.

"And I, you."

Alisa struggled to make conversation. "Is . . . is your mother well?"

"Oh, she's always well. She'll live to be ninety, I'm sure." Matt dismissed his mother with a shrug.

"And the children?"

"Julia has had two bouts with tonsillitis, but Henry has been well. He is being tutored now to prepare him for private school. He still talks about his old teacher during the fire. I think my son had a crush on you." Matt talked of his son, all the while continuing to drink the brandy, his cheeks gradually growing more flushed.

Alisa sipped her own drink, her heart pounding with nervousness. Had she brought Matt here only to quiz him on Henry's Latin and Julia's piano lessons? Why *had* she asked Matt here? But of course, she knew very well. . . .

"Alisa, you look beautiful when you sit like that, looking so pensive. Why do you look sad, my dear?"

"Do I?"

"Yes, you do. Is it me? Do I make you sad?" Matt rose and came to crouch before her, taking her right hand in both of his. His palms felt very warm, their skin softer than Riordan's. And Matt's blue eyes were pale and colorless compared to Riordan's dark ones. *Oh, God,* the protest rose in her. *Stop thinking of him.*

"I suppose I was too bold in writing to you as I

did," she began, lowering her eyelids. "But I . . . I had to."

"You had to?" Then Matt's face changed and she sensed his dawning awareness of what was happening, what her letter had meant. He moved toward her and pulled her into his arms. She smelled his hair pomade and brandy, felt the alien touch of arms that were not Riordan's.

"Alisa . . . Alisa . . . you know how I feel about you, how I've always felt."

"Yes, Matt, I know."

"When I got your note tonight . . . Well, I couldn't help it, I wondered why you'd sent it. I haven't heard from you in months, you've been totally enthralled by that Daniels man. It's been hard," Matt went on in a choked voice, "feeling about you as I do . . ."

"How do you feel?" she prompted. As she said it, she felt a cold, hard knot bunch itself inside her. This was what she wanted, what she'd hoped would happen. Yet . . .

Stop, she ordered herself savagely. *Stop thinking about Riordan Daniels, because he isn't yours, he never has been and never will be.*

"Do you know what you mean to me, Alisa? I love you . . . I always have. I want to take care of you, do things for you, make the way easy for you. But you never would let me. You insisted on working. On working for Daniels."

She forced herself to look at him from under her lashes. "I didn't realize I'd hurt you."

"You did, but it's all right. Alisa, I have to ask it yet again. Will you marry me? Please say you will."

"Yes."

Matt's voice broke with incredulity. "What?"

She drew back, tried to smile at him, and felt the smile collapse on her lips, turning into a terrible trembling. "Yes, Matt," she whispered, putting her face against his chest. "I'll marry you."

He crushed her against him, almost clawing at her in his joy, pushing her face against his coat so that she could barely breathe. "Alisa! Did I hear that right? Say it for me. Say it again."

She spoke with difficulty. "I'll marry you, Matt."

Later, after Matt had left, flushed with brandy and with the prospect of marrying her, Alisa paced around the house turning out gas fixtures. She had drunk half a glass of brandy, but it hadn't affected her, other than to create a gauzy, filmy curtain that seemed to insulate her from reality.

She had just consented to marry Matt Eberley. She had done it deliberately. Soon, perhaps even later tonight, she would weep over her decision. But for now she could not seem to feel any deep emotions, one way or the other.

Slowly she walked upstairs, listening to the deep, steady pound of the rain on the roof. Matt had promised her an engagement ring that had been in his family for more than eighty years, worn by his grandmother and then his mother, a heavy old ring made of diamonds set *en pavé*.

As Matt's wife, she would be Henry and Julia's stepmother, and Ida Eberley's daughter-in-law. She would go back to live in the Eberley house, she would . . .

She would hurt Riordan Daniels. She would pay him back for the way he had tormented her, for the scene she had witnessed between him and Linette, for his arrogance.

She stopped, trembling, at the top of the stairs, feeling the hatred shake through her body.

"What? You've done what? You're going to marry Matt Eberley? Have you gone utterly insane, Alisa?"

The next morning, Riordan paced back and forth, his movements lashing, like those of a tiger about to spring. His face was dark with fury, a muscle knotted dangerously in his jaw, and he looked cold and hard, every inch the man who had once fought a duel, who from early childhood had battled enemies and won.

Alisa faced him, willing serenity to her expression. "Yes," she said evenly. "I am."

Riordan's lip curled. "Matt Eberley is no match for you, and you know it. He's a weakling. Why, you'd eat him alive!"

His words were like arrows, penetrating the protective fabric of the emotional shield that Alisa had built around herself, last night battling her emotions in the privacy of her bedroom. She drew herself proudly to her full height. "How dare you say such things about my fiancé?"

"I dare because they are all true. Matt Eberley is a tabby cat." Riordan sneered. "A man who follows the orders of other men. Is that the sort of husband you want?"

"Yes, it would seem so."

He laughed harshly. "I doubt that. I doubt it very much. You'd tire of him in five days—probably sooner. *If* you were to marry him, which you are not going to do."

"I am!" she cried. "I am going to marry him,

I'm going to wear his grandmother's ring, it's been in his family for—"

"I don't wish to hear any more about it," Riordan said, turning away.

Furious and thwarted, Alisa sat down at her worktable and tried to concentrate on stacks of correspondence about the Daniels Link-Belt Machinery Company. But the copperplate handwriting of various clerks seemed to weave in and out of her sight, tormenting her. Her mind felt raw, screaming with emotions so new and strange that they were frightening.

Oh, she didn't even know *what* she really felt. She wanted to shout at Riordan at the top of her lungs and hear him shout back at her. She wanted him to try to take her into his arms, so that she could battle him, pounding her fists against his hard-muscled chest.

But she knew deep in her heart that she also longed for him to hold her. Then, remembering the greedy way Riordan's mouth had kissed Linette, she pushed the thought away violently. She was going to marry Matt Eberley. She'd do it soon, before she could change her mind. And she hoped it hurt Riordan, she hoped it hurt him a lot.

"Miss Amsell? I wanted to ask you . . ." Will Rice barged into her office, interrupting her disordered thoughts.

She sprang up. "Can't you knock first?"

The accountant stiffened. "It's the way I've always entered your office, but I'm sorry if I've offended you."

"It's all right," she whispered. "I'm sorry I was

short with you, Will. It's just that I . . . I'm getting married."

"Married!" The man stared at her.

"Yes, to Matt Eberley, an attorney of note in the city. We are going to set an early wedding date. After all, there is no sense in waiting."

Will looked stunned, and she knew he was wondering about their partnership. "But . . ."

"I will continue to work here, of course," she told him sharply. "All else will be the same as before. *All else*," she emphasized.

"Yes, of course," he said, looking both relieved and puzzled.

That evening Matt again called at Alisa's house, taking dinner with her. Afterward Fifine winked at Alisa and excused herself, saying that she had to deliver some bonnets to the opera house. In the kitchen, cutlery and china clattered as Nella cleared away, assisted by her elder son.

"You only have two servants, and one of them is a boy," Matt remarked as they walked into the parlor. "You live with a common seamstress. I'm going to treat you much better than that, Alisa." He encircled his arms around her. "All day today I told myself that last night was only a dream, that I'd wake up to find that it hadn't happened at all.

"But it's real, you are going to be my wife. Henry and Julia were delighted to hear the news. And my mother—she will soon grow to adore you too, I'm sure."

"Yes," Alisa agreed obediently. But she doubted it. She couldn't imagine the stiff, complaining Ida Eberley loving anyone.

"In fact," Matt went on, digging into his pocket,

"I brought something for you. I imagine you know what it is."

Alisa knew. She waited while Matt brought out the ring, a heavy, old-fashioned piece of jewelry that slid easily onto her finger, exactly the right size. Alisa gazed down at it. The diamonds were large and brilliant, with a faint bluish cast to them, the old-fashioned gold setting worn from years of use.

"I can get the stones reset, if you like," Matt offered.

"No, no, this will be fine." She didn't care what the ring was like. She could just imagine the kind of ring that Riordan would have bought her—a huge stone, no doubt, worth many thousands of dollars, something that would glitter on her finger like raw sunlight, attracting the attention of everyone, impossible to ignore.

But Riordan wasn't going to give her a ring, she reminded herself savagely.

"There," Matt said. "Hold your hand out, I want to see how it looks."

Alisa did as he asked. The antique ring felt heavy on her finger, and she imagined she could feel its gold itching her skin. She fought the sudden urge to scratch.

"Yes," Matt gloated. "It looks wonderful. *You* are wonderful, Alisa . . . I never thought I'd have you . . ."

He nuzzled kisses at her like an anxious puppy— or the very "tabby cat" that Riordan had mockingly mentioned. How she wished Riordan hadn't said that. Returning Matt's kisses, she wondered what he would be like in bed, and quickly pushed away the thought.

"Of course," Matt said after a while, when his breathing had gone heavy and ragged and it was obvious that a break was needed if he were not to overstep the bounds of propriety, "some things are going to have to change."

"What things?"

"Well, for one thing, there's Riordan Daniels. You certainly can't work for him anymore, now that you are to be my wife."

She felt her cheeks grow hot. There was her father . . . her plans for the Amsell mill . . . Her thoughts swirled. "But I can't quit my job."

"Nonsense. Why not? Now you have *me*, and there's no more need to work. I've been thinking that we should be married at Christmas."

Her heart sank. "Christmas?"

"Yes, would Christmas Eve suit you? But that doesn't give you much time to prepare for our nuptials. There will be parties, showers, all kinds of social events. And shopping. Of course you'll quit your job, there's no question of it."

"I won't stop working." The stubborn words popped out.

"Oh, now, Alisa . . ." Matt laughed uneasily. "My darling girl, be realistic. You are going to be much too busy to do clerking work for Riordan Daniels. But I promise you won't regret your decision. I'm going to make you happy, Alisa. So happy. I do love you, you know. I really do."

They began kissing again and Alisa allowed Matt to push her back on the sofa. His hands caressed her back, sometimes brushing the soft mounds of her breasts. In the thickened excitement of the kisses she gave him, Matt forgot that she had never agreed to quit work.

After a proper time she pleaded a headache, and finally, reluctantly, he left. He told her at the door, "I'll see you tomorrow, Alisa. It's Saturday and there's a symphony concert. Then I'll take you to dinner. Oh, darling, we're going to be so happy together."

Alisa could hardly wait for him to leave. She closed the door behind him and shot the bolt, leaning against the heavy oak, her body suddenly seized by violent tremors.

My God, what had she done? She'd made a mistake, a terrible, terrible mistake. She didn't want to marry Matt Eberley. She didn't want to mother his children, she didn't wish to cope with his spoiled, snobbish, unpleasant mother. She'd only been trying to hurt Riordan.

For long moments she stood rigidly, her eyes focused on a brass gasolier where blue-and-yellow flames cast a circle of light into the hallway. She was a fool. A dangerous, hurting fool, for now she'd dragged Matt into it, and even if he was a "tabby cat," as Riordan claimed he was, he didn't deserve to be misused.

Oh, Riordan, why? The silent cry filled her mind.

Fifine was home, smelling of wine, from what appeared to have been a party in a hotel room attended by several of the actresses to whom she had sold hats.

"What are you doing up, Alisa? Why, I thought you'd have been in bed long ago, dreaming of your fiancé." She winked drunkenly, her movements loose and wobbly.

As Alisa murmured something, Fifine leaned toward her with the air of a conspirator. "Now, on your wedding night you will have to conceal that you are not a virgin. You must act shy and frightened, and when he begins to enter you, you must tense your—"

"Stop!" Alisa shuddered. "I don't want to talk about such things."

The Frenchwoman drew back, her sallow cheeks reddening. "Ah? You are too good to talk to Fifine? Fifine who changed your dirty petticoats and drawers when you were only seven years old? Fifine who could have been your stepmother?"

Alisa stared at her former maid in shock and revulsion. "What . . . what are you talking about?"

"You know very well what I am talking about, *chérie*. You are not stupid."

"But I . . . I don't know."

Fifine giggled drunkenly. "You don't want to know, do you? You don't want to admit it."

"Please," she whispered.

"He was going to marry me." Angrily Fifine began taking the pins out of her black hair, so that it fell thickly around her shoulders. "The bastard."

"Don't . . . don't talk about my father like that. It isn't true, none of it. He wouldn't—"

"Pfah!" Fifine spat the word. "You are *stupide*. A silly little girl hero-worshipping her Papa. Every night after he said good night to you, *I* went to his room. How else do you think I got to him so quickly the night he shot himself? Why do you think I cried so at his funeral? But he promised

me he would set me up in a shop, then he killed himself before he could do it. Why could he not have thought of me, eh? I, who had served him well."

Alisa felt cold with an anger that went deep to the bone. All these years . . .

"Ah, well." Fifine shrugged drunkenly. "Eben is dead and I am struggling to make my little business a success. When my quarters in your house are far too small and cramped for me."

"I see." Alisa's voice was hard. "That's what you really want, isn't it? Even when you worked for me, you really wanted to own my shop. And when you ran from the fire, what did you think to rescue but a bonnet? Very well, then. I will lend you money to move to your own place."

"How much?" the woman asked greedily.

"As much as you need," Alisa sighed. Weariness, deep, fundamental, swept over her like a gray fog. "Now I'm going to bed. I'll provide you with a bank draft in the morning."

Fifine hiccuped and leaned toward Alisa. "It's only what *he* owed me."

"No," Alisa snapped. "It's the price I pay for getting you out of my house, Fifine."

Two days later Alisa was at Cousin Malva's, surrounded by girls in long silk dresses, who screamed in pleasure at the sight of Alisa's extended hand, the antique ring that gleamed discreetly on her left hand.

"Ooooh! It's pretty, *so* pretty!" Cordelia Landsdowne was effusive in her admiration of the ring. She herself had also recently become engaged and already had acquired the habit of draping her hands over the backs of chairs so that her own ring could be admired. "And when will you be married, Alisa?"

"Christmas Eve," Alisa explained.

"Oh! How exciting. I'm going to be married the week after. The holidays are going to be such an exciting whirl, I can hardly wait!"

Others crowded up, cousins of Matt's and girls with whom Alisa had made her debut. Alisa smiled and smiled, displaying her ring for all of them and accepting several offers for bridal showers.

"Of course you are going to quit your job with Riordan Daniels now," Cordelia said when most of the others had drifted off to gather around the pianoforte, which one of the women was playing.

"I don't think so."

"But won't he expect it? I mean, you were very brave to go to work like that, we all admired you so much. But now you don't have to."

"I like to work. I have no intention of quitting."

Cordelia giggled and nudged Alisa. "Wait until Matt hears you say that—he'll be furious. Oh, you are a minx, aren't you? You're just going to keep on saying that until he is forced to buy you a very expensive wedding gift in order to console you when you do quit."

In vain Alisa protested that this wasn't true.

"I won't tell, I promise. Oh, it's going to be such fun, isn't it, both of us being married within a week of each other? Let's go shopping together for our trousseaux. I know the most charming dressmaker, Mrs. Capeziano. Her things are quite stylish, and if you have a real emergency and need a dress quickly, she is very willing to oblige."

Somehow Alisa managed to escape the chattering Cordelia. She fled to Malva's well-stocked library, where she stood in front of glass-enclosed bookshelves wondering if she was going to lose her sanity. First Fifine and her lies about Alisa's father that might not be lies, but truth, and betrayal. Then this marriage. With every day, every hour, she mired herself deeper into folly. She never should have accepted the ring from Matt.

"Well, Alisa, you look as if the funeral is to be held in about half an hour."

Alisa turned, startled, to see Malva enter the room, wearing her usual black, pearls gleaming on her full bosom.

"The funeral?" But there was nothing Alisa could say, no excuse she could make, for Malva had known her since she was a child, and she could not hide her distress.

"Alisa, what on earth is the matter with you? For an engaged woman, I never saw anyone look so miserable in my life."

"I . . . Oh, Malva, my father . . . he had a mistress. He took Fifine . . . I'm such a fool, such an idiot." Alisa wept uncontrollably, and Malva took her into her arms, holding her tightly and patting her shoulders in little wordless thumps of comfort.

"Are you? Why?"

"It's Matt. I don't love him. I . . . I just said I'd marry him to . . . Oh, to . . ." She sobbed and gulped, the rest of her confession buried in the softness of Malva's ample frame. How good it was, how wonderful to be held. She gave herself up to the soft comfort, until finally her shudders grew less intense and she could pull away.

"I *am* a fool, you know," she said quietly, holding up her hand. "Look, Malva, look at this awful ring. I hate it. I hate knowing that Ida Eberley wore it, I hate knowing that *I'm* going to have to wear it. I wish I hadn't taken it. I wish I hadn't shown it off. But I have. I . . ."

"You've done this to hurt someone, haven't you?" Malva questioned gently.

Alisa looked downward, shamed.

"You wanted to hurt Riordan Daniels, of course," her cousin mused. "And that's why you haven't corrected the mistake you made with Matt. Because you still wish to hurt. You are a very proud woman, Alisa. Perhaps too proud."

"I . . . I know. I don't care." Tears were rolling down Alisa's face.

"On the contrary, my sweet, you do care, very much. But you mustn't carry this too far, Alisa. You must back out of your engagement to Matt Eberley as quickly and gracefully as possible."

But some inner, stubborn core of Alisa would not allow her to admit defeat, and the horrible things that Fifine had said about her father only seemed to make her more adamant.

She had told Matt she would marry him, and she had told Riordan Daniels of that decision. If she backed out now, she'd be admitting to Riordan that she hadn't meant it in the first place. That he had affected her so strongly that she had taken another man on the rebound.

No, she vowed. She wouldn't give him that satisfaction. Let him come into his office every day, let him glare at her with that cold expression on his face, let him speak sharply to her and berate her for petty business matters. *Let him hurt.*

These days it seemed that stress surrounded her on all sides. Fifine accepted the bank draft that Alisa gave her with greedy eagerness, again claiming that Eben Amsell owed it to her.

Alisa shuddered. "No, he didn't owe it to you, not in the way you mean. You were one of his household servants. If he had had the money, he would have left you something in his will, I am sure. I'm only giving you what any decent mistress would give a servant who wants to leave her employ."

With every repetition of the word "servant," Fifine seemed to stiffen. Insolently she shrugged. "Well, what does it matter now? My shop is too crowded and cramped in your house. I definitely require more room."

Alisa said it tiredly. "Then look around town, Fifine, and find yourself some good workroom space. Rentals are at a premium here, with the housing shortage, so you will have to look well."

"I don't need you to tell me how to do things," Fifine muttered, but she turned away, carefully folding up the bank draft and thrusting it into her apron pocket.

Several days later, Matt and Alisa also quarreled. "I thought I asked you to quit working," Matt burst out to her after he had arrived to call on her, bringing her a huge bouquet of forced daisies.

"I decided not to," she told her fiancé stubbornly. To stop working for Riordan now would be like admitting that her father was Fifine's lover, that her entire world had slipped crazily awry, that everything she'd lived for over the past two years had been wrong, an error.

"Well, I wish you to, Alisa! You are going to be my wife, and I can well afford to keep you, and in a far nicer style than you're living in now," he added, looking around at her cozy little house with all the furnishings arranged exactly as she wanted them.

"I like the way I live now," Alisa said, bristling.

"Of course you do," Matt placated her. "But the truth is, my home is larger and much more elegant than yours. We can entertain, we'll give parties and balls. . . . What have you done about a trousseau?"

"Nothing."

Matt frowned. "This is awkward. . . . Is it because you can't afford it?"

"No, I am well able to afford to buy myself the bridal clothing I'll need. It's just that I haven't had the time. I work a very long day, you know—"

"You *did* work a long day. You don't anymore. You're to go into Daniels' office tomorrow morning and give your notice, Alisa. I insist on it."

She glared at him, amazed at the force of the feelings that surged through her like a grass fire. "And I insist that I'm not. I'm not going to stop work."

Matt took both of her hands in his. "You're so spirited, Alisa, so wonderfully alive—maybe that's why I love you so much. Of course you enjoyed working, but I assure you, you'll be far too busy as my wife to have time to think of business matters. In fact . . ." He brightened. "What about a European trip for us, a Parisian honeymoon? What do you think of that?"

Paris. Alisa finally nodded. She wondered what pride felt like, if it felt like a steel rod inserted through the core of her body, its raw-metal ends rasping at her throat.

She wanted to laugh. She wanted to cry.

She was going to marry Matt Eberley, and she'd honeymoon with him in Paris—her terrible pride was forcing her into it.

19

Alisa finally, reluctantly, began shopping for her trousseau, and had purchased a "bridal set" that included, as was the custom, a half-dozen night-gowns, chemises, and drawers, all lavishly trimmed with Valenciennes lace and needlework medallions.

Taking these items from their tissue wrappings, she laid them on her bed. There were also two lacy caps, sewn with tiny satin bows, coy and ruf-fled for flirtations at the breakfast table.

What every well-dressed bride wears, she thought dully. Hadn't Cordelia, who had gone shopping with her, purchased the same items, bubbling over with silly excitement?

Alisa sighed and put away the clothes, slamming the drawer shut. She didn't feel any excitement, silly or otherwise. All she felt was tired. She was making a mistake; every day proved it more and more vividly. Riordan, stalking his offices like a grim-faced general, barely talking to her. Her grow-ing feeling of oppression whenever she was with Matt, their constant quarrels over her continuing to work. It was as if, she thought rebelliously, she

301

had become Matt's property even before the ceremony.

Now she moved about the room, releasing her thick honey-colored hair from its pins to brush it, her hands moving automatically in the familiar task. What was she going to do? If she had any sense at all, she'd take Malva's advice and break the engagement. What wicked devil kept her from doing so? Did she really want to hurt Riordan so much that she'd injure herself to do it? Or was it somehow Papa, too, that she wanted to hurt, for his failures, for not being the idol she had once thought him?

But she didn't know for certain that Fifine had been his mistress, she reminded herself. All she had was the woman's word, and Fifine had often proved herself to be venal and calculating.

Then too, Fifine had been drunk that night. Maybe she had lied. Yes, perhaps for strange reasons of her own, she'd hoped to shock Alisa into giving her money to start her own millinery establishment.

If only Fifine could locate proper working quarters so she *would* move out! But housing shortages had hampered the Frenchwoman, and now that their enmity was in the open, nerves on both sides were wearing thin.

Interrupting her thoughts, she heard a rap on her door. "Alisa, there is a caller waiting downstairs to see you. And he does not look happy," Fifine added.

Alisa ignored the gloating tone in her former maid's voice. "Very well. I'll go down."

Was it Matt, arrived unexpectedly? Or Will Rice,

with some important concern of their joint business ventures? Or even Riordan . . . ? Her heart
thumping, Alisa hurried to pile her hair into a
thick, loose knot, fastening it with pins. But when
she went downstairs, she found that her caller was
indeed her fiancé.

Matt paced the foyer, clad in a striped afternoon coat, his right hand figeting anxiously with
his cravat. His usually florid face was pale, and as
she appeared, he gave a guilty jump.

"Matt? Whatever is wrong?"

Matt cleared his throat. "Alisa, something has
come up."

"What are you talking about?"

"Why . . . why, it's nothing serious, nothing to
be alarmed about. It's merely that our nuptials are
going to have to be postponed for a while, that's
all."

"Postponed?" Alisa stared at Matt, wondering if
she'd heard him properly. Only a week ago, he'd
vowed undying love. "But why?"

Matt's smile was quick, placating. "Oh, it isn't
anything bad—it's only that a rather large case has
come up. An important one. The principals are
the Union Stockyards and, of course, Mr. Philip
Danforth Armour and Mr. Gustavus F. Swift."
These were the meat-packing kings of Chicago.
"The case is going to require a lot of time. I'll
have to work night and day. For a while we won't
see much of each other. As for a long honeymoon,
that's entirely out."

So there went Paris.

"I . . . I see." Alisa wondered why this had all
happened so suddenly; Matt, who talked to the

point of boredom about his practice, had never mentioned Armour or Swift before. "Why, yes, I suppose we can postpone the date."

"We can? Oh, darling . . ." Matt looked at her, his eyes pleading. "You see why I have to take this case, don't you? Armour and Swift are big names in meat packing, and once I gain their trust . . . Well, you can see where it might lead. Frankly, it's the chance of a lifetime for me—it would be for any lawyer."

"How long do you think this litigation might go on?"

"Things move slowly in the courts, Alisa. And this case is very complex, involving several railroad lines and a major shipping dispute."

Philip Armour, Alisa suddenly remembered, was one of the frequent business callers to Riordan's office. The two sat together on several boards and even owned joint shares in a pipe-fitting company. And hadn't Riordan told her in a fury that their marriage "wasn't going to happen"? That Matt was a man who "took other men's orders"?

Her heart had started to pound with thick, irregular beats. What if Riordan had somehow engineered this whole thing? Deliberately created this "big case" in order to postpone her and Matt's wedding?

Impossible, she thought. But the idea persisted. Wasn't Riordan just arrogant enough to employ such Machiavellian tactics?

"I hope you understand," Matt was saying. "I hope you'll be patient."

"Of course," she agreed, barely aware of what she said. She took Matt into the parlor, served him tea, saw the relief dawn on his face as he realized that she was not going to put up a fight or talk about breach of promise.

He had wanted to marry her, Alisa told herself incredulously, only a day ago. Now he was happy to postpone. What had happened? But she could see only one explanation—Riordan.

After Matt left, giving her an embarrassed kiss, Alisa closed the front door behind him, her cheeks burning. Riordan had done this! Like a giant reaching down from Olympian heights. Riordan had chosen to intervene in her life. The audacity of it, the sheer egotism! Did the man really think that his money could buy him anything he wished?

Yet, oddly, the emotion she felt was not anger, although she knew that it should be. No. She was beginning to feel an odd lift, a swirling sensation of reprieve, a pounding, fierce joy. Riordan did care about her. He did. This amazing, arrogant act proved it.

When she arrived at the Daniels mansion the following morning, tired from a sleepless night in which her thoughts had spun around and around in her head, the first sight that met Alisa's eyes was a flash of blue cashmere coat. It was Tessa, toddling out from behind a protective hedge, her frantic nurse running after her.

"Tessa ... Tessa ..." Fanny called, chasing the baby on legs painful with varicose veins. "Sweetie ..."

The little girl turned, crowing with delight at the sight of Alisa, but when she tried to elude her nurse again, she stumbled and sat down. However,

Tessa was a plucky baby; Alisa did not hear a cry
as the nurse scooped her up and bore her off
behind the hedge to the private garden again.

Alisa went into the house, not knowing whether
to smile or be angry. How dare Riordan keep a
baby locked away like that? Did he think himself a
god, permitted to do anything he pleased? Obviously, he did! Regretfully she longed for her
former visits to the little girl, now forbidden. She
had been growing quite fond of Tessa, and still
was.

She opened the library workroom and went
around turning on the gaslights, for the day was
overcast. A fire had already been lit in the marble
fireplace and burned cozily, pine knots snapping.
The room was tranquil, or would have been, she
thought, if she had not had so much on her mind.

She worked undisturbed for several minutes,
until Riordan rapped on her door.

"I have some instructions for you today." He
sank into a chair, his long legs stretched out in
front of him, his eyes glinting as if with suppressed excitement. "Are you ready to take them
down?"

Alisa found her notebook and scribbled down
her orders, which included starting several re-
ports and making visits to the Amsell mill and the
Daniels Pipe Mill. Finally she dared to tell her
employer what had been on her mind all last
night, so that she had barely slept at all.

Riordan raised one dark eyebrow to stare at her
coldly. "What do you mean, do I know anything
about the new case Matt Eberley has got? Of course
I don't. Why would I?"

Alisa's breath tightened. "But I thought ... I have seen Philip Armour here often—you have business dealings together ..."

"I have dealings with many men."

"But I ... I thought you might have ..." She stopped, her cheeks flaming.

Riordan threw back his head and laughed, the sound rich, deep, and mocking. "You thought that I might have had something to do with the postponement of your wedding? Don't be ridiculous. I don't give a damn about your fiancé's legal cases. Besides, I might remind you that the ceremony has not been canceled but only postponed. Sooner or later, you'll still be Matt Eberley's wife. And you'll still regret it, believe me."

Alisa felt a rushing spurt of anger mingled with a sharp, stabbing disappointment. How dare Riordan ridicule Matt and herself? She had thought ... but she had been wrong. He had not cared enough to stop her marrying Matt. No, on the contrary, he had mocked her, made a fool of her.

She rose, seething with resentment. She snatched up her brocade purse and slapped its drawstrings tight. Only minutes ago he had asked her to visit his pipe-fitting mill, and she decided to leave at once, only too glad to get away from him for the day.

"Well, when I do marry Matt, I won't regret anything," she snapped, gathering her papers. "I love him."

"*Love?*" he mocked.

"Yes, love! Why not? It's a wonderful emotion, in case you've never thought of it yourself. It's the purpose of living for some people, the epitome of existence."

"Ah? Such a romantic you are, my charming Alisa."

"Don't make fun of me! Matt Eberley is a fine man, he has a good future here in Chicago—"

"As someone else's employee."

She faced him, dangerously near to tears. "Oh! Oh, you are so . . . so *arrogant*! You think you're better than anyone else, don't you? An all-powerful god who can do exactly as he chooses with others' lives. Just because you are in a position of power, because you can buy and sell most of the men in Chicago—"

"It's true." With easy grace, Riordan rose from his chair, his tall, muscular body looming like the very god she had accused him of being, filling the room with his presence.

His eyes glittered at her. "I *am* indeed arrogant; I have a dozen rivals who could verify that fact, to their sorrow. And I *am* in a position of power; that, too, is real enough. I have certain things I want, and I intend to get them. I am, in fact, very near to it."

What did he mean? But Alisa didn't even care. She felt almost sick with her fury and her thwarted love. Why did she allow him to torment her like this? Blindly she turned to the cupboard where she kept her outdoor wraps.

"You're going to the mill, I presume?"

She whirled savagely. "Yes, sir! As instructed!"

"Good. Well, save some time to pack. I have a trip to St. Louis this week and I need your services. I expect you to go with me."

"You expect . . . what?"

His voice was bland. "You are my assistant, aren't you?"

She faltered. "Yes, but . . ."

"I have some appointments set up to look at a steel mill there and to investigate several lumber and shipping ventures. There will be much paperwork and I want someone competent at hand, someone who can work the same long hours I do and who knows my business intimately."

Well, that certainly described her. She stared at him, feeling a wild-bird tremor in her stomach. She knew that Riordan had recently purchased two private railroad cars, and had ordered both fitted out for travel. He had not yet used them, but had been wanting to do so.

Her anger was suddenly gone, drained away. She moistened her lips, abruptly very aware of him physically, the bold, sensuous cut of his mouth, the philanderer's cleft. The black hair that curled at his sideburns would be crinkly soft, silky beneath her fingers. "I . . . I can't travel with you."

"Why not?"

"You know why not." She thrust her hands behind her back so that he would not see how moist with sudden perspiration they were, how her palms trembled. "How arrogant and stupid can any one man be? We aren't married. It's bad enough that I work for you in your house. But if I went to St. Louis alone with you . . ."

Dark eyes coldly locked with hers. "The solution is simple then. Find a chaperon."

"But I can't just—"

"You can and you will, if you expect to remain

in my employ. I am leaving in four days' time and I expect you to be at the railway depot with me at dawn on Monday, ready to board. There will be space for one woman servant. Inform her that she is to assist my chef in preparing our meals and will otherwise keep herself busy with cleaning or other tasks. I will provide a valise for her, traveling garb, and a handsome bonus."

Alisa opened her mouth and stammered out a reply, feeling indeed like the mortal who looks up to see a giant's hand descending out of the clouds. Blood squeezed into her face, alternately hot and cold, burning and chilling her.

This was insane. Insane! Riordan wanted her to go with him to St. Louis. Was insisting on it, would pay her chaperon. Threatened to fire her if she did not go.

And she wanted to go. Despite her engagement to Matt, despite all good sense, the desire to be with Riordan in that opulent new railroad car was growing in her blood like a wild dangerous fever.

She decided to ask Nella to be her chaperon. When the German woman learned that she would receive a new valise and a traveling dress, plus a sum of money, she was overjoyed, and at once made arrangements for her two boys to stay with her sister, who lived in the Fifth Ward, near the Brighton Trotting Park.

Alisa spent the next days in a fever of packing. She sorted endlessly through her closet, pulling out bonnet after bonnet, only to discard each. One was too drab, another out of style, and the ones trimmed by Fifine all seemed too gaudy, not

appropriate for business. Nor could she find any
gowns to suit her. She felt like a debutante dressing for her first party of the season—uncertain,
frightened, tremulously eager.

On the night before she was to leave, Fifine
came into her room with a bonnet that she had
remodeled at Alisa's request. Alisa tried on the
hat, frowning into the mirror, while Fifine watched
sourly. It was plain that she felt insulted that Alisa
had chosen to redo her creation.

"You ruined it by taking away the flowers," Fifine
remarked. "What is a hat without *frou-frou?*"

"I am a businesswoman. I want to look simple
and plain."

The Frenchwoman shrugged eloquently. "Ah,
well. Perhaps that drab little hat will help to keep
him away from you."

"He's not . . . He isn't going to . . ."

"Don't be *stupide*. All men want women's bodies,
unless they have something wrong with them, unless they are *pédé*. And I assure you, Riordan Daniels is not. I have heard that he is fully a man, that
he—"

"Enough!" she said hastily. She had no desire to
hear more. *He is fully a man.* Where had Fifine
heard such things? Alisa feared her source was
none other than Linette Marquis, with whom Fifine
had grown increasingly thick. "Thank you for your
services, Fifine. Here . . . for your trouble."

She found some money in a carven box and
gave it to the woman, who took the bill, inspected
it, and then folded it away in an apron pocket. "I
suppose that will do," Fifine said grudgingly.
"Although I have been receiving much more than

that for alterations from my actresses—they are very generous."

As soon as Fifine had left, Alisa closed and locked her bedroom door. She sank onto her bed, staring upward at the ceiling. She couldn't believe it, the state her nerves were in, merely at the prospect of traveling in the same railroad car as Riordan Daniels.

They would be gone for seven days. *Seven days,* she thought with a choking excitement that almost made her sick. What would happen in that time? What would they say to each other over breakfast, over lunch? Would they dine together? Would—?

But swiftly she squelched the speculations. She closed her eyes, putting both hands to her chest, where her heart seemed to be clenched like an enormous pulsing fist.

A thin gray light pervaded the railway station.

"Well, what do you think of my efforts, Alisa? I am the first man in Chicago to have his own private Pullman car, and I ordered these made fit for a king. In fact, I didn't think the workmen were going to finish in time, but I threatened them with mayhem and they worked twenty-four hours a day."

Riordan was like a joyous, eager boy this morning, Alisa thought in wonderment, watching as her employer paced back and forth in the depot beside the train, his face wreathed in smiles. The objects of his pride were two new "palace cars," their clean, shiny black sides embellished with golden curlicues and scrollwork and the initials "R.D."

Alisa pulled her woolen mantle tighter about her shoulders. There had been a thick white rime on the grass this morning, and on the way to the station they had seen their horse's steamy breath in the air, along with their own.

"Miss! Oh, miss, we'll be boarding soon. Isn't it a pretty, pretty train?" Beside her, Nella, in her new black traveling dress, was exclaiming in pleasure, her eyes following the sight of the train starter, who trotted past them with an air of importance.

"The cars are certainly impressive enough," Alisa agreed with Riordan. Although she herself had paid the bills to upholsterers and cabinetmakers, she had not yet viewed the results of their labor.

"Impressive! Is that all you can say?" His grin flashed. "Wait until you go inside, Alisa. They are as opulent as I could make them. They've got everything. They are . . . I guess you could even call them voluptuous."

At the choice of words, Alisa laughed. "Voluptuous?"

"Of course. Come on in. I'll show you what I mean."

Riordan held Alisa's elbow while she climbed the two hanging steps, each a masterpiece of shiny black enamel and gilt embellishment, until it seemed almost a shame to mar them with footprints.

The door opened into a tiny vestibule and then into the car itself. Entering it, Alisa suppressed a gasp. Riordan had not exaggerated. From its ornate walls to its curved ceiling, the car had been paneled in rich Santiago mahogany that had been carved into lushly rounded leaves, flowers, and pheasants. The reddish wood seemed almost to glow from within, so highly polished was its gloss.

"Oh, Riordan." Her eyes moved to the blue satin curtains beautifully pleated, that were looped at the windows, held back by gold velvet ties. "The curtains . . . and the *rugs* . . ."

For on the floor were Persian rugs of deep ruby and blue, intricate, stylized lotus flowers woven on a sapphire background.

"I thought you'd like it." Riordan took her hand, leading her into the elegant drawing room, which was arranged with plush blue velvet chairs. "But this isn't all, you know. There are three bedrooms, each with its own attached bath equipped with fixtures of the finest Italian black marble."

Dazed, she allowed him to lead her through the office, paneled in rosewood, containing a complete library, smoking chairs, a fully stocked liquor cabinet, and a large pigeonhole desk equipped with every writing amenity, including a solid gold penholder and inkwell.

"Do you think you might have forgotten something?" she couldn't help teasing.

To her delight, Riordan scowled. "What could I have forgotten? I wanted a complete office and that's what I've got. If you find anything missing, I'll . . ." He stopped, seeing the grin on Alisa's face. "Oh, I see. You poke fun at my private rolling office? You think it too elaborate? Foolish?"

"No. Oh, no . . ."

"Understand something about me. I like money, I like comfort, I like having the best. It's like a payment to the past, to the days when I was a butt of ridicule and taunts, a small town's bastard boy."

His tone was suddenly so bitter that Alisa impulsively reached out for his hand. "Your palace car is lovely. Lovelier than one could imagine."

Mollified, Riordan took her to the back of the car to show her a large open observation platform with a wrought-iron guardrail. Here passengers could lounge in wooden chairs to observe the passing scenery. Although Alisa, shivering in a sudden gust of November wind, thought this would be rather a chilly pleasure, and wondered about the possibility of flying sparks.

But something else had been puzzling her. "Where is Nella to ride?"

"I've provided for that in the second car. It's got a very nice dining room, a gallery, quarters for four servants, and a capacious luggage room."

Her heart pounded up in her throat until she could scarcely force the words out. "Do you mean to say that Nella, my chaperon . . . is not even to be in the same car with me?"

"The cars are connected by an enclosed passage with full access between them." His boyish mood suddenly gone, Riordan spoke sharply. "Or do you want me to have a bell installed in your bedroom so that you can ring your servant if I make unwelcome advances? I'm certain she'd be happy to come in to rescue you—assuming you'd need rescuing, which you won't."

Her cheeks scarlet, Alisa lifted her chin. "I'm certain your arrangements are satisfactory."

They glared at each other like two stubborn children, and then Riordan's mouth twisted in a sudden crooked grin. "Alisa. Are we to spend the entire trip at loggerheads, quarreling with each other over trifles?"

She felt a smile tug at her own lips. "I ... I suppose if we made an effort we could be civil to each other."

"For a seven-day trip, I'd say we'd better make more than an effort. Unless you intend to make me so angry that I toss you out over the observation rail in Peoria, or Stephens Gulch, or somewhere else equally colorful and godforsaken."

She dared one reckless glance from under her long lashes. His eyes were fixed on her, a smile glinting in their depths. "I'll be good," she promised.

"You'd better be. If not, I'll fire your chaperon. Then where would you be? Alone with me and at my mercy. A fate worse than death," he teased.

Their lighthearted mood was like a fragile soap bubble, easily broken and therefore all the more precious. It continued throughout the day as they pulled out of Chicago, rolling past new brick buildings, warehouses, mills, stockyards, and the small homes of workmen. Views of Lake Michigan delighted them, the water gray today like some enormous pewter bowl reflecting a silver sky, the whole world shimmering with light.

As scenery flashed by, they played chess with a set of ivory pieces. Riordan beat Alisa so badly that, groaning with mock chagrin, she suggested that they turn the board, he taking her losing pieces, and she his winning ones.

"You know, of course, that I'll still trounce you."

"Go ahead," she challenged. "Since you seem to be such an expert at chess."

Riordan scowled at the board, decisively moving Alisa's beleaguered queen. Ten minutes later he called out, "Check. And mate. There, I've done it," and they collapsed in a flood of foolish laughter.

Then Alisa beat him at backgammon, and followed up her victory with card tricks her father had taught her. At dusk they went into the adjoining car to eat dinner in an elegant dining room hung with Waterford crystal chandeliers that reflected diamonds of light in the plate-glass windows, beyond which dark fields and trees flashed by.

Nella and one of Riordan's menservants waited on them, bringing in course after course, from turtle soup to stuffed veal, cheeses, and a delicate pear sherbet.

However, both of them only toyed with their food, their eyes meeting again and again as their mood gradually grew quieter, fraught with subtle tension. The occasional flare of a house light or carriage lantern in the darkness outside the train seemed to emphasize their isolation, the only diners in this opulent salon.

Nella, neat in a black silk apron, hurried in to take their plates and serve the sherbet. Flushing guiltily, Alisa looked down at her napkin. For a "chaperon," Nella was being kept conveniently far away. The neighboring railway car in which the servants rode might as well have been on the moon, she thought, for not once had any of the employees entered the other car except when Riordan had rung for them.

Was all of it planned to keep them alone together? Of course, Alisa answered her own question. Any "chaperonage" had been meant strictly for public show, not for private reality. The truth was, she and Riordan were more alone now than they'd been in weeks—months.

Her spoon clinked against the fragile crystal sherbet glass. Trembling, she put it down.

"Alisa?" Riordan's voice had a husky timber to it. "My God, the way the light from the chandelier picks up the highlights in your hair—your hair is like the purest wild honey, so thick, so . . ." He rose suddenly, pushing his chair back from the table. "Come with me, back into the other car."

"But . . ."

"I have to make love to you. Now."

She could have refused, could have exploded with anger at him for violating their agreement, could certainly have rung for Nella to serve as a buffer against his advances. And, briefly, all these thoughts flew through Alisa's mind. And then, like a fluff of dandelion seed, they flew away again before she could act on them.

Riordan's eyes were dark on her, glowing with desire. Silently Alisa rose, doing as he asked.

∽20∾

Inside the parlor car, Riordan turned a heavy key in a lock and turned to take Alisa in his arms, lifting her up to carry her through the car. She clung to him, feeling dazed, almost drugged with her desire. Her heart slammed wildly, weakness pervading her like opium.

She wanted him. Oh, how she wanted him! And yet, she hadn't meant for this to happen; it was why she had brought Nella, so that it would not occur. Yet now she did not see how she could stop herself, or him. It was *happening*, and the rich, forbidden sweetness was ten thousand times more delicious than the sherbet they had just enjoyed.

He was carrying her over a threshold into one of the darkened bedrooms. "I had this room made especially for you," Riordan whispered, laying her down on a coverlet of smooth, sensuous satin.

Her arms were still draped around him. "For me? What do you mean?"

His eyes glittered. "It was a fantasy of mine, and I decided to fulfill it. This room is . . . you, Alisa."

She didn't understand.

"I'll show you." Riordan reached upward to switch on a gas fixture. Immediately a soft golden light flooded into the room.

For a moment Alisa stared around her, stunned, still not understanding. The entire room—bed, hangings, walls, ceiling, chairs, even the door—had been upholstered in a dusty, honey-colored satin. Transfixed, Alisa stared at the compelling color, subtle, muted, yet glowing from within like pure meadow honey poured into a crystal goblet and lit from behind by the sun.

She gasped. *Yes.* She felt a growing tightness in her groin, a thrill of sexual pleasure. The color of this room was exactly matched to her own hair, the thick, heavy locks that Cousin Malva called her "crowning glory."

Nude, her hair loosened to flow like silk about her on the pillow, she would be displayed to perfection in this incredibly sensuous room.

"What do you think?" Riordan murmured.

"I . . . It's . . . I've never seen . . ." She didn't know what to say. There had never *been* a room like this. Now she saw the huge bouquets of roses in shades of pink, some the warm coral of love-flushed cheeks, others the delicate peach of soft skin. Where, where had he found such stunning colors, to glow with the rare beauty of a woman?

Drawing a shaky breath, Alisa realized that perfume pervaded the air; was it roses? Jasmine? Or something else tropical and rare?

"Riordan . . ." She shook her head from side to side, trying to take in the full meaning of it.

"Alisa, I created this room to display you. Your body, your wonderful beauty. I hope you like it."

Like? She opened her mouth to speak, but no words would come out. She felt choked, damned up with her desire for him. It had been so long . . .

"Undress, darling," his whisper urged her.

For an instant she hesitated, her mind battling the tatters of her good sense. This was Riordan Daniels, her enemy, the man she'd vowed to hurt, who had hurt her father, who had . . . But all of her careful thoughts slid away, beyond her power to recall them. There was only now. This moment, this thrilling and endless moment when Riordan had asked her to undress for him.

She did so. Slowly, deliberately, with all the sensuousness this incredible room deserved. First came her blue foulard traveling jacket with its tiny jet buttons. Then the dress, with its row of buttons, its plackets and ties. Slowly she removed them, making a ritual of it, an art.

The lacy camisole straps slid off her shoulders. As she stripped, her skin flamed with the knowledge that Riordan watched her with slitted eyes, a smile of desire on his lips.

At last she lay naked, completely exposed to him. In a gilt-edged mirror that hung on one wall, she saw herself, her skin glowing against a backdrop of dusky golden honey until it looked almost translucent, the skin of a goddess.

Riordan drew in a long, deep breath. When he spoke, his voice shook. "Alisa. My God . . ."

He came to her.

They made love for hours, by the soft glow of the lamp. Alisa moaned with pleasure, opening like a rose under Riordan's touch.

They moved together in fierce, hungry pleasure that ended with an explosion of feeling so violent that Alisa screamed under its impact, only half-aware of Riordan's own groaned climax as he spasmed within her.

They slept for a while, drowsy, replete, at peace with each other. Then Riordan stirred. He reached out to touch her, and soon he was kissing her softly everywhere, her knees, the delicate flesh of her inner thighs, and finally her central pink bud, his tongue teasing, drawing stunned quivers of sensation from her.

He mounted her again, this time his thrusts slow and deep and controlled, her flesh so sensitive that it seemed every stroke would explode her again. But when this seemed about to happen, he deliberately slowed. Then he rolled her over so that she was on top, and she saw that his eyes focused on her with a glaze of intense desire.

They moved together in the sinuous dance of love.

"Now!" he groaned. "Now . . . and now . . . and now . . ."

He pounded into her, scourged her, created her. She screamed again, climaxing in rivers of sensation that flowed out of her, so intense that she had to grip Riordan's back with all her strength, or surely she would have been swept away in that flood of rapture, lost forever.

The Mississippi river gleamed molten silver under a pearled sky. The levee was densely crowded with steamers, boats that had names like *Colossal, Spread Eagle I, Bayard, Minnesota,* and *Emma C.*

Eliot. Endless sheds and warehouses lined the waterfront, along with wagons, stacked bales and barrels, processions of sweating stevedores.

In years to come, Alisa would never think of St. Louis without thinking of Riordan, smiling as he helped her to clamber around a huge coil of rope in a shipyard. Or scowling as she tugged at his arm, begging him to catch a ride on one of the brightly colored horse trams that clattered along the streets of the high-bluffed river town.

"Nonsense, why should we ride public transportation when I can hire the finest carriage in the city?"

"But I *want* to ride in one!" Alisa teased like a child until Riordan chucked her under the chin and told her she was impossible. Then he made her ride and ride all afternoon, until they were both jounced half to death and laughing uncontrollably.

They were like honeymooners, oblivious of everything and everyone except themselves, exploring the old river town as if it had been created especially for them. They had arrived four days too early for his meetings, Riordan said, so why should they be bored sitting in the palace car when they could be enjoying themselves?

Recklessly Alisa allowed herself to be persuaded. While Nella shopped for her children or helped Riordan's chef to prepare elaborate meals, she and Riordan poked along the riverfront, where hundreds of workmen toiled on the new St. Louis Bridge that was being built across the glittering span of water.

They strolled arm-in-arm through what Riordan

said was the largest horse and mule market in the world, an incredible, jostling cacophony of animals, auctioneers, buyers, mule skinners and herders, bedeviled by buzzing flies and the dust churned up by the hooves of the shifting herds. From the sheds and holding pens rose such a thick barnyard reek that Riordan offered to lend Alisa a handkerchief to put over her nose.

She laughed at him. "Why would I want that?"

He looked bewildered. "Because you're a lady, Alisa. And, frankly, this place has an odor that is . . . ripe, to say the least. Why you'd want to come here at all is beyond me. I'd think that you'd prefer to do some shopping on Broadway or Fifth Street—that's where all the really good shops are. Mermod and Jaccard is one place you might like—their large jewelry showroom is devoted to the sale of precious stones, brick-a-brac, and art goods."

"Darling Riordan." Ignoring the stare of a passing mule-boy, Alisa slid both arms around Riordan's neck. "Do you really think that that's what I want—to go shopping? If I did, I could do that in Chicago." She gestured toward the noisy market that teemed with rich, smelly life. "I happen to like this place. It excites me. Every day thousands of dollars change hands here. This is where real life is happening, the real world of sweat and work!"

He eyed her curiously. She was revealing too much of herself, she knew. But it seemed important that Riordan realized she wasn't just a *lady* whose delicate sense of smell had to be protected.

She belonged to commerce, to money and power and excitement, just as much as he did. She was just as competitive as he was. And if he only knew it, it would not be long before she'd won back the Amsell mill from him.

"Watch it—here comes somebody's string of mules," Riordan said, pulling her aside against the weathered walls of a stock shed, his strength such that he nearly lifted her from the dusty ground in doing so. "So you love the 'real world,' eh? The world of sweat?"

She faced him defiantly. "Yes, I do."

Riordan's grin widened. "Then when we finish here I'll take you to see Philip Armour's new meat-packing company here in St. Louis. That will be well worth the trip for you, I'm sure, although they say the smell is enough to gag a goat. But then, you won't require a handkerchief over your nose, will you?"

He went on. "And there is a brewery you might like. Ever smell hops and malt? It's pungent, but you'd love it. Oh, yes, and St. Louis is famed for its tobacco factories. They produce huge quantities of plug chewing tobacco. I'm sure you'd find the manufacturing process delightful . . ."

She smiled back evenly. "Stop teasing me."

"Me? Teasing? Oh, no."

"Yes, you are. Well, for your information, I *would* like to see all those places—and more." She pulled out her chatelaine watch and inspected it. "It's noon now. What about the meat-packing plant first?"

Riordan grimaced. "You're serious, aren't you? But not until after lunch, my sweet. Even I don't wish to spoil a good meal."

They spent three more days exploring the gritty

town with the air that reeked of a hundred wonderful, terrible odors: river sewage, hops, horse manure, tanneries, coal dust, the yeasty smell of a biscuit factory. There was even a brickyard, twice as big as Pots Ogden's, twice as redolent of sooty smells.

"Miss Amsell . . ." Nella, her expression troubled, began to protest once, but Alisa, flushing, turned away from her servant. Riordan, she suspected, was paying Nella a handsome bonus to look the other way, and how could she, Alisa, object? Not when she was enjoying Riordan's company so much!

On the fourth day, Riordan began the meetings for which he had come here, with railroad men who discussed endless plans for extending railway lines.

"One day," Riordan told her, as if all of this were his own personal doing, "we'll extend spurs and lines to cover large parts of Missouri and Kansas. We'll reach Denver and Boulder, the wheat fields of Nebraska, the sugar plantations of Louisiana. All that land, Alisa, just crying out to be covered with rail."

His eyes sparkled at the thought, and Alisa, too, felt a surge of excitement. While cigar smoke blued the air, she took notes in the meetings, ignored by these loud-talking men who at first had objected to her presence.

One night she and Riordan made love in the satin-lined room. Afterward, sated with pleasure, they lay in bed and talked. Beside them on a side table stood an ice bucket and a magnum of champagne from which they poured each other glasses of bubbly, fizzy liquid. Alisa felt as if some of those bubbles had fizzed directly into her brain, making her thoughts as effervescent as air.

"It's been . . . oh, wonderful," she sighed. "This whole trip has been like a dream to me, a revelation."

"The lovemaking has been superb, I must say." Riordan grinned, pouring her another glass. "*You* are superb, Alisa."

She smiled teasingly. "Oh?"

"Yes, indeed. You're everything a man dreams of in his bed. Warm, passionate, abandoned . . ."

She loved his compliments, but this time she wanted to be taken seriously. "Yes, but . . . there's more to it than that—about this trip, I mean. There's St. Louis. I love it."

He raised an eyebrow. "Manufactories, shipyards, mule markets?"

She drank deeply of the exquisitely dry champagne. "Oh, I loved everything. Even the brickyard."

"The *brick*yard? What a funny girl you are." Riordan stroked her flank as if she were a kitten, absorbed in the texture of her skin. "You're like silk, Alisa. I don't think your skin has a single flaw. Even those little burns you got during the fire are completely gone now, as if they'd never been."

"No, listen to me." She was laughing, champagne bubbles flowing through her like a heady elixir, aerating her own giddy thoughts. "I liked that brickyard. Yes, I did. Bricks mean money, you know."

"Money?"

"Oh, yes." Was she drunk? Her tongue certainly

felt loose, and it was an effort to pronounce her words clearly. "Do you know that bricks are immen . . . immensely valuable? Well, they are. All of this is so new to me. But one day when I have enough money from my bricks, I'm going to . . ."

At the slip of the tongue, she stopped short in horror. But it was too late.

"*Your* bricks?"

She tried to recover herself. "Well, our bricks; after all, I do work for you."

"No. That isn't what you meant at all, is it, Alisa?"

"I think I've had too much champagne." She sat up, gathering the luxurious satin sheet around her. Her skin suddenly felt cold, goose bumps prickling her. She might have drunk too much, but Riordan had not. His eyes were sharp and hard on her.

"You talked of bricks," he persisted. "What bricks?"

"Why, the brickyard we visited, of course."

"No, I don't think so. Alisa, I received a very odd letter last week from a gentleman who called himself Mr. Pots Ogden. Have you ever heard that name before?"

"I . . ."

"In the letter he stated that he was planning to visit Chicago sometime in the near future and wondered if he might stop by my office again, since we had had dealings together, and this time he hoped to find me there. He said 'this time,' Alisa. At the time I merely put the letter aside, thinking that possibly an error had been made, since I had never heard of Mr. Ogden before. Now I am beginning to wonder."

Alisa sat very still, huddled in the satin coverlet, which suddenly seemed shroud-cold about her shoulders. She stared numbly at the twin humps made by her quivering knees, all too aware of Riordan's hard scrutiny.

"Well? Can you explain that letter, Alisa?"

Gaslight flickered in the satin-lined room that had suddenly become, not a bower for love, but an interrogation room. And Riordan, his expression hawklike, his eyes blazing, became not a lover, but an inquisitor.

He fired question after question at her. Hadn't she known that it was unethical for her to have dealings with a man who had come to him to seek his business? How much money had she made from the brickyard? How much of his time had she stolen in order to line her own pockets? How long had it been going on? Were others of his employees involved? Why had she done it?

"Stop, stop, stop! I don't want to hear any more!" Alisa clapped her hands over her ears, wishing she could be anywhere, anywhere but here, stark naked and humiliated, clad only in a satin sheet.

"Well, you're going to listen—and you're going to talk, too." He lunged toward her and yanked her hands away from her ears, pinning them down to her sides. In the process the sheet fell away from her, so that she lay totally bare to his gaze, vulnerable and guilty.

"Stop . . ." she gasped. "Stop manhandling me. And let me cover myself."

"Very well."

He released her and she snatched up the bed-covers again, feeling a hot red flush burn all over her body. Sobs gathered in her like hard, terrible fists. Oh, and to think that only minutes before, she'd been happy. But she refused to weep—not now. She was Alisa Amsell, she could not cry in front of her enemy. Which, at this moment, Riordan most assuredly was.

"All right," she said dully. "I'll tell you everything, since you demand it—but it's going to take a while to explain, and I'd prefer to get dressed first."

"Fine. Dress yourself, then. We have all night. And I don't think we need any more champagne, do we? I'll ring for coffee."

He turned his back and she pulled on the dress she had worn today, her hands shaking so violently that she kept getting the buttons in the wrong holes. She felt shocked, stunned by the suddenness of it all.

My bricks. Two little words had done this.

But, she thought miserably, hadn't she known this would happen one day? It had been inevitable, from the day of her father's funeral. *I'm going to make you sorry, Mr. Daniels, very, very sorry for what you've done. And I'm going to get my father's mill back, too. It was meant to be mine, he wanted me to have it!* Her own words, spoken more than two years ago, rang in her mind like a taunt.

Yes, she'd made Riordan sorry . . . yes, she'd nearly accomplished what she'd set out to do. But along the way it had all changed, hurtling out of control. She hadn't known she'd love working for him so much, be so swept away in the power and fun of empire-building. And she hadn't known she'd fall in love with Riordan. Desperately, totally, recklessly in love. . . .

Finally she was dressed, and so was he. Oh, God, she thought, her mouth dry as cloth. What would happen now? Riordan's valet—thank God it wasn't Nella, she couldn't have faced her own maid-servant now—brought a silver pot of coffee, steaming with fragrance.

Suddenly Alisa felt shaky. The champagne giddiness had drained out of her, leaving her almost sick to her stomach. She wondered if Riordan would shout at her. If he would hit her. If . . .

Calmly he poured two cups of coffee and added cream to one, stirring it with deliberate care. He handed the cup to her, and she had no choice but to take it, praying he would not notice the way the cup shook.

She saw his eyes go to her hands. "All right, Alisa," he said. "It's time you told me everything, from the beginning."

So, her voice sometimes firm and angry, at other times nearly inaudible, she did as he asked, leaving out only Will Rice, whom she did not want to implicate. She told him of her father's letter, of her own vow to get the Amsell mill back no matter what it cost. Of her elation at getting the job with him, and the unexpected call of Pots Ogden which had shown her the way her objective might be accomplished.

Riordan made her repeat it over and over, all

the details of her visits to the brickworks in Fort Wayne, the sales she had made, her other investments, even the amount of her bank account.

"Didn't you know that you were cheating me? Betraying me?" He said it softly, his lips curved in a terrible smile.

Alisa prayed she would not faint or be sick. "Of course I knew it. I did it for my father, don't you understand? He *died* as a result of your perfidy, your machinations in business—or don't you remember that anymore?"

"I was at his funeral, and I did *not* kill him."

The night hours dragged by, the two of them locked in verbal combat. "And who are your accomplices in this 'venture' of yours?"

She shook her head. "There are none," she lied. "I did it all alone." She had begun to perspire lightly, all over her skin, at the idea of Will Rice being implicated in this too. Not that Will hadn't known there was a risk. Still, Will had a family to support. She was the real guilty party.

Then she froze as she realized where her thoughts were taking her.

"You treat me as if *I'm* guilty," she cried. "Well, maybe it's the other way around. Maybe *you* are the one who's guilty—of a man's death. As for the punishment I meted out to you, I'd say it's pretty small, wouldn't you? Compared to your vast fortune—you own so many railroad lines you can't even count them; you're talking about opening up a whole continent to rail, and all I want is one little mill!"

"Which you are not going to get."

"I am—I will! I have only five thousand dollars more to set aside and then I—"

Riordan tipped back his head and laughed, the sound harsh. "Alisa, Alisa. What a fool you are. What a damned stupid little fool! Do you think it's that easy? That all you have to do is save up enough money and you can buy back whatever you believe I have robbed you of?"

She paled; she had spent two years believing exactly that. "I will—"

"No, my dear. No, you will not. I won't sell you that mill—not for any amount of money, any at all. It simply isn't available to you and it never will be."

She shook her head wildly. "But . . . but you have to! It's mine, he wanted me to have it, he—"

"He was a fool too, my dear. Your father was a compulsive gambler, didn't you know that?"

"You're lying!"

"Am I? He spent about six hours a day at Conley's, he was one of the man's prime customers. That's where I first encountered him, at the tables. He lost your precious mill at roulette."

"*No.*" She could feel her mouth go dry with shock, the gold-satin-lined room spinning about her like her own pounding blood. "No . . . I don't believe you."

"It's true, Alisa, I'm sorry to say. Ask your cousin Malva, if you don't believe me. Or that frippish French maid of yours, *she* knows a good deal, believe me."

Alisa clapped her hands to her ears again, trying to shut out the inexorable voice. "No one wanted to tell you because you idolized the man and refused to listen to anything you considered bad about him."

Alisa swayed, ice and fire battling in her veins. She tried to speak and could not.

"I'm sorry, Alisa, but your father killed himself from shame, because he had gambled away all of his assets. There is the real truth of it. You have devoted yourself to avenge a feckless gambler!"

"I haven't, I haven't!" Shamed, goaded beyond endurance, she flew at Riordan like a wild animal, scratching, clawing, biting.

Savagely she raked his jawline with her nails, and the side of his face, digging at him, wanting to obliterate him with the sheer force of her hate. How could he do this to her? How could he say he was "sorry" and tell her such hurtful, untrue things? She sobbed and gasped, screaming out her anger. No, Papa hadn't done that. She knew him, she'd lived with him for nineteen years.

"You're hysterical—stop this, Alisa." Riordan pinned down her flailing arms and clamped them to her sides, conquering her easily. She shuddered like a trapped hare. "It's true, all of it, I swear it. You had to know."

"I . . ."

"Breathe deeply, Alisa. Big, big gulps of air."

She did as he told her, seeing the rivulet of blood that ran down Riordan's face, the scratches she had given him already coming up livid. Gradually the worst of the hysteria passed, leaving her cold, clammy, and drained.

"My father was a fine man, a wonderful one," she said dully. "And I'm still going to get his mill back—his letter asked me to, and I promised him."

Riordan held her rigid, not allowing her to escape. His eyes glittered like obsidian, black volcanic rock. "I'm sorry for you, Alisa—I pity you for your illusions and I admire you, in a way, for your courage. But you used my name, my influence, my offices, and possibly even my own employees in order to further your own purposes. You betrayed me. I can't forget that and I won't.

"But what's worse," he went on, "is that you came to my bed deliberately, in order to betray me. And that's the real reason why I'm going to fire you."

Fire her.

Alisa gripped her fingernails into her palms, welcoming the pain that shot through her. Anything to help her withstand the thought of not working for him anymore, of not being a part of his world. Oh, she'd loved that world so much. She'd loved him, too. The loss hammered at her. *Riordan* ... They'd clashed before, angrily. But never before had their conflict been like this, so savage.

"How dare you fire me?" she cried out. "How dare you say that I betrayed you? *You* betrayed *me*, using me sexually like any cheap woman of the streets!"

"What?"

"You did, you have, you *are*." She gestured furiously. "Look at this room, Riordan, this ... this mirrored boudoir, this love nest, this 'tribute' to my body!" Her voice shook. "Are you going to bring Linette Marquis here too, when you've finished with me? Or Maria Capeziano? Or—"

"Enough!" he roared.

"No, it isn't enough, not at all. You've had women, lots of them, myself included—how many of them do you need, a whole chorus line full?" Insults popped out of her mouth like bullets, impossible to hold back. "Further, you keep a baby girl immured in your house like a prisoner—who *is* Tessa's mother, another of your paramours?"

"Alisa, shut your mouth before you say too much."

But she could not stop. "What's to become of Tessa? What, Riordan?" She was satisfied to see him wince, his face paling. "You've got her locked away, with only a nurse to care for her or love her. . . . You destroyed my father, Riordan, now you're destroying that child. Oh, you don't care about anyone or anything. Only money!"

With each of her words, Riordan's face had gone more gray, except for dark blotches of anger that stained his cheekbones. She was shocked to see moisture glitter in his eyes like diamonds. Tears? Was he crying?

But then he lunged forward again, to clamp his fingers around her upper arms like steel manacles.

"I suggest that it is *you* who loves money, Alisa. Isn't it really money that drove you to do everything you did? Not high ideals and daughterly love, but cold, hard cash?"

"No! Money wasn't important."

"Wasn't it? Money is everything with you, girl, money and power. Why, your behavior in St. Louis these past days only illustrates that. Factories and mills, that's all you wanted to see."

"But it wasn't like that!" she tried to explain, knowing that it was all hopeless, he'd never understand her, the fact that she was *just like him*, enjoying the game of money as much as he did.

"It was, Alisa. You're a liar, a gold-digger, and a deceiver. I order you to turn over to me at once your holdings, your bank notes, bank accounts, all your investments."

"You can't really believe I'd do that."

"You will, or I'll take them from you."

"By intimidating me?" Alisa felt a flare of hate. "No, Riordan, I'm not going to give up anything I've earned—not my brick profits, not anything. I worked too hard for them, and they legally belong to me."

"Morally they are *mine*. I can buy and sell you, Alisa, don't you realize that? I could put your Pots Ogden on the streets, and likewise your greedy lawyer fiancé, Matt Eberley."

And you, too, was the unspoken addition.

They stared at each other. Alisa could hear the thick, angry draw of Riordan's breathing. They had reached an impasse, she realized, a point from which they could not retreat. They had both said terrible things and meant them. There was no going back now. Ever.

Alisa stood proudly straight, refusing to show by a flicker of expression how suddenly devastated she felt, as if a fire had blazed amok across her very life, destroying everything that was joyous and wonderful, leaving only ashes.

"I . . . I think I had better leave now," she said heavily. "I'll find Nella and we'll go to a hotel. We'll book passage back to Chicago in the morning. You needn't pay her bonus, of course. I'll do that, and I'll reimburse you for both of our expenses here in St. Louis. In a day or so I'll send Nella to the office to collect my things."

She'd never see him again, of course. Never want to. She'd failed at everything. The mill. Riordan, the love she'd felt for him, the joy they'd found together. . . .

Shaking, she went to the beautiful satin-quilted dressing table where she had put her clothes and began to take them out, willing herself not to break into the sobs that were building inside her, craving release.

"Alisa." His voice was hoarse, so low she was not sure at first that she even heard it. "Don't. Don't pack, not yet."

"Why not?" Grimly she threw a petticoat into a canvas bag. "I told you, I'm leaving. As soon as I can get train tickets. Didn't you just fire me? I assume that my severance is to begin immediately."

Riordan looked at her, his eyes dark stones, perspiration dotting his forehead. "No. Perhaps not." He spoke hoarsely. "I have a proposition for you."

～21～

"What proposition?" Alisa demanded hotly. "There can be no proposition, no agreement between us."

"Can't there?"

"I . . . I don't understand." She walked back into the scented, satin-lined room and sank down in a pink chair. This room—once she had thought it a paean to her, a wonderful, sensual tribute. Now she saw it for what it was, a trap. An insult to her, to her love for him, for it would be used to bed down other women, it wasn't specifically for her at all. Why had she supposed it was? He could tell any woman that he had designed it for her.

"You were very right about some things, Alisa." Riordan astounded her with his next sentence. "And I realized, as we quarreled, that my plans must come to fruition now, before any more time passes."

"Your plans!"

"Yes. I would like to make an agreement with you."

She stared at him. Only a moment ago they had been shouting at each other, saying dreadful things, irrevocable things. Now Riordan was talking to her in this conciliatory voice. Immediately she was suspicious. "What sort of agreement?"

"I will give you your mill. The Amsell mill, lock, stock, and barrel."

"What!"

"And that house your father owned—it has since been sold to new owners, but I'll buy it back from them and give it to you as well."

She could feel her lower jaw dropping; she knew she must look foolish in her surprise. What did he want? *Why was he doing this?*

"I don't understand," she said at last in a low voice. "What have you to gain from this?"

"My daughter."

Alisa swallowed. "Tessa?"

His eyes held a fierce look, fixed into the distance, as if they gazed at some long-ago painful scene. "I have told you about my childhood, the cruel taunts that goaded me every day until I was old enough to fight my tormentors. But even after that, there were the whispers, the innuendos. No matter how tough he is, how can a boy fight back against that? He can't. In a way, I suppose my illegitimacy made me strong, but I don't want strength to have to come to Tessa in such a terrible manner. Is it wrong of me to want to smooth her path, to make life as easy for her as possible?"

"No. Of course it's not wrong. But what has that to do with me, and with the Amsell mill? *My* mill," she added stubbornly.

"It is not your mill, it is mine, but I assure you, this is the only way you can ever possibly get it. You have something I want, Alisa, something I need, a quality that I've come to see only you can give me."

"Oh, I do, do I?" She spoke impatiently, jumping up from the soft chair. "Stop speaking in riddles, Riordan, and tell me what's on your mind. I have packing to do if I am going to catch a train in the morning."

"No." His hand reached out to stop her. "I told you, no packing, no train. Marry me, Alisa."

"Marry you!" Her voice trembled, and the fiery, icy waves rippled through her again, lacerating her. "Marry you! I can't believe I really heard you say that."

"I did say it."

"But . . . why?" She stood rigidly, wanting to laugh, to cry, to smack him across the face for his terrible cruelty. How dare he do this to her? He must know that she loved him—how could he not be aware? And to deliberately use it against her! He could not have thought of an act calculated to hurt her more.

Riordan continued, his features a mask that made of his mouth a straight, hard line, his jawline a fortress. "Because I want to legitimize Tessa. You were right, Alisa, utterly right when you told me I was wrong to keep her hidden away in my house. But you were wrong about something else."

"And what is that?" she asked faintly.

"Her nurse is not the only one to love her. I love her. More than I'd ever dreamed I could love a child. And I intend to remake her life."

Alisa began to shake all over, feeling as if she'd been plunged into an ice bucket like the champagne they'd drunk—was it only hours ago? This was incredible, she thought. Utterly incredible! "And how do I come into it?"

"You are Alisa Amsell. Your family fortune is gone, but your antecedents are still impeccable." Riordan's eyes glittered at her. "You have a fine old name and your bloodline is good on both your father's and your mother's sides."

"Oh! You mean I'm bred like a Kentucky racehorse?" she snapped. "Out of Tessa, sired by Eben?"

Black eyes bored into hers. "Something like that. You date back to the *Mayflower*. In your veins runs the blood of several signers of the Declaration of Independence. I know because I had your family tree traced. You do own a legitimate place in Chicago society. You have friends, contacts, people whom you can call on to help my daughter."

How arrogant he was! Alisa thought angrily. He wanted to use her as a calling card into Chicago's drawing rooms!

Fury lent her voice tight calm. "It isn't as easy as you seem to think. Tessa is more than a year old now. We can't just get married and produce her as our child. People will talk. She'll be no better off than before."

"I've thought of that. No one knows she's here in my house, except for the servants, and they're well paid not to talk. After we marry, we'll receive a telegram. Cousins of yours have died, leaving an infant girl orphaned. We'll make a sad trip to bring her home with us and we'll adopt her as our own child. We'll bring Tessa up with the cream of Chicago society—she'll make her debut with Mc-

Cormicks and Biddles and Armours. She'll be secure."

"But . . . but it's all to be a lie!" Alisa managed to say, shocked as she had never been before.

"A lie! My God, Alisa, don't you go holy on me! Haven't you told plenty of lies? You spent half the night admitting them to me. We're talking about Tessa. *About my little girl.* I'll do anything for her, do you hear me? Anything!"

Her voice crackled. "Including marrying me?"

"Yes. Even that."

Even that. As if she were some sort of unpleasant liability, an onerous hardship!

She faced him, her color high. "I won't even consider it unless you tell me who Tessa's mother is."

"I don't intend to tell you that."

"Why not? After all," she mocked, "I would be your *wife.*"

"Because I have sworn secrecy. Because all depends on secrecy!" His nostrils flared, his mouth twisting angrily. "If you can't understand that, Alisa, if you can't deal with it . . ."

She turned, unwilling to let him see the swirling maelstrom of emotions that tormented her. He had said nothing of love. Not one word. He had refused to tell her who Tessa's mother was. He could easily intend to keep Linette Marquis or any other woman as his mistress—to bring her along with him on trips in this very palace car, making love to someone else in the same satin bower where they had shared such rapture.

Alisa's heart thumped wildly, until she thought

she would go mad with its insistence. Her thoughts were like a train, rushing on. *And yet this was victory.*

Well, wasn't it?

For she would gain, too. In exchange for her part in this charade, Riordan intended to give her back the Amsell mill he had taken from her father. She could fulfill her promise to Papa, the thing he'd begged her to do in his last, pathetic letter.

No matter that Eben Amsell had been a gambler, he'd still loved her, she told herself grimly, and more than life itself, he'd wanted Alisa to inherit from him. Now, if she married Riordan, she could. It would be revenge ... of a classic type she'd never even envisioned.

But that wouldn't be all. As Riordan's wife, she'd have more money than she could spend in a lifetime, a dozen lifetimes, and the unlimited power that went with it. Freedom to invest in all the factories and brickyards and railroads that she wished, to play the power game that Riordan loved so well, and to do it, at last, on his own level. Not as his employee, but as his equal.

Alisa's heart throbbed in her throat; she thought she would be sick with the terrible force of it. *Victory*, she thought, putting her hand to the pulsing hollow of her throat.

"I ... I have one stipulation," she heard herself begin in a low whisper. "Your mistress—if you are to have one—I must never be shamed...."

She was shocked at the sudden angry change in his expression. "I am not a monster. I will treat you impeccably. Damn you, Alisa, damn you ..." For a moment his voice thickened. "But I expect honesty from you. Honesty. Do you think you might possibly manage it?"

She was trembling all over with the insult. But she forced out her hard reply. "Yes."

They glared at each other.

"Good. Then I am certain our bargain will work out excellently for both of us. And now, if you don't object, my dear 'fiancée' "—his sarcasm was as sharp as a surgeon's knife—"I'm going out for a walk. I need some fresh air, and I need to take it alone."

He was gone, turning abruptly on his heel to slam out of the ornate satin bower, leaving Alisa shaking, barely able to stand. Her body felt racked with crisis. She felt as if she'd survived a bout with pneumonia. As if she'd nearly drowned and had been brought back to life with only seconds to spare.

She had said she would marry him. She had struck the bargain. My God, how had it happened, and how would she live with it?

Was it minutes later, or hours, that she finally summoned the strength to go over to the dresser and resume the job of removing her things? For she couldn't sleep in this room now, not after all they'd said to each other, the lashing words, the hurt. She would sleep alone until they were married.

Feverishly she bundled up piles of petticoats and nightgowns and lugged them into one of the other bedrooms, a room paneled in mahogany and carpeted with red Turkish rugs. She flung the clothes down on a chair and went back for her gowns, throwing them on top of the other things.

In the morning she'd have Nella put them away. Or she'd have Riordan buy her new things—from the skin out. She could, now. She was rich beyond imagination.

Dully she threw herself on the new bed. *We're poor but blue-blooded*, Papa had said once. *That means we survive on our wits, using what faint glamour our name still possesses.*

He'd said other things, too, jesting words that came back now to haunt her like a cruel joke. *I don't suppose you could marry for money, could you, chicken?*

Instead, she would marry for Papa, she thought, turning over restlessly to bury her face in the unfamiliar goose-feather pillow. Then a cold knot tightened in her stomach. No. That wasn't it at all.

Be honest, Riordan had demanded. And if she were truly honest with herself, deep inside her soul where no one had ever looked, she knew that she loved Riordan Daniels. She always had; there had never been a time, even on the day of that first wild buggy race, that he had not been able to make her pulse race, to take full possession of her thoughts and her heart.

She loved him then. She loved him now. In spite of their terrible quarrel, in spite of the dreadful loveless bargain they had just struck between them.

Further, she knew it was beyond her power to hate him for what he had demanded of her tonight. Nothing would kill her love. Not ever. She'd love Riordan until she was a very old woman rocking in some sunny parlor, she'd love him until she was in her grave, she had no control over that.

But he didn't love her, she thought, feeling the first hot tears begin to slide down her cheeks. Riordan didn't return her feelings; he despised her for her betrayal of him. But now, she told herself, there was at least a chance. She'd be his wife, living in the closest intimacy with him. There would be days, weeks, years of being with him.

She lay quietly, letting the tears come, letting them flow like soft release, healing the lacerations of her spirit. Years, she thought, drifting off to sleep in the thin morning light. A lifetime with Riordan.

Five days later they were back in Chicago, and Alisa managed the difficult task of telling Matt Eberley that she was breaking her engagement to him.

He looked shamefaced, his freckled cheeks flushed. "I'm sorry, Alisa, that it turned out this way."

"I am too. But you had something to gain from postponing our marriage, didn't you?" She asked it sharply, remembering Riordan's remark about her "greedy fiancé," admission enough, if she had needed one, that Riordan had interfered in her life.

"I . . . I can only repeat that I'm sorry," Matt said miserably, and Alisa had to be satisfied with that. He was a man who tried to dominate women when he could, she realized, but he had himself been dominated by Riordan. How glad she was that she'd been saved from marriage to Matt!

A few days later Riordan presented her with the largest diamond ring she'd ever seen, a baguette-shaped stone mined in the De Beers mine in

Kimberley, South Africa, its faceted glory blazing with light.

"It actually feels heavy on my fingers," Alisa breathed, staring down at the fiery gem.

"It ought to," Riordan growled. "It weighs fifty carats."

"But it's so large. Perhaps too large; won't people stare?"

"Nonsense. Let them. I am Riordan Daniels, and my wife must be outshone by no one."

The ring symbolized, Alisa thought bitterly, the bargain that she and Riordan had struck. She would receive the Amsell mill, her father's house, and unlimited money to spend. In return, she would legitimize Tessa.

She took Malva into her confidence, for this was something she knew she could not do on her own. When Malva heard the full story, she drew back to stare at her cousin with unconcealed shock and dismay. "Why, Alisa! This all sounds like a penny novel."

Alisa flushed. "It's real, though, and I don't see what's so wrong about it. It's simply an arranged marriage. A marriage of convenience. People have been doing *that* for centuries."

"But it's almost 1873 now, my darling, not the sixteenth century." Alisa seldom saw her cousin angry, but Malva was angry now, her usually generous mouth compressed into a tight line.

Tears spilled out from under Alisa's eyes. "But . . . I love him, Malva. That's the whole trouble! It has to be this way, don't you see? This is how he wants me—and it's what I want, too. I . . . I want the mill, I want what my father meant me to have. *And I want Riordan.*"

"I see." Malva sighed. "Very well. I must tell you, though, that I don't approve. He is handsome, of course. But he is well known as a rake and a womanizer and he has long been excluded from real society. But I suppose once he is married to a woman of your stature . . . we could do something."

Alisa laughed through tears and hugged Malva, whirling her around. "And Tessa? Will you help me with that? Riordan has stipulated that no one but us is to know. There must be no taint of her name."

"I can manage it," Malva said grimly. "But we'll have to map out a battle plan. It will take plenty of time and work to carry this off."

Alisa's smile faded. "Riordan doesn't want to spend months and months—he has already made that clear to me. He wants us to be married within weeks, if possible. He is a man of action, Malva, and once he makes up his mind to do something, he pushes ahead until it is done."

"Well, this is one time when he cannot push. There must be time to prepare people, time to relaunch you into the winter round of teas and parties and balls and introduce him. Then there is the matter of the child. The groundwork must be well prepared there, too. You must make it known that you have a cousin, that they have a child. Then, later, you must be suitably worried when you learn that your cousin and her husband are deathly sick with . . . yes, with influenza."

Alisa stared at her cousin. "Why, Malva, I believe you have a real talent for deceit."

Malva grinned. "Perhaps I do at that. Anyway, Alisa, you can tell that fiancé of yours that I will help, and all I wish is one reward, something so easy for him to grant that it will be nothing to him at all."

"What reward is that?"

"Why, that he handsomely endow my orphanage for young girls. They are a worthy cause, my girls, and since he possesses such indecent amounts of money, someone might as well get some good out of it."

So it was begun, the "battle plan," as Malva called it, that would change three lives—Riordan's, her own, and Tessa's. The first objective was to reestablish Alisa in society, and Malva set about doing this with the same relentless energy that had made her one of Chicago's *grandes dames*.

First she insisted that Alisa quit her job with Riordan and devote full time to her social life.

"But, Malva, I *like* to work!" Alisa protested in vain.

"Perhaps, but a full social life is work too, believe me. Dress fittings alone are going to take you days."

And days they took. They were endless visits to dressmakers, milliners, shoemakers, jewelers, glovemakers, for Alisa must be outfitted with the elegant good taste that would cause her to be admired by her women friends, rather than envied by them.

"I wish he hadn't given you such a damnably *big* ring," Malva lamented. "It will turn women green with envy, and the men will be jealous too, chagrined that they cannot provide such huge stones for their wives. Ah, well, it's too late now, already a number of people have seen it. So we will have to live with it. Perhaps . . . yes, perhaps we'll make it an asset. People do respect, even fear money."

To Alisa's relief, Fifine had finally managed to find a small shop of her own and moved out of Alisa's home in a flurry of good spirits, promising free bonnets if Alisa would talk up her creations among her friends.

But Alisa privately vowed that she would never use Fifine's services again. She could not look at Fifine these days without wondering what her father had seen in this woman, and these were thoughts she did not wish to entertain. The thought of going to Maria Capeziano made her feel equally uncomfortable, so she made excuses to Malva, avoiding contact with the pretty, dark-haired widow.

Riordan cooperated fully with Malva's plans, although he seemed often preoccupied. Once, when Alisa called at the office to pick up a cash advance to pay her large dressmaker's bill, she heard him inside his office shouting at someone with low, controlled fury.

She couldn't help pausing to listen; she was almost certain that she had heard Tessa's name. But she could hear no indication of who the other person in Riordan's office might be, and when he emerged, he looked cold and businesslike.

"Yes, Alisa? What is it you wanted today?"

"I . . . My clothes," she managed to ay. "You wanted my wardrobe to be extensive, but—"

Brusquely Riordan handed her an envelope full of cash, making her think uncomfortably of times in the past when he had done the same thing for Linette Marquis. "I'm establishing charge accounts in your name, Alisa, at all the best stores. Use them. Spend whatever you have to."

"Thank you," she began. "You're most generous."

He shrugged. "It's hardly generosity, only a part of our bargain."

Alisa stiffened. "Our bargain! Is that all you ever think of?"

"What else should I think about, Alisa? Would you prefer that I not keep my word?"

"No. I . . ." Then, reddening, Alisa turned away. How could Riordan be so unbelieveably dense? Didn't he know that she loved him, that she would have given anything, done anything, to hear a soft and loving word from him?

The Christmas season came, and in the drawing rooms of Michigan Avenue and on the near North Side, tall fir trees blazed with candlelight. In her tasteful marble-fronted mansion Malva gave several dinners to launch Alisa and Riordan.

Guests, dressed in their glittering best, arrived at seven o'clock, and the ladies took their wraps to a downstairs cloakroom, while the gentlemen took theirs upstairs. In the gentlemen's cloakroom, white envelopes were arranged on a silver tray. Inside each was a card with a woman's name on it—the lady he was expected to escort in to dinner.

The guests then reassembled downstairs, where Malva met them, splendid in black silk sewn with thousands of tiny jet beads. A stunning necklace of diamonds flashed at her throat. She skillfully made introductions and guided conversation.

"Carlotta, have you met Riordan Daniels? He is

one of the best supporters of my orphanage. Do you know he is building us a new dormitory and school, in addition to six private cottages for our teachers and headmistress?"

Riordan would smile warmly at whichever bejeweled matron he was asked to greet, his eyes full of slow, intriguing fire. Soon he would have charmed his way onto yet another invitation list.

However, Riordan chafed privately at these dinners, insisting that he felt like a trained monkey on display.

"What!" Malva, who had struck up a surprising friendship with the dark-eyed financier, laughed heartily. "I hardly believe you are that, Riordan. In fact, you are the most interesting man to attend my gatherings in years. All the ladies are quite taken by you. Have you noticed them giving you discreet little glances?"

"I suppose," he responded grumpily. "Still, I find these dinners strange. That little ritual you call 'changing the conversation,' for example. We all have to keep an attentive eye on you, our hostess. When you shift your attention from the man on your right to the one on your left, the entire dinner table has to turn heads too. Do you realize how laughable that is?"

"Laughable?" Malva grew suddenly icy. "It's not so laughable when you consider what's at stake—your daughter. Haven't you and Alisa been receiving a goodly number of invitations?"

"Yes, we have." Riordan glanced at Alisa, who was examining guest lists, trying tactfully to stay out of this discussion. "It's what I wanted, Malva, and I can't thank you enough. I'll do anything to smooth the way for that little girl. Anything I can."

Malva looked somewhat mollified. "Good, at least you're cooperative. Now, to Tessa. She must be kept in more secrecy than ever—there must be no chance of a gossip leak ruining everything we've tried to build. If you have any servants who can't be trusted, I want to know about it now."

"My servants are all trustworthy."

"Good. New Year's is coming, and I am giving a large ball, a gala the likes of which has seldom been seen here in Chicago. You both will attend, of course." She turned to Alisa. "I want you, Alisa, to mention your little niece, Tessa Eames, and the fact that you have recently heard from her mother, who has been sickly. Express your concern, then change the subject. Be very casual."

"All right."

"We're going to make this work," Malva said. "But no matter what happens, Tessa's welfare is assured. *I* have taken her under my wing, and that guarantees her. No one will dare to reject her without making *me* an enemy."

"Malva. You are wonderful," Riordan murmured, leaning forward to kiss Alisa's cousin, the gesture natural and easy.

Watching, Alisa felt her heart tighten.

Riordan! He could be so loving sometimes, such a complex mixture of charm, boldness, and hard obsession. The thought of being married to him was frightening to her, as if by saying vows she would be stepping onto a perilous, powerfully driven carousel from which there could be no escape.

* * *

New Year's Eve arrived in windblown drifts of snow that clogged the streets in three-foot drifts, so that everyone had to travel to Malva's home on Michigan Avenue in horse-drawn sleighs. Snowflakes glistened in sable and fox wraps, on elaborately dressed hair, and were caught in diamond tiaras and pearl chokers.

In Malva's ballroom, thousands of white tapers glowed. A towering twenty-foot Christmas tree, trimmed with holly and hundreds of white Meissen porcelain bells, dominated the room. Seven lead-crystal chandeliers lent glitter, the central one of such huge magnificence, its pendants flashing like sun-diamonds, that all of the guests gathered around it to exclaim.

Thousands of white roses also banked the room, heavy with scent, depleting the stock of five greenhouses, which had grown them especially for this occasion. At least six hundred and fifty people waltzed to the music of a twenty-piece orchestra.

"Good evening, Alisa," Matt Eberley murmured as she walked past the huge buffet tables laden with a hundred rich delicacies, from caviar-stuffed potatoes to galantine of veal and scalloped oysters.

"Matt!" She stopped short.

"I see you are wearing an enormous diamond. It looks a bit large—do you think you can hold your hand up under its burden?"

Alisa reddened, stifling the urge to clasp her hands behind her back. Was Matt trying to make her feel guilty because she had broken their engagement? But he himself had allowed greed to push him into postponing their wedding, she reminded herself.

She turned, to see Riordan behind her, rescuing her from the uncomfortable moment. "Darling . . . I believe we have this next dance, don't we?"

Black eyes shot a glare in Matt's direction, and the attorney bit his lip and melted away into the crowd.

"You are a marvelous dancer," Riordan murmured to Alisa as he held her as tightly as the waltz would allow, twirling her about effortlessly.

"And you." She said it in wonderment, for she hadn't realized he could dance so well.

"If I can dance, you have your cousin to thank. Malva has been polishing my skills."

"Malva has been giving you lessons?" But before Alisa could absorb this fascinating fact, Riordan suddenly danced her toward the center of the room, where he maneuvered her directly underneath the huge blazing crystal chandelier. His grip at the small of her back was so strong, so sure, that they moved as one unit, Alisa's body and movements totally caught up in his mastery.

He dipped her gracefully and Alisa trusted her body to him in the elegant movements she had been taught as a girl, trying not to show her surprise as the other guests moved back to a polite distance to admire the show.

He was *chandeliering* her, she realized, showing her off, in the center of the ballroom beneath the most important chandelier, performing the most spectacular dips and twirls and turns of which he was capable. What would people think of such show-offishness? Couldn't he do anything, anything at all, in moderation?

"Riordan!" she whispered as soon as they were upright again and he turned and swirled her with an ease she had not imagined in a million years that he could possess. "Riordan, you're attracting attention!"

"Of course I am. Malva told me about the practice of chandeliering, and I just wanted to see if we could do it. We can. Very nicely, too."

"But . . . people are looking! They're clapping!"

"Let them clap. Let them notice us, Alisa. We are in their world now, and they are going to have to accept that."

Later that evening, Alisa followed Malva's instructions and dropped the hint about her "niece." And at the stroke of midnight, just as several clocks were chiming the new year, six servant boys dressed in white entered the huge ballroom and released basket after basket of white doves.

Winging their way into the air, amid the screams and cries of the women guests, white birds dipped and soared, scraps of living, extravagant beauty.

Alisa laughed in giddy delight. "Who is going to catch all those poor creatures later? Whose idea was this?"

"Mine." Riordan's grin was triumphant. "I thought doves would be just the thing. And did you notice that each of them is wearing a necklace of rhinestones?"

He swooped down to kiss Alisa. As boldly as if they were alone, his tongue parted her lips with sweet insistence. Numbly she gave herself up to the sharp pleasure of it.

"There," he said jubilantly, pulling away. "This is going to be our year, Alisa. Next comes the wedding. And soon after that, Tessa will be out in the open, and I can begin to show her off. She'll be mine, legitimately."

Alisa stiffened. She had thought . . . The birds, that kiss, so warm and loving . . . But he hadn't been thinking of her, only of Tessa and his goals for his baby daughter.

"Yes," she said dully, all of her pleasure gone. "Tessa will be yours."

22

They were to be married on St. Valentine's Day, in a ceremony that had grown in lavishness by leaps and bounds, until it promised to be the social event of the season.

Emerging from yet another dress fitting, Alisa sucked in a lungful of crisp February air and plunged her hands into a deep furry muff. A gust of wind rippled the sable fur luxuriously.

Alisa and Cordelia, who had accompanied her, hurried to reach the relative warmth of Riordan's phaeton, with its woolen lap blankets and glowing brick foot-warmers.

"Oooh! It's cold, so cold! Alisa, aren't you tired of dress fittings by now? Good heavens, I think you've bought enough to stock an entire shop if you chose."

Alisa smiled, waiting for Riordan's driver to help them both into their seats and tuck the thick blankets around them. Today a cold sun blazed against snowdrifts, so that winter light seemed to glare all around them, hurting the eyes.

The liveried driver flicked the reins and they started off, steam puffing from the horse's nostrils.

"Goodness." Cordelia was in an odd, exhilarated mood, perhaps caused by the obsequiousness with which the middle-aged dressmaker had treated both of them. "Alisa, you're to be married in ... what is it, four more days? And you don't even seem excited."

"Of course I'm excited."

"Well, you certainly don't act it. One would think that you did this every day, marrying the biggest catch in Chicago."

Alisa gave a slight, ironic smile, thinking that a year ago Riordan had not been considered a "catch." It was Malva and her efforts that had made him so, along with Riordan's sheer, grim determination to be accepted for his child's sake. "I suppose I'm used to the idea by now," she lied.

"Used to it! Oh, Alisa, he is so handsome, everyone says so. *I* would never be used to it." As always, Cordelia chattered on and on, saying whatever came into her head. "But he is such a kind man, isn't he?"

"Kind?"

"Why, yes." The other girl turned to stare at her. "To adopt your little niece, Tessa. That poor baby, orphaned at such a young age—it's a good thing that you and Riordan are going to take charge of her. Otherwise she might have to go to Malva's home for orphaned girls."

Alisa nodded. "Riordan is a very caring man," she finally managed to respond.

"Oh, he is! And I think it's so sweet that he wants to formally adopt Tessa. Not every man would do such a noble thing, you may be sure. Oh, your wedding is going to be so exciting, Alisa.

I know I'll cry. I always do at weddings, I even did at my own."

For Cordelia had been married over the holidays and was a mint-new bride, full of blushes and hints as to the glory and mystery of married life. "But I know *you* won't cry, Alisa," she went on. "You're such a sensible person, so capable. I can't imagine you doing anything silly."

Alisa dropped Cordelia off at her town house, then proceeded to her own home, her mind drifting to the events of the past weeks.

The excitement of the coming nuptials, coupled with ... yes, with what Alisa could only call apprehension. For, Cordelia's chatter to the contrary, all was not as it appeared.

Riordan a "caring" man? Yes, Alisa thought bitterly, if by that you meant his affection for his illegitimate daughter. Although Malva had urged him to wait until several months after their wedding before introducing Tessa, Riordan had refused.

"No, dammit. She's mine and I've waited long enough, keeping her behind closed doors. I want to bring her out, I want to make her mine—that's the purpose of all this, isn't it?"

The three of them were having tea together in Malva's neat, elegant drawing room filled with her collection of Sèvres and Capodimonte porcelain.

"But it's risky to—" Malva began.

"No, it isn't risky. What difference between a lie now and a lie later? As we planned, Alisa will travel to Detroit and return with Tessa, telling everyone that the child's parents are both dead of influenza. Everyone will believe that story—it's the winter season and sickness is common. She'll bring Tessa back to her home. She'll insist that she wants to adopt her little niece. I'll finally consent to it, in order to please my bride." Riordan shrugged. "It will work."

Malva frowned. "No doubt it will. Still, such hastiness . . ."

"I insist. It's going to be done my way, and I personally will see to any loose ends that need to be taken care of."

"Loose ends?" Alisa had questioned.

"Never mind," Riordan said. "I told you, I'll take care of it."

So Alisa had followed the script Riordan had outlined for her. She had made a train trip to Detroit and returned with Tessa, who had secretly been taken there a week previously. Now Tessa and her nurse, Fanny, lived with her, the small girl romping through the parlor, bedrooms, and kitchen of Alisa's home as if it were a new and glorious playground.

And Alisa could not help taking the child to her heart. She took Tessa to Malva's afternoon teas and to watch the ice skating on the lagoon at Lincoln Park.

"What a pretty baby!" Malva's friends gushed, vying to play with the pretty toddler. Everyone admired Alisa for wanting to adopt the little girl, and they considered Riordan noble and self-sacrificing in attempting to please his new bride in this way.

Only Alisa, Malva, and Riordan knew the full story, along with the servants whom Riordan paid well to remain silent.

Life grew hectic as the wedding date neared. Flowers from Riordan arrived daily, along with wedding gifts of crystal boxes and goblets, bone china, porcelain, silver tea services, and furniture. There were parties, teas, receptions. By day, Alisa lived the life of the joyous engaged woman.

But at night, all was different. She had begun having difficulty sleeping and would toss and turn, her restless dreams haunted by disturbing images.

In one of the dreams, she was trapped inside the long tunnel-kiln at Pots Ogden's brickyard, while a carload of cherry-red blazing-hot bricks rolled toward her. She watched it come, too horrified to scream. Just as bricks tumbled over on her, she would awake, to lie in her bed shaking all over.

Other dreams were worse. Riordan himself was in them, a stranger who wore a mask that showed only his eyes, filled with dark emotion.

"You betrayed me," the dream-Riordan accused. *"You're a traitor. Give me back that ring, you have no right to it."* Then he would snatch the heavy South African diamond off her finger. Flashing in the air, the ring would roll away and fall through a crack in the earth.

"It's only a bargain," Riordan taunted. *"An agreement, a contract, no more."*

Alisa would wake up, her cheeks wet with tears she had not known she had cried. She would sit up in bed and switch on the gaslight, holding her engagement ring up to its glow. Only the knife-hard, sharp glitter of the diamond could convince her that she still wore it, that she still was Riordan's fiancée.

There were times when she thought that Riordan, too, suffered. She was certain that he had lost weight, that his body was leaner, that the lines of his face were bolder, craggier. Often he seemed distracted, as if his thoughts were many miles away. On those occasions, he spoke shortly to her, refusing to be drawn into conversation.

Once she saw him staring at a mother and child on the street, his mouth set with a curious expression of pain.

"Is anything wrong?" she dared to ask him later, when they had returned to her house and were playing on the floor with Tessa.

"No." He said it harshly. "Why should anything be wrong?"

Tessa had crawled away to investigate the fringe of the Turkish rug. Alisa cleared her throat. "Why, I just thought . . . you look so fierce, so angry. It is as if there is something amiss, something you aren't telling me."

"There's nothing wrong that can't be fixed."

"Then there *is* something wrong!"

He glowered at her. "I told you, I'll fix it."

"But if you'd tell me what it is, then maybe I could help."

Involuntarily his eyes flicked to his daughter. "If I needed your help, I'd ask. Yes, something has come up. But it's something that can be handled—I'll deal with it." She had never seen Riordan look so agitated, as he rose from the floor and left the room.

What could have happened to turn Riordan's mood so savage? Some holdup in the mysterious adoption proceedings about which he had told her little?

Today Alisa's body was tense with worry as she hung up her wrap and put aside a small length of lace from the shopping expedition, climbing the stairs to her cozy bedroom.

She reached her room and went inside, closing the door with relief. She began to take off her dress, deciding to lie down and try to nap before she had to dress for yet another of Malva's elegant little suppers. What should she wear tonight? She had a choice of a dozen elegant silks, failles, surahs, and satins, each one a tool that would help Riordan to get what he wanted.

As she stood in her petticoats, Nella rapped at her door. "Miss Amsell, you have a caller downstairs. I tried to tell her that you weren't receiving today, but she wouldn't listen."

"Who is it?"

"She wouldn't give her name."

Annoyed at the intrusion, Alisa quickly redressed. Social custom required that each hostess set aside certain hours in which she would receive callers, but this was not one of Alisa's "afternoons." Perhaps, she thought, her visitor was a newspaper columnist, here to glean more information about the wedding, details of which would occupy columns in the *Tribune*.

"Well, if it isn't the lovely young bride-to-be, toast of all Chicago!" Linette Marquis greeted her with a derisive smile, not even rising as Alisa entered her own parlor. A mingled aroma of perfume and brandy drifted around the actress like a fragrant fog, and her cool little face held an expression of utter determination.

"Good afternoon, Miss Marquis. I take it that you don't have a matinee to give this afternoon."

"No, I don't." In the hallway they heard the jubilant sounds of a small child banging on the floor with some hard-edged wooden toy, then Fanny's voice attempting to quiet her. "I've heard about that little girl you're going to adopt. I heard it at Fifine's. I go there for all my hats now. I love her styling—she knows just what sort of designs are going to tip my fancy."

"I see." Had Linette come here merely to talk about her milliner?

"She's a pretty kid, isn't she? I peeked at her while I was waiting for you to come down. And I've seen her before, too, when you and Riordan had her out in the carriage. All that cloud of black hair . . ."

"Why have you come here?" Alisa demanded, a sudden, terrible suspicion filling her.

"Why do you think?"

Perhaps she'd always been expecting this, in spite of what she'd been told by the stage manager and by Maria Capeziano.

Perhaps that was why Alisa was able to hold herself so straight and tall, and to speak to Linette with icy calmness. "You're Tessa's mother, aren't you?"

"I am."

The two women stared at each other, each taking the other's measure. Alisa, wearing a cool blue tea gown, her lace collar lending understated elegance. And Linette, every inch the flamboyant actress, wearing bright red silk trimmed with yards of black Parisian lace. On her head Linette wore one of Fifine's gaudiest hats, red velvet bows piled one upon the other, topped with a pair of stuffed songbirds that seemed to stare at Alisa with hard, beady eyes.

Alisa jerked her glance away from the dead birds. Her heart was pounding oddly. "But how can you be Tessa's mother? You've never been pregnant! That is, they said ... Mrs. Capeziano told me ... the stage manager said ..." Her cheeks flamed. "You never missed a stage performance."

A smile twisted Linette's lips. Alisa could smell brandy as she leaned forward. "I'm an actress, aren't I? There are ways, for those who are clever enough to think of them. Anyway, it doesn't matter now how I did it. *He* has been after me to sign papers about that kid. Wants me to sign her over to him."

Alisa started, feeling a horrid prickle run over all her skin, like a premonition of disaster. So this was why Riordan had looked so haggard lately! Why hadn't he told her? Why had he kept this from her?

She moistened her lips. "Of course you're going to sign the papers, aren't you? Tessa must grow up leading a normal, happy life, and be cared for in every way possible. Surely—"

"Surely I have some brains in my head," the actress interrupted scornfully. "He thinks he can manage me with a bit of sweet talk and a little lump of cash, some promises. But he can't. He wouldn't marry me. Now I want everything from him, I want his damn life's blood. And I intend to get it. I've taken steps to see that I do."

Horrified at the vicious purpose in Linette's voice, Alisa took an involuntary step backward. "But think of Tessa . . ."

"No. Think of me. I've always had to—no one is ever going to take care of me unless I do it myself. And think of that big wedding of yours, Miss Amsell, with all those hundreds of society guests you've invited. Oh, I read the papers, I've read all about it."

Alisa froze. Her wedding? This was a nightmare, Alisa thought. And suddenly she knew, with a sinking heart, that Riordan, for all of his money, all of his power, was vulnerable. He could be hurt, terribly so.

She forced herself to speak. "Explain yourself, Miss Marquis."

"Oh, you'd be surprised if I told you. There are things I know about your fiancé. Things he's done that would surprise everyone here in Chicago, that would make them all think twice about him. Then he wouldn't be such a big cheese in all those fancy society drawing rooms, would he?"

"What are you talking about?" Alisa whispered.

Linette shrugged. "Ask him. He'll tell you."

Alisa was trembling all over; she didn't think she could stand another moment in the presence of this vicious, greedy, self-serving woman. She could scarcely believe that Linette could be Tessa's mother. She was like a wicked stepmother, returning to the christening to demand some terrible favor.

"I want you to leave, Miss Marquis. Leave my house right now."

"Oh, I'll leave, all right." Linette tossed her head, her eyes narrowed, a hard little smile carved on her lips. "But I just wanted to tell you, Miss Fancy, that I can ruin your wedding. I can ruin everything for you if I choose to do it. You'd better talk to him, that's all I can say. You'd better make him see sense, if you know what's good for both of you."

With that threat, Linette turned and swept out of the room, her red skirts rustling angrily.

"What did she mean? What was she talking about? What can she do to Tessa, Riordan?"

Alisa had not been able to wait even a few moments longer, but had summoned a buggy and driven immediately to Riordan's mansion, where she had hurried into his office and demanded admittance.

Riordan rubbed a tired hand over his forehead. "She can do a great deal, Alisa, if she chooses."

Alisa's nerves felt tightly wound up, like steel buggy springs about to snap. Her eyes hurt with the tears that prickled at the backs of her lids, the tears she'd been blinking back ever since Linette had left her house. "I just don't understand all this! Is Linette Marquis really Tessa's mother?"

"Yes." Riordan sighed heavily. "She is."

Alisa wanted to shake him in her pent-up frustration. "Well? Is that all you're going to say? Why didn't you tell me before? However did she manage to hide it? What did Linette mean when she said there were things you'd done, terrible things, that would ruin you in Chicago?"

Riordan rose from his desk and paced the room in the movements she knew so well now—the loping, tight strides of the pent-up jungle animal that meant Riordan was in deep mental anguish. "I don't want to discuss it with you, Alisa."

"You don't want to discuss it! Well, isn't that just fine? We're going to be married in four days, we are planning to adopt your child, and you can't be bothered to talk about it!"

"Alisa. Calm down, please. It isn't as you think."

Her voice rose, shaking with indignation. "I don't know what I think anymore, Riordan. I just don't know. You wanted to marry me apparently only so you could get open possession of Tessa. Now there is some hitch in that plan. What is the hitch? What's going wrong? If you don't tell me, I . . . I think I'm going to smack you."

For the first time she saw a slow, weary grin twist Riordan's lips. "You wouldn't dare."

"Of course I'd dare! Do you think that I wouldn't?" She pulled back her right fist and brandished it, as she'd once seen a pugilist do at a street fair. "I'd *love* to punch you, Riordan Daniels—right on your big arrogant nose!"

Riordan was six inches taller than Alisa and about eighty pounds heavier, looming over her; if he were to hit *her*, he would knock her clear across the room. They glared at each other, and finally Riordan's lips widened in a genuine smile. "Go ahead, then."

"What?"

"Punch me."

"But . . . I might make your nose bleed."

"Let it bleed."

Again they glared and then Alisa released a string of helpless giggles, sinking back against a cabinet and giving way to the horrid, rollicking force of them. Soon Riordan laughed too, and finally they staggered together and held each other, laughing until tears ran from their eyes and their sides hurt.

"All right," Alisa said, when finally they had reached equilibrium again. "Now you have to tell me, Riordan. Because I was half-serious when I said I'd hit you, and I'm certainly not leaving here until I find out."

The story was brief, sad and sordid. Nearly two years ago, Riordan had been still in New York, pouring most of his energy into his work, which occupied nearly all of his time. But one night he had been persuaded by friends to attend the theater, and there he had seen Linette Marquis in *Pique.*

"She was saucy, charming, magnetic—you've seen her on the stage, Alisa, you know what she is like. Afterward, I went backstage and my friend introduced us. I took Linette to supper."

"I see." Alisa spoke slowly. "And . . . did you love her?"

"Love? No. I did find her fascinating, though. She was a type of woman I'd never met before— tough, charming, and totally independent."

"Oh," Alisa said in a small voice.

"To make a long story short, we became lovers and Linette got pregnant. Apparently she first tried to abort herself with medicines and drug-

store tonics, but was unsuccessful. So she concealed the pregnancy."

"Concealed it!"

Riordan scowled. "With all the layers of corsets
and petticoats you women wear, with waistlines
that can be raised, and flowing mantles and
overjackets that conceal the figure, apparently that's
quite possible. It must have been terribly hard,
but she never missed a stage performance and
gave birth alone in a hotel room, with only a
servant to attend her. I didn't learn these things
until much later. By then I'd come to Chicago,
with only occasional trips back to New York."

"I . . . I see."

Riordan looked troubled. "In fact, I knew nothing until one night when Linette came to see me
with the infant—Tessa—in her arms. She swore
that the child was mine. At first I wasn't sure
whether to believe her or not. But I took one look
at Tessa and saw myself in that beautiful little
face. I knew, in my bones, that she was mine."

"She does look like you," Alisa whispered, her
heart hurting as she waited for the rest of the
story.

For a while Riordan paced the room, his face a
stony mask. But finally he spoke again. "I offered
to adopt the child, but Linette angrily refused.
She wanted more—she wanted me as her husband."

"As . . . Oh!" Alisa's heart squeezed.

"I couldn't marry her, Alisa. I just could not. I
had already seen enough of Linette to know . . .
well, that we were much too different. And Linette
was furious! She went into a rage, shouting that
she wanted two things—me, and money. I would

be her lover—publicly, irrevocably. And I'd give her all the money she wanted as long as she wanted it. She said if I didn't do those things, she'd take the child and go to another city and abandon Tessa on some doorstep—I'd never see the baby again, never even know what had happened to her."

"Oh, no," Alisa whispered, appalled.

Riordan stopped his pacing, his expression anguished. "She was such a lovely baby. Her eyes were so bright, and when I reached out to touch her, she gripped her tiny fingers around mine and wouldn't let go." His voice broke. "I knew then what I had to do."

Alisa waited tensely, feeling a little thrill of alarm.

"I remembered the misery I'd experienced from my illegitimacy. The stigma of it, the curse, the filthy brand that tainted me! I didn't want it to be that way for my little girl. I ... I couldn't stop myself, Alisa."

"What did you do, Riordan?"

"I kidnapped my baby."

"You what!"

"Yes." His mouth was twisted with grim pain. "I wrested the infant from her mother's arms and left with her, ignoring Linette's screams. I departed that night for Chicago, taking Tessa with me. Later I sent Linette a large sum of money in reparation. Was I right or wrong in what I did? Did I commit a crime or a humanitarian act? Only God can judge me on that."

And man, Alisa thought, swallowing hard.

Kidnapping was a crime, punishable by law. She was shaking as she tried to absorb the shock of

this news. To take a baby from its mother's arms
. . . But what if that mother didn't love it? What if
she'd already threatened to abandon it, was using
her baby only to get money?

"But didn't Linette report you to the police?"
she asked.

"No." Riordan looked weary. "Instead, as soon
as she could, she followed me to Chicago. She
forced me to resume being her 'lover,' making me
dance to her tune."

"You danced extremely well," Alisa breathed.
She felt sick, dizzied from surprise after unpleasant surprise.

"She demanded much of me." Riordan looked
shamed. "I gave what I had to, Alisa. Presents,
money, attention. I even attended her performances, dancing attendance on her just as she wished.
But it was all for Tessa. I kidnapped my baby.
What would happen if Linette talked? Scandal.
Total, severe, damaging, and permanent. Added
to the taint of illegitimacy, it would ruin Tessa's
future forever."

"Oh . . ."

She heard Riordan go on. "I settled on a sum to
pay Linette, enough money to support her for the
rest of her life, if she would sign adoption papers,
giving up all rights to Tessa. She agreed to
everything, and I launched our plans to be married."

Alisa felt her stomach grip like a clenched fist.
She remembered Linette's stony face, her vehemence as she said she would take Riordan's very
lifeblood. Linette had wanted him for herself. Now
she, Alisa, had him. Was going to wed him in a

huge, splashy wedding. No wonder Linette was so angry!

"And now she doesn't intend to sign?"

"She'll sign. All I need to do is pay her more money."

"Are you so sure, Riordan? It seems to me that Linette is jealous and angry, that she hates us both."

"Don't worry about it. She's a vicious little blackmailer, no more than that. I can take care of her easily. You forget—I'm rich." With that, Riordan drew Alisa into his arms, crushing her against him.

She bit her lip, pulling away, again feeling those shivers of apprehension. "I don't like it, Riordan. You make it all sound so easy; you can solve everything with money. But suppose you can't? I talked to her, I heard her. She's utterly determined to hurt you."

Riordan looked grim. "No one is going to hurt me, Alisa, nor will anyone harm my Tessa. In a few days we'll be married, and I intend to sign those adoption papers, and all of these worries will be over."

Alisa prayed that he was right.

～❀ 23 ❀～

Alisa woke from a troubled sleep to the sound of pounding on her door.

"Miss! Miss!" Nella called. "You asked me to wake you, and I did . . . it's time to get up and get ready. I have your bath run, and breakfast is waiting downstairs, I'm keeping it warm."

"Oh . . . very well. Thank you, Nella." Alisa's voice was still thickened from sleep. She struggled up from under piled comforters, slowly becoming aware of the hard, clear February sunlight that streamed through the icicles hanging like crystal pendants from her window.

It was her wedding day.

She pushed aside the quilts and slid out of bed. Barefoot, she went to her dressing table, where she leaned forward to stare at her reflection in the glass. She saw with relief that her nights of sleeplessness had not left dark circles under her eyes. Once the day had begun, she knew, excitement would lend a flush to her cheeks, enhancing her looks.

Was she making a mistake? The question slithered

into her mind like a serpent, and once it came, could not be dislodged.

Alisa bit her lip as she pulled on a dressing gown and gathered her bath things. Linette's threats. The fact that Riordan didn't love her. The cold-blooded "bargain" that they had struck between them. None of these facts were auspicious for marital harmony; Alisa knew that as well as anyone.

If she had any sense at all, she knew she would dispatch Nella's son to Riordan this morning with the message that she could not marry him. Then she would pack her things and take a trip—to California, perhaps, or to Europe, where the distraction of new sights would help her to forget.

But she knew that she was not going to do those things.

She sighed, opening her door to pad barefoot down the corridor to the small bathroom, where Nella had already filled the claw-footed tub to brimming. The truth was, mistake or not, she had no intention of backing out now. How could she?

She sank into warm water, giving herelf up to its soothing heat. She longed to be with Riordan, craved his kisses and embraces as an addict craves opium. Oh, God, she thought. What would become of her, feeling as she did? Would Riordan ride roughshod over her emotions, hurting her deeply?

She thought about the day ahead, the lavish ceremony, the scheduled signing of the adoption papers, the reception and dance to follow, and finally, the moment when all masks would be dropped and she would be alone with her husband.

Then, she thought, swallowing, Riordan would have to express his feelings for her. Whatever those were.

She felt a nervous clenching of her stomach. Love. Even if he did not feel that way now, Riordan would surely grow to love her in time. He had to! Meanwhile, there was at least a start. He had assured her he would treat her well and that he would not humiliate her by flaunting his mistresses in her face. Didn't that count for something?

Uneasily she reached for a vial of bath oil and added several fragrant drops to the water, wondering if Riordan would like the soft rose scent. If this marriage was to work at all, she told herself, she must put aside her doubts and plunge ahead, trusting that all would be well.

But could she do that? If only her body would relax, her heart stop thumping in that thick, erratic manner!

The ceremony was to be at five o'clock. At two Malva arrived to help Alisa dress, along with Cordelia, who was to be the matron of honor. Both crowded into Alisa's room, where Nella labored to press out invisible wrinkles in Alisa's veil of Brussels net, so exquisitely fine that it seemed mistlike, hardly a thing of substance.

The wedding dress, white satin trimmed with pleated satin ruffles and rare handmade *point-duchesse* lace, hung from a door, while all around the room were laid out the petticoats and other articles Alisa would wear. In a satin-lined box gleamed the lustrous pearl-and-diamond necklace that Alisa once had worn to the theater. It was Riordan's wedding gift to her.

"Oh," she had breathed two days ago as she opened the box lid. "You went back to the jeweler's, Riordan, and bought this."

He had smiled crookedly, as if well pleased by the effects of his surprise. "I did. You refused to accept it once, but now you are going to flaunt it, my darling. And this is only the beginning of the jewelry I will lavish on you. None can say I am not generous in striking a bargain."

"Of . . . of course."

That last remark had completely spoiled Alisa's pleasure in the gorgeous necklace. Had he be-liberately set out to mar her joy by reminding her of her obligations toward him?

Now she only half-listened to Cordelia's excited chatter. "Alisa, there are already huge crowds in front of the church; we saw them on my way here. Throngs and throngs of people, all waiting to see you arrive. I hope you're ready for that!"

"People?" Alisa bit her lip. "But surely the wedding guests would not arrive hours early."

"They aren't guests," Cordelia gloated. "They are gawkers! Shopgirls and housemaids and heaven knows who else, common people who like to follow what the upper crust is doing. Haven't you been reading the papers? Why, columns and columns have been devoted to your wedding, naming every detail, from your veil and bouquet to the gold-engraved place cards you're having at the wedding supper. Even the little girl you're planning to adopt."

Alisa reddened, thinking that this day was going

to be turned into a sideshow. She felt thankful
that Tessa was safely ensconced again in the nursery at the Daniels mansion, with Fanny, her nurse.

"I provided the details for the papers, my dear,"
Malva put in. "I felt it best." She looked signifi-
cantly at Alisa, and Alisa understood that the lavish display had something to do with Tessa's
acceptance. Well, if that was the case, she certainly
could tolerate it.

If only she were not so nervous! The closer the
minutes ticked to the moment when she would
leave for the church, the more apprehensive she
became. Her hands and feet felt cold, with an icy
chill that seemed to penetrate directly to the bone.

"Here," Cordelia said. "Let's get Nella to lace
you, and then you can put on your petticoats,
Alisa. That dress looks so heavy—I think it's going
to be hard work just to pull that long train behind
you."

The three women converged around her, Nella
lacing, while Malva and Cordelia offered advice.
Then Alisa was being helped into the layers of
petticoats, then the crinoline *tournure*, which tied
around the waist, its back padded and ruffled to
provide support for the heavy dress.

But at last she was dressed. The tiny pearl buttons were meticulously fastened in their loops,
each fold of satin carefully adjusted to hang
perfectly. On her right hand Alisa wore one small
garnet ring that had been her mother's.

Nella held up the long train to preserve it until
they got to the church.

"Oh, Alisa," Cordelia sighed.

"Alisa." Even Malva's voice held a tone of awe.

"You are lovely beyond words. Your husband is going to be awestruck." *Your husband.* The words seared across Alisa's soul like a burning brand. "Come, my dear, look at yourself in the mirror."

Obediently Alisa walked to the mirror. She caught her breath, staring at herself transfixed. The terror she felt did not show. The image that gazed back at her was calm and ethereal, a tall, stunning woman whose heavy loops of honey-colored hair were fastened by a coronet of orange blossoms and large pearls. More pearls and diamonds gleamed at her throat. Her pale cheeks were delicately flushed, and her eyes flashed deep blue.

"You are a beautiful bride," Malva pronounced.

"Something old, something new," Cordelia crowed. "Alisa, Alisa, we've forgotten all about that! What have you that's old?"

Alisa held up her hand with the garnet ring. "That was my mother's."

"And *new*, of course, that's your dress and veil," Cordelia chattered. "But 'something borrowed' —what is that to be?"

"My wedding necklace," Alisa said firmly. "I borrowed it once."

"I have 'something blue' for you," Malva put in. She handed Alisa a small linen handkerchief, its scalloped edges exquisitely embroidered in blue thread. "This is my own work. You may tuck it down your bodice, Alisa."

"Malva." Alisa stood holding the scrap of linen, feeling absurdly touched, far out of proportion to the gift. Tears stung her eyelids, threatening to spill. "Oh, Malva, to think that you did this yourself . . . I don't know when you could have had time."

"Of course I had time, dear." Malva swept forward and hugged Alisa to her breast, pressing her close so that Cordelia would not see the crystal tears that glittered on the cheeks of the bride.

A carriage guarded by a driver and two postilions took Alisa, Cordelia, and Malva through the huge crowd that surged in front of the church. The gawkers were packed ten and fifteen deep, nearly trampling over low wrought-iron fencing in their eagerness to see the bride arrive.

Alisa looked at their staring, avid faces. A tired-looking woman of thirty had a small boy clinging to her skirts. A grizzled man wore the leather apron of a blacksmith. A woman dressed in shabby black pressed close, her face avid for any glimpse of the nobility she could get.

Little more than a year ago, these people had fled the towering conflagration of the Great Fire; perhaps, on that frightening night, she had rubbed shoulders with some of them. Alisa forced herself to relax a little. What was wrong with her, seeing enemies in these eager people? In their way, perhaps they even wished her well.

As the carriage slowed to go through the church gate, mounted policemen drove back the crowd.

"Oh, Alisa, look!" Excitedly Cordelia pointed. A sketch artist scribbled madly, taking down his impressions of Alisa's face as seen through the window of the brougham. From this, a woodcut would be done, and this would appear later in the newspaper.

The gates swung open and the carriage rumbled through. Just as it turned to the right, toward the chapel entrance, Alisa saw another buggy pull toward the church. In it was Linette Marquis, the actress, wrapped in a long sable cape that framed her face dramatically. She was accompanied by a balding man in black; an attorney?

Alisa could not help drawing in her breath.

"Nervous?" Malva asked, leaning forward. "Of course you are, it's only natural. How many wedding days does a girl have? But I assure you, all is going well."

"Is it?" Alisa asked numbly.

The church anteroom was furnished with stiff Chippendale furniture and smelled of beeswax, scented candles, and soap. Alisa had been ushered here to wait for the ceremony to begin and for the adoption papers to be signed. Present would be Alisa, Malva, Riordan, Riordan's attorney, and Linette and her lawyer.

But thus far only Malva was here. The wait stretched into long minutes, while Alisa paced restlessly back and forth, going to the window to stare out at the circular brick drive, flecked with patches of February ice. Even here, within the stone walls of the church, they could hear the noisy crowd.

Alisa stared at the frozen puddles, thinking that her stomach felt as if it, too, were coated with liberal amounts of that very ice. Nervous shivers rippled up and down her skin. Something was going wrong. She felt it.

"What is taking so long?" she fretted. She felt

sure she had heard sounds coming from another room—the sounds of angry, raised voices.

"Patience, Alisa," Malva counseled. "You know attorneys—there is always something in the fine print to distract them and cause a delay. It's only part of the game they play."

"But surely all the details of the adoption have been worked out in advance. And they know it's our wedding day. Oh, where is Riordan? The least he could do is to come in here and tell us what's going on!"

"Shall I go to find out, then?"

But before Malva could leave the anteroom, its door swung open and Riordan entered, followed by his attorney, a man of fifty with a crest of distinguished-looking white hair. Alisa took one look at Riordan's thunderous expression and felt her heart sink down to her satin slippers. Wordlessly she went toward him.

"She won't sign." Riordan voice was thick. "She wishes to wait."

"What? But she promised. She said—"

"She wants to wait," Riordan said savagely, "And there is nothing we can do about it without revealing Tessa's parentage, as she well knows!"

Chilled, Alisa turned for confirmation to the attorney. The man looked troubled. "He is right, I'm afraid. Apparently Miss Marquis had decided to try to hold out for more money."

Alisa shivered violently, remembering Linette's cold expression when she had talked to her, and her feeling that the actress was like a wicked witch at the feast, intent on some angry retaliation.

"Money?" Riordan was scowling. "If that's all she wants—"

"But it isn't all she wants." Alisa had been thinking about this for days. "That's the trouble! Linette wants revenge, Riordan! I'm sure that's it. You refused to marry her."

He glowered. "Oh, come now . . ."

"No. She is a beautiful actress, she must have received the adulation of many men. And then to be refused—it must have been a humiliating blow to her pride. As a last blow, you took her child. Even if she doesn't want the baby, even if she intended only to use Tessa, still, she must have had *some* motherly impulses. Perhaps—"

But Riordan angrily brushed aside Alisa's speculations. "Nonsense! She is a greedy woman who lives and dies for money. Smither, see to it that a bank draft is drawn up." He turned to the attorney and named a figure, stunningly high, enough to keep Linette in luxury for the rest of her life.

The man nodded, hesitating.

"Well?" Riordan's brows were beetled together in a savage scowl. "What are you waiting for? Go and make the arrangements, or I will find myself another attorney, one capable of following orders!"

"Yes, of course." The lawyer retreated, leaving the door to swing shut behind him. In the ensuing silence, Malva cleared her throat and Alisa could hear the thick pound of her own pulse.

"Riordan . . ." Nervously she approached her husband-to-be. "I don't like this. Linette isn't meekly going to accept a bank draft and get out of our lives on demand. You know that as well as I do. She wants more. She—"

"Be still!" Riordan shouted. "I don't want to listen to your doubts and fears, Alisa. We've come too far for that." She had never seen his face look so dark and stony, his expression so terrifying. She swallowed hard. Instead of a loving bridegroom, he looked more like an angry devil.

"Riordan . . ." To her dismay, her voice shook. She wanted to reach out to touch him, but was afraid he would shake her hand away, afraid he would turn on his heel and storm out of the anteroom, never to return. It was that kind of moment; she felt it spinning perilously in the air.

Beside her, Malva, too, stirred uneasily. If Riordan wished to wed her only because of Tessa, and he were thwarted in regard to his daughter, then why would he need Alisa? Their bargain was useless; therefore there was no need for a wedding.

Would Riordan jilt her?

Alisa felt herself sway. Small black dots crowded in front of her eyes, dancing like dark, evil snowflakes.

"What of the wedding?" she asked in a thickened voice that did not sound like her own.

Riordan shrugged impatiently. "The wedding? What's the matter with you, Alisa? Let's get on with it, of course. I'll see to Linette Marquis within the next few days."

She turned and walked to the window, her long satin train rustling behind her. Outside, sunglare glittered on the ice patches, hard and burning on the eyes. He intended to go through with it. But didn't he realize, didn't he see? Linette Marquis wasn't going to let him alone. Why should she sign adoption papers when she could continue to buzz around him like an ugly horsefly, demanding bits of blood?

Riordan didn't love her at all, was marrying her only for the sake of the child, a social future for the little girl that now hung in jeopardy. If for some reason that failed to materialize, then what would hold their marriage together?

Alisa shivered. Nothing would.

She felt tears burn her eyes, and knew, as she turned, what she must say. She could not marry him, not under these doomed circumstances; she'd be a fool to do so. An utter fool. Yet when her mouth opened, the words of refusal had somehow flown away.

"Very well," she heard her voice say. "Let us call the minister, then, and begin the ceremony."

Alisa stood at the altar beside Riordan, the nave so heavily banked with roses, orchids, and stephanotis that their scents were cloying, almost sickening. Nausea lurked at the back of her throat, and grimly she swallowed it back.

This was her wedding—what was supposed to be the happiest day of her life. She'd concentrate on that, she'd forget Linette, she'd *will* happiness into existence.

The sonorous words of the marriage service filled the air. Alisa repeated her vows, her voice low. From behind the long gauzy veil she cast a look upward at Riordan. How handsome he was, with his craggy face that today made her think of an angry warrior, perhaps even Genghis Khan, after the loss of some stragetic battle.

Riordan was saying his vows now. His voice was

hoarse but firm. Numbly Alisa listened to his promise to love and honor her. Her heart felt as if it were clenched into an enormous fist that would keep tightening and clenching until finally it was a burning core of pain.

She realized with a start that it was over, that they had been united in holy wedlock, pronounced husband and wife. Riordan's eyes met hers and she saw pain in them and a dark yearning.

Riordan! I love you, love you. Could he sense her thoughts, the deep, shocking wave of emotion that suddenly swept over her, leaving her weak?

He leaned forward to lift her veil, the fine netting faintly scratching her cheeks as he pulled it away. He bent toward her for the wedding kiss. His lips met hers, warm, smooth, and suddenly the hard knot that was Alisa's heart began to melt away. A quiver of joy radiated through her; she felt it rack her like an explosion.

She was Riordan's wife now, *his wife*.

She felt giddy, almost delirious with her relief. They were married now, for better or for worse. Whatever happened, whatever shocks or scandal or horror Linette Marquis had for them, they would face it together.

~❧24❧~

More crowds were at the Daniels mansion, being held off by policemen and by a staff of Pinkerton men that Riordan had hired for the occasion. It was here that the reception was to be held, and Riordan's home had been lavishly decorated for the occasion, banked with thousands of white roses and orchids, orange blossoms mixed with pearls strung in garlands down the magnificent staircase.

As Alisa stepped inside the house on Riordan's arm, she couldn't help gasping. The sight of the flowers was overwhelming, and their scent wafted toward her like afternoon in a June garden.

"Riordan," she breathed. "Oh . . . oh, it's wonderful!"

He smiled down at her, seeming pleased, although she saw that a tense muscle still flickered in his jaw.

One of the home's two ballrooms had been opened to the wedding guests, most of whom had already arrived at the house and were milling around, eager to inspect the wonders of the Daniels mansion. Among them was every important name in Chicago, from meat-packing kings, lumber and railroad barons, to those whose antecedents were based on very old money.

Later, after the receiving line, an elaborate supper would be served, the menu prepared by a Parisian chef whom Riordan had imported especially for the occasion.

As a favor, each woman would receive a silver dove, its neck set with a circlet of *pavé* diamonds and pearls. These favors alone had cost Riordan thousands of dollars, Alisa knew; and the flowers had depleted the supply of every florist in every city within train distance.

"Riordan . . . it hardly seems real." She clung to his arm, feeling weak with excitement, the sheer dreamlike quality of it.

"You can thank your cousin for most of this," he said. "Her ideas were splendid. Let's go upstairs and get Tessa," he suggested. "I want her in the receiving line with us. People might as well meet her right away."

Alisa began to object; this had not been in their plans.

"I told the nurse to have her ready."

So there was no choice but to stifle her apprehension and do as Riordan wished. Surely, Alisa thought, Riordan would not place his daughter in the receiving line if he were not assured that her adoption would be brought off without a hitch; she was being a fool to worry.

"Dada!" Tessa toddled to the nursery door, dressed in white muslin trimmed with pale blue ribbon, her cloud of dark curls held back with another blue bow.

"Darling girl." Riordan stooped to pick up his daughter, who squealed joyfully, clinging to his neck. Then, in a gesture of babyish generosity, she reached for Alisa too. Alisa felt a tug of emotion. Tessa *was* adorable, her every move loving and eager; it would take a hard heart indeed to reject her.

"Da! Lisa!"

"She's trying to say Alisa," Riordan said, grinning widely, the somber look gone from his face. "Fanny tells me she knows dozens of words now, she's a regular chatterbox. Come on, chicken, it's time to go downstairs and meet a lot of people. They're going to love you, you can bet on that."

Triumphantly he carried the little girl downstairs, Alisa following, and they went into the ballroom.

Later, it would all form a blur in Alisa's memory—the endless receiving line, women leaning forward to kiss her until the smell of their powder and scent was cloying in her nostrils. Her hand ached from being shaken, and her mouth felt frozen from constantly smiling.

She was a beautiful bride, everyone said, the most breathtaking bride Chicago had seen in a decade, and surely Riordan was the most handsome bridegroom.

But the real hit of the receiving line was Tessa. Perched in Riordan's arms, the bright little girl gurgled, smiled, or, when an attack of shyness overwhelmed her, buried her face in the starched front of Riordan's shirt.

"She is simply beautiful," matron after matron gushed, won over. "Such a charming child, and she is yours now, you say?"

"Yes, we adopted her just before the ceremony," Riordan said. "She is now officially Tessa Daniels. It's a pity her real parents couldn't have been here today to see how pretty Tessa looks, but we plan to take very good care of her, don't we, Alisa?"

"Yes, of course," Alisa agreed through stiff lips, wishing that Riordan hadn't chosen to lie.

Later, when music drifted through the house and Tessa had been taken upstairs to the nursery, Alisa was briefly alone with her husband near the banked flowers and shrubs that concealed the fifteen-piece orchestra.

"Riordan, why did you have to make the announcement about us signing the papers so *definite*?"

He scowled down at her. "What other choice did I have? Think about it. We had already told everyone her parents were dead. You went to fetch her, we had told everyone we would sign papers. Was I to say that we couldn't sign, that an impediment had come up? What sort of impediment could there possibly be?"

Despite the warmly heated house, Alisa felt a chill. "But what if Linette does something to spoil it?"

"She won't. I have sent her a large sum of money."

"But what if that isn't enough?"

"It will be." His face had again acquired that frighteningly angry look that she had seen in the church anteroom. "Will you spoil our wedding day with worry, Alisa? Do you want people to see you looking tense and anxious? They'll guess something is wrong."

"I . . . I'm sorry." She tried to force her features into a smile again, although she felt perilously close to weeping. She was an unwanted bride, wed only to fulfill a purpose. That was the bitter truth of it. She had held herself proudly together for so long, she'd smiled and smiled until her very face hurt. Now she longed only for privacy, to be alone for a while to regather her courage.

"Darling." As if sensing her sudden vulnerability, Riordan slid his arms tenderly around her. "You don't have to apologize to me or to anyone. You've done splendidly today and of course you are worried; we both are. Please, just hold out for a few hours longer. Then we'll be alone together, and it will seem better."

Wordlessly she clung to him, needing the feel of his strong arms holding her. Several of the wedding guests stared, but Alisa didn't care; after all, weren't they newlyweds, and didn't lovers indulge in such intimate displays, especially on their wedding day? She had nothing of which to be ashamed. And if there was worry on her face, she decided, people would only attribute it to the natural nervousness of a bride.

It was midnight before the last guest departed and Alisa and Riordan were able to go upstairs to the suite that Riordan had had redecorated for their use. There was a dressing room for each of them, Alisa's lined on three walls with closets for all the many gowns she would one day possess. A smaller closet contained built-in drawers and shelves for petticoats, fichus, breakfast caps, and other accessories, and there was even a small floor safe for temporary storage of her jewelry. Built-in racks could hold hundreds of pairs of shoes.

A sitting room had been decorated in tones of gold and white, but the large master bedroom had, like the palace car, been adorned entirely in dusky honey-colored satin. Roses in wonderful shades of salmon, coral, and peach were arranged everywhere, their scent sweet.

Alisa had seen these rooms in various stages of completion, so they did not come as a surprise to her this night. Leaving Riordan in the sitting room, she walked into her dressing room and opened one of the closet doors, gazing inside at a closet as yet unfilled with gowns.

"Do you want me to call Nella or another maid to help you undress?" Riordan called from the other room. "I'm sorry, Alisa, I should have thought of it."

"No. I don't want Nella, not tonight." She stood looking into the empty closet, feeling suddenly empty herself, as if all the emotion had seeped out of her, leaving her bereft. Perhaps she was tired, and certainly excitement had taken its toll. She just felt drained.

Wearily she stooped and, managing the long train with difficulty, managed to slide off the satin slippers.

"That dress is bound to be heavy," Riordan called. "I'll help you with it, then, since you refuse to have a servant."

"No, I . . . I can manage."

"I will help you, Alisa." Suddenly he was beside

her, his fingers already warm at the back of her neck as he released the clasp of the pearl-and-diamond necklace. Alisa stood trembling, feeling like a gazelle captured at the mercy of some wild hunter.

"It is a beautiful necklace," she whispered. "I do love it."

"It was yours all along, you know," he murmured, putting it aside. "Did you think I would let you take it on loan, like some shopgirl wearing a bauble she could not afford?"

"It wasn't necessary for you to give it to me."

"Ah, but it was. You are my wife now, Alisa. My wife." He bent down and she felt the butterfly-soft touch of his kiss at her nape. The sensation sent warm, shivering thrills deep into the center of her.

"It's been a long day. I'm so tired," she whispered. "More tired than I had thought I would be."

"Of course you are, and we'll have you out of this gown quickly." He was behind her now, his hands managing the long row of looped buttons as skillfully as any lady's maid, lingering on the curve of her back. Feeling dreamily removed from reality, Alisa allowed him to undress her, to lift away the heavy gown with its yard upon yard of flounces and long train.

Finally she stood in petticoats, which Riordan stripped away in gentle caresses that at last left her standing bare to his gaze, her eyes averted in sudden shyness.

Smiling, he tilted up her face to meet his. "You are beautiful. Don't be shy, Alisa, you mustn't shrink away from me, not now, after all we've been to each other."

She felt an absurd leap of her heart. *After all we've been to each other.* Was he about to declare his love for her?

"Alisa, Alisa, Alisa," he murmured, nuzzling more kisses into her neck, kisses that strayed to the soft curve of her collarbone and then trailed down the slope of her breast.

"Riordan . . ." She clung to him, her body shaking all over now, willing him, willing him to say the words.

I love you.

Such simple words, only three of them, and yet what meaning they'd have for her. They'd provide the real joy of this day, they would make it all worthwhile for her, the struggles and anxiety, the worry and heartbreak.

But the words she longed to hear did not come. Riordan lifted her up and carried her to the wide satin bed, pausing to undress himself, until he, too, was naked, resplendent in his maleness.

"You are beautiful," he repeated, scooping her to him. "So beautiful, Alisa, so very, very lovely. Ah, I'm lucky, lucky beyond all worth. . . ."

Long into the night they held each other and he rained kisses and caresses on her. Soft, tender, demanding, fierce. He stroked her skin and called it satin, he kissed her neck and called it the sweetest he had ever tasted, he rocked her in his arms, powerless to his strength. He took her and made her his forever, in a way no man would ever, could ever, do again.

But Riordan did not tell her that he loved her, and it was a lack that took away the fine edge of joy, rendering Alisa's wedding night bittersweet.

It was nearly dawn when Alisa lay next to Riordan, still bleakly awake. She stared into graying darkness and tried to force away the searing disappointment that filled her. He didn't love her, he couldn't. Otherwise, he would have told her; did not all men tell their wives they loved them on their wedding nights? If not *that* night, then when?

Despair filled her as she listened to the slow, even, regular cadence of Riordan's breathing. Already she loved the sound of that breathing, because it meant that he was near her, it meant intimacy with this puzzling, complex, disturbing, wonderfully lovable man. God, how she adored him! And he didn't love her. He had only married her to make a position in society for his little daughter.

Closing her eyes, Alisa thought about Tessa. It wasn't the baby's fault that Riordan was obsessed with achieving for her what he'd never been able to accomplish for himself. How easy to be jealous of Riordan's regard for his daughter.

Alisa shivered, thinking that Tessa must not be blamed ever. The little girl needed love, and Alisa vowed that she would give it to her unstintingly. This was a part of the "bargain" that Riordan had not even mentioned, nor had he said anything about the other children that would surely follow one day.

Children upon whom Alisa could lavish her love,

gaining the fulfillment that possibly never would await her in her relationship with her husband.

Dear God. She voiced a half-wordless prayer. *Please* . . .

She heard a deep sound beside her. Her husband turned over in bed, reaching for her in his sleep, enfolding her in his warm, strong embrace. Alisa felt tears sear her eyelids as she folded herself into the curve of Riordan's naked body so that they lay spoonlike.

If he loved her at all, surely he would have told her so this night.

Still, he did feel warmly toward her, she consoled herself; she would have to be a fool not to see that. And they were husband and wife now. She heard her own breathing grow more regular, and finally, just as dawn was breaking, she was able to let her body relax deeply enough so that she fell asleep.

"Mrs. Daniels, it's time to wake now . . . I have lovely orange juice for you, and it's a sunny day, the snow is almost melted!" Nella's voice woke her, as it always did, full of early-morning cheer.

Alisa sat up in bed, noting that Riordan had already risen to go to work in his office, leaving her to breakfast alone in bed.

How quickly and easily her new routine had slipped in upon her, seducing her with its luxury. Breakfast in bed—once she had scoffed, thinking that only spoiled, lazy women permitted themselves such self-indulgence. Even a year ago she would never have dreamed of doing such a thing.

But today she stretched and yawned, smiling as Nella brought in the silver tray upon which were arranged fresh croissants baked by the Parisian chef, jam, and pats of butter. Freshly ground coffee gave off its rich, steaming aroma.

Breakfast in bed was perhaps even a necessity, she thought as Nella left. For her new social routine was as exhausting as it was busy. These few moments alone in her bed with breakfast were sometimes the only privacy that Alisa would get in her entire day. Teas. Dinners. Receptions. Excursions to the opera, where Cousin Malva had seen to it that the Danielses were able to acquire a coveted box, from which they could see and be seen.

Time to think was what this solitary meal gave her. To plan the busy day, each activity designed with but one end in mind—to launch Tessa safely and permanently into Chicago society.

Alisa nibbled at her food, finishing only the coffee. Finally she put the tray aside and rose, going into her dressing room to select the first of several gowns she would wear today.

First, of course, was her "morning gown," in which she would greet Riordan in his office, then go to another office on the second floor, where she would meet with her new social secretary, a snobbish but impoverished widow hired to help with the countless details required to launch Alisa as one of the city's top hostesses.

"But, Malva!" she'd protested in vain when Malva had suggested hiring Mrs. Rivers. "I don't want ... I can't—"

"Delia Rivers is a veteran social secretary. She knows society inside and out; all you have to do is listen to her, and you can't go wrong. You *must* entertain, Alisa. I have accomplished much, but if you do nothing, it will all slip, and we will be exactly where we were before. Tessa's position must be solidified."

"I . . . I see." Alisa's heart sank. "But I'm not sure I can give large parties."

"Nonsense. Like any project, if you try to do your best, the challenge becomes absorbing, and certainly you are amazingly capable, Alisa. I am certain you will charm Chicago as it has never before been charmed."

"I hope so," Alisa said dubiously, thinking that this, too, was part of her bargain, and there was no reneging upon it now.

If only she could devote some time to work, to the management of the mill she had coveted, the life of financial power that drew her with such glittering allure! But there wasn't time anymore. It required endless expenditures of time and energy to entertain on a lavish scale, as she was finding out.

But in a few years, she assured herself, when Tessa was secure, she would have the routine of party-giving down to a science. *Then* she'd work again, and Riordan could not stop her.

"Mrs. Daniels, good morning." It was Betty, her new wardrobe maid, a slim woman of twenty-five whose sole duty it was to see to Alisa's clothes, to mend tears in hems and seams, to wash and press the dresses Alisa wore every day, and to help her put them on.

"Good morning, Betty. I think I'll wear the celery-green morning dress, if you could have it ready."

Alisa opened the second closet door and walked into the closet, which now held dozens of new gowns. Carefully she inspected the dresses: a brandy-colored silk, a cobalt faille with elaborate ruched trimming, countless others.

"Then, for receiving this afternoon, I think I'll choose the écru foulard. Later, when Mr. Daniels and I go out for a ride in the carriage, I'll wear the new carriage dress of striped lavender and white silk with the bias flounce."

The maid nodded, promising to have these gowns ready. "And tonight, madam? For the ball at the McCormicks'?"

Alisa frowned, going to the third closet, where ball dresses in a dozen hues hung on padded satin hangers. "The rose-colored faille, I suppose," she said at last, pointing to a gown fashioned in medieval design, with a low-cut chatelaine bodice, a lace frill, and an elaborate looped sash that emphasized the soft, feminine curves of the dress.

Four gowns in one day, Alisa thought as the maid collected the first dress and all of its accessories. It was life on a scale to which she had never really aspired, and she wasn't sure she liked it.

What had happened to the simple pleasures in life? Taking Tessa to Lincoln Park to watch her grub happily in the sand. Curling up in bed with a good book. Or jumping into her dashing new buggy to set off downtown at a brisk, spanking trot. Eventually to rattle over one of Chicago's busy bridges, savoring the dirty, smoky, industrial life of the city, the smoke and grit that meant power.

Those were the things that Alisa really liked to do.

She waited while Betty fastened the morning dress, feeling a stab of envy that Riordan could still do as he liked. Why was it that their bargain resulted only in a change in her life, not his? For he went on exactly as he had before, working long, hard hours, stopping only to escort Alisa to the various social functions that required his presence.

It wasn't fair, she fumed as Betty fastened hooks and eyes and looped buttons.

On the surface, from the viewpoint of any curious onlooker, Alisa's marriage was picture-book happy. Riordan was the perfect lover, the handsome, doting husband who gave her anything material that she wished. They had a beautiful adopted daughter. Yet in private Alisa knew it was all a sham.

Just as her heavy, sparkling ring was for "show," so was Alisa herself. An object with a use, she thought angrily. And that was all.

"Anything else, madam?" Betty wanted to know, in the prissy, stiff accents of a trained lady's maid.

"No, Betty, that will be all."

Alisa could hardly wait until the woman left. She turned to inspect herself in the full-length mirror with which one of the closets had been hung. She saw a tall, beautiful woman impeccably dressed in the height of fashion even to do her household accounts and meet with her secretary.

Rebelliously she whirled, hearing the silken rustle of her skirts. What if she *didn't* consult with her secretary today? What if she did exactly as she pleased for a few hours?

Riordan, deeply involved these days in a railroad merger, would probably never even notice. And she could give snobbish Delia Rivers the task of making up the invitation list of two hundred guests for the reception Alisa intended to give in three weeks' time.

That, Alisa thought gaily, would surely keep the woman busy for a while!

She laughed to herself, reaching up onto a closet shelf for a bonnet trimmed with pale green and yellow silk roses, trailed with an airy little veil. Yes, she thought, she would do it, she would! She would escape from the house and visit the Amsell mill.

Before she left, however, she stopped to say good morning to Tessa. She found the child seated at a low nursery table messily engaged in feeding herself her own breakfast, to the accompaniment of oatmeal spilled on face, hands, dress, floor, and nurse.

At the sight of Alisa, Tessa chortled, reaching out both sticky arms. Alisa hugged her, promising to come back later to read the little girl a story.

"Story! Story! Story!" Tessa crowed.

Alisa went out to the carriage house to claim the newest, shiniest black runabout, marked with the Daniels initials in gold relief. It was a soft April day, full of the moist, intriguing smells of new earth. Alisa breathed in great gulps of air, enjoying, too, the faint waft of stockyard and factory smoke that always permeated Chicago.

It felt good to be outdoors today. More than good, she told herself, slapping the buggy reins. For the first time in weeks she felt free. She could do as she wished, go where she wished, and there was no one to stop her.

She drove to the Amsell mill, noting with pride that the twin pine trees in front of the door had grown taller and fuller and greener over the winter. This month a new blast furnace had been added to the mill, and piles of brick, timbers, and steel girders were still stacked in the yard, lending an air of untidiness.

But Alisa looked around covetously, loving every untidy pile and stack. This was her mill. *Hers.* She had worked for this mill, she had schemed and plotted and sold herself—well, hadn't she, wasn't that what her marriage to Riordan amounted to, if she were bitterly honest?

But at least the mill was now hers, Riordan having honored his commitment by deeding it over to her, and she gloried in its possession.

"Well, Alisa! It's good to see you. Are you here to see what we've been doing?" Felix Morgan, the manager, greeted her effusively.

"It's good to see you, Mr. Morgan. I just had to come out today to see the new blast furnace. Would you show it to me?"

"But the ground is terribly muddy. That last thaw . . ." Morgan seemed visibly to pale. "I'm sure Mr. Daniels wouldn't want you to soil your beautiful dress."

"Oh, that's all right. It will wash." Alisa brushed aside his concern. "About the new furnace. I've been interested in its capacity. About how many . . ." She stopped. Morgan's eyes were riveted on her gown.

Involuntarily she, too, looked down at the morning dress, with its rows of pale green flounces, its delicate hand-woven lace trim that could not withstand a harsh washing. Flushing, she realized. Before, she had always come to the mill wearing simple and serviceable clothes.

Now she looked what she was—a society woman toying in business.

She lifted her chin. "I suppose my dress is a bit fragile. But we'll take care of that. Do you have an old coat lying about? And a serviceable horse blanket or two?"

Facing down the man's objections, she made a point of protecting her gown from mud so that she might tour the new furnace.

She left the Amsell mill in an odd, defiant frame of mind. Although she had been intending to go home, she found that she had turned the buggy, instead, toward the house that had once been her father's. Along with the mill, Riordan had also deeded that over to her, and its previous tenants had vacated.

She drove there. It sat as it always had, a corner house in a row of large homes crammed on tiny lots, each guarded by elaborate wrought-iron fencing. Carriage houses in an alley served the dwellings.

Alisa pulled up in the drive of the one her

father had used. How many times, as a girl, had she raced out to that very carriage house to meet Papa? It was there he had hung the rows of buggy whips he'd won in races, and there, too, that he had begun teaching her how to drive.

Now the carriage barn looked shabbier than she remembered, and much smaller. Or was it simply that she was accustomed to greater luxury now?

An unfamiliar-looking stableboy, his face pocked with acne, appeared to help her to climb down.

"I'm Biff. I work the stables next door, too, and shovel the walks in winter."

"I see. I'd like to go in and look at the house. Is it possible?"

"But it's closed, ma'am." This boy looked something like Billy, she decided, who had come to work in her millinery shop. But after the Great Fire, they had lost track of Billy, and she supposed that, like thousands of others, he had left Chicago.

"Then find the caretaker for me, Biff, and I'll let myself in."

"Yes, ma'am."

The boy trotted off, while Alisa waited near a clump of forsythia bushes, pale green with new buds. She looked at the house, feeling a strange, thumping sensation of the heart.

Was it really nearly three years since she had lived here? Since that day when she'd rushed home from racing her buggy so as not to be late for that final luncheon with Papa? That horrid lunch when he'd been so distracted, talking wildly about sharks and predators?

She shook herself, thinking how different she was from that girl of three years previously. She'd been so *young*, she thought painfully, so . . . new. Yes, she thought, looking at the bushes, she'd been as new as those fresh yellow buds of forsythia.

Then had come her father's suicide, the fire, Riordan, her struggles to win back the mill, and finally the bargain she had struck with her husband, a marriage of convenience.

"Ma'am?" A stooped-looking man appeared on the walk. "I'm the caretaker here. You must be Mrs. Daniels."

Alisa shook away her dark thoughts. "Yes. I'd like to inspect the house, if you please."

25

She walked through the house, hearing her footsteps echo on wooden floors now bare of rugs, feeling haunted by ghosts. Papa, his head flung back in laughter as he chased her up the stairs, teasing her. Her fifteen-year-old self, shouting something saucy back at him. Fifine, scolding in French, or whispering through the halls in a long silk robe.

Papa, she thought with a painful spasm of the heart, *oh, Papa*.

Nearly all of the furniture the Amsells owned had been sold, but a few of the larger pieces remained, carefully draped with muslin cloths. Alisa peered into her father's library. Almost, it seemed, she could smell the blue curl of good Havana cigar smoke.

Hastily she backed away. She poked her head into the conservatory, where, strangely, the plants still remained, lusher than ever, obviously still being watered by the stooped old caretaker who had given her the key. Among the greenery stood the little Greek boy, his marble eyes dancing with merriment.

Alisa stared at him. When she had been eight years old, the marble boy had looked exactly like that, his smile frozen forever. He was still the same, only she had changed.

Suddenly wishing she hadn't come, she left the conservatory and went upstairs. Studiously she avoided Papa's bedroom, where he had shot himself. Somehow she didn't feel like walking into that room, where, if this house held any ghosts at all, surely his would lurk.

Then she shook herself, trying to smile. Papa, lurking? Nonsense! Papa had loved her. Cared only for her. Wanted her to have this house, the mill, her inheritance.

I have them now, Papa, she told the empty house. *I got them, just the way you wanted me to, so you didn't die in vain.*

She hurried past the closed door, seeing in her mind's eye the agitated face of Fifine as she tried to stop Alisa from rushing in after they'd heard the gunshot.

Fifine had been Papa's mistress, she told herself calmly. For the first time she was able to accept this fact. That was why Fifine always treated Alisa with the acerbic possessiveness of a stepmother, why she'd acted as if the family still owed her something, for all those years in Eben's bed.

And who was to say that Fifine wasn't right to expect such things?

Alisa thought it tiredly, allowing this new thought to enter her mind. In a way, Papa had used Fifine just as Riordan was now using Alisa—to get something he wanted. Only, it occurred to her, Papa hadn't paid Fifine nearly as well.

She continued down the corridor, reaching the narrow staircase at the end that led to the third floor, where there were servants' quarters and a small attic. Fifine had had her bedroom here, separate from the others.

Some impulse made Alisa start up the staircase. Here, apparently, the caretaker seldom came, for there were dust balls on the stair treads, and the banister, too, wore a coat of dust. Upstairs, the servants' rooms still held narrow beds, dressers, wooden chairs, and china ewers for washing. Alisa peered into several of the rooms, wondering why she had come up here, what she was looking for.

She poked through the room that had been Fifine's, finding little to remind her of the French-woman save for a discarded hair net flung over the back of a chair. The bed was a little wider than the others, its feather ticking definitely softer, and there were two chairs here, and a little mahogany whatnot, as if Fifine had been given certain small luxuries to compensate for her position.

Alisa shuddered and closed the door. She strode to the end of the corridor to where a door opened to the house's half-attic.

Why not? she thought dully. She pushed open the door to step into the attic. As a child she'd climbed up here on rainy July afternoons to play among the old boxes and discarded furniture. An entrance led from here to the brick cupola room, where once she had marched her toy soldiers or peeked down at the street below.

Now Alisa breathed in deeply of the smell of dust and mildew, feeling as if she'd stepped right back into her childhood.

Nothing had changed. There were even the same boxes, although she saw that more boxes had been added, as if the previous tenant, in going through the house, had stuffed unwanted items up here, out of the way.

Curious, Alisa poked through an old wooden file box that she remembered being in the library. It contained old letters from creditors, most of them, she noted with a reddening of her cheeks, regarding accounts months overdue. She was about to close the file when a dusty cigar box tipped to its side. Pulling it out, she opened its lid. Sheets of paper had been stacked loosely inside.

Alisa picked one of them up, reading brief notes in Papa's handwriting. *Faro,* one of them said. *Owe Clifford Johnstone $500. And Philip Armour $1,000. Remember.*

There were more slips—dozens of them—scrawled with cryptic notations about gambling wins and losses. A few of the slips contained notes that the debts had been paid, but most did not. Alisa wondered if the debts had ever been paid. She closed the cigar-box lid and slid it back in the file cabinet. As she did so, a little puff of dust drifted up in the air, causing her to sneeze.

Papa, she thought, pushing back tears as she left the attic. *So you were a gambler, you really were one. I never wanted to believe it.*

She went downstairs and found the caretaker, giving him back the key.

"Are you aiming to put this house up for sale, Mrs. Daniels?" the man asked her, replacing the key on a large ring and pocketing it. "It'd make a nice big dwelling for someone that likes to live with a little class, eh?"

"I . . ." She shook her head, feeling confused and uncertain of herself. "I don't know. I hadn't thought."

She lifted her skirts and fled back to her buggy, thinking that she would be late for her afternoon receiving hours.

The shopgirl hovered obsequiously nearby, hoping that Alisa would purchase one of the luxurious shawls displayed in a fanlike arrangement.

Examining the shawls with centers of steel gray or black, and elaborate corner designs of double palm leaves in rich India hair, Alisa felt unfriendly eyes on her even before she turned.

"Well, *Mrs.* Daniels!" Linette Marquis' high-pitched, dramatic voice held malice. "What a surprise to meet you here shopping. One would think that you already owned more than enough shawls."

Alisa narrowed her eyes at Tessa's mother, wondering whether to snap out a sharp reply, nod, or simply ignore the woman. To cover her indecision, she reached out to finger a shawl with a center of creamy white.

"How is your little girl, Mrs. Daniels?" The actress asked it mockingly.

"Tessa is in very good health, thank you." Alisa managed to force out the words, feeling her heart sink with dread. Riordan had written a large bank draft and they'd heard no more from Linette. Alisa had even begun to relax a little. These past weeks she'd managed—they both had—to push out of their minds the fact that Tessa wasn't legally theirs.

"Is she?"

"Yes, she's a very active child."

The shopgirl was staring, and hastily Alisa found some money in her purse and bought the white shawl, telling the clerk to wrap it up.

She hurried out of the shop, while Linette followed her, dropping several items contemptuously on the counter, as if they weren't worth her purchase. Outside on the street, Linette turned.

"I wanted to talk to you, Mrs. Daniels."

"Yes?" Flushing, Alisa prayed no one she knew would see her here conversing with Linette. She did not know how to deal with this woman. She could hardly cut her dead and walk away as she longed to do—not without jeopardizing Tessa. But she did not have to put up with rudeness, either, she told herself. She decided to listen to whatever Linette had to say, but make the contact as brief as possible.

"I hear," the actress said, sneering, "that you are giving big, splashy parties these days in that fancy house that Riordan owns."

"We have given a few, yes."

"You're giving one next week. Two hundred people coming, I read in the *Tribune*."

"That's right."

Linette's eyes glittered. "What wouldn't I give to see that for myself? What are you serving? Pheasant under glass? Truffles? Smoked oysters? The finest French champagne?"

"The menu is still being planned," Alisa said cautiously, wondering where all this could be leading. Surely ... oh, surely Linette wasn't hinting for an invitation to attend? A visit from the flamboyant actress could only mean disaster.

"Well, good," Linette said, her tone deceptively sweet. "Is my little girl going to be there, then? I suppose she is, since she lives in your house."

"Yes, Tessa will be there."

"Kiss her for me, will you? I miss her sometimes. It's hard to give up your own baby, your own blood. Especially when she was snatched from you and you screamed and screamed and could do nothing about it." Like the actress she was, Linette suddenly assumed an expression of piteous bereavement.

Alisa's throat had suddenly closed up and she felt as if she could not speak. "I'm sorry," she managed to say.

Linette's smile erased the grief as if it had never been. "Indeed, I'll bet you are. Anyway, it looks like that bank draft that Riordan sent me isn't going to be nearly large enough to do what I want with it."

Alisa stared. "But the check was huge—he told me it was enough for you to live on for the rest of your life!"

"I told you once what I want from him. I mean to get it."

As she said this, Linette was smiling, and she even nodded to two well-dressed women shoppers who at that moment walked past them, carrying parcels. "So I might come up there sometime and see my little girl, just see that you're taking good care of her, if you know what I mean."

"We are taking excellent care of her, she lacks

for nothing," Alisa breathed, horror spinning through her.

"I'll be the judge of that. I want my little girl taken care of. And my man."

"Your man?"

"He was mine long before he was yours, if you'll remember. And maybe he'll be mine again, who knows!" Linette gave a harsh, theatrical-sounding laugh and started toward a carriage that waited near the corner, its driver pacing about and smoking a cigarette.

Linette was helped in, and the vehicle pulled away in a rattle of trappings and buggy wheels.

Alisa stood frozen, feeling as if she could not get enough air to breathe, her breath coming in shallow gulps. So, she'd been right. The check hadn't been enough, and Linette was simply letting them know that she hadn't forgotten, that she still had the upper hand.

I told you what I want from him. I mean to get it.

Linette's boast taunted Alisa with a terrible meaning, for hadn't the woman told her once that she wanted Riordan's very life's blood from him?

Alisa drove home in a fever of indecision and anxiety. Should she tell Riordan of her encounter with Linette? Of course she should! And yet, the closer she neared their home, the more reluctant she felt to do this. First, Riordan would explode in helpless rage. His solution to the problem would be to pay Linette yet more money, money that would never be enough.

And now Linette seemed to want more—acceptance into their home as an equal. Did she also want Riordan back as her lover? That, too, seemed implicit in the hints she had dropped. Alisa felt cold, chilly with her fear, and she knew that if she told Riordan too much, he'd only explode into action—action that might very well make things worse.

Troubled, concealing her worry from Riordan, she managed to endure the final week of planning before the reception. Mrs. Rivers had turned out to be a workhorse who could juggle a thousand details in her head, knowing the guest list by heart. Gratefully Alisa allowed her social secretary to run the event. Anything, so long as the party went well and Riordan was pleased.

The day of the reception a light May rain had dampened the streets but by six P.M. sunlight peeked through the new green leaves again, giving the street a festive air. A phalanx of flowering crabapple trees bloomed in front of the house, deep pinks and magentas lending magnificent color.

Inside, five buffet tables were laden with elaborate foods, the house decorated with hundreds of pots of hyacinths in glorious mixtures of blues.

Tessa toddled among the guests, the sash of her dress a vivid hyacinth, her laughter merry. How pretty Tessa was, how sweet. Alisa loved her more every day. If something happened to Tessa, she would feel as if her own child had been ripped away from her.

As Tessa giggled and flirted, women guests vied for the privilege of picking her up, and dozens flocked upstairs to see the nursery, to which Riordan had added a child-sized "house," built so that Tessa herself could crawl in and out of its rooms.

Matrons exclaimed and cried out in pleasure, begging Riordan for the plans so that they could go home and reproduce such a toy house for their own children or grandchildren.

Alisa kept a dazzling smile pasted on her face, her stomach clenched with dread. These were the women on whom Tessa's future depended. They were the mothers and grandmothers of the small girls with whom Tessa would someday go to school, make her debut, dance at cotillions.

Right now she and Riordan were in these matrons' good graces.

But what if Linette Marquis were to sweep through their front door this evening wearing one of the flamboyantly noticeable gowns for which she was famous, the ensemble topped off by a horrid hat on which a dead bird perched?

What if Linette were to announce to these women that Riordan had kidnapped her child, telling the tale with the appropriate tears and sighs? Alisa felt sick with worry.

Riordan approached her at the buffet table, bearing a laden plate. "Alisa, I've been watching you—you haven't eaten a thing."

"I . . . I'm excited, I guess."

"But you ate very little luncheon either, I noticed. Here. I've filled a plate for you and I expect you to devour every bite. I can't have my wife wasting away to nothing."

Obediently she nibbled at the rich, rare food, thinking that she would have been far happier with a simple piece of fruit and a glass of milk.

She was relieved when Malva and a group of her cronies swept toward them, pulling her away to exclaim over a new painting that Riordan had purchased.

The reception seemed to last interminably long. Coached by Malva and her social secretary, Alisa remembered the names of all her guests, and she made the rounds of every one, engaging each in personal conversation.

Once during the evening her eyes met Malva's and her cousin nodded. Alisa felt a brief thrill of pride. Riordan could not fault her here, she assured herself. He had asked for acceptance for Tessa; he was getting it.

Only Linette cast a cloud. . . .

Finally the guests began asking to have their carriages summoned, and after the last couple had departed in a flurry of good-byes and last-minute conversation, Alisa gave a long sigh.

"Well, that's over. It went very well, don't you think?"

"Superlatively well," Riordan said. "You do everything with wonderful ability, Alisa."

"I . . . I suppose." Disconsolate, she stooped to slip off her shoes, relieved that at least Linette hadn't appeared to ruin everything.

They walked slowly upstairs.

"Alisa," Riordan said, "something's wrong, isn't it?"

"I . . . why, no, what could be wrong? I'm simply tired, that's all. It was an exhausting party and I still don't know how I managed to remember the names of two hundred people."

"But you did." They were walking into their

bedroom now, Riordan stripping off his silk cravat as they went, to toss it on a chair. "Come on, now, Alisa. Out with it."

"Out with what?" she resisted.

"I know you, Alisa. I've worked with you, I've lived with you, and seldom do you pick at your food as I saw you do all day today."

Once she might have been flattered at his close observation of her, but tonight it annoyed and alarmed her. He knew she was hiding something. He would keep after her until she revealed it.

Her voice shaking, she admitted, "There is something. I don't wish to alarm you, but . . ."

Reluctantly she told him everything about her encounter with Linette. "I believe she hoped to attend our reception, Riordan—I think that was what she really wanted. And she made it plain that the money you paid her was not nearly enough."

"Alisa!" Riordan's face had gone white. His voice rose. "When did this happen, more than a week ago?"

"Yes. I—"

"Why did you wait until now to tell me?"

"What could you have done," she flared, "other than what you're doing right now, shouting at me? We haven't got adoption papers signed. Linette Marquis has a hold over us, she can tell the world that you kidnapped her child and everyone will know about Tessa's illegitimacy. You can pay Linette more money, you can pay and pay, but it's never going to be enough!"

"Dammit, Alisa! Dammit! Why couldn't you have

told me! Maybe there was something I could have done!"

"Such as what? Invited her to our party? Allowed her to flaunt herself here, parading in front of our guests with her secret? Is that what you want, Riordan? Or do you want Linette back again as your mistress, is that what you think ought to be done with her? Take her to bed and shut her up!"

They stared at each other, both of them breathing heavily in their thick, fierce anger, and Alisa realized with a sinking heart that this was their first quarrel as a married couple.

"I don't want Linette as my mistress," Riordan said at last.

"Don't you?" she taunted. "Oh, surely she pleased you well enough once. I saw how you enjoyed her that time in your office—"

"Enough," he roared. "Let's drop the subject. I will take care of Linette Marquis."

She felt a horrid, squeezing pang of her insides. "How?"

"No need for you to know."

"But you can't just . . . you can't just take action without telling me! I want to know what you're going to do!"

He leaned close, his eyes hard black stones, stubborn and angry. "I married you to provide respectability for Tessa. Thus far, you've been carrying out your end of our agreement admirably. But now it's my turn, and there are some things I must deal with. Linette is one of them. If she won't take money, then I'll solve the problem in some other way."

He turned on his heel to leave, and she knew he would return downstairs to his library and its inner workroom, his sanctuary.

"How, Riordan?" She hurried after him. "How? What are you going to do?"

He whirled savagely. "I'm not going to tell you, Alisa. I don't want you to mention it again, nor do I want you to do anything yourself about this. Now, leave me alone, *leave me alone, please!*"

Alisa felt a terrible energy consuming her, an energy she did not know how to expend. Restlessly she paced the corridor, hearing from downstairs the sounds of the servants as they dismantled the buffet table and cleared away scattered punch cups. From the nursery came Tessa's loud protest at being put to bed, her small temper already as fiery as Riordan's.

Alisa stopped in the nursery to hug the little girl. Tessa smelled of talcum from her bath, her adorable black curls moist. She squeezed the baby to her, feeling as if a band of molten metal constricted her throat.

Tessa. My God, what did Linette Marquis want, and what did Riordan intend to do about her? How did he plan to stop her from being a problem to them?

Alisa went back into their bedroom and closed the door, uneasily remembering that Riordan had, by his own admission, kidnapped his little girl, snatching a newborn baby from the arms of its mother. No matter that Linette was a bad mother, a greedy one, it still had happened.

Her thoughts thickened. Riordan had been in a

duel once, she remembered, shooting another man in the thigh. If his opponent had died, then Riordan would have been a murderer.

There were other acts of violence, too, in Riordan's background. Those fights he'd had as a boy defending his name. Altercations in the mining camp in Colorado.

Then she shuddered, pushing away the thought as if it were a scorpion. Whatever his faults, she knew Riordan would never physically harm Linette. But what would he do to solve this problem?

She sank onto her bed and stared sightlessly at looped brocade draperies with expensive silk ties.

May slid by in glorious days of sunlight and blossoms, followed by a hot June and an equally warm July. The Fourth of July was celebrated in Chicago with parades and speeches. Guns and fireworks were shot off in the streets, loud explosions that seemed to shatter their way into the Daniels mansion.

As if sensing the unease in the household, Tessa grew fretful, crying angrily at the loud noises and resisting being put to bed. She refused the soothing of her nurse, and it was Alisa who rocked her until at last she fell asleep in her arms.

In September, it would be Tessa's second birthday, and Alisa began to make plans to throw a large birthday party for all the little girls with whom Tessa would one day attend school. The guest list was being compiled carefully. As Malva insisted, it was never too early to begin making connections.

But Alisa could not put her heart into such

preparations. Since that night that she had told Riordan about Linette, nothing seemed the same. Riordan was now the one to eat little, and he spent hour upon hour holed up in his office or out on unexplained errands, absences that caused Alisa to grow cold with worry.

Where was he? What was he doing?

Questions ate at her like acid, and it seemed to her that her husband was drifting far away from her into the vortex of his private agony. She imagined a hundred different scenes. Riordan giving everything he owned to Linette in a staggeringly huge bank draft, only to have her laugh and tell him it wasn't enough.

Riordan paying regular calls on the actress, taking her back as his mistress, deliberately putting her under the considerable spell of his lovemaking in order to silence her.

Riordan, engaged in blackmail of his own . . .

Here, shuddering, Alisa would force away her speculations. She didn't know. Had been told not to ask, not to interfere. She was only tormenting herself with questions to which she had no answers.

She, too, had lost weight, and now she seldom slept an entire night through, lying half-awake in bed until Riordan came, sometimes nearly at dawn, to crawl between the covers.

Did he smell of perfume? Had he come from Linette's arms? *Oh, God!* She felt sure he had to be sleeping with Linette, that he might be desperate enough to do almost anything short of actual violence.

The actress's words haunted her. *He was mine*

*long before he was yours, you know. And maybe he'll be
mine again!*

One evening Alisa was descending the stairs, on
her way to consult the chef about a small dinner
party they were giving, when she happened to see
Riordan on his way toward the back door that led
to the mansion's carriage house.

Some instinct made Alisa pause before he could
look back and see her. Earlier, he had indicated
he planned to stay in his office and work. Now he
was going out.

As soon as she heard the rattle of Riordan's
buggy wheels in the drive, she hurried herself to
the carriage house and ordered the boy to hitch
up a second buggy.

She waited impatiently while the boy took his
time hitching a black mare in the traces. It was too
late to spot which direction Riordan had driven,
but she had a good idea where he might have
gone, and as soon as she was in the buggy, headed
it out through the gate and toward the old opera
house.

Overhead, a full moon was a luminous silver
disk casting silver light on a ridged formation of
clouds that partially obscured the stars. It was as if
the sky had been splashed with a giant silver brush,
on such a lavish scale that the concerns of mere
mortals were dwarfed.

Even the streets seemed caught in the magic
spell of that luminous light. Gaslights cast yellow
circles into summer darkness, and somewhere Alisa
heard laughter and the distant clip-clopping of
horses' hooves on brick pavement.

She felt a pang. It was a night made for lovers, for kisses and enchantment, and here she was following her husband on his way to what she felt sure was a rendezvous with his mistress.

She approached the old theater, where, as always, the line of carriages was parked, their waiting drivers gathered to talk, smoke cigarettes, or gamble. The performance hadn't yet let out, apparently, or the carriages would now be dispersing.

Alisa drove down the line, spotting Riordan's runabout at the very end, the horse tethered to a hitching post. He must have gone into the theater only moments before she arrived. Did he plan to watch the third act? Or was he in Linette's dressing room at this very moment awaiting her?

She drove around the block again, wondering what to do. Her heart was pounding thickly in her chest, and she felt her cheeks throb with the rapid beat of her pulse.

He was with Linette. That much at least was apparent. She felt sure he would remain until after the performance, whereupon he would take Linette somewhere for supper, or perhaps there would be a more intimate meeting.

White arms reaching upward to slide themselves around Riordan's neck. Long legs with beautiful curves that would wrap themselves around Riordan, hips urging him on to passionate lovemaking. . . .

Alisa sat rigid in the buggy, wondering if her heart would beat out of her chest here and now. *Riordan.* Was he lost to her forever, because of his illegitimacy and his obsession that his child should not suffer the way he had?

Grimly she drove around the block again, and then drove some more, widening her circles so that her buggy rumbled through newly rebuilt sections of town, clattering over new bridges and passing rebuilt factories and shops, the ornate marble Grand Pacific Hotel, soon to be opened. Overhead, the glorious moon mocked her.

She did not know how long she drove, or how many times her buggy circled the opera house, each time passing Riordan's parked buggy. The play let out, carriages being called by the cryer up to the front entrance of the theater to pick up their owners. And still Riordan's buggy remained.

The moon slid behind a piled-up screen of clouds, giving to them a wild, swirling brilliance. Alisa realized that she was crying, and had been for some time. Her cheeks were wet, a night breeze chilling the moisture against her skin.

Then she started. A dark figure strode toward Riordan's buggy, his walk all too familiar. Hastily she spurred on her horse, hoping to round the corner before he spotted her.

But it was too late.

"Alisa?" He stopped in his tracks, his voice low, tormented. "That can't be you."

Panic flooded her and she didn't stop, cracking the buggy whip over the mare's head to speed her away.

"Alisa!" he called after her. *"Alisa! What are you doing here?"*

She managed to arrive home before Riordan did, turning in the buggy to the stableboy, then racing upstairs to throw off her clothes and jump under the covers. She lay very still, her breathing rapid and uneven. Would he come upstairs and confront her? Demand to know what she'd been doing, why she'd followed him to the opera house?

But her husband did not come upstairs for a long time, and when he did, he just climbed into bed and lay beside her. She could tell by the sound of his breathing and his other movements that he wasn't asleep, but stared upward into the darkness just as she did.

Once she heard his breathing go sharp and uneven, as if he were crying silently. *Riordan, crying?*

She longed to reach over and touch him, to roll across the feather mattress and take him in her arms. But she could not. Never had she felt so distant from him, so far away. He was a stranger to her, a man she didn't really know at all. Tonight, more than anything, proved it.

He had married her for one reason—to provide security for Tessa. Now that had been threatened. A terrible thought stabbed her. What if the worst happened and Tessa were revealed to the world as illegitimate?

Then Riordan wouldn't need Alisa anymore. For their bargain would be negated, its usefulness finished.

She lay stiffly, willing her body not to shake with the silent sobs that filled her. She loved him so much, so much. And he didn't love her. Linette Marquis hung over their marriage like a mocking witch. Beautiful, vengeful Linette with her demands.

Linette wanted Riordan. Perhaps even tonight she had told Riordan that she would give him his daughter if he were to put Alisa out of his life forever. Divorce her and marry Linette.

The more she thought about it, the more Alisa knew, deep in her stomach and bones, that this was what had happened. No wonder her husband wouldn't talk to her. No wonder he was such a stranger!

26

The following morning Alisa woke to find Riordan already gone, and Nella knocking on her door with the customary breakfast tray. She sprang up.

"I ... I'm not hungry this morning, Nella. And you can tell Betty I won't need her either. I'll dress myself this morning."

Nella retreated, and Alisa went into her closet, searching at the back until she found one of the more modest work dresses she'd worn months before, a neat blue silk. She hurried into it, brushing her hair into a thick, shining roll. Then she left her bedroom and went downstairs to the library, where she knew she would find her husband.

"Yes?" When she knocked at his inner office door, Riordan's voice was gruff and impatient.

"It's me, Riordan. I want to talk to you."

There was a pause, as if he were going to refuse her, but finally he came to the door and opened it, ushering her inside. "Yes, what is it, Alisa? Is there something wrong with Tessa?"

"No, there isn't anything wrong with Tessa," she mocked. "Don't play games with me, we both know why I'm here. I saw you last night, and you saw me. Let's admit it to each other and talk about it!"

His jaw knotted, his mouth pressing together in a straight, hard line. She could see the deep pain in her husband's eyes, the anguish, and she longed to reach out to him, but again could not.

"There is nothing to talk about," he said.

"Nothing to talk about! Riordan! I can't believe you would say such a thing to me. Linette Marquis is *blackmailing* you—that's what it amounts to! She wants you to divorce me and marry her. Doesn't she?"

"I really don't wish to discuss it," he told her coldly, turning away.

"Oh! You don't!" She stepped after him, her fury so intense that she could have scratched his eyes out. "Well, I *do* want to talk about it. I insist on it!"

"Your insisting will do no good, Alisa. Haven't I treated you well as a wife? Haven't I given you everything you could possibly wish for, more than most women could even dream of having? Didn't I deed you back the Amsell mill, and that house of your father's you were so intent on having at whatever the cost?"

She lifted her chin furiously. "Yes, you gave me those things, you fulfilled your end of our *bargain* very well, Riordan Daniels. But you broke a promise to me."

"What promise?"

"That you wouldn't humiliate me by flaunting your mistress in front of me!"

A black eyebrow quirked up, and a bitter smile

twisted Riordan's mouth. "I didn't flaunt her, Alisa. As I recall, you followed me to the theater, intruding yourself where you had no business to be."

"Oh!" Before she could stop herself, her hand snaked out and slapped Riordan full across the face. For a startled instant they stared at each other. Alisa's palm stung from the contact with his flesh, and she saw with horror the reddened mark across his skin.

Riordan's expression hardened. His eyes seemed to flare hatred at her. "That's quite enough, Alisa."

"I . . . I'm sorry," she whispered, her entire body shaking in horror at what she had done. But he had already turned and was striding out of the office, leaving her to stand there alone.

She stayed in Riordan's office for long moments, willing her body to stop shaking, and composure to return to her features.

Why, why had she slapped him? What could she have been thinking of? She had only placed more distance between them, creating a chasm so wide she didn't see how it could ever be bridged.

Finally she fled the room, walking aimlessly into the large central hallway, where she found herself walking again toward the back door that led to the carriage house. Ten minutes later she was on her way to Malva's.

"He . . . he doesn't love me, he never did," she wept to her cousin, unburdening herself at last. "He only married me for Tessa's sake. Now Linette is thrusting herself at him, using the one sure hold she has over him—the child. She wanted to marry him when Tessa was born, and he refused.

She's resented that and now she sees a way to make it happen."

She collapsed in more sobs, and when Malva took her into her great warm arms, Alisa clung to her cousin, weeping until there were no more tears to cry.

"Oh, Malva, what am I going to do?" she whispered at last.

"You are asking me?"

Alisa pulled away. "Of course I'm asking you! Malva, I . . . I'm at a loss. Riordan is a stranger to me, a cold, hard stranger. I . . . I have just come from a quarrel with him in which I slapped his face. It was an unforgivable thing to do and it only shows that . . . that we are far apart, that he doesn't love me."

"I'm not sure how it shows *that,*" Malva remarked dryly. "Nevertheless, Alisa, I am sure you are wrong about one thing, and that is your husband's love for you. He adores you. It's written all over his face and always has been—ever since I've known him, anyway."

Alisa lifted her head to stare at her cousin. "I . . . I'm sure you're wrong."

"And I'm sure I am not. Love is a deep feeling and some men have trouble putting such feelings into words. But that doesn't mean that the emotions aren't there, running deep and true."

Alisa thought of Riordan and how firmly expressive he was in every other area. If he loved her, he would have been able to find the words. "I can't agree with you, Malva."

Malva frowned. "Then you are blind, Alisa—as

blind as he is! As for the other problem—Linette—I'm sure you'll find a way to solve that as well."

"How? Malva!" Alisa began to pace her cousin's boudoir restlessly. "She is blackmailing him with the thing that he loves most dearly—his child. You *know* he is going to capitulate; what else can he possibly do to save Tessa? I can't solve that."

" 'Save' Tessa?"

"Why, yes. You, of all people, know what a stigma illegitimacy is!" Alisa was losing patience with her cousin, who suddenly seemed to be making remarks that made little sense. "Taunts, innuendos—Tessa would grow up tormented, called names ... she'd never be able to make a decent marriage, she'd be socially ostracized. You know that would happen, Malva!"

Malva looked troubled. Finally she sighed. "Illegitimacy is indeed a trial and a stigma. Perhaps in another, more enlightened era, such a child could live a different life. But you will solve this, Alisa. You are one of the strongest and most capable women I know, and if there is a way, you will find it."

Alisa wanted to weep again from sheer frustration. She whirled angrily. "Oh, what nonsense you talk, Malva!" she snapped. "I'm not capable and strong, not in the way you mean. I have made so many mistakes, I—"

"Stop it. You're only feeling sorry for yourself. Look in your heart, Alisa. Look deeply, and you'll find the way. And now, my dear, I have to go summon the carriage and visit my orphanage. I am taking some new dresses and other fripperies to my girls."

Before Alisa could argue further, Malva had swept out of the room and was gone in a swish of black taffeta skirts.

Alisa sat for a moment in her cousin's boudoir, among the scents of Malva's sachet and perfume and the collection of small porcelain boxes that the older woman had collected for years on various trips to Europe. She felt thoroughly ashamed of herself. She had cried on Malva's shoulder, she *had* felt sorry for herself, and finally she had ended by snapping at her cousin, who was only trying to help her.

But how was she going to get Riordan back? She didn't feel capable and strong, as Malva suggested, and she certainly didn't see what there was in her heart that could shed any light on the problem. The only thing that her heart held was pain!

She left Malva's and drove aimlessly, unwilling to go home but not really caring where she went next. It was a hot summer afternoon, sun glinting on puddles left after a rainfall the previous night, the air thick with city smells. From somewhere Alisa could smell pungent river sewage and the odor of a granary.

But even those odors, which usually excited her, today couldn't rouse her from her misery. Her throat felt thick with unshed tears. What good was the exciting game of money and power without Riordan?

He had always been there, she realized, to challenge her, to test her, to be her mentor and opponent. Now she did have the Amsell mill and the chance to use that as the stepping-stone to a new fortune. But it was empty, empty.

Driving past a grain warehouse, Alisa saw some playbills plastered to its brick walls, one of them advertising Linette Marquis in *East Lynne*, the play that was now showing at the opera house. She pulled up her buggy to gaze at the lithograph of the actress, a stylized portrait of Linette that emphasized the swanlike, graceful curve of her neck and the dark, flashing eyes.

Linette, she thought dully. The actress was really at the center of all this, and had been from the very beginning. Was there a chance—any chance at all—that she might persuade Linette to change her mind, to stop the ugly game she was playing?

Hope quickened her breath. Maybe there was still something she could do! Riordan had told her in very strong terms that she was not to interfere, not to try to do anything on her own. But what did she have to lose now?

Certainly matters were as bad now as they could get, and if she did not do something ... She shivered, not even wanting to think about how deep her loss would be, how searingly painful.

Slapping the reins, she turned the buggy in the direction of the opera house.

"Linette Marquis?" The stage manager grinned, rubbing one hand through his wavy, pomaded blond hair. "I suppose she is still around here somewhere—I think she is having a wardrobe fitting."

"I ... I'd like to talk to her, please."

The man shrugged. "Suit yourself. Me, I stay

away from her these days. Her temper is as mean
as a junkyard dog."

Her heart sinking, Alisa followed his directions,
finding her way down a narrow, damp-smelling
corridor to a staircase that led to a basement beneath the stage. Ancient, battered doors marred
with generations of initials and penciled marks led
to a series of dressing rooms.

Alisa saw a shadow scuttle in front of her, and
shuddered violently. A rat! Theatrical paint was
made of animal glue, and probably actors often
left food in their dressing rooms, good fare for
rodents.

Why was she thinking about rats now? It must
be this oppressive theater, she decided, all of its
glamour on display in the auditorium and lobby,
with the real, underlying shabbiness revealed below stage all too plainly.

In a green room someone was battering an old
piano, singing a music-hall song, and Alisa heard
feminine laughter coming from one of the dressing rooms. She tried to force herself to relax.
Linette was only a woman, after all, with human
and understandable motives. Somehow, Alisa would
appeal to those motives. She'd . . .

She stopped short at a door labeled "WARDROBE,"
standing ajar. She stood trembling, trying to gather
her courage to knock. From inside came quarrel-
some voices.

"I don't like it, I tell you!" Linette Marquis
snapped. "Those flounces are simply not hanging
straight and I'm going to look ridiculous in this
dress, everyone is going to laugh at me!"

"Merde!" Fifine uttered the curse in a muffled

voice, her mouth sounding full of pins. "It will be charming, I tell you—in a moment when I have resewn it."

"Fool! I don't think so. That top flounce needs raising, and then that will put the train out of order . . ." There were scraping sounds, and then the door suddenly banged open. "I thought I heard someone out here. Well! If it isn't Mrs. Riordan Daniels, the queen of Chicago's social set!"

"Hello, Linette. Fifine." Alisa drew a deep breath and entered the room, smelling the thick muskiness of Linette's perfume, mingled with the scents of rouge, powder, and perspiration. A small silver flask sat on a table nearby, and Alisa suspected that both women had been drinking from it.

"What are you doing here?" Linette's mocking laugh rose. "Surely you're a little early to catch tonight's performance."

Fifine had risen to her feet, and the Frenchwoman gazed sullenly at the daughter of her former lover.

"I didn't come to see the performance," Alisa said tightly. "I wanted to talk to you. Alone, if I could," she added, looking at Fifine.

"Perhaps I don't wish—" Fifine began, but Linette shushed her with a quick movement of her head, and the Frenchwoman sniffed, sweeping out of the dressing room and slamming its door huffily behind her.

"There," Linette said. "She resents you, you know. You never came to her for your bonnets or dresses, and she would have liked your business."

"I'm certain she would have. However, I didn't choose to give it to her." Alisa took a few steps farther into the room, aware, as always, of the contrast between herself and Linette. Linette wore a dramatically cut stage gown with a neckline that skimmed her shoulders, revealing inches of white bosom. There were yards upon yards of flounces and ruched lace, and much trim that showed Fifine's love of ornamentation.

In contrast, Alisa's own dress was of plain blue silk, its cut simple.

"Isn't Fifine good enough for you?" Linette sneered. "Apparently she was good enough for your father, eh?"

Alisa stiffened. "I'm not here to discuss my father or Fifine either. I'm here about Riordan and your blackmailing of him."

"Blackmail? That's a very strong word." But Linette seemed to grow nervous, stroking her hands down the elaborate lacework of her gown.

"It's the right word as far as I can see," Alisa said. "Isn't that exactly what you're doing, Linette? Asking for money, using Tessa, an innocent baby, in order to get what you want?"

The actress shrugged, turning to sweep to the far side of the small room, where a table held scraps of fabric and Fifine's open sewing box. She poked fitfully at the box. "Perhaps I am."

"What is it that you want, Linette?" Alisa burst out. "Tell me, please. I need to know. Surely it can't be money—Riordan has already given you so much; what could you possibly have spent it on?"

"An actress always needs money." Linette again moved her soft, powdered shoulders in a shrug. "We grow old, we get wrinkles, one day we are forced to take character parts instead of leading roles. And the men who come to the green room afterward bring roses to other women, not to us."

Alisa was silent. Linette certainly did not look in any immediate danger of old age; her cheeks were flushed and vibrant, her dark eyes flashing.

Linette went on. "What is to happen to me then, when I can't go on the stage any longer? I am simply planning for my future, that's all."

"But at the expense of a little girl! Think of Tessa," Alisa began as persuasively as she could. "You miss her sometimes—you told me so yourself. I'm sure you harbor some love for her. You must know what a hard life it would be for her, being stigmatized as illegitimate."

Linette looked sullen, her color high.

"Not to mention," Alisa pressed on, "the fact that your own career would be ruined if her existence were to be mentioned."

Linette snapped out the words. "No one would believe she is my child. I have those who can testify I was not pregnant, I've never been pregnant."

Seizing her opportunity, Alisa pounced. "Then how can you say Riordan kidnapped your baby—*if you've never had a baby?*"

"Damn! Damn you!" Linette whirled, giving the sewing box a shove that sent it clattering to the floor. "You think you're so smart, don't you? Well, you're not so smart as you think. No, not at all. He wouldn't marry me. He had high social aims, he thought he was far too good for the likes of me. Now he's settled on you."

Linette's mouth twisted. "Little rich girl with a society name . . . but let me tell you something."

Each word was a punishing slap. "He only picked you for one reason, your name. And it wasn't because you're good in bed," the actress added, looking Alisa up and down insultingly. "You look so cool and calm, I'll bet you're an iceberg between the sheets."

Alisa felt her cheeks flame red. She stifled the urge to shriek at Linette like a fishwife, venting her fury and hurt. "My private relationship with my husband is none of your concern."

Linette's eyes glinted savagely. "Oh, yes, it is. He's told me all about it—all about you, Miss Iceberg. How cold and unfeeling you are, how you lied to him, tricked and deceived him, how all you want is money, money."

Alisa stepped backward, feeling as if she had been slapped hard.

Riordan—his name was a wordless cry in her, of anguish and despair. Had he really talked about her—about their lovemaking, their life together— with this horrid, vengeful woman? She felt unbearably dirty and soiled. And yet maybe Linette was lying. Yes. It had to be. Even Riordan wouldn't sink that low.

Would he?

She gathered her courage and stood tall, to the full extent of her height, knowing that she dwarfed the actress by several inches, and here held an advantage. "Is it true, Linette, that you intend to try to take my husband away from me?"

Linette's eyes met hers, dark, stony. "I not only intend to, I will. He is about to give in to me, too." Her grin was angry, yet triumphant. "He is besotted with that little girl, he would give her anything in the world, sacrifice anything for her, anything at all. He's going to sacrifice you, Alisa. Oh, yes," she added as Alisa paled. "You're going to go."

You're going to go. Linette's words spun in the room like shiny, lethal knives.

Alisa swallowed, her throat gone so suddenly dry that her tongue seemed to cleave to the roof of her mouth. It was one thing to suspect such a thing; it was another to hear it spoken with savage bluntness. Oh, God, could it be true?

She feared in her heart that it was, and she thought she would be sick with the sheer impact of it.

Riordan didn't love her. He didn't, didn't . . .

With a shock, she realized that Linette was still speaking. "Oh, yes, we're going to get rid of you, all right. Riordan has already figured out how to do it. In order to get a divorce, he needs to prove you have wronged him through adultery—"

"A-adultery!" Alisa reeled back, shaken to her core. "What do you mean?"

"Why, with Matt Eberley, of course."

"Matt! He has never been my lover!"

"Indeed. Hasn't he?"

"No! Never! What are you getting at, what are you trying to say?"

"What does it look like?" Linette's grin was slow and full of meaning. "He was bought once. Riordan confessed about how he threw Eberley a large legal case in payment for postponing your wedding. Matt Eberley looks so proper and tidy on the outside, but inside he is as greedy as any of us, and every man has his price, believe me."

Would they really use Matt against her? Alisa

thought she would be sick. Her knees felt weak with the ugly shock of what she had just heard. It was only a supreme effort that kept her from swaying, revealing her humiliation in front of Riordan's mistress.

Her voice shook as she responded. "I don't believe you. I don't think Riordan would ever stoop so low as to do such a cruel thing to me."

"He will, to get his daughter."

They glared at each other.

"No," Alisa whispered, hurt to the quick.

"Oh, yes, and you won't be able to do a thing about it, not one thing. I'm going to take your husband, Alisa. I'll move into that fancy mansion of his and I'll take over as Tessa's 'stepmother.' "

Linette's lips had formed another angry, triumphant smile. "I'll have it all. Him. That house, wealth, position. I'll give the fancy receptions soon. And I'll make Riordan pay for rejecting me. He'll pay in full! If this were a card game, I'd possess all the tricks!"

Alisa shivered, feeling the nausea rise in her throat. Grimly she held it back.

"Tricks." She said it in a low, strange voice that she did not recognize. "That's all you really are, Linette—tricks and sham and deception. Do you really think that Riordan wants to live with that? That he'll tolerate duplicity and lies for very long?"

"He'll tolerate them," Linette gloated, "until Tessa has made her debut and is married—that's at least eighteen years, maybe longer."

Eighteen years. Linette was absolutely right. Alisa went rigid, wanting to scream out from her agony. Instead, she turned and, holding her spine erect, walked carefully out of the wardrobe room into the musty theater corridor.

Linette flung open the door, her strident voice following Alisa. "I'm going to get him, do you hear me? He's always wanted me, ever since he first saw me. How dare he say that he wouldn't marry me? That it would never work, that we were too different. We aren't different! We aren't! We are two of a kind. *And I'm going to have him, and there is nothing you can do to stop me!*"

27

Alisa hurried up the narrow theater staircase, blind with grief and anger. How could Riordan do this to her, treat her so cruelly? What had she ever done to him that she should be discarded as less than unwanted trash, humiliated and degraded in court?

She knew that she had not even begun to feel the full enormity of the pain yet. That would come later, when she flung herself across the bed in the privacy of their bedroom and gave herself up to a tumult of agonized weeping.

Riordan, Riordan! His name filled her with hopelessness. She loved him . . . she loved him . . . She still did, in spite of this, in spite of everything. It was her curse: she would continue to love him until the day she died; nothing he did to her could ever change that.

Dully she saw that Fifine was waiting for her at the top of the stairs, the Frenchwoman's skirts blocking her way so that there was no choice but for her to stop.

"So you are going to lose your husband," Fifine

said in a gloating tone. "As I lost my man, now you must pay, too. His daughter. It is fitting justice, eh?"

Alisa caught her breath, too numbed at the memory of Linette's strident voice even to react fully to Fifine's spite. "If you are angry at my father, then I am sorry, Fifine, but it isn't my fault and I had nothing to do with it. Please let me pass. I'm very tired and I'm going home."

"Home to prepare for your divorce?" Fifine stood back, arms akimbo. "Your adultery charge? Ah, that should be interesting, should it not? Alisa Amsell branded an adulteress in court—an adulterer like her father!"

"It is none of your concern, Fifine," she managed to say.

"*Oui*, perhaps not. Men!" Fifine made a spitting sound. "They are all the same, they all want something from us, and as long as we give it to them, they are happy. But when they can't get it anymore, or tire of what they get too easily ... pfah! One might as well bow to the inevitable— what will happen, will happen!"

Alisa stared at Fifine, wondering why she had never seen it before, this woman's deep resentment. Had it been there all along, only she had been too blind, too stupid to see it? Fifine hated Papa—and hated her.

And—Alisa suddenly sensed this with sharp intuition—this was why Fifine had cultivated Linette Marquis.

Fifine longed for revenge. It was Fifine who had coached Linette on the details of Alisa's engagement to Matt Eberley, who had probably suggested using him as a lever to force the finish of Alisa's marriage. Perhaps she had even suggested other things to the actress, egging her on whenever possible.

Alisa's thoughts raced on. If that was so, then perhaps Riordan had no idea of what these women were really planning.

A tiny flame of hope leapt within her, then almost as quickly died. What difference did it make whether the ugly adultery threat was Riordan's or Linette's or Fifine's? There still had to be a divorce if Riordan was to gain possession of his child. That was hard, cold reality and could not be denied.

Surely Riordan would make it as easy on her as possible; she believed he was not a cruel man. Still . . . it would happen.

With a start, she realized that Fifine was looking at her strangely. How long had she been standing here, lost in the torment of her thoughts?

"I . . . I must leave now," she mumbled to the Frenchwoman.

"Who is stopping you, eh? Certainly not me!" And Fifine gave a gloating little laugh as Alisa hurried past her toward the cavernous backstage area and the door that led to the stage alley.

Back in her buggy, Alisa sat shivering, her hands trembling too violently at first for her to pick up the reins. What was she to do now, what could she do? She drew shaky breaths, suddenly wishing desperately that Papa was here sitting beside her in the buggy, that she could talk to him, pour out her grief and longing and despair.

But he wasn't here. He was dead. Steadying

herself, Alisa picked up the bridle and slapped it firmly, and the mare began trotting at a brisk pace. Papa had said he would buy her a new buggy once ... yes, he had said it at luncheon that day, the last meal she had ever taken with him.

"How would you like a brand-new runabout? Handmade, the best, with a good hardwood frame?"

Alisa had hesitated. *"But I already have a fine buggy."*

"Then you shall have another one, my darling. I'll buy you a beautiful Arabian horse with the clean, fine lines of a champion—because you are a champion, Alisa, you are clean and fine, too, the very best. . . ."

Why was she thinking of that now? She blinked back angry tears as a big lumber wagon rumbled around a corner, its burly driver shouting at her angrily. "Out of the way, lady! You're blocking the road!"

"I'm not!"

He waved a fist at her.

The challenge came almost as a relief, assuaging her misery. Alisa half-stood in the buggy, raising her own clenched fist back, as Papa would have done, and urged her mare to a fast trot. The man shouted gleefully, whipping on his own team so it would take up all the road space, forcing Alisa to stop.

But Alisa's buggy was smaller and lighter, and her mare was quick. Before the larger wagon could move, she had darted her buggy around it, taking satisfaction in the choking cloud of dust that drifted into the driver's face. She heard his curse and then she was past him, waving back at him triumphantly.

She could fight, she *was* strong. Feeling suddenly much, much better, she veered the buggy toward State Street, knowing what she had to do next.

"Matt, I know this is awkward, you probably don't want to talk to me about it, but I need some answers, and I intend to get them."

Matt Eberley's new State Street office had a high ceiling of molded plaster and long, narrow windows that opened on a street crowded with carriages, omnibuses, wagons, and pedestrians mopping their faces because of the July heat.

The office itself was luxuriously furnished with Turkish rugs, heavy mahogany furniture, and a beautiful long-case clock covered with floral marquetry. Two clerks busied themselves in a beautifully appointed law library, and, Alisa noted, there was now a second office where a younger associate interviewed clients.

"What are you talking about, Alisa?" Matt looked nervous. He rubbed at his upper lip, his hand partly concealing his mouth as if he wished to hide something from her. They had already spent some moments in conversation, and Matt had talked at length about his new, expanded law practice, evidenced by the expensive furnishings and his general air of prosperity.

"You know what I'm talking about! First, I know that you were given that big Armour law case if you would postpone our wedding—I *know* that, Matt," she added as he began to shake his head.

"It wasn't quite as it seemed, Alisa," Matt said, flushing. "It wasn't that I didn't love you—I did, very much. I was planning to marry you ... I never would have reneged on that. But when I was given that case, I saw no harm in postponing the date for a while. Surely that wouldn't hurt anything, and besides ..." He stopped.

"Yes?" She prompted.

"I knew then that ... well, that things could have been better between us."

"What do you mean?"

Matt rose from his desk and went to stand at the window, which was open because of the warm weather. A warm breeze lifted the hem of a brocade curtain, rattling it against the molding. "There were things he said to me ... things I did not want to repeat to you."

"What things? Matt! I ... I'm in trouble, my marriage is deeply at issue, and I need to know. What did Riordan say to you? Please tell me!"

"He was in love with you. That was very obvious." Matt said it harshly. "He told me frankly that he was buying me off. That you were his woman. That you were his life."

As Alisa reacted with a gasp, Matt turned, scowling. "There. Does that satisfy you, is that what you've come to hear? So I capitulated. Is that so wrong, Alisa? He is a strong man, a determined one, he could buy and sell me a thousand times over, he could make me suffer, and I knew it. He wanted you, he intended to have you, and he was not going to let me stand in the way."

"I see." Although Alisa had suspected much of this before, she had not known what Riordan had said to Matt. *He loved her.* She felt rocked, shaken to the core by this revelation. But that had happened months ago, she remembered with a sudden clenching of her stomach. Much had occurred since then. "I need to know one more thing, Matt, and I beg of you to tell me."

"What is it? I'm very busy today, Alisa. I have an important meeting that is due to begin in ten minutes, and I still have to prepare—"

"We were never lovers. Has anyone come to you . . . has anyone hinted in any way that . . . that we might have been? That . . ." But Matt was looking so incredulous that she could not go on. "Never mind," she finished. "I see that I was wrong. I'm sorry to have bothered you, Matt. I'll find my own way out."

"No, I'll show you to the door. It was good to see you," Matt said heartily. "You'll have to stop by sometime soon, Alisa, when we have more time to talk."

He clasped her hand as if this had been only a social call and ushered her past the clerks and out of the door, all the while talking volubly about the summer weather and a small factory fire, as if nothing whatever had transpired between them.

Alisa drove home, feeling exhausted by all she had learned, a thousand times weary. Riordan loved her—had loved her once, she amended in her mind. It was Fifine and Linette who, plotting together, had conceived the plan of using Matt Eberley as corespondent in a divorce.

There had been truth in Fifine's gloating gibe: *You might as well bow to the inevitable.*

Tessa, beautiful, adorable Tessa, was Riordan's weak point. That and the illegitimacy against which he had fought all his life. And Alisa knew with bitter certainty that Linette Marquis would use both these weapons to the hilt.

What could Alisa do against that?

Fight, came her first thought, *fight hard. You can win.*

Then another voice whispered in her bleakly: *But what if you do manage to hang on to your marriage, then what?*

Knowing the answer, Alisa shuddered. Linette was not going to give up. She would still be there, a wicked witch lurking at the periphery of their lives, demanding money and attention, even public acknowledgment as Riordan's mistress.

Yes. Alisa's heart shrank in certain knowledge. If Linette could not have Riordan as husband, then she would insist on taking him as her lover— true to her vow, she would take his heart and guts, she would make him pay and pay.

Alisa had reached the block on which Riordan's mansion stood. She drove up the avenue, beneath the large trees that met overhead, forming a canopy of leaf and shadow. The big house dominated the street, the arched colonnades lining the massive porch, the decorative archways, balconies, and fretwork all newly painted, glistening in the afternoon sun, everything crowned by an enormous cupola.

She slowed the mare, gazing at the house with eyes that brimmed with tears. Once she had thought this mansion too ostentatious, gawdy and showy. Perhaps it was.

But she'd grown to love this house with its vistas of large gilt-decorated rooms, and now those rooms held memories. Riordan and herself bent over ledgers in the library, laughing together. Riordan serious at the dinner table, or carrying her up the staircase to make love.

And Tessa, toddling, wreathed in giggles, or crawling through the wooden house that Riordan had had built for her . . . Tessa wide-eyed as Alisa read her a story, or falling asleep in Riordan's arms.

A thousand memories, so precious.

Now Alisa was to leave them, the two people she loved most. She had to. For she knew as she slowly pulled her buggy through the wrought-iron gates and around to the carriage house that she had no right here anymore.

She pulled up the buggy and climbed out, forcing her face into lines of composure so that the stableboys would not see how upset she was.

Yes. The realization grew. She had no right to hold Riordan anymore. Linette's being his wife would solve everything. He would have his child safe, and Linette would be where he could watch her, keep control over her, all of her threats nullified. She could hardly threaten Riordan with blackmail if she was his wife!

Did she love Riordan enough—and Tessa—to want what was best for them?

The thought of the little girl sent a black shiver running through Alisa, but swiftly she assured herself that Tessa would not suffer. Fanny, whom the child deeply loved, could continue to be her nurse, and Tessa would never lack love from her father. Perhaps Linette did harbor some love for her daughter. But even if she did not, Tessa would still receive enough adoration to make up for it.

And there was always Malva, Alisa reassured herself. Malva liked Riordan and adored Tessa, so surely she would continue to sponsor the little girl. Since Riordan had already been accepted into society, Tessa would still be able to attend school with all the right children, and make her debut exactly as planned.

Without her.

"Everything all right, ma'am?" Josh, an older stableman, approached her. "You didn't have an accident or nothing, did you? You look kinda shaken up."

"No, I . . . everything is fine, Josh. Just fine."

She even managed to smile at the man before she turned and went into the house. She decided to tell Riordan that she would go to Boston, where she had distant relatives. She would pack her things and leave immediately.

A quiet divorce could follow. There would be notoriety because of that, for a time, but Malva would help, Alisa assured herself. Gossip would die down, and things would be smoothed over. . . .

As she stepped into the house, it seemed to reach out and surround her with its dear familiar smells of beeswax and the lemon oil used to polish the furniture. She felt a hard, painful clutching of her heart. Her throat closing up, she turned toward Riordan's office.

She found him bent over an open ledger, frowning at a column of neatly penned figures as he brushed one hand wearily across his forehead. Alisa saw the dark circles under her husband's eyes, new lines of worry and pain etched into his face. All these long weeks, Riordan had been in torment too, she realized. It was written plainly there for her to read.

"Riordan?" she whispered. "Can I come in and talk to you?"

"Why?" He asked it coldly.

"We . . . we have to talk. I'm so sorry I slapped you. I don't know what possessed me to do it, I'm so ashamed of what I did."

He nodded. "I'm sure you are."

She felt her cheeks burn red as she sank into a chair beside him, forcing herself to look directly into his eyes. Black eyes, compelling ones, that now looked into hers with piercing scrutiny, seeming to see into her very soul.

"What do you want, Alisa?"

Her heart was hammering and her whole body felt clenched with dread, with a wild, wild grief. "I am going to give you what you want," she blurted in a low, agonized tone.

" 'What I want?' And you imagine that you know what that is?"

Why did he have to make this so hard for her—was he deliberately torturing her, stringing her emotions out to the breaking point?

"You want legitimacy for Tessa, you want acceptance for her, you want everything for her, the best that life has to offer." She moistened her lips and forced herself to continue. "I want that for her too. And I want you to be happy, Riordan. Your happiness is important to me."

Steadily he scrutinized her, and although her throat closed and she wondered if she would be able to talk, somehow she heard her voice continuing.

"I love you, Riordan. I always have. But I know you don't care for me in that way, and I know that our bargain, our marriage agreement, can no longer be valid. Linette has taken care of that. I . . . I'm going to leave Chicago."

"What!" Riordan went rigid, his cheeks suffused with a sudden influx of blood.

"If you divorce me and marry Linette, then Tessa has a chance at a normal life."

"Tessa!"

"Yes, Malva will help you with her. I will personally ask her to see to it before I go. Linette will be silenced and . . . and you'll have what you want."

She could go no further. Choking back a sob, she jumped from the chair and started toward the door.

"Alisa!"

"I have to pack," she choked, pushing at the knob with blind fingers.

"Alisa!" He had started to his feet, but she was already fleeing, lifting her skirts to run upstairs to the master bedroom, where she closed the door behind her with shaking hands.

Downstairs, they had a caller. Alisa knew this, because she had heard the rumble of carriage wheels and had gone to the window to peer out. She had watched the landau pull up the drive, its occupant a woman wearing a bright red velvet gown elaborately trimmed with rows of black French lace.

She had not seen the woman's face, but she had not needed to. Linette. Riordan's mistress had come here boldly, blatantly, was even now closeted with the master of the house.

Planning what to do with her spoils, Alisa surmised, surprised at how calm she felt, as if all the sharp emotions had been blunted in her.

Grimly she moved about the room, gathering up the few things that she would take with her. Her modest work dresses, she decided; they would be serviceable whatever job she chose to do, and work she certainly would.

She did possess the Amsell mill and her father's house; Riordan had deeded them to her. Before she left, she would ask Will Rice to sell them for her and send her the money. With her other holdings, these would be enough to finance some other business.

She would absorb herself in building a new fortune. It would not be the same without Riordan—in fact, life would be empty and pointless—but there would be something to fill her time and she was determined not to feel sorry for herself.

She rang for a servant and had him bring up several trunks, into which she began packing petticoats, mantles, shawls, books, and other personal items. With a stab of sorrow, she picked up the pearl-and-diamond necklace that Riordan had given her as a wedding gift. It shimmered in her hands, the pearls large and lustrous, the diamonds refracting the sunlight that streamed through the windows.

What memories this necklace held! That day when Riordan had insisted she go to the theater with him, and had taken her to pick it out; their wedding day, with its bittersweet joy. Other occasions on which she had worn it, proud that he had given it to her.

She put the necklace back into the safe, deciding to leave it. And then she remembered Linette. When Linette took over, she would scour through the house from top to bottom, Alisa had no doubt, searching for every trophy she could find. With what glee she'd take over Alisa's jewelry, wearing it as her own!

Decisively Alisa took the necklace, put it in a small satin-lined box, and added it to the trunk. She would never let Linette have this. It would be her memory of Riordan, something he had given her, to treasure forever.

There was a knock on her door and Alisa's heart leapt into her throat.

Riordan.

She couldn't talk to him now—she couldn't, couldn't. If she looked at him now, if she even touched him, she would break into wild sobs of grief. And she didn't want him to see that. She would leave proudly, as befitted an Amsell.

But it was not her husband, it was Nella, in tears, wadding her apron into bunches with agitation. "Ma'am? You're not going, are you? I heard them say, down in the kitchen . . . that you're going to Boston! And you're not coming back."

"It's true."

"But why? Oh, ma'am!" Nella's eyes were genuinely reddened with tears.

"I have to, Nella. It's Tessa. There has been trouble regarding her mother, and there is no other way."

"But he loves you so, Mrs. Daniels. You can't do this to him. You can't go away like this."

Alisa slammed down the lid of the first trunk, feeling sharp tears stab at her eyes. "Nella, perhaps he does love me, and I do love him. But it doesn't matter, because he needs to protect his daughter, and that comes first, and it's the way it has to be."

She had unconsciously raised her voice and was nearly shouting. "He can't have both—he can't have Tessa and me. And anyway, he doesn't want me at all. He never did. Only my name. My name, Nella, as if I were a blooded racehorse. only that! So I'm going to Boston. I'm going to work there. I'll make a new life. I . . . I'll forget Riordan, I'll forget all of this."

"Ma'am . . . ma'am . . ." Nella was openly weeping now. "The poor baby—"

"Tessa will be fine. You'll be here, and Fanny, and Riordan, and Malva. She'll be fine . . ." But Alisa broke down. "Nella, please leave me be. I want to finish packing so I can call the carriage. I'll leave as soon as I can."

"No." The voice, full and deep, came from behind Nella and belonged to Riordan. He moved forward, nodding to the woman, who scurried off down the corridor toward the stairs, leaving them alone.

"Alisa, Alisa." Riordan came into the bedroom, closing the door behind him and turning the key in it, locking it. He pocketed the key. "You are wrong, you know. So very wrong."

"I don't think I am." She stood shaking. She couldn't bear it. "Go away," she begged in a muffled voice.

"No, I won't go away, and I won't give you the key to unlock this door and leave, not until I say a few things to you." Never had she seen Riordan look so pale, his black eyebrows fierce, his jawline knotted grimly.

"Please leave," she pleaded. "Don't do this to me. I have made my decision and it's the best one for us—the only one."

"What!" He threw back his head and laughed bitterly. "You can't be serious! To leave me here in this house wed to that harridan Linette Marquis? That cruel, opportunistic woman who used her own baby as a tool to get what she wanted, who loves Tessa not one whit? Who would deliberately throw you to the wolves, dragging you through court with an adultery accusation, ruining your reputation forever!"

"I . . ." She stared at him, remembering the threats that Linette had screamed at the theater. "But I thought . . ."

"You thought wrong, Alisa. So very wrong." Riordan came to her and enfolded her in his arms, holding her close. "Oh, my darling, my little darling. You would go to Boston, leave me, make such a sacrifice for me!"

"It's the only way," she whispered. She tried to hold back, but his arms were so sheltering, so strong and warm, that she could not help going into them. She clung to him, knowing that this might be the last time she'd ever be so close to him.

"It isn't. Alisa, it isn't!" He gripped her arms, holding away so that she was forced to look into his eyes, soft and dark with pain. "I love you, you little fool—I always have!"

"But—"

"I never would have married you if I didn't love you. I couldn't ever have done it."

She thought she would collapse from the rush of emotion that filled her. "But I thought . . . You never told me . . ."

His jaw knotted. "I never told you because I didn't think you loved me. I was sure you married me only for my wealth and position, to build the vast fortune that obviously excited you so much." He pulled her closer and they melded their bodies together, his lips grazing kisses on her neck and cheeks. "Alisa, I was wrong. You do care, you do love me, you've loved me all along, haven't you, darling?"

"Oh, yes," she whispered.

"And you would sacrifice yourself for me . . . Darling, my darling . . ." His kisses were tender, seeking.

"But Tessa," she finally said miserably, remembering their flamboyant visitor. "Linette will destroy her, Riordan, if you don't do as she wishes."

He looked at her, his eyes hardening. "Do you really think I would allow anyone, anyone at all, to blackmail me or to hurt my little girl? Come."

She was bewildered. "But—"

"Come, Alisa, I want to show you something."

He put his arm around her, while, with the

other hand, he unlocked the door and held it open for her. They walked downstairs to his office, Riordan's hand clasped around her own, warm, strong.

"There," he said when they had reached his inner office. "Look." He picked up a sheaf of papers and handed it to Alisa, his eyes flashing.

Alisa scanned them, reading quickly. "But . . . but this is . . ." She looked at Riordan in wonderment. "This is a paper in which Linette admits she is Tessa's mother and gives up all rights to her— *these are adoption papers!*"

"Yes." Riordan looked grim. "I told her, Alisa, that I would not marry her if she was the last woman on earth, that I would rot in hell before I would do such a thing. That I personally would call a press conference and announce to the world that she is Tessa's mother and I'm her father and we're both proud of it."

Alisa thought she would sink to the floor from sheer shock. While she'd been preparing to leave him, Riordan had done this! Her eyes burned with quick, hot tears of joy. Riordan, too, had sacrificed. He had done this for her.

"And . . . and what did she say?"

Riordan's eyebrows gave a quirk upward, and for the first time he smiled. "At first she didn't believe I would really do it. When she realized, she screamed with fury. For above all else, Linette is selfish. Her career will always come first. When all the chips are down, she hates and fears bad publicity."

But Alisa, suffused with rushes of emotion, of glad love and joy, still could not relax. "But,

Riordan," she asked worriedly, "what of Tessa? What will happen to her?"

"Darling, I love my daughter deeply and I always will. I never want her to suffer as I've suffered. But I cannot live without you, I never want to be without you. Illegitimacy is a stigma, that's true. But I survived it. I grew strong fighting it, and if necessary, Tessa can too."

"But . . . she's still a baby. She mustn't have to fight . . ."

"God willing, she won't." Riordan again pulled her close and kissed her, soft, tender touches of his lips that gradually gave way to more and more. "We are going to leave Chicago, Alisa. Will Rice will be in charge of my office here, but we are going to take my palace cars west to Denver, and I'm going to start a new railway line there. We are."

"Denver! And . . . us?"

"Mmmm, yes." Strong arms encircled her, Riordan's hands caressing her shoulder blades with loving, urgent tenderness. "You'll be my partner, Alisa, we'll work together. The West is all new, Alisa, so much freer than the tightly bound society of Chicago and Boston and New York. In Denver, Tessa will simply be our little daughter. She'll grow up free. But if Linette should ever talk, if any gossip should ever fly that far west, it won't matter, not on a frontier."

"Oh . . ."

"Alisa, my love, my darling, darling love. Come with me wherever I go. Be my life, my heart, my wife, in every real meaning of that wonderful word. For true and forever."

It was as if they spoke their vows all over again, this time just for each other, committing themselves in promises that had not been made before.

"I will," she breathed, her voice low and strong. "And you'll be my husband, Riordan, in love and trust and joy, for all of our lives."

"Yes. Yes. Ah, Alisa, thank God. Thank God I have you." He swept her tightly into his embrace, his kisses brushing away all sorrow, all doubt, all fear forever. Joyously Alisa gave herself up to her husband, the full, rich assurance of his love.

Sensational Reading from SIGNET